THE ASH TRIALS

THE SEPTERRA SERIES: BOOK ONE

AMY SUTO

SUTOSCIENCE LLC

Paperback Edition ISBN #979-8-9926190-0-3

Hardcover Edition ISBN #979-8-9926190-1-0

First Edition.

Edited by Kyle Cords.

Proofread by Sierra C. Campbell, Founder and Editor of Editing by Sierra (www.editingbysierra.com).

Cover design by Ashley Munson (www.libra-collective.com).

Map design by Melissa Nash (https://www.fiverr.com/mnash884).

To learn more about the author, visit: AmySuto.com

To Kyle—you are the partner and creative genius of my heart's wildest dreams. Thank you. For everything.

CONTENT WARNING

The Ash Trials is an action-packed romantic fantasy novel that takes place in the brutal world of deadly trials set on a mystical island. As such, this story contains violent scenes, strong language, depictions and discussions of suicide, and sexually explicit content shown on the page. Enter the trials at your own risk.

N

W · E

S

Dragon's
Tail

Siren's
Rest

The
Temple of
Orsi

Eternal
Sands

Lake
Aetherna

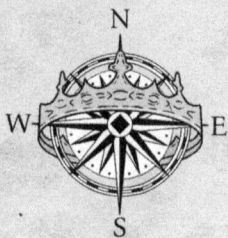

The
Cimmerian
Sea

The Foggy
Forest

Ashguard
Prison

The
Saltspire
Palace

The
Stone
Coliseum

-Isle of-
EMBERMERE

PART I

THE RUNAWAY BRIDE

1

Who am I?

In the dark, I didn't know my name. My present. My past. I was nothing.

I pressed my palms to the stone floor. It was so cold in this dark place, but the air was still. I crawled forward, realizing that I had a body in this darkness and that I could move. I crawled until my hands met cold metal bars.

I was in a cell.

That scared me, just like the suffocating dark scared me. Where had I been *before* this cell?

The suffocating dark held no answer for me—only a terrifying realization as my question echoed in the emptiness of my mind.

I had no memories.

The fear that rose in my chest was chased away by a sound.

Footsteps echoed, and lanterns illuminated the endless dark that had surrounded me. As my eyes adjusted, I was finally able to look around my dark cell, which held a single dirty cot with a threadbare blanket.

The lantern light grew brighter, and I turned to see two prison guards approaching. The guards wore gold and white uniforms with an upside-down fire insignia emblazoned on them. One was broad and ox-like, the other was smaller and fidgety.

"Looks like she's finally awake," the fidgety guard sneered at me, stopping in front of the bars of my cell. The lantern light flickered around the empty hallway. I was in some sort of stone dungeon, the stone arcing above my cell.

"Missing something? Or *someone*?" The ox-like one asked. They snickered as I looked down at myself on the dirty floor of the cell.

I was wearing a torn wedding dress. A delicate lace curled along my arms and blossomed from my small frame into petals of soft fabric like a white rose. My dress looked like it had been dragged through the dirt. That *I* had been dragged through the dirt. Pieces of leaves clung to my long white-blonde hair—still holding the ghost of soft curls. A small dirty handkerchief also sat discarded on my cell. It was embroidered with a strange emblem of a hand gripping a lightning bolt.

"Put up a fight at the altar, did you?" the fidgety one asked.

"Where am I?" I asked. I didn't recognize my own voice, a realization that made me shiver.

"Better make amends with your fate, girl," the fidgety one jeered at me. "Because you'll either die on this island or become gods-blessed."

"Gods-blessed? Her? The monster we have over on floor six will eat her for lunch in the first trial," the ox-like one said, spitting at my cell. "That's if the fire sprites don't barbecue her on sight."

"What do you mean, *trial*?" I asked, my mouth dry.

"You'll be fun to watch die," the ox-like guard said and pulled away.

"What's going on? Where am I?" I tried to shout after them, but my voice felt so small in. Their footsteps echoed in the stone hallway as they walked away from my cell, taking their light with them as they continued on their way.

I felt an instinct to cling to the bars and claw at the men and... do *what*, exactly? What had happened between when this dress had looked pristine and now?

Where was I... and *who* was I? Suffocating terror filled my throat. I clawed at my brain for memories. I had to remember *something*... but nothing came. The encroaching dark entombed me, and I felt my throat close up, smothering me—

Another pair of footsteps approached—and then ran toward me, another lantern bringing warmth and light once more to my world. My head shot up to see a large figure standing at the bars of my cell.

"Saffron?" he bellowed, and I swept my eyes over him. The guard standing at my cell had tousled blond hair, deep green eyes the color of a verdant forest, and he was easily twice my size and built like a warrior. He wore a uniform similar to the other guards, but with extra insignias on his uniform that marked a superior rank. His broad chest, strong frame, and those pleading eyes—he was handsome, I realized. The light from the lantern he placed on the ground by my cell bathed every corded muscle of his in its golden light.

I felt myself inching closer to the bars where he stood, gripping them with white knuckles.

"No, it can't be," he said, devastation flashing across his face as he grabbed for my left hand. He pushed back my lace sleeve and revealed an upside-down golden flame inked on my skin in a kind of shimmering tattoo. "What did you do, Saffron?"

"*Saffron*," I said, tasting the name. It felt right. It felt like *mine*. "I'm Saffron. Who are you?"

The man crouched down to my eye level, as if he were trying to calm a wild animal. "It's me, Saffron. I'm Callum. It's *me*. Don't you remember?"

The pleading look he gave me cracked a piece of my heart. I reached into my mind with tendrils of curiosity... but I was met with a cold emptiness of *nothing*. I so badly wanted to remember this man looking at me with such longing in his eyes—but my mind was silent.

"I don't," I whispered.

His face fell. "I'm Commander Callum Wells. We grew up together. I'm... I'm a friend. You can trust me."

A *scream* echoed down the corridor of cells, and Callum's gaze shot to the activity just down the hall from my cell.

"Prisoner loose!" a guard called. "We need backup!"

"Stand back," Callum warned, but I didn't. I needed to see what was going on.

Callum moved toward the sound of the noise, and I watched him as he started walking down the long hallway to where I saw a cluster of four guards standing. As Callum's lantern illuminated the darkness, I noticed that all the cells around mine were empty except for this one, which was ten or twenty paces away and at a diagonal from where I was being held.

The guards stood at the ready, their swords drawn.

Clang! A dark figure stepped out from the cell, the door slamming open.

A *crash* sounded as one of the guards dropped his lantern...

...and started *floating*, suspended in the air...

...surrounded by a swirling mist of *blood*. His *own* blood.

"He's a blood wielder—don't bleed in front of him!" Callum yelled at the other guards.

Another guard shot forward, shoving his sword at the blood wielder, but with a sickening *crack,* the floating guard's body broke in half, and the rushing blood struck the other guard, flowing into his mouth and ears, drowning him in the dead man's blood.

I couldn't tear my eyes from the brutal scene even as my body started to shake from fear. As the guards and Callum stumbled back, the blood wielder dropped his hands. Callum went to one of his men, crouching down as he tried to staunch the bleeding from the fallen guard's wounds.

But the blood wielder slowly turned toward me. An owl-like swiveling of his head—but with a dead gaze that bore into the depths of my soul.

I knew I needed to step back, get away from the bars, but I was frozen in fear. I couldn't move, my terror keeping me locked in place.

The blood wielder strolled down the hallway to me, stepping over the bodies of the guards he had slain. He wore a tattered black cloak with a hood. His steps were silent as if he was merely floating above the ground instead of walking upon it.

He reached me and lowered his hood so I could see his face. It was bone-white and deathly pale. I felt my heart speed up, my entire body reacting to the predator before me.

"Saffron, get back!" Callum yelled, jumping from where he had been crouched. He started striding toward the blood wielder, his blade outstretched. But I still couldn't make myself move as the blood wielder just... sniffed me.

And grinned.

"What's this? You're a *hollow*? And a pretty one, at that. You didn't earn your death sentence. But you'll get one anyways."

The thin flesh peeled back from his powdery lips into a terrifying smile. But before he could make a move toward me, a sword pierced into his heart from behind. Blood suddenly started dripping from his mouth. He looked down at it, touching it and holding it up.

Callum wrenched the sword out from the blood wielder. "Get away from her."

"You dare try and stop me?" The blood wielder said as he whirled on Callum. Droplets of blood began to levitate and shift, turning into a bloody, flaming cutlass.

The blood wielder held the cutlass aloft as he made to slash at Callum—

—only for Callum to drop to one knee, crossing his arms above his head and conjuring a glittering blue shield that seemed to electrify the air around us as it formed out of nothing. As the glowing shield grew and made contact, it blasted back the blood wielder, who hit the far wall with a dull *thud*.

The fallen blood wielder didn't move, his cutlass now just a puddle of red beside his slumped body.

Callum lowered his shield, rising to his feet. The two remaining guards ran forward as Callum stood.

"Commander! Are you hurt?" one of them asked.

But Callum ignored the guard and turned to me.

"Saffron, are you okay?" Callum asked, his eyes darting over my body to look for injuries.

"Where am I? What is this?" I asked, trying to keep my voice from shaking.

"You're in Ashguard." When the name didn't register with me, Callum took another step closer to my cell, despair in his eyes. "This is the most remote prison in all of the realm. It holds the most dangerous magical criminals whose powers are too strong to be contained anywhere else. Every single prisoner here has committed heinous crimes, Saffron—and each have been sentenced to death. Including... including you. *You shouldn't be here.*"

Sentenced to death. The words clanged through me, and my legs finally gave out as I crumpled to the floor.

"I'm going to die?" I whispered, trying to calm my racing heart.

One of the guards called for him, and Callum looked conflicted. "Not if I can help it," he said softly. "I have to go, but I'll be right back. I promise."

I watched Callum turn and walk away from my cell, his dying lantern light leaving me alone in the dark once more.

~

My prison was windowless and doused in darkness, but I knew morning must be approaching when the torches that lined the prison hallway flickered to life.

I sat on my small cot, holding my knees to my chest. All night, I had tried to remember something—*anything*—about who I was and what had led me here. I must not have been a terrible person my entire life if Callum had remembered me not as a criminal, but as a friend.

As the torches flickered and illuminated my cell, I rose and walked to the small mirror above a chamber pot in my small cell—no running water for inmates here. The grimy mirror showed me a stranger, someone I didn't recognize. The mirror showed me myself, and she meant nothing to me.

I shuddered, but forced myself to keep my gaze on my reflection. I had ice blue eyes and long blonde hair that reached my mid-back. I guessed that I was most likely in my early twenties, but I couldn't be certain of my age. I could be considered pretty, but I looked battered. Dark circles pressed underneath those shocking blue eyes, and my collarbones poked through my skin. I was too skinny, and the ruined wedding dress hung a bit too loosely on my petite frame. I was to be wed awhile ago, then. *How long have I been here?*

I was pacing the length of my cell when I heard footsteps once more, and I darted to the cell doors to greet Callum as he strode to me.

"I returned as quickly as I could," he said in a low voice as he approached my cell. Now that the hallway was lit with the warm glow of the torches, I could better see him. He had a sword strapped to his back with a golden hilt, and a bit of stubble that gave him the look of a man even with his boyish, bright eyes. He carried himself like a man comfortable with having total authority, but there was a softness in his gaze when he looked at me.

Callum held a bundle of fabric under one arm, and in his other hand he carried a bucket and a washcloth. "This is for you. And water to wash off."

I took the bundle, unwrapping a freshly laundered off-white button-down tunic, a pair of black leggings, and a black cloak. He set down the bucket with the cloth by the cell's bars.

"This doesn't look like standard prison attire," I said.

"Your timing is... impeccable. As always," he said, brushing back some of the honey-blond hair that had dipped into his face. "The trials are starting in a matter of days. All of the prisoners here are now... *contestants*... and with that comes certain privileges."

"I'm a contestant in some sort of trials? What does all this mean? I thought I was brought here to die?" I asked.

"Put on these fresh clothes and I'll explain. I can't be away from my men for too long," he said, turning away from the cell to give me some privacy.

I reached through the bars and dipped the washcloth into the water. I withdrew it to wash away some of the dirt on my hands, grimacing at the layers of grime that came off in the process. "Your men. So you're a..."

"Commander of the Royal Guard. I'm normally stationed back in Luminaria. But I'm here on the Isle of Embermere to serve the King for the trials."

I started to peel the lace from my body, tearing off the ruined wedding dress as I spoke. "Who are you? Beyond your name and your rank, I mean."

"You really don't remember me?" Callum asked, his back still turned to me.

"Were you who I was to be wed to?"

Silence.

I frowned, wishing that I could see his expression and what was hiding there. "Callum?"

"I was not," he said, but I noted that his voice wavered. *Interesting.*

"Do you know how I got here?" I asked as my hand stilled with the washcloth over my chest as the water dripped down my skin.

"I don't. But whatever happened, it was enough that you've been sentenced to your death here in Ashguard."

"So I'm to die?" I asked.

"You are," Callum's voice sounded thick. "Right alongside this entire prison filled with thieves and murderers of the worst kinds."

A chill settled over my wet skin as I shivered. "Am I... *was* I... a bad person?" I asked, finishing washing myself. I began slipping into the clean fabric of the shirt and pants.

"The Saffron I knew couldn't hurt a fly," he said. "You being here is a misunderstanding, I'm sure of it."

I tugged on the leggings, finished getting dressed. "You can turn around now."

He did, and I saw in the light of the lantern that his eyes were glistening. He blinked, his gaze flickering to the discarded shreds of the wedding dress that lay on the floor.

"Did you love him?" he asked.

"Did you miss the part where I don't remember anything?" I asked, quirking my head as the quip jumped past my lips.

Callum's eyebrows shot up... and then a small smile crept across his face. "It's been too long since we saw each other last, Saffron." But the smile dropped as all of the torches flickered from red to green and back to red again. Callum stiffened, shaking his head. "I don't have time. Listen, we have to get you out of here—"

"Aren't I a contestant now?"

"Not if I can help it. Only one prisoner can win The Ash Trials and earn their freedom—unless the King grants you mercy."

"Does the King normally show mercy?"

Callum's expression went dark. "No. But maybe he'll make an exception."

"How do I win them, then? These trials?"

Footsteps echoed down the stone hallway, and Callum quickly picked up the bucket by my cell. "I can't stay any longer. Just... stay alive. I'll try and figure out why you ended up here in the first place. And keep to yourself at meals. Don't engage with any of the other wielders or shifters or—well, don't engage with *anyone*. They'll kill you before the trials even start if they realize you're a hollow."

"What's a hollow?"

Callum hesitated. "The word... it refers to humans who are powerless."

Powerless.

The word echoed in my mind.

"I'm... powerless?"

But Callum was already moving to leave. "You don't have magic, Saffron. That's why you have to be careful and stay away from the rest of the prisoners and *don't let them find out*. Listen, I have to go. If anyone asks—you don't know me. It would cause problems for us both if the others knew."

"Okay," I whispered as Callum turned and headed away from me, casting one last glance over his shoulder at me—worry in his gaze.

Without magic, without a single memory... how would I survive this place?

2

After Callum left me, Ashguard Prison began to wake up, and I heard all of the horrible noises that came with it. Screams, moans, shouts, yelling of the guards, footsteps—they all echoed down the long hallway outside of my cell. The sounds were too far away to make out individual voices, but I knew I didn't like what I heard.

Footsteps sounded once more outside of my cell, and a bored-looking guard arrived, holding two bands of iron.

"Commander Wells said you were to put these on," he said, thrusting them at me through the bars of the cell.

I stared them down, wary. "What are they?"

"They prevent you from using your powers." He looked me up and down. "Not that you probably have very much to begin with, if you weren't leashed when you got dropped off."

Oh, so that's what Callum must have run off and done. He probably ensured this guard came back with these so I could keep my secret of being a... what was it again? Right—a *hollow*.

I raised my chin, pretending to be offended. "My power is none of your business."

He shoved the bands at me. "I don't give a fuck. Put them on."

I grasped the two thick metal bands and yelped as they went transparent, slid down to my wrists, and became cold iron that fitted exactly to my skin. They weren't too heavy, but they were a bit uncomfortable. I reached down to try to move them or take them off, but they didn't budge, clamped tight to my wrists.

"Let's go," the bored guard said, pushing open my cell door.

"Where?" I asked, my stomach growling. The noises of the prison were growing louder, and while I didn't want to get near the den of lions that surely awaited me, I knew I had little choice. Plus, I needed food if I was to regain my strength for whatever these trials were.

The guard, tired of waiting on me, grabbed my arm and threw me into the hall. I bounced off the bars of the empty cell across from me, wincing in pain.

"Walk," the guard said, pointing forward.

As I walked ahead of the guard through the winding maze of empty cells, I felt like I was sleepwalking. Memories felt just beyond my grasp—as if I had forgotten something important, but it had just slipped from my mind. Memories that eluded me all the same, no matter how hard I tried to recall them.

The stone floor of the cells started to slope upward. I realized that all of the cells I had passed were empty.

"Am I the only prisoner in here?" I asked.

"The floors are segregated by power level. Which is why you're here—you're probably as close to hollow as they get," he muttered.

I was on the floor with prisoners who had the *lowest* level of magic? I shuddered as I realized that meant the blood wielder that Callum had killed was one of the *weaker* among the types of powerful beings I would face in this prison. *Great.*

Ahead of us, the endless corridor was finally beginning to lead up to a large round room...

...where prisoners were starting to line up around the outer rim of the circular space.

The guard nudged me forward, inclining his head. I followed his gaze to where I was to go stand. And as I looked up, I *gasped*.

I was on the ground floor of an incredible silo that had to be at least twenty stories tall, rimmed by a staircase that spiraled up each floor. At the top of the silo was a glass ceiling, frosted slightly so that light could drip in. *Sunlight.* From what I could see from the ground floor and the floors above us, there were offshoots of endless dark stone corridors, leading to what I assumed were different cell blocks and other areas of the prison.

To house the most dangerous prisoners, Callum had told me.

The same lethal prisoners who were all standing and staring at me as the guard shoved me toward them. As I walked to my place at the end of the line, I took in those around me—all of them wore the same metal bands I did, and a few of them wore thick metal anklets, too. *Perhaps because they had more power that needed to be contained?*

"Saffron Vale," a guard at the front called, and I stepped forward, taking my place at the edge of the circle as he continued to call out names for what seemed like a roll call ritual. Across from me, prisoners were still filtering down from the upper levels by way of that sloping, spiral staircase. I watched them as they descended, taking note of their names as the guard called them out.

"Otto Lynch," the guard called, and the man who descended was greasy-haired and could barely walk in a straight line. He kept dropping into a crouch and hissing at the other prisoners who gave him a wide berth.

"Priscilla and Felicity Hayes." A pair of willowy brunette twin women walked down, swaying with their hands intertwined as the iron bands at their wrists clanked like eerie windchimes in the echoing prison silo.

"Ajax Drake," the guard called, and a hulking mass of a man seemed to vibrate the stone underneath him as he barreled down the staircase to the ground floor. He didn't join the end of the semicircle in an orderly single file like the rest of the prisoners had, but instead crossed the circle and shoved aside a few other prisoners so he could stand next to a few guys who greeted him with slaps on the back. I instantly found a distaste for this man, and made a mental note to stay away.

The roll call continued as nearly seventy prisoners filed into the outer rim of the circular floor of the silo. The prisoners were a wide range of ages, with Issac Pike, a boy who looked not a day older than eighteen years, fidgeting on the other end of the semi-circle, and Otto, the greasy-haired man with greying hair—clearly the oldest as well as the most mentally unstable. Most of the prisoners looked fairly in shape, with the exception of a larger woman with buglike eyes and a more rotund figure. All of the prisoners wore clean tunics and pants as if their uniforms had been swapped out recently in preparation for these trials. The guard who had finished calling roll lowered his scroll and stepped back, waiting in silence for something to happen.

"We're bored! When are you going to let us start the trials?" Ajax said. He clenched and unclenched his massive fists like he was imagining squeezing the necks of other prisoners within his meaty grip. I tried to step back in line, out of his eyesight, but he leaned forward and grinned when his dark eyes latched onto me, scraping down my body with a greedy glint. "Oh, look at this, a new tribute to the precious gods. Looks like we have some fresh meat today, boys."

A few of the others snickered.

"Why don't you dance for us, girl?" Ajax said with a leering smile.

"I'll dance in your blood," I spat at him before thinking twice. I felt my hands twitch... as if they were trying to grasp something. But what? As he laughed at me, I felt an overwhelming urge to ring his neck—

Or did I? I was to be married just before coming here. Why did I feel violent anger rushing to my blood in a way that made me feel like I was capable of doing destructive things?

The Saffron I knew couldn't hurt a fly, Callum had said.

I felt like I was losing my mind—or whatever was left of it.

Ajax just grinned, wiping where I had spit at him with his palm... and then licked it with a sickening grin. My stomach churned with revulsion.

"I look forward to our first trial together, girl," Ajax said with a grin. He looked up and down the line as if looking for someone. "And where the hell is Derrick?"

"He murdered my men in cold blood while trying to escape, so he got what was coming to him," a voice boomed, and out from the shadows strode Callum. No, this wasn't Callum as I had met him. The soft and kind man had been replaced by *Commander* Callum Wells, a man who maintained order in the prison at all costs.

Ajax growled, his fists clenching so hard I thought they would explode with the sheer force. "You assholes *murdered my fucking brother*—"

Callum just stared Ajax down—not intimidated by the huge mass of man and muscle that stood before him, as if Callum knew his own skill and strength would still be enough to take down Ajax even as the brute seemed like he was about to explode with rage. "And I'd kill you, too, if you were stupid enough to think you could escape. That goes for all of you." Callum's gaze lifted to the other prisoners, resting for a split second on me before bouncing away. "You saw what happened to Lucille—and now Derrick—when they tried to escape. The trials will begin, and you *will* compete. If you don't, you choose death outside of the ring rather than a chance at a new life within it. If not at my hands, then at the hands of your High Sorceress."

As if on cue, a trio of guards went to the metal doors at the far end of the circular room, which had been bolted shut and seemed to be connected to an off-limits part of the prison.

A way out?

Before I could start to put together the pieces of how one entered and exited Ashguard, the doors flew open and *she* walked in.

She was a force to behold. She wore an ice blue robe and hood, her dark brown curls tumbling free as she walked. She was a vision of piety, wearing a white gown and a smooth golden circlet that rested above her brows. Her features were delicate, sensual in a way that contradicted her vision of innocence. Her lush lips seemed to promise sex even as her wide honey brown eyes shone with doe-like innocence. Behind her, three priestesses in the same ice blue robes followed her in, all of them flanked by a small army of guards.

I expected the other prisoners—like the hulking man who had jeered at me—to do the same when this vision of a woman walked in.

But no one made a sound. It was silent except for her satin shoes padding across the stone to the center of the circle before us. It was as if the others were... afraid of her. She parted her lips into a sweet smile.

"Good morning, contestants," she said, her voice warm, inviting, flirtatious. The lilt of every syllable promised certain pleasures even as a dark cruelty seemed to writhe in her layered gaze. "I pray you all have been training and resting up before what's to come?" She surveyed the group, but no one dared answer her.

Suddenly, a scream echoed at one of the higher levels, and everyone's gaze shifted.

"I refuse to compete in the trials!" a man's voice screamed. "You can't make me!"

My eyes tracked a man sprinting away from guards on the higher level. He was running until he stopped short—boxed in by more guards who had just cut him off. He was trapped.

Even though he was nearly six stories up, I could sense in the way his body stiffened and then slightly relaxed what had gone through his mind. *Resolve.* He was making a choice.

"RESIST THE ASH TRIALS!" he screamed, and then held up something that glinted in the stream of sunlight—a crude weapon. He moved as if to spear himself in his own heart—

"Stop him," she said with a voice that oozed total control. Right before the man was able to drive the makeshift weapon into his heart, one of the guards lunged for it, wrestling it out of his hand—

—and shoved him over the banister of the spiraling staircase. The man fell, landing in front of us with a sickening *thud* that echoed in the stone room. He had landed on his back, blood pooling out from every orifice, and his limbs were cracked in horrible, unnatural ways.

One of the guards moved to the body, but the woman held up a delicate hand. "No, let me." She reached down to the soupy mess of a man and punched through his chest with a kind of strength I didn't realize she was capable of. With horror, I realized she was digging around in the dead man's chest cavity for his heart, which she withdrew and squished between her fingers as blood rolled down in crimson rivulets from her hand, staining her white dress.

What was even more strange, however, was the glittering crystal that remained when the crushed heart fell away, just smaller than her fist. Her eyes flickered up to us.

"Have you ever seen a heart crystal before? Isn't it so beautiful, how the gods bless us with magic to be refracted in so many different ways, granting us each with our unique powers? It's an honor that you all get to be here to thank them yourselves with your participation in the holy Ash Trials. Wouldn't you all agree?"

Murmurs of agreement spread through the prisoners, and even the crouching madman Otto with the greasy hair bobbed his head in emphatic agreement as if he had known the pain of disagreeing with the woman before us in the depths of his bones.

The woman held up the bloody heart crystal and one of the priestesses ran over with a small square of fabric, wrapping the crystal. Cassandra waved the priestess away, her own hand still stained crimson. "You all know that heart crystals can implode upon death by suicide, especially when speared with a weapon. The man on the ground before you wished you all dead, and you are lucky the guards were able to spare you. It is imperative that you protect yourselves from those of you who wish to go against the will of the gods—and send you to the lands of eternal damnation. That's not what you're all here for, is it?" The woman's eyes swept over the rest of the prisoners and landed on me, and she floated toward me with a smile. "Now, I know some of you are our new guests. I am High Priestess Cassandra Wraithborn, keeper of the Temple of Orsi for the Order of the Serafim. It is nice to meet you, Saffron Vale." She held out her bloody hand for me to shake, as if daring me to squirm away.

I held my chin high as I took her hand and shook it, trying not to think too hard about the still-warm blood that coated it. I didn't reply, but I held her gaze, refusing to be intimidated.

Cassandra let my hand drop, and turned to the rest of the prisoners. "As you all know, the six Ash Trials are about to begin. This is why things are going to run a bit... differently around here as the trials begin. You will still have time for meals and allotted training and study time, but there will be no room for insubordination when it comes to the rules we do set for you. We only want the best to compete for King West and the Kingdom of Luminaria. Understood?"

"*Understood*," the prisoners echoed.

Cassandra smiled, turning to Callum, who stood like a statue of a war hero by the fallen body of the crushed prisoner. She ran a hand across his back as she circled behind him, and I saw him stiffen slightly under her touch. "Commander Callum Wells will take good care of you. And if you're lucky, you'll be out of here and staying in Saltspire Palace within a matter of weeks for the remainder of the trials. If you're not, you'll be nothing more of a mess that the rest of us will have to clean up."

Cassandra gave a sniff of her delicate nose as she cast a glance at the puddle of a man a few feet away from her.

"Illumia be with you," she said and nodded at all of us.

"*Illumia be with you*," voices responded in unison, and then everyone turned to their right, following the prisoner in front of them down another hallway. I followed the others, not breaking the single file, feeling Cassandra's gaze on my back.

The single-file line curled through another dizzying set of stone hallways adjacent to the silo's ground floor until we reached a large mess hall that felt like it was born out of the earth. Tables and benches seemed to have burst forth from the ground, covered in thick vines and wood. Even the buffet line—manned by staff in gold and white uniforms—seemed to originate from the soil. Food trays were refilled from the hollow of a tree, steaming as if it were some sort of oven. The line connected right to the end of the buffet table, prisoners grabbing wooden trays with the ease of repetition.

I watched the redheaded woman in front of me and copied her movements. I took my lunch tray and went down the line of surprisingly fresh-looking foods that seemed to have been offered up by the loamy soil itself.

"None for you, Rachelle," one of the servers said to the redhead. I zeroed in on her and her empty plate.

"You've got to be kidding me," Rachelle said, vibrating with anger, her wavy red hair and freckles making her look as fiery as her temper. "It was *one* time!"

"You're lucky you attempted to escape *last* week," the worker replied. "The punishment this week is much worse than a missed meal."

Raachelle's face flushed, and she stepped out of line with a sigh. I watched her from the corner of my eye as I moved through the line and collected mushrooms and strange root vegetables of different textures that were offered to me.

As I reached the end of the food line, I turned and surveyed the mess hall.

Prisoners had already chosen the groups they were sitting with at different tables. There was that hulking man, Ajax, and his equally large goons beside him. The willowy twins, Priscilla and Felicity, sat at a table with some of the more fair female prisoners. Then, there was a table of prisoners who looked deeply unhinged, which included Otto. Another of them stood silently by his table, doing pirouettes and locking eyes with me with each turn. Lastly, there was a table of smaller and weaker prisoners, including the young boy I had taken note of earlier, Issac, who eyed me with curiosity. Everyone had their own social caste and friend group here—everyone but me.

I shuddered at the unnerving presence of those around me, shifting my glance as I tried to size up the different groups...

...but my gaze snagged again on the red-haired woman, Rachelle, sitting alone with her head in her hands at a far table that looked even more covered in vines than the others, sloping at an odd angle.

I felt myself walking over to Rachelle. *I needed an ally.* But as I sat next to Rachelle, who was holding back tears in front of an empty plate, I knew my reasoning ran deeper than just finding an ally.

The truth shuddered through me as it floated to the surface. In my past life, I had known hunger. And I didn't wish it on anyone.

"Have some," I said, sitting next to Rachelle, who looked up at me with watery eyes. I slid onto the wooden bench beside her and pushed my plate in front of her.

"I can't," she said.

"Why not?" I asked.

"You need it just as bad as I do," Rachelle said, nodding down at me and my pointy collarbones protruding with silent protest against my skin. But I didn't care.

"Have some," I insisted once more, pushing my wooden tray to her like a treaty.

Rachelle took it as gratitude filled her gaze. She stabbed a large mushroom with a wooden fork. "I'm Rachelle Deveraux."

"Saffron. Saffron Vale," I said, remembering the last name that had been called out for me at roll call. It felt right when I tried it on my tongue.

"You're new, aren't you?" Rachelle asked.

"That's what they tell me."

She eyed me. "You're here to compete in the trials?"

"As far as I know," I said, the truth just one layer down.

Rachelle grinned. "You're right. What do I know? Maybe *you* are the first trial. You could just be a wraith come to fuck with us from The Foggy Forest of Embermere."

"Embermere?"

Rachelle raised an eyebrow as she stuffed another forkful of food into her mouth. "You don't know the name of this island? Gods, maybe you are a wraith. In that case, just drain my life energy and get on with it, already. The trials are going to be brutal and slipping into a quick death might be a mercy."

"How bad can they be?"

"Win and become a hero for Luminaria, or die on this island and become worm food," Rachelle quipped. "That's what they always tell us, and the kingdoms beyond these trials only know whisperings of what happens here. Each year, The Ash Trials are thrown to honor the gods and the prophecy—not that gods have walked this earth for millennia. All of our gods are dead—well, as close to death as gods can be. But if you win, you gain your freedom—after five years in service to King Owen West's army in the fight against Stormgard and the rebel kingdom they've formed after breaking off from Luminaria fifty years ago. The winner gets the honor of being bestowed the role of a high general—and all of the riches, land, and freedom that goes along with it. Survive the trials, and you get to live a renewed life. That's the closest to godliness any of us scoundrels can hope to get close to after our crimes, anyways. At least, that's what our precious King would have us to believe." Rachelle stabbed a vegetable with her fork with so much force I thought the metal utensil might splinter.

"Not a fan of the King?"

Rachelle laughed, a sound that was surprisingly singsong for the dire situation she was in. "The King is a loathsome royal, which is why death might be nicer than being back under his thumb."

"So that's why you were trying to escape?"

"Yes," Rachelle sighed. "I am magnificent, my dear Saffron. When you see me roar in the trials, you'll understand." She pointed her fork in my direction, a gleaming smile curling across her face. "But even I in all of my magnificence know that The Ash Trials are a death sentence. A way to cull magical prisoners in a way that entertains the King's courtiers and his allied kingdoms that he invites to come and watch. And *I* do not perform for *them*."

"There will be an audience?"

"As with everything the King does, yes, to an extent. So what did you do to end up on the wrong side of his laws?"

"I don't know."

Rachelle snorted. "That's what they all say. Fine, you don't have to tell me."

"I would if I remembered. All I remember is waking up in a cell in a wedding dress. The rest is just... nothingness before that."

Rachelle's fork froze. "Oh. Shit. You're being serious." She put down the fork, studying me more closely. "Do you even know what your power is?"

I hesitated, but something in me wanted to trust Rachelle. I needed her as an ally, so I made the risky decision to be vulnerable. "I think I may be a... *hollow*. One who doesn't have powers, I've been told."

Rachelle's eyes widened. "Gods, Saffron. You're not going to last a day here."

I leaned forward, folding my hands underneath my forearms so Rachelle wouldn't see them shaking as I swallowed my fear. "I know. I overheard that you tried to escape. How?"

Rachelle dropped her gaze, and she seemed to go to a different place. "Not just me. Lucille and I."

"Lucille," I said, remembering what had been said earlier this morning. "She..."

"Didn't make it," Rachelle said through clenched teeth. "She made a run for it just as the guards caught me. The island made sure she didn't get far."

The words made something on the back of my neck prickle, as if I was being watched. "What do you mean *the island* made sure she didn't get far?"

Rachelle stared me down. "No one who is branded with the mark of The Ash Trials may leave this island, Saffron. Not unless the gods will it. That's why you have no choice but to try and survive the first trial."

"I hope to last much longer than that," I said. As soon as the words tumbled from my lips, I realized they were true. I had a resolve that came from something I didn't fully understand.

Suddenly, a bloodcurdling scream echoed through the prison. All of the prisoners stopped eating, looking around for the source of the noise.

The guards who were stationed in the mess hall turned and ran back to the center of the silo, leaving us alone.

"What's happening?" I asked.

Rachelle watched every last guard run out of the hall. "I don't know, but I want to find out," Rachelle said, pulling me after her. "This way."

Rachelle dragged me down a separate weaving tunnel, toward the sound of screams. A *boom* tore through the prison, a rattling aftermath of an explosion that shook the walls. Dust and pebbles rained down on us as we ran through a narrow stone corridor.

Rachelle and I came to a stop at a tunnel opening that led into the circle of the silo where we had been earlier. As the dust from some kind of blast started to clear, I tripped on something below my feet. As I tumbled to the stone floor of the silo, I turned back to see that a guard's dead body had caused me to fall. I raised my head, and saw dozens of bodies of fallen guards littering the silo floor with piles of debris and fallen stone. The damage was massive—crumbling stone was littered everywhere.

"Saffron!" Rachelle called a few paces behind me where she stood half-hidden by the lip of the tunnel.

"What—" I started, but I screamed and jumped back as another body fell from above, another blast rocking the silo.

I looked up just one level above where I stood, and my eyes caught on a flash of dark green-and-blue flame—*shadowfire*, a voice from within me supplied the name. Even from here, I could feel the flame, but instead of rippling heat, I felt a blast of cold air—so cold I could see my breath.

But it wasn't the vast, all-consuming ripple of raw magic that nearly brought me to my knees. It was the immensity of the man who wielded it.

Ten guards lunged at him, and he lazily raised a hand, sending them flying over the banister with a smirk. He strolled past another dozen guards, descending down the spiraling staircase, giving me a better view of him as he strode across the ground floor of the silo, just ten paces away from me. He had dark black hair and high cheekbones that could cut glass. A swagger in his stride that looked casual, but belied a lethal grace. His black cloak flowed behind him as he summoned shadows that curled out of the ground around him. He was terrifying and devastatingly handsome—and I could feel the waves of absolute power rippling off him.

It was then that Callum emerged from the shadows opposite this strange man. Callum unsheathed his sword, standing strong and undaunted in front of this new threat.

"Stop. There will be no more bloodshed today, *Assassin*," Callum spat at him.

The man growled. "When I get what I want, the bloodshed will end."

"Will it?" Callum challenged.

"Where is—" the man started to yell but then stopped. The air shifted. Suddenly, he took a step back from Callum, and Callum followed the line of his gaze—

—to where I lay on the ground amidst the rubble and the bodies of the guards.

The world seemed to pause in that moment as the stranger's deep black eyes locked with mine. His gaze was intense, as if galaxies were unraveling and being reborn in his irises. His dark black hair framed his face, his hands glowing with the power of shadowfire. He seemed to be illuminated by a glow that was otherworldly, and having all of his attention—all of that power radiating off him—focused on me felt heady. Intoxicating, even in the danger that rippled from this predator.

The stranger took a step toward me, transfixed.

"No!" Callum shouted, and in that instant, he dropped to a knee, blasting his shield over himself, and stretching the shimmering magical shield over to where Rachelle and I were with a grunt of effort.

But the stranger kept walking. As if in a trance, he headed toward me with that piercing gaze that felt like it was dismantling every fiber of my being and rebuilding it again and again. It kept me glued to the floor, unable to move even as Rachelle lunged for me, trying to get me to move. To *run*. But I couldn't.

"Who are you?" I whispered. The question forced him to stillness, just a few feet in front of me. Some deep battle raging inside of him.

"Careful," Rachelle warned, gripping my arm. I couldn't tell if she was warning me or him.

But instead, a smirk stretched across this dark stranger's lips, and he bowed. "I am the Shadowfire Assassin. But you may call me Tristen Greywood."

The shield glowed around Rachelle and I in warning.

"Get away from them," Callum called from behind the stranger—

Tristen Greywood—and Callum slowly rose to stand while keeping his arms crossed as he continued to channel his magic into the shield.

Tristen turned and, with a flick of his wrist, sent a bolt of shadows after Callum, who was thrown backward, his shield lifting.

"Callum!" I yelled, but Callum was up in an instant, his sword glowing as he deflected Tristen's darts of magic. Tristen turned fully and shot a powerful blow of shadows toward Callum, but Callum expertly dodged. He threw out another blast of his shield, tossing Tristen off his feet, but Tristen quickly recovered, landing catlike in a fighting stance.

"We're done here," Tristen said, flicking his wrist as more shadows poured out from around him, the temperature in the silo dropping a few more degrees. I shivered as the shadowfire continued to gather at his hands, the building shadows making Tristen look like a god of death.

"We're done when I say we're done," Callum said, unsheathing his sword.

Tristen stalked toward Callum, his body glittering with raw power. Then, Tristen raised his hands, and the deadly blue-green flame shot out. Callum was shoved backward, hitting the stone wall behind him with a groan as he slid down it, his shield buckling under the force of Tristen's blast.

"I'm just here to take what's mine," Tristen said.

Callum struggled to his feet, and I could see the pain in that movement as he squared off against Tristen, his shield glowing around him once more. "I won't let you."

Something pushed me to a run just as Tristen's power began to build once more.

"STOP!" I screamed, and I slid in between the two men, throwing my arms around Callum. "Please," I said, looking up at Tristen.

The flames on Tristen's hands flickered, pausing. "You throw yourself in front of this man? To die for him?"

"He... he's the only one here who knows me," I confessed, my motives laid bare. "He's my friend." Or, that's who he said he had been to the past version of me. I needed Callum to help me uncover the puzzle of the void that threatened to swallow my sanity.

But I also didn't want any more blood to be shed today. I was exhausted by it—all of those who had been killed in front of me in the mere hours since I had awoken in my cell.

Tristen watched me, that piercing gaze heating with what felt like... hatred? Anger? I couldn't tell, but I was still made breathless by that heated intensity, the chill of his strange shadowfire causing goosebumps to rise on my skin.

Would I die here, before the trials even began?

But the shadowfire died on Tristen's hands. As it did, I realized that he was wearing a wedding band on his left hand. *He was married?*

"Very well, *Sael*," Tristen said to me. "If that is what you wish."

I frowned at the odd word—*Sael*—but Callum's expression hardened as he pulled me close.

"*Now!*" a voice called from behind Tristen.

As Tristen whirled, a dark net with a glowing aura was cast over him. The moment the heavy iron net landed in a sea around his body, the guards swarmed him. I felt an immediate dampening of the power in the room as the net closed in on him. The immensity of his shadows receded back into him, lifting the darkness that had dampened the room, the torches on the wall flaring once more.

Callum held me closer. "Shackle him in iron and take him away," he directed his guards.

"Yes, Commander," a chorus of guards replied, and they descended on Tristen, who emerged from the dark net with new iron bands on his arms and legs like the other prisoners. But despite his loss, he still looked unbothered. Nearly lounging in his new iron bands, he threw a smirk over his shoulder—

"See you soon," he said to me, his eyes sparkling. And then he strolled away, the guards leading him back to that staircase, toward the higher floors. Maybe even the highest, as the lethal nature of his magic would warrant the most secure cell block as his cage.

I unwrapped myself from Callum as he pulled away to look at me.

"Are you okay?"

"I think so. Who was that?"

Callum glanced around, seeing a few guards cast curious gazes our way. "Not here. Go back to the dining hall. I'll find you later."

I walked back to where Rachelle was standing in the corridor, her face pale.

"Fuckin' gods, Saffron," Rachelle said.

"What?"

"You threw yourself in front of the realm's most powerful magic wielder. Tristen Greywood, the *Shadowfire Assassin*. You're lucky he didn't shatter you with his power."

I shivered, my instincts about him being a predator being proven right. "Why didn't he?"

"I don't know, but you have to stay away from him. He's not just one of the most powerful wielders—he's a *mindweavyr*. And not the kind that respects your privacy."

"Mindweavyr?"

"This way," Rachelle said, pulling me back down the maze of tunnels to the mess hall. "Mindweavyrs can jumble your memories. Compel you to do things you don't want to. Tristen Greywood has been working with the rebels for a long time. He's killed many of King West's highest-level advisors—by warping their minds and leaving them for dead. Some he has the mercy to kill after he's ransacked their minds."

"Can he do that here?"

"Not while he's wearing those iron bands. But once we begin a trial... all bets are off. When the iron is gone, so is our protection from him." Rachelle leaned in closer. "The rumors say he once killed an entire village of Luminaria loyalists—just by convincing them to walk off a nearby cliff to their own deaths. Including the children. He's *that* powerful—and ruthless."

"If he's so powerful, how did he end up here?"

Rachelle shrugged. "Betrayed by his own, maybe? Our dear old King West has quite the spoils of war to feed his never-ending reserves of blackmail and persuasion. The King must be overjoyed to have such a powerful rebel leader in his clutches—all the better reason for you to stay away from him."

"Noted," I said as we slipped back into our corner table just as the guards returned. Rachelle didn't have to convince me to stay away from a man who had taken down a dozen guards with next to no effort. But I still wondered what had stopped him from destroying me.

"Everyone back to your cells!" the guards called, and there was a sea of white and gold as the guards started yanking prisoners up, herding them back down separate tunnels. The guards made it to our table, pulling us up by our arms.

"They never do this," Rachelle said before she was forced by her guard to head in a different direction. "Usually they give us some time to train."

"Then why now?"

"I bet we have the special *guest* to blame for this. I hope it doesn't last," Rachelle said. "See you soon, Saffron."

Rachelle was led down another hallway, and a single guard herded me down the maze of dark hallways that I was trying to commit to memory.

I was once more locked in my dark cell lit by the single row of torches, and I folded myself onto the cold cot. I tried to calm my sprinting heart, but everything I'd witnessed that morning kept replaying in my mind.

I hadn't lied to Tristen when I had flung myself in front of Callum. I knew that Callum was a key for a door in my mind—a door I would pay to unlock at any cost. Anything to banish the suffocating darkness of not knowing who I was and how I got here. And, selfishly, I saw Callum as an ally. Someone my past self trusted. I needed him to survive here.

Footsteps made me jump up as Callum rounded a corner with a lantern. As he found my gaze, he smiled. A brilliant, easy smile that softened his warrior's appearance.

"Here, I brought you something from the guards' mess."

His other hand held out a tin mug that was steaming with something hot. He bent down and slid it under the bars by the door where there was enough space for it to get through. I gently rotated it to pick it up by its handle, bringing it to my mouth as I stood back up. It smelled warm, earthy—and had a rich chocolate smell. Despite the steam and heat coming off the mug, I desperately tried to take a sip.

"Don't burn yourself!" Callum said, laughing, but it was too late.

I felt my tastebuds scream out as I stuck out my burned tongue, but I stared at the mug longingly. "What is this? It's so good."

"I thought so. Cocoa root tea. You used to drink it back in Riverleaf."

"Riverleaf?"

"Our village. Would you like me to tell you about it?"

"Yes."

Callum smiled, but it didn't reach his eyes as a sadness crept into them. "Rolling hills—endless green grass and fields with wildflowers that were so vibrant. The main town square was cut by a wide river that the shopkeepers used for trade. There were so many beautiful boats that bobbed down that main channel. We used to watch the boats go by together from the top of our favorite hill, but you always loved Artisans' Square, where all of the chocolatiers and seamstresses showed off their wares. Riverleaf was... peaceful."

"Was?"

"Many battles have been fought on Riverleaf's soil as it's a neutral border village that stands between Luminaria and the Stormgard rebels. But I'll always remember it as what it was before the war. Back when I used to steal tarts from your freshly baked supply. You got so mad at me—but you always baked more than your mother needed to sell. I think you saved them for me on purpose."

I blushed. "Sounds like I liked you."

Callum swallowed. "I think you did, too."

His description of me had melted my heart a bit—just like the hot drink I was cradling in my hands, the sweet smell teasing my senses. But there was no time for nostalgia. I had to get the answers I needed to survive. "What do I need to know about The Ash Trials, Callum?"

Callum sighed, looking at the ceiling—our moment broken.

"They are a series of six trials held every year. All prisoners must compete—but only one can win. The rest die trying."

I shivered, my new friend Rachelle blinking into my memory. "Only one survives?"

"It's your life or theirs. The final trial is usually just a deathmatch to decide the winner."

"And what should I expect from the other five trials?"

He winced. "They're brutal, Saffron. They are true trials of the mind and body, each one conjured by the island above a different burial site of a dead god. And no one knows exactly what they'll be each year, as the island decides—"

"The island? You're talking of the one we're on right now?"

"Yes. The Isle of Embermere. And it's listening to us. Deciding what trials are fit for its inhabitants. Its only goal—a directive given to it by the gods who are imprisoned here—is to turn mortals into heroes to carry out the gods' wishes."

I stared at him. "A sentient island is going to decide what trials we're going to go up against?"

Callum darkened. "Embermere is ancient. And it demands payment each year."

"Why?"

"The Isle of Embermere is trying to claw back what it wants. To destroy every living inhabitant on it. To eat every manmade structure. To reclaim every inch for itself. And if you can survive what it thinks it is owed—then you'll be strong enough to head up one of King West's armies. The old gods knew that our world would need heroes. This island is the antidote to that. It prevents our kingdom from becoming weak and succumbing to the rebels. The only thing safe from the island is Saltspire Palace. It's made from salt crystals and warded with magic so the island thinks it's organically part of itself. The King and his court live in Saltspire every autumn during the trials."

I nodded, trying to hide my sense of unease. "Okay," I said, processing.

"But you can't enter the trials, Saffron. You have to beg the King for mercy. When he comes to address the prisoners tomorrow morning, offer anything he wants. Try and get out of it—"

It dawned on me then. What he was truly saying. "You think I can't win," I said.

Callum's face softened. "You're smart, but the odds are stacked against you."

"Because I'm powerless?"

"Yes. But also because you're... *you.*" Callum reached through the bars and took hold of one of my hands. "You're the daughter of a baker. You make a mean tart, but... you're not a mean fighter, Saf. I lost you before, and I don't want to go through that again, not after I just got you back. So, *please.* Beg the King for mercy. For your sake. And mine."

I looked down as Callum's hands clasped around mine, the still-steaming mug warming my skin. He was right—I wouldn't last one of thes trials if the blood wielder and Tristen Greywood were any indication of what types of monsters I'd be up against. Even Rachelle could be something deadly. I would have no idea who any of my fellow prisoners were until their iron bands came off and their magic was unleashed in the first trial.

So why did it feel wrong to give up before the trials even started?

"Please," Callum said, his hands tightening around mine.

"Okay," I said, and he nodded, relief evident on his face. "I'll do whatever you think I should to get out of here."

"Get some rest," Callum said.

I curled back on the cot as Callum disappeared with the warm light of his lantern. I cradled the hot drink I used to love from a memory far, far away.

3

I spent the rest of the day pacing in my cell, breaking only for the brief meals the guards brought to me on a wooden tray—not allowing us to leave after the carnage caused in the wake of Tristen's entrance. The guards were wordless, ignoring my questions and leaving me alone with the stone walls and quiet cell block.

The silence around me echoed in my mind—and I found myself reduced to sobs several times as the darkness of my cell threatened to close in on me. It was as if I was drowning in the unknown, being dragged deeper into despair as I tried to grasp at something, *anything* to keep me tethered to this reality.

Who was my mother? My father? Were they alive? What about my wedding day? Who was there? Who had been left at the altar when I was ripped away from that day?

When sleep finally did claim me, it was like an endless dark. It rippled and swirled around me, sucking me deeper into the void of my mind until I jolted awake, gasping for air. Even my nightmares taunted me with the nothingness that filled the place where memories once lived.

"I'm stronger than this," I said aloud into the dark of the cell.

The choking darkness did not give me a reply.

❧

"GET UP, GIRL," a guard sneered at my cell, unlocking the door and holding it open. I recognized his wolfish grin and the ox-like build of his body. He was one of the ones who had jeered at me when I arrived.

"Or what?" I said as I pulled my stiff body off the hard cot, the morning chill causing my body to shiver as I appraised him in the light of the torches that illuminated the hallway.

"I can think of a few things," he said, licking his lips as he appraised me.

I felt my anger rise, boiling my blood. Screaming at me to *fight*. I held my head high as I stepped out of the cell, keeping my distance from the guard, but he grabbed my arm and pulled me close.

"Just try me, sweetheart. Nobody will care what happens to you down here."

"Get the fuck away from her Rook," a booming voice echoed down the cell.

The guard—Rook—slinked back from me, dropping my arm and bowing his head. "She was giving me trouble, Commander—"

Callum stopped just a foot in front of Rook, still several inches taller than the imposing guard. "I'm reassigning you to the mess hall."

"But Sir—"

"*Now*," Callum demanded with a cold authority that promised pain if Rook didn't obey.

Rook leveled a glare at me, but Callum grabbed him and threw him against the wall of the corridor with surprising force.

"Don't look at her. Look at me. You touch her? You die."

Rook scrambled to his feet, nodding before turning and running down a separate hallway.

When we were alone once more, Callum turned back to me. "Are you hurt?"

I shook my head, but my mind was reeling with the casual

strength he had just thrown the guard around with. "What did you do, back in our village? Throw bags of rocks around for fun?"

"Why? You think I'm strong or something?" he asked, a half-smile slipping up his stubbled cheek on his square jaw.

I flushed, but ducked my head and pushed past him to hide my feelings. "No. Aren't you supposed to escort me somewhere?"

"Y'know, I could tell you I was the most revered warrior in all the realms and you'd have to believe me," Callum said as he placed a hand on the small of my back, leading me through the maze of the prison corridors.

"Until I found someone else who knew me. So be careful how much you exaggerate. Would hate for someone else to tell me the truth," I teased, but Callum fell silent. My footsteps and the dripping water were the only sounds cushioning the strange silence between us. I frowned, picking up on a thread. "Callum, is there anyone else in here who knows me? From before?"

"No," Callum said, not entertaining my questions. "Now focus. The King will be arriving to address his *contestants*. You need to make sure that you're *not* one of them."

"Okay," I said. "I know Rachelle had mentioned her friend tried to escape—"

Callum gently put his strong hand on my shoulder, stopping me and turning me to face him in the dimly-lit stone corridor. "Lucille had the best chance of escape out of everyone here. Her heart crystal gave her the power to turn invisible, one of the more rare powers out there. She somehow got her metal bands off and was able to access her full power, slipping out while Rachelle caused a distraction. Lucille was running down to the beach with the intent to steal a boat —and she was found with a lung pierced by the sharp branch of the tree, her arms and feet bound by vines. She was still breathing when Cassandra found her."

"So she lived?"

Callum grimaced. "Cassandra made sure the girl didn't see morning."

I blew out a breath. "So escape isn't an option. And... I'm not a fighter."

Callum took my right hand and placed it on his heart. "Feel this?"

I felt the strong beat of his heart, realizing how close I was to him. "I do."

"Watch," Callum said as he pulled me down to kneel next to him as he called upon his power, my hand still at his heart. As his hands rose over his head in a cross, I saw his heart glow slightly underneath his uniform, feeling a warmth underneath my hand—just for a second before it faded and his shimmering blue shield shot up around us, glittering in the dark hallway.

"It's beautiful," I whispered, the shield taking my breath away, glimmering around us.

"Most of us have an ability that is refracted from our heart crystals. A power that protects, harms, or shifts our beings entirely. My power is strong, but there are others whose heart crystals only refract pain and suffering—like the Shadowfire Assassin. They'll kill you in an instant to get closer to freedom."

He let go of my hand and I mourned the loss of the heat of him underneath my palm. "You have no idea how I ended up here?"

Callum helped me to my feet, and we stood in the hallway once more. "I've tried to get access to your file, but the Order of the Serafim did not deign to consider my request. Only the *witches*—I mean, the High Pristesses and her followers, know the crimes of those who are brought here to rot—and the powers held by each of the prisoners, if those powers are known. But I know you've committed no crime. It's not in your nature to be violent. That's why you have to make your case to the King. *Today.*"

Callum kept walking, and I followed. "And if he refuses?"

"A King's blade will be a quicker death than the one you would meet in the ring," Callum replied, but his tone was strained. My stomach churned as I contemplated the nearness of my death.

Callum walked beside me for the last bit of the tunnels. But right before we turned the corner to the main floor of the silo, he grabbed my hand and squeezed it. I looked up at the warrior's face, and was surprised to see unshed tears glimmering in his eyes.

"Beg for his mercy. For me, Saffron."

I swallowed, nodding. Before I could say more, footsteps sounded behind us and Callum turned away from me. He turned into Commander Wells, taking his place at the front of the semicircle of prisoners. I walked onto the silo's ground floor once more, joining the circle of bloodthirsty prisoners, ready to beg for my life.

4

I stood by Rachelle at the end of the semicircle of prisoners as roll call came to a close.

"Morning, Saffron," Rachelle whispered to me as the same guard from yesterday called out names as we filtered into the circular space. "Get some good sleep in your new home?"

"Best night of sleep I can remember," I said, earning a giggle from her at that.

Then, a hush settled over the group. I followed everyone's gaze to one of the stone staircases, where twenty guards escorted Tristen down to the ground floor of the silo. He prowled down the spiral staircase, iron bands at both his arms and his ankles, darkness trailing in his wake as if the power dampening bands barely contained him. His powerful frame nearly brushed the weathered stone walls, each step a dance of predatory grace.

Rachelle let out a low whistle. "Damn, if he wasn't a murderer I would totally jump his bones. He's so hot."

Tristen's deep obsidian eyes landed on mine while a knowing smile played at his lips, filled with dark promises.

Rachelle noticed just as I averted my gaze. "Uh oh, does the Assassin have eyes for you, Saffron?"

"It doesn't matter if we're all going to die, does it?" I asked, gritting my teeth. Tristen was a heartstopping sight, and the feminine part of myself couldn't deny that. But I had also seen a wedding band on his left hand. There was no room for fantasizing about a married killer when I was here to try and escape with my life.

When Tristen joined the semicircle across from me, the guards seemed nervous to step away from him, crowding all around him as if ready to spring into action and try and take him down.

"Call off your hounds, *Commander*," Tristen said in a bored tone, his hands in his pockets. "I wouldn't want anyone to get hurt." The threat was delivered in his honeyed voice, extra sweet to get under Callum's skin.

Callum glared. "You've lost, *Assassin*. Your capture will send a clear message to the separatist rebels of Stormgard that the time has come to rejoin Luminaria. You'll either die here or live long enough to become a traitor to the rebel crown. The will of the gods always prevail."

"The gods' will means nothing," Tristen said to a chorus of surprised gasps from the other prisoners—who clearly feared the gods I knew nothing of. In response, I swore the ground below us let out a low rumble. "Not only are they trapped beneath the soil of this cursed island, but they only seek to use this cruel bloodsport you call *trials* to free themselves of this island and conquer the world once more. The gods want nothing more than total destruction. Mark my words."

Whispers rippled through the other prisoners, and Callum closed the gap between him and Tristen. Callum unsheathed his sword, bringing it to caress Tristen's neck.

"You forget. *I* carry out the will of the gods here, Assassin," Callum said, drawing a thin line of blood from Tristen's neck with his sword.

"Go ahead. I like it rough," Tristen said with a wink.

Bloody murder shined in Callum's eyes, but he pulled away and sheathed his sword as the metal doors behind him started to creak open.

"Attention! The King arrives," Callum called, the guards letting out a unified stomp, standing up straight. "All kneel for His Majesty, King Owen West, Wielder of Ilumia's Light, Savior of the Kingdom of Luminaria, Defender of the Fallen."

Callum stepped back, and turned to the open doorway, kneeling. The other prisoners did the same. I caught on and followed suit. On one knee, I watched King West enter the silo's ground floor, flanked by several decorated guards in white uniforms with gold trim.

King West looked no older than thirty-five years of age, and he strode in like an aristocrat used to wearing a heavy crown and all the jewels that came with mastering the art of politics. His beauty was soft, and he had dark brown-gold hair like the color of spun straw that had heated into gold. He looked regal, but lacked the kind of rough brutality that Callum and Tristen and some of the other prisoners had in spades. He was no warrior, that was clear by his milky smooth skin. His body had not seen hard labor. He was decorated royalty through and through.

"You may rise," King West said, his voice like music. With the sound of scraping boots and iron, we rose on his command. "As you all know, the trials are due to start in just a few days' time—"

"Please," the woman with huge buglike eyes said, throwing herself at his feet. "Mercy! I beg of you, Your Majesty. I beg for mercy."

King West paused, looking at the woman at his feet. The guards tensed, ready to jump in and restrain the prisoner, but they waited for their king's reaction.

"Please," the woman wailed again. "I don't belong here. I have a family. Children—"

"What is your crime?" King West asked, low and quiet.

With a hitching breath she looked around, and then back at the King. "I didn't know."

"Didn't know what?"

"That he was a guard. I..."

"What is your crime?" the King boomed.

The woman flinched. "Murder. I didn't realize it was a royal caravan—"

"You were just trying to rob any merchants who crossed your path, just not those from my court, is that correct?"

"Yes. No. I—I have children I need to get back to. Hungry mouths to feed—"

"Anyone else looking for mercy?" the King asked, looking around.

I felt Callum's eyes on me, but I didn't look his way. But it didn't matter, the King caught Callum's gaze.

"Commander Wells? Is there something you'd like to tell me?" King West asked.

"No, my King," Callum said simply.

But King West was already walking over to me, curiosity in his gaze. "Is there something you'd like to ask me?"

I sucked in a breath, ready to do what Callum suggested. The smart thing. The safe thing. Begging for mercy so I could live instead of die.

But as I opened my mouth to speak, it was not my voice that rang out across the silo.

"She does not, because she doesn't deserve your mercy," a smooth, dark voice said from across the room. All heads whipped to Tristen, who leveled a harsh gaze at me. Those dark obsidian eyes flashed with that same intensity.

"Excuse me?" King West asked.

"You do not recognize the face of The Lord Killer after so many attempts at her capture?"

A hush settled upon the entire room. Then, it was immediately broken by frenzied whispers. The prisoner on the other side of me shuffled away slightly as if recoiling from my presence. To her credit, Rachelle didn't flinch away, but I felt her eyes on me, watching my reaction. Even the King dropped his chin, an eyebrow raised.

"I was not informed by The Order that The Lord Killer was within the walls of my prison."

"Then you have a High Sorceress to punish, don't you?" Tristen said. "You're looking upon the most lethal serial murderer of all the

realms—one who seduces and kills her male prey in all matter of...
creative ways."

My heart dropped. *The Lord Killer.* I couldn't be a murderer. *Could
I be?*

"Those are baseless rumors," Callum stepped in. "My liege, we do
not know the true identity of The Lord Killer. Saffron can't be her.
She's an innocent daughter of a baker—one who should be excused
from the trials."

King West slowly turned his head to Callum, studying him.
"Commander Wells, since when do you speak for the prisoners? Let
alone, know their names?"

Even wearing his stony demeanor, I saw the slight wince that
cracked Callum's facade. My heart skipped a beat. Callum was
wading into risky waters for me, and I almost wanted him to stop—to
protect himself against whatever punishment would surely follow for
this.

"Please, Your Majesty, show mercy." Callum bowed his head with
respect.

"I'll be her mercy. Leave it to me, my King," said the meaty man
who had made a pass at me yesterday. He sneered at me from down
the line, licking his lips. I clenched my fists, trying to keep myself
from stalking over and punching him in the face—despite him easily
being two or three times my size. The others were whispering and
snickering, and I still felt Tristen's heavy gaze on me as the prisoners
sized me up.

"Silence!" King West bellowed, stunning the group into quiet as
he continued, "From the light of Ilumia herself, I am here to issue a
warning and a promise. The Isle of Embermere and The Ash Trials
never fail to provide us with the hero that Luminaria needs to win its
battles against the rebels intent on slaughtering our families and children. As quelling the rebellion grows more challenging, you have an
opportunity in these trials. You can leave here not just a warrior, but a
hero amongst our people. Maybe this will be the year that the
prophecy will come to pass, and the one will rise who will silence this
revolution once and for all, uniting the Kingdom of Luminaria again

with its wayward brethren of Stormgard. Together, we will find peace. Isn't *that* worth fighting for?"

A roar of cheers erupted from some of the more violently inclined prisoners. I stole a glance at Tristen, who was watching the King with narrowed eyes.

An assassin for the rebels, I remembered. Of course he wasn't thrilled by the King's speech—he was on the other side of the fight.

Beside me, Rachelle straightened as King West briefly gazed at her, a half-smile on his lips before he turned away. Before I could whisper a question to her about it, King West crossed to the shuddering woman who had begged for mercy earlier. "Do you still wish to forfeit the trials?"

"Yes," she said, and the King inclined his head toward one of his royal guards to lead her away from the line.

The King leveled his gaze at me. "I would have considered a plea of mercy from an innocent villager, perhaps. But from The Lord Killer? You will need to find your own brand of mercy in the ring."

Snickers emanated from the rest of the prisoners, but they kept their distance. Did I now make them uneasy with this new reputation? I looked over at Callum, but he was glaring daggers at Tristen, who had a self-satisfied smirk on his face. The bastard had just ruined my chances of escaping the trials—and gaining the King's mercy.

"Take her to the surface," the King said to the royal guards, who escorted the woman to the doors behind us. "And may Illumia be with you, contestants." King West nodded and turned, walking back to the doors, flanked by his guards.

As the King and his cadre left the silo, my heart dropped.

I was officially a contestant of The Ash Trials—and perhaps I had even unlocked part of my past. A past where I was The Lord Killer— so monstrous that I was not worthy of mercy, only disgust.

Had Tristen been telling the truth about who I really was?

5

Since the damage was repaired from Tristen's entrance, we were allowed back into the regular routine—and permitted out of our cells after the King left. As we were shuffled to the dining hall, I felt Callum's hand on my arm, pulling me in step with him at the back of the line where I was out of earshot of the others.

"Did you know?" I whispered to Callum, slowing my pace so I walked beside him.

"You're *not* The Lord Killer," he said.

"How can you be sure?" I asked. "You didn't even know I was to be married, or to whom. How much do you even know about me, anyways?" My sharp tongue cut deeper than I intended, but I couldn't help it. Was I a maiden? Or a monster? Not knowing the full truth was slicing at me like shards of broken glass.

Callum hid the flash of pain that sparked across his face at my words. "We grew up together, Saffron. I knew you until you turned twenty-one. The day you were taken."

My eyes widened. "Taken?"

"Riverleaf was a neutral village. A place where merchants from Stormgard and Luminaria could come and exchange goods and services. Where separated families could meet safely. But the rebels didn't like how King West was eyeing our village. They decided to make a stand. And you were kidnapped. It's been nearly a year since I've seen you last."

My heart pounded as this piece of information clicked into place. "Is a year enough time for me to become a cold-blooded killer?"

"Don't believe the lies of these people. Tristen is a degenerate and labeled you to eliminate any chance of the King letting you go free."

"Why?"

"Because he's a sadistic monster," Callum said, as if it was obvious. "Tristen Greywood is in enemy territory. He will do anything to hurt the King and anyone who isn't aligned with the Stormgard cause."

"Who is The Lord Killer, anyways?" I asked.

"They're stories, Saf."

"Then tell me them."

Callum sighed, finally giving in. "The Lord Killer is a notorious black widow who went after nobility. Killed them for their fortunes—often after seducing them. Legends say that she would sever their manhood and feed it to them, choking them to death." Callum grimaced at the image.

A shiver slipped down my spine. If I truly wasn't The Lord Killer, Tristen had been quick to throw me into the fire. How would I survive him—or any of them—when they all had access to their powers in the ring?

"Hey," Callum said, pulling me into an alcove just outside of the dining hall. He brushed a stray white-blonde curl of hair out of my face and tucked it behind my ear. "You'll get through this."

"How?"

Callum steeled his expression. "You may not be able to win with magic. But you can win with wits."

"Is there a bread baking trial I'm not aware of?" I asked, attempting to lighten the mood.

Callum smiled, but his gaze still held so much sadness. "I'll do my best to protect you, but I can't do anything once you set foot inside the trials. You need to be careful—the island has already begun to try and cull out the weaker ones."

In that alcove, I was aware of Callum's strong frame so close to mine. He was a warrior, all right. His broad shoulder carried his heavy weapons with ease. His warm green eyes were like freshly cut grass. Comforting and warm, with the promise of a sunny day in them. In that moment, I could see him wanting to say more, but he stopped himself. Callum stepped away from me, and I felt a piece of myself mourning his nearness. I took a deep breath and forced a smile to my face.

"Thank you, Callum," I said, my voice coming out more quiet and unsteady than I'd intended.

"Stay alert," he said, and just like that the Callum I knew morphed back into the Commander role he wore so well.

"I will, Commander," I said with a small smile, and he pulled away from me, disappearing into a crowd of other guards who were waiting for him. I split off toward the mess hall line, but as I did, I was hit by a strong, familiar scent. A scent that set off ripples amongst the prisoners—*darkspice*, a tea that smelled so warming and familiar to me. Just the smoky aroma of the beverage perked me up as I noticed the steaming stone carafes that sat on the earthen tables, begging us to pour them into stone mugs.

"Oh *gods* that smells good," Rachelle said from beside me in the mess line. Some of the prisoners couldn't resist, even peeling off from the line for food in order to coax the liquid into mugs, risking their breakfast in exchange for first dibs at the luxury before them. "I haven't had darkspice since I visited Frell." Then, glancing at my blank expression, she filled me in. "Major port city in Luminaria. *Sublime* sweetbread, which pairs even better with the bitter taste of darkspice."

"It smells like home," I said, watching a strong man with a hulking set of muscles pour himself a cup of darkspice tea and savor it with eyes that rolled back into his head.

"And where's home to you?" Rachelle asked gently.

I reached back into my mind, probing for the answer... but came up with nothing. Only what Callum had told me. "Riverleaf, I'm told," I said. "But maybe sense memory could help me. Maybe..." I stepped out of the mess line, walking toward one of the carafes. The scent of the darkspice grew stronger, earthier. Reminding me of specters of slow mornings, wrapped in bedsheets. Soft caresses. Breakfast in bed. Someone trailing kisses up my thigh—

"I wouldn't do that if I were you," a smooth voice purred.

I had one hand on a carafe when a man's hand shot out to grip my wrist, stopping me.

Not just any man.

Tristen Greywood. *The Shadowfire Assassin.*

Electricity shot through my body at his touch. Up close, he was even more breathtakingly handsome. His eyes were dark obsidian that seemed to warm slightly as he studied me. His lips were quirked into a smirk. But this close, I could smell the scent of him—spice and oak, like magic sparking in the forest. Like... something else I couldn't quite place.

But Tristen was standing between me and a potential memory—I wouldn't allow it. I needed to learn as much as I could about myself before whatever was coming. Besides, he had made it clear that he was here to fight dirty—and had oh-so-kindly *gifted* me the reputation of The Lord Killer that had kept me from receiving the King's mercy.

"I can pour my own cup," I said, reaching over to remove his hand.

He let go, watching me pour the dark liquid into one of the stone mugs that was slightly misshapen as if it had been forged by the earth itself.

"I never said you couldn't. I just don't think it's wise. Considering..." he inclined his head in the direction of another table.

I looked up, following his gaze...

...and saw the strong man from earlier foaming at the mouth, seizing as half-drunk tea was spilled in front of him and a hush descended over the dining hall.

"It's poison," I breathed, dropping the mug with a *crash*. I turned back to Tristen, catching his unreadable dark gaze. He had saved me. The feared *Shadowfire Assassin* had saved me? "Why did you warn me?"

"I think you'll be of use to me in the trials. Would be a shame for some hot beverage to take you out before things get... interesting," he said, shrugging.

"Playing favorites over there, Tristen?" a mocking voice called, and the beefy man I recognized as Ajax ambled over. "I hate to inform you, but I've already called dibs on the new girl. She still owes me a dance."

"Back off, Ajax, or *I'll* be your new dance partner," Tristen said, and there was something deadly in his tone. But that didn't stop Ajax giving me a once-over with his hungry eyes. The man was built like a wrestler, all rolling muscles and pure strength like a human boulder.

"What are you going to do about it? Turn my mind against me? I'd love to see you try," Ajax goaded.

Tristen leaned back, putting his hands in his pockets. "It's not me you have to worry about. After all, *you're* the one trying to call *dibs* on The Lord Killer."

Ajax took me in. Others around us watched our interaction with morbid curiosity and fear. Fear of me? Or of what Ajax would do to me?

"Well, I speak for the rest of the prisoners when I say I can't let you in the trials. Which is a letdown—I would have liked some play time with you. Nothing personal, *girl*."

"Don't call me *girl*," I said, my voice low and deadly.

Ajax lunged for me, but something took control in that moment. A heat flashed in my veins, and my body moved almost without thinking.

I snatched the hot carafe of poisoned darkspice and hurled it at Ajax. It made contact, smashing open on his face, the liquid still steaming hot. He screamed, staggering backward as he clutched his eyes. Shattered ceramic was embedded all over his face, and he clawed out pieces of the stone carafe, the hot poisoned drink mixing with his blood.

"You bitch!" Ajax yelled and then charged at me.

A baker's daughter would have cowered. Or ran, maybe.

But I knew I wasn't just some baker's daughter.

I crouched low, swinging out a leg just in time to trip Ajax. He fell to the ground with a loud *thump*, and I didn't hesitate. I jumped on top of him, burying a knee into his chest, my forearm at his throat, choking him. My movements were natural, instinctive.

This is who I am, I realized, my body telling me a kind of truth.

I didn't hear the thundering feet of the guards as they ran toward me. I just felt the molten roiling in my veins, the ringing thought in my head.

Kill him before he kills you.

But as the guards pulled me off Ajax, I caught sight of Tristen, who was watching me with an eyebrow raised. He looked... *impressed.*

It took several guards to drag Ajax out of the mess hall as he screamed a mixture of curses and threats my way. I doubt a little bit of poison was enough to kill a hulking man like him—especially considering the energy behind his screams. I had only made my enemy angry with me.

"What's going on here?" a voice boomed, and Callum took in everything, zeroing in on me. "Who hurt you?"

Rachelle hurried over from across the mess hall. "Ajax attacked Saffron—"

A hush settled over the mess hall, and Callum stiffened, as if sensing the female presence before she showed herself.

Cassandra and a trio of priestesses entered the mess hall. "Commander. I have a new order from King West—one that is to take effect now as the island has started to see fit to cull the herd." Her eyes flickered to the carafes. So the *island* had poisoned those drinks?

"What is the order?" Callum asked, his expression cold.

"As of this moment, our guards will interfere with nothing other than escape attempts, which will be met with a swift death. The prisoners are all on their own—no help or aid may come from any of us. Or you, Callum." Then, Cassandra turned from Callum, addressing us directly. "Survival is in your hands now. Might as well get some training in. Your first trial has been called for tomorrow," Cassandra said. She then walked away with her cadre of guards and priestesses, and Callum backed away, looking furious as he was forced to follow.

I was on my own now.

~

I FELT Rachelle pull me into our corner table in the dining hall, saw the food she placed in front of me, but my mind was still stuck on the fight I had just had with Ajax.

I fought him. And won.

"Saffron, you have to eat something," Rachelle said, and I realized I hadn't touched anything on my plate as we sat side-by-side in the mess hall. "You can't train on an empty stomach."

"Why was Ajax so eager to try and kill me?" I asked, my mind still catching up with me.

"It was a dirty move for Tristen to bring that up in front of everyone. Because if you *are* The Lord Killer—and that's still *just* a rumor right now—you pose a gruesome threat to everyone in here. But, for the record, I don't think you're The Lord Killer."

"Thanks, Rachelle," I said.

"In fact, I think you're way more evil and violent than that," she said, a grin on her face.

I rolled my eyes as she laughed, clearly fucking with me. "Well, that would be helpful in the trials, at least. But why would Tristen spread a rumor like that if it wasn't true?"

Rachelle studied me. "The Ash Trials aren't just about surviving the trials themselves. It's about surviving the people around you. Tristen was clearly trying to paint a target on your back." She sighed. "Unfortunately he seems to be both hot *and* a manipulative genius."

"Why would he paint a target on my back only to try to save me from the poisoned tea?"

"He can't have everyone just ganging up on him when the trials start. You're as good of a target as anyone, so he probably saved you to be his shield. He will keep on shifting the target to you as it suits him.

Just keep an eye on him—I know mine already are," Rachelle said with a swoon and a sigh.

I smiled at her exaggerated admiration of Tristen's good looks and speared some vegetables with my fork, trying to fit together what had happened that morning. Everything felt blurry, wrong. Like the thoughts running through my mind hadn't quite hit on the right answer. Puzzle pieces were floating, but not locking into place yet.

Breakfast finished quickly—no one really wanting to dine with the lingering corpses and the reminder of luxuries turned weapons— a cruel start to our trials.

As breakfast concluded, the guards didn't shuffle us back into our cells. Instead, they corralled us down another network of stone hallways that were cracked with vines, as if the lush veins of the island were snaking their way into the heart of Ashguard.

What was even more strange is that these hallways started to slope *upward*. As the damp smell of the prison started to recede, I felt a strange fresh breeze hit my skin.

I fell in step next to Rachelle. "Are we leaving the prison?" I asked, having only known near-darkness since waking up in Ashguard.

"Don't get too excited, rookie," she said.

But I couldn't help myself, pushing forward to the front of the group as the upward-sloping tunnel gave way to my first glimpse of the island.

The guards stood by the entrance of the training grounds as the rest of us prisoners spilled out onto the lush grassy training ring. This wasn't just some field, however. The circular training ring was a wide clearing surrounded by tall rose bushes that bore black roses, their petals littering the edges of the training arena with ominous black spots—as if the forest itself was crying black tears. A few strange-looking trees dotted the interior of the training grounds. The breeze was temperate with just a hint of humidity, the smell of exotic plants sweet and spicy on the light wind.

"C'mon, let's warm up," Rachelle said, grabbing me and leading me to a pile of springy moss that surrounded the raised fighting ring at the center of the training grounds. As we walked, I saw other prisoners reaching up to rip off branches from the trees. But they weren't branches—

"Are those swords growing from the trees?" I asked in surprise, watching as some of the more menacing prisoners went to go tear off huge wooden practice swords and other intimidating weapons that the trees in the training ring seemed to have made just for this purpose. Another prisoner ripped off a wooden dagger that seemed to have been growing from a lower branch, and the edge of the practice blade looked blunt—but still sharp enough to do some damage.

"The Isle of Embermere provides for us all," Rachelle said, mocking Cassandra's singsong tone. Rachelle and I reached the mossy patch, and she started to stretch atop its springy surface. "The rules are simple. Training time is free time and you can grab practice weapons, do exercises, or just wait for it to be over. You just need to avoid the sparring ring." Rachelle inclined her head to where four glowing mushrooms grew out of the ground, boxing in the sparring ring that was elevated above the rest. Two ropes made of vines encircled the sparring ring, closing it off from the rest of the training grounds. A single stone wall lined the back side of the training ring, and I wondered how many heads had been bashed into that wall during a fight.

"Why should I avoid it?" I asked.

"Because the only *other* rule here is that each prisoner can be called to the sparring ring once per training session to spar with another prisoner. If you get multiple invitations to spar, you must accept at least one of them per training session. It's how we settle things around here—we fight until the other prisoner yields. But with the guards no longer allowed to intervene, who knows how far those matches will go now," Rachelle said.

I watched as the other prisoners went to lift heavy stones or sprint through agility courses, each trying to hone a unique advantage beyond their magic, which was still leashed by their magic-dampening iron bands. Still, others went to some of the stout tree stumps covered in moss that were perfect striking height, bashing their wooden weapons against them in frightening displays of force.

I sucked in a deep breath as I watched those around me prepare to fight—to kill.

Would I even stand a chance when their bands came off and their magic was set free?

"My sister has come to spar with you," I heard a female voice say.

I turned to see the two willowy twins awaiting me.

"I want to see what you can do, Lord Killer," one of the twins—I think it was Felicity—said, baring her teeth as she flipped a wooden practice dagger. "I'd like to see you try and live up to your reputation, you psychopath."

A crowd was forming, and my heart dropped. The rules were the rules—I was going to have to fight in the training ring. Rachelle stepped up next to me, but I knew she could do nothing in the face of Ashguard's rules.

"No. She's mine," a low voice said. Every word sounded like sweet molasses as they dripped from *his* lips.

The crowd parted to allow Tristen to pass. Murmurs echoed his name. Despite the heavy iron bands on his wrists and ankles, he still *strolled*. As I took him in, I felt the breath punch from my lungs. A dusting of dark stubble gave him a roguish look. But it was his deep obsidian eyes that melted me—yes, deeply *melted* me as his gaze settled on mine. Something flickered across his irises as he stared at me. The revered Shadowfire Assassin was now stalking me as his prey.

Hadn't he thrown me to the wolves already by claiming me to be some sort of killer?

"I am not yours," I said, keeping my voice level to hide my anger.

"Don't accept his challenge," Rachelle warned in a low voice. "Fight Felicity instead. You only have to accept one of your challengers, and it shouldn't be him."

Tristen shot Rachelle a dazzling smile and winked. "Ah, another lady who has heard of my talents."

"Back off, Tristen," Callum said from where he circled the outer edges of the training grounds. Suddenly, he was unsheathing his sword, placing it and the rest of his gear on a bench made of roots and branches as he approached, now unarmed. "I will spar with Saffron."

"Callum," I admonished, noting the way the other guards looked at me too closely. Callum was bringing the wrong kind of attention to himself—to us.

"Didn't dear Cassandra say you couldn't interfere with our fights?" Tristen taunted. "Or do you think Saffron is so defenseless that she can't take the rest of us on in a fight?"

"No, I'm here to personally ensure that she can wipe the floor with all of you. You saw what she did to Ajax. Let's go, Saffron," Callum said, nodding to the sparring ring.

But Tristen stepped swiftly in his way. "It would be strange for a Commander of such a high standing to challenge a trainee. Wouldn't it?"

Callum paused.

"That's right," Tristen said. "Now let me pass. As the High Sorceress said, it's *our* prison now. No guard involvement allowed any longer now that the trials are upon us. Come, Saffron—let's fight."

The way he said my name sounded like sin. It heated me in ways I could not admit to this smirking man who was putting me on display yet again. Forcing me to show up, rather than cower in anonymity.

"Scared?" he asked, leaning closer to me. His eyes were taunting, and something in me couldn't back down.

"In your dreams," I said. It would have been wise to accept Felicity's challenge instead, but my body was already moving to the sparring ring. I held on to the top rope of the sparring ring, and swung my legs over the edge, walking to the far side and falling into a fighting stance as I turned.

Tristen grinned, joining me on the raised platform. The mushrooms at each corner of the sparring ring seemed to glow slightly, as if the island itself was acknowledging our presence. "Then show me what you've got."

I didn't hesitate. I launched myself at him like a pit viper, unleashing the pent-up muscle memory that had been curling in my body ever since I had awoken in my cell. He deflected my first punches with ease.

"Rusty?" he asked, drawing back and stretching his neck.

I narrowed my eyes. "What's your problem with me?"

He quirked his head. "Problem?"

"You could have picked anyone else."

He shot out at me, but I dodged, going to sweep his leg like I had with Ajax, but Tristen caught my ankle—crouching down and yanking me toward him in a smooth motion as I yelped.

"The others aren't nearly as fun," he said, his body on top of mine, the whisper of his breath by my ear. I felt every part of him pressed against my body—and I was so hot with anger at yet another man trying to *claim* me.

"I'll show you how *fun* I am," I said, snatching his wrist and catching him off-balance so I could roll out from underneath him—

—and then I allowed him to fall face first on the springy moss of the sparring ring. I twisted his hand behind his back, shoving him into the ground.

"Yield or I break your wrist," I threatened.

A half-smile crept across his lips as he turned his face to me. "I will not yield," he said, but before I could register what he was doing, he used his legs to swivel himself out of my grasp. Quick like a panther, he rolled us over. I found myself pinned once more underneath him. I squirmed as a deep part of my mind was about to execute my next move when those lips of his were by my ear once more.

"Yield," he said with a quiet intensity. "Yield to hide the strength you so desperately want to prove to me that you have within you."

Was he asking me to let him win? *Absolutely* not.

"Saffron!" Callum yelled from the sidelines. "Tap out!"

A fire stoked in my veins. "I will not yield," I said, throwing Tristen's words right back at him and ignoring Calllum. *I would not be seen as weak.*

And then we were on our feet once more, fighting, meeting each other's blows like a brutal dance that my body strained and struggled to keep up with, his lithe smoothness always one step ahead of my kicks and jabs.

But I saw an opening. Saw how Tristen had a slower left side. Just slow enough—

—I went to land a blow, but he had me. *It was a trap.* He spun me around, pressing me up against the only solid wall of stone of the sparring ring, my arm at an uncomfortable angle behind my back.

"Yield," he said, his voice husky.

"No."

"Are you sure? A little bird told me that you might need this arm for an upcoming trial or something," he growled.

"Why do you care?" I shot back.

"I don't. But you should," he said, adding just enough pressure to show he was serious without injuring me. "Yield!"

Pain shot up my arm, but I *couldn't* yield—wouldn't—

Out of the corner of my eye, I saw Callum stalking to pick up his sword where he had laid it down earlier. About to break his promise, his duty to his role. *He would do that to save me.*

As Tristen twisted harder, nearly bringing my arm to an unnatural angle as pain lanced through me—

"STOP! I yield," I yelled, my voice cracking with pain.

Tristen dropped my arm and I felt my breath *whoosh* back into my lungs.

I whirled, glaring at Tristen, whose dark black hair was mussed from our fight. "You fiend," I growled at him, feeling like the animal within me was starting to claw its way to the surface.

Tristen's eyes glittered black. "I'm your enemy, Saffron. Just like everyone else in this place. Don't forget that. *Ever.*"

Slowly, the crowd around the training ring dispersed. As I turned from Tristen, I still felt his gaze upon me as I jumped out of the sparring ring, rejoining a wide-eyed Rachelle down below.

"Saffron... that was..."

"I lost," I said with a frown. Across the training grounds, Callum was glaring at Tristen, unrestrained rage in his expression. Tristen pretended not to notice, pulling off his shirt as he moved on to do

pull-ups from a thick branch of a nearby tree, a gaggle of female prisoners and guards lurked around him—both groups watching him
intently for different reasons.

"But you're a fighter. A good one," Rachelle said, awe in her voice.
"You fight like you were trained. For a long time."

I nodded, that piece clicking into place, at least. It felt right. And it
would maybe give me a chance against these vicious opponents. "It
makes sense," I murmured.

"Let's go do some drills. Get some space between you and him,"
Rachelle said as she cast a look in Tristen's direction. "Not that you
would want space from that specimen of a man, damn."

I nudged her. "Tristen's all yours," I said, and she just laughed.

"If only we were fighting for something more fun," Rachelle said
with a sigh as we crossed the training hall.

As we moved through the other drills in preparation for the first
trial, I couldn't help but notice how the other prisoners started to give
me a wider berth. They were avoiding me. For now.

In claiming me in front of the others and showing them what I
was capable of, Tristen had unwittingly given *me* a shield. I hoped it
would keep me company through the first trial—when everyone's
magic would be finally unleashed.

6

I spent the rest of our allocated training time running drills with Rachelle—who was evil incarnate as a trainer. There were a set of root patterns on the ground by a big tree that she used for agility drills, having me run through them wih high knees. She tied stones around my waist and yelled at me to run, and I fought against the heavy weight as they dragged me down. Rachelle tied stones to herself, too, but somehow she was able to run literal circles around me, playing both drill sergeant but also giddy best friend as she clapped and jumped up and down every time I finished a set.

"You're a beast," Rachelle said as we drank from our waterskins. I sat on the ground, trying to catch my breath as she stood and stretched.

"I feel like jelly," I whispered as I tried not to heave up my meager breakfast, not wanting to appear weak in front of the others.

"You just gotta keep fighting, Saffy my gal," Rachelle playfully punched me. "You may say you're not The Lord Killer, but you did kill that workout."

I rolled her eyes. "Whatever you say, boss."

The training grounds were slowly emptying out as prisoners

headed back to their cells. As Rachelle went to the small stream at the edge of the training grounds to refill her waterskin, I followed her. But instead of going to the stream, I walked to the tall hedges of black roses that circled the training grounds, keeping us in.

I edged closer to them, trying to see through to the other side. What might await us beyond these bushes. Curious, I started to put my hand into the bush to try and part it—

"STOP!" Rachelle said, and she yanked my arm out just in time as the bush grew sharp thorns the size of daggers.

I stumbled back, staring at the bush in shock. I watched as the thorns slowly receded. "What is this place?" I breathed.

Rachelle shook her head, leading me back to the patches of moss where we had been stretching before. "All of the gods were imprisoned on this island generations ago by our ancestors. This island might have been normal before, but it's not now. The gods—if they are truly waking up—want us to participate in these trials. That's why the island keeps us here. Only those with Illumia Crystals can move freely without the island attacking them."

"Illumia Crystals?"

"Supposedly crystals that are blessed by the goddess Illumia herself. The King, his court, and the courts of allied kingdoms he invites to watch the trials have them. Same with the guards. But us?" Rachelle held up her left hand, showing the upside down flame inked on her flesh that was a symbol of being a participant in The Ash Trials. "We're marked for death or whatever fate comes with winning these trials."

"So escaping..." I started.

"Isn't an option, which you just saw," Rachelle said glumly. "After Lucille... I promised myself I wouldn't try again. I didn't want to doom anyone to that kind of fate."

I saw the pain in her expression, and I wondered what she had endured before ending up here. "What was your life before this?" I asked.

Rachelle grinned at me "Seeing if you can trust me?"

"Just wanted to know who I'm allying with. Maybe you could also tell me what your power is, as I assume you have one."

A ghost of a smile graced Rachelle's lips as she sat down, tugging me down to the moss with her, taking a swig from her waterskin. "You're smart, Saffron. Even though you were basically as good as born yesterday."

"Flattery won't let me forget the questions I asked."

"As for my power? You'll see very soon. As for what got me here..." Rachelle looked away, and I caught a flicker of pain in her gaze. "The King no longer saw me fit for his harem. And I didn't want to train another generation of girls to please him. So I tried to fight my way out. Killed a bunch of palace guards with the help of Lucille back when we were in Luminaria's palace on the nearby mainland. Maybe we got a little too... *eager* in the process. Ended up here a few months ago. Lucille, as you know, discovered the consequences of trying to escape —but her death was still more merciful than being the King's whore for the rest of her life. Her and I left behind a life of golden cages."

My hand flew to my mouth as her history settled in. "I'm so sorry."

"You're not the King. You have nothing to apologize for."

"That's why you don't want to compete. Why you tried to escape before I got here."

Rachelle shrugged. "Before you came, there wasn't a point to the suffering I was about to endure. But after? It's nice to be around someone with fight left in their bones. Even if you need to bulk up a bit," she teased, pinching my side.

I swallowed, and felt like I had to admit something to her. "Callum—the Commander—was trying to convince me to ask the King for mercy. So I'm not sure if I truly have the fight in me that you think I do."

"I would never fault you for trying to save your ass. There are many different ways to fight, you know. But you have to tell me this, Saffron: how did you get both Tristen and Callum to take interest in you? Please spill your love potion recipe, I beg of you."

My cheeks reddened. "Callum's not—"

"Oh come on, Saffron. I used to serve as a royal whore. I know the look a man gets when he sees something he wants."

"It's not like that. Callum knew me when I was growing up. We were from the same village and he's trying to protect me. But to be honest, I just... I don't know if I can make it out alive—through any of this. I'm in way over my head," I confessed. "And it might be stupid to tell you that, as I know we're technically competing against each other, but it's true." I met Rachelle's gaze, and she put a hand on my shoulder.

"First, most of us are terrified. If you're not scared, you're a fucking bridge troll with a taste for human suffering," Rachelle said.

I laughed, the feeling of it making my body relax—just a little.

"Secondly," Rachelle continued, "we *are* technically competing against each other, but we'll both be in trouble if we can't even make it to the sixth trial. So I propose an alliance. We'll both do everything we can to help each other get to the end, and let the gods sort it out from there. Deal?"

I smiled at her outstretched hand, and took it. "Deal," I said, and we shook on it.

A guard came over, nodding his head to Rachelle. "Training's over. I have to take you back."

Rachelle turned to me. "I'll see you in the first trial. Try to get some rest," she said, giving my hand a reassuring squeeze.

"I'll try," I said. I watched Rachelle get escorted away, presumably back to her cell. Then, I stood and turned—nearly running into Rook, the guard Callum had reassigned the other day.

"It's time to take you back to your cell," he said, but there was a coldness about him that shone in his beady eyes.

"You're no longer my assigned guard," I tried, but the training grounds had completely emptied out, the afternoon sun starting to dip into the sky and casting long shadows across the field. There was no one for me to ask for help.

"The others are tied up in Crown matters. Let's go," he said, shoving me toward one of the entrances back down to the prison. Guess I had no choice, then.

He led me down the sloping ramp back into the belly of Ashguard, and I followed him through endless twisting hallways. We continued past a block of empty prison cells, lit torches lining the walls and illuminating the stone hallways in the dark. While most of the cells looked the same, I noted that after a few turns, they didn't seem to be going in the direction of where I thought my cell was.

"This isn't the way back to my cell."

Rook was silent, not turning to me.

"Hey, we're going the wrong way—" I said, reaching out to grab his arm.

Rook whirled around, throwing me against a wall. I cried out as I hit the cold stone, and a spark of pain rattled through my bones as I slid to the floor.

Rook advanced toward me. Some instinct awakened within me, and I scrambled to my feet. He set his lantern down and unsheathed his shortsword.

"You murdered my father, and for that, you will pay, Lord Killer."

Lord Killer. Would this stupid rumor be the death of me?

"I didn't do anything. I'm not The Lord Killer," I said, watching my death advance toward me. What could my fists do against a sword?

"You lie."

"Don't you think if I was strong enough to kill some lord I would have done away with you by now?"

"LIAR!" Rook yelled, fire in his eyes as he raised the sword, slashing wildly.

I rolled out of the path of his blade, snatching the discarded lantern in the narrow hallway. I held it up like a shield, my body shaking out of a combination of fear and pure exhaustion.

"I'm not who you think I am!" I yelled, blocking another swing of his blade with the lantern—

—which shattered upon impact, and I clenched my teeth through the pain of the cascading broken glass biting into my skin. I tossed the open flame of the bare lantern directly at the guard, and he roared as part of his uniform caught ablaze. His sword clattered to the ground as he tried to put out the flames.

That's all I needed to turn and sprint down a hallway that I hoped would lead me back to the others—to *someone*—my heart pounding in my throat.

I turned down a musty tunnel, slipping on some slick stone—but regained my balance and turned down another hallway.

"Don't you run from me, Lord Killer!" Rook bellowed after me.

Faster.

I sprinted down another corridor of empty cells. I pumped my legs, sprinting to...

...a dead end.

No no no no no no.

I heard the sound of advancing boots from behind me, and I whirled, backing up against the wall, my chest heaving.

Rook turned the corner. Seeing me trapped, he slowed his pace. A predator toying with its prey.

"Let's try this again, girl." His sword glinted in the light of one of the wall-mounted torches, and I got a burst of pride from seeing the burn marks and deep wounds the lantern had inflicted upon him. That *I* had inflicted upon my would-be murderer.

But it wouldn't be enough.

I crouched in a defensive stance. "Kill me with honor and drop your sword. Unless you're afraid of a *girl*."

"You deserve no such honor," Rook said, advancing toward me and raising his sword once more with wild eyes as I felt my heartbeat hitch as I squeezed my eyes shut—

—but no death blow swung down on me. Just the squelching of a sword slicing through a body. I gathered the courage to open my eyes.

Rook coughed up blood and staggered backward as Callum yanked his sword from the man's heart. It was the second time in just as many days that I had seen Callum kill a man with that piercing blow from behind.

Rook fell with a gurgle, and Callum raised his sword. He once more plunged it into the man's heart. Making sure that Rook was truly dead before he turned back to me, walking over and crouching down.

"Saffron," he said, his hands going to me. "Are you—"

I winced, my hand going to the back of my head, and coming back with blood. *My* blood.

Callum's eyes went wide, and moments later his strong hands slipped underneath my legs and my neck, cradling me to his strong body as my mind went foggy.

"Where are we going?" I asked, fisting my hand in his shirt to try and steady my spinning vision.

"This wing has an old alchemist's office. I think they have some supplies down here," he said, but I noted a dash of panic in his voice.

"I thought... you weren't allowed... to interfere..."

"Not when other prisoners are trying to kill you. One of *my* men, on the other hand? They must have a death wish."

Words felt harder to get out, but I tried to push them from my lips. "He thought... I was The Lord Killer..."

Callum's jaw tightened, and he pulled me closer as he picked up his pace and turned down another hallway. "I'll never forgive that fucking Assassin for painting a target on your back."

"He helped me. Earlier."

"When he almost broke your arm?" Callum ground out.

"No, when he... I almost drank the tea..."

Callum swore. "Who do you think poisoned the tea to begin with? He's moving pieces around on the board. Don't be one of them."

Before I could reply, Callum kicked open a door that swung on its hinges. He walked me into a dark room, torches flaming to life thanks to the prison's magic. As the light filled the stone room, I saw that there was a metal table against one wall, but the rest of the room was filled with plants dripping over every surface—and boxes of what looked like medical supplies.

"What is this place?" I asked as Callum placed me on the high metal table, my back against a wall in a sitting position as he stepped between my legs.

"It's an alchemist's old lab. The healers use it from time to time and keep the supplies they need here. Just be careful of the Spark-seed plant, it explodes if you throw it at a wall. I think that's how we lost the alchemist who used to work here, actually." He tilted his neck, towering over me as he bent to examine my head injury.

"Don't fuck with the plants, got it," I said, but my breath hitched as I was nearly flush against Callum's chest as he held me, and I smelled his musky leather and citrusy scent. He smelled of forests and greenery, of the outdoors, and tumbles in dirt. He smelled... familiar. As if I could envision the two of us running around a leafy village together. No memories came to me, but I could see how Callum could have fit into my past.

"Your head doesn't look too bad," Callum said as he examined the wound. "A simple healing elixir should be just fine for now, but I'll come check on how it looks tomorrow."

He pulled away, turning to the cabinet and I shivered, feeling the loss of his body heat and closeness. Seeing my shiver, Callum wordlessly pulled off his guard's jacket.

"I don't need—" I started, but he just shook his head and tucked the jacket around me, bundling me in it.

"Keep it. It's only going to get colder down here."

"You don't think it's suspicious if the other guards see me with your jacket?"

"Let them talk," Callum said, turning to ransack one of the shelves.

"That hardly sounds wise," I said. "I can't let you get hurt because you're helping me."

"Don't worry about me," Callum said, setting down an armful of medical supplies on the table next to me.

I frowned. "You have to be careful, too, Callum."

A smile twitched the edge of his lips. "I'll try if you try." He wet some linen strips with a colored liquid. "Here, lean your head on me."

I did, nestling my forehead in his shirt as he gently parted my hair on the back of my head where the wound was.

"This might sting a bit," he murmured, and I could feel the rumbling of his chest as he spoke.

I hissed in pain as the linen coated with the healing elixir stung my injury. I fisted his shirt again, this time to pull him into me as he worked, cleaning the wound with his gentle fingers. I felt a tingling sensation on the back of my head as if my flesh was slowly knitting back together.

"There. All done," Callum said, his voice gruff, setting down the bloodied cloth on the counter beside him, going to wash his hands in the metal sink before turning back to me.

But as I lifted my head and looked up at him, he didn't pull away, still standing in between my dangling legs, his hands shifting to hold mine. His right thumb drew small circles on the back of my left hand.

"Feeling better?" he asked.

"A little," I said, feeling a bit intoxicated by his closeness. Maybe it was the heady rush of escaping death, or the fear of the upcoming challenge, or the comfort of having an ally—but I didn't want to leave him. Didn't want to go back to my cold cell.

"The first trial is tomorrow. It will be some kind of fight in the Stone Coliseum. You'll need to find a weapon in the arena and defend yourself. Do you know what kind of weapon you'll pick?"

"I'm not sure," I said. "I didn't get a chance to handle many of the weapons today, so I'll just make do with what I can find in the trial."

"Good. Whatever you do, don't go for the sword in the stone."

"The sword in the stone?"

He nodded. "In every previous trial, one of the weapons that an unlucky prisoner tries to go for is the Bluesteel Blade. It's a sword embedded in a stone, and every prisoner who has gone after it has died a gruesome death."

"Why? What's so special about it?"

"Honestly? Only the gods know. The properties of Bluesteel are unknown, but I've just heard so much about how those who try to wield it get their arms burned to ashes and the like. Avoid it and just go for another weapon."

"Don't go after the Bluesteel Blade. Got it," I said.

"Just keep a low profile and stay alive," Callum said.

"Why are you helping me?"

His expression softened, and I fought the urge to run my fingers through his wavy blond-brown hair. "Because. I want us to go back to the way things were before."

"Which was?" I asked. He was so close to me, his eyes dipping to my lips at my question. It was difficult to keep thoughts together.

"It depends," he breathed, and raised his right hand to gently cradle my jaw, his thumb swiping across my bottom lip. I felt a strange urge to lean into it, to part my lips for him, to take his thumb into my mouth...

I tilted my head up to him, but winced as my body's injuries and bruises came creaking back into my consciousness.

Callum let his hand drop. "You should rest. Dinner will be sent to your cell soon, and tomorrow—" he paused, the words hard for him to get out. "Get through tomorrow and we can pick up where we left off."

I nodded, and Callum didn't wait to ask me how I was feeling before he swept me up in his strong arms once more, carrying me past that room covered in plants and potions, nudging the door open with his body and carrying me in silence down the stone hallway toward my cell. Once we arrived, he gently laid me down on my cot, tugging his—now *my*—jacket around me to keep me warm.

"One more thing," Callum said, and he withdrew a small blade covered in a rag from a pocket in his breeches, handing it to me. I started to unsheath it, but he stopped me. "Keep it sheathed for now. It's got a fast-acting paralyzing elixir on the edge of the blade. It's a small enough dagger that you should be able to keep it hidden, but be careful with it if you do need to use it. The paralyzing elixir won't work long, but long enough to hopefully give you a chance to escape whatever... *situation* you might find yourself in."

"Thank you," I said, and his warm green eyes were so close to me in the dark. He was once again risking his position to help me.

"Knock 'em dead, Saffron. I mean it," he said, and rose up and left my cell. But each step seemed like it took effort. As if he didn't want to leave my cell.

But I knew I couldn't let Callum distract me, even if I wanted him to. Even if I wanted to beg him to help me escape and take me far away from this island, this prison, and these godsforsaken trials I was about to face.

However, no matter what tomorrow brought, I would rise to the challenge. If I was to die, I would die fighting with everything I had.

7

When we arrived at the silo's ground floor that morning for roll call, the sky looked stormy as gray light filtered down from the skylight. As I surveyed the group as everyone filtered in, I saw that Ajax was sporting a brand-new eye patch. The poison must have seeped into his eye, but he was still capable of sending me a dirty glare with his remaining one.

He deserved it, I thought, a bit surprised by the brutality of my reaction. But I was here to survive—and my only regret was not killing him when I had the chance, as I knew I had made a brutal enemy who wouldn't hold back in the trials.

Tristen arrived last—once again descending from the upper floors with no fewer than fifteen guards surrounding him. His entourage all had their swords unsheathed, looking anxious. Tristen acted as if they weren't there, looking perpetually bored with the procession surrounding him.

A ruthless killer. That's what everyone knew him as. I shivered, wondering if his reputation would prove true when we entered the killing field.

The High Sorceress Cassandra Wraithborn emerged next from that set of metal double doors across from where we stood. She was wearing her usual ice blue hooded robe, but today the dress she wore underneath was white with a gold trim—Luminaria's colors, I gathered, as they were the same colors as the guard's uniforms.

Callum joined Cassandra, and she stepped forward as roll call ended.

"Some of you have spent nearly an entire year underground, waiting for your shot at freedom," Cassandra said in her sultry voice. "But now, each of you will rise to the challenge of the first Ash Trial. You will fight for your place on the frontlines of your King's crusade to victory and for the honor of clearing your name and protecting your home. You will fight for your *freedom*. If you lose, however, you will be plunged into the darkness of eternal night. A hero's death. May each of you face your fate with bravery through all six trials. Now, we rise."

With that, the floor of the silo started to *move*. I tried to stand steady as the entire platform that had been the ground level of the silo started to rise—a huge cement elevator that brought all of us to the surface, one level at a time.

The sunroof at the top of the silo retracted, and I could feel fresh air flood in to greet us as we rose. When the platform arrived on the surface of the silo, my breath stilled in my throat.

I had seen just a tiny corner of the island from the training grounds, but from the top of the silo, I could see much more of the surrounding area from the hilltop the silo peeked out from. We were in the middle of a lush island, greenery dripping everywhere. The air was only lightly humid, and a soft fog rolled in through the trees like creeping specters, just barely obscuring a huge Stone Coliseum that towered over the silo. Between us and the coliseum was a winding dirt road that curved through a forest that hid the rest of the landscape from view.

And from the coliseum, I could hear a crowd *roaring*.

"Walk," Callum commanded all of us prisoners, and we were forced into a single-file line by the guards.

I felt compelled to memorize as many details as I could of the tiny swath of the island between the silo and the coliseum as the fog and thick forest allowed. It also helped me slow my heart rate and keep the anxious thoughts at bay.

I'm going in blind to this, I felt my bitter thoughts threatening to bubble over. *At least the others have their godsdamned memories.* But I shook my head and tried to push the thoughts away. Something deep down reminded me that I couldn't afford to curse my lack of power. I was working with what I had been given—and at least I was a good fighter. That was something.

The single-file line of seventy prisoners passed through a smattering of trees, winding through the edge of the forest...

...and the sight before me made me *gasp.* There, with iron nails nailing their hands to a makeshift cross that stuck out above the trees, was the woman from yesterday.

The woman who begged for *mercy.* She had been crucified.

As we walked closer, murmurs sparked. Something had ravaged the woman's body. Large chunks were missing, as if a beast with a huge maw had taken big bites of her before growing bored and wandering away.

I forced myself to look away. Tried not to listen to the rustling in the forest just beyond the treeline, where the tendrils of fog curled like beckoning fingers of a lover.

The Isle of Embermere was not fucking around. And neither was the King who ruled here.

I tried not to let it shake me, tried to still my trembling hands as we continued the pilgrimage to the coliseum, the roaring of the crowd growing louder.

I almost died yesterday. But would that death had been kinder compared to the death I might be about to face today?

I wrapped my arms around my body, trying to breathe. Callum was at the front of the line, and he couldn't be seen helping me or he would risk the others taking too much of a note of his favor for me. Even Rachelle had a determined look on her face, striding ahead at the front of the pack with her head held high.

We were close to the Stone Coliseum now, and outside I noticed an odd shimmering pool about the size of one or two men. It was being guarded by a few armed guards, and shaded by a few large trees. *Strange.*

But my gaze went back to the towering Stone Coliseum ahead of me, and we passed through one of the rounded arches of the first set of gates to enter the cavernous tunnel that led into the main ring of the coliseum.

As we entered the coliseum, the roaring grew to a fever pitch. My eyes went to the stands, which were packed full of a few hundred courtiers and their help. I scanned the crowd, trying to get a sense of who was in attendance. The royalty wore incredible finery, from crimson gowns to headpieces made of jewels. Men in tailored shirts and golden armor were accompanied by guards in fighting leathers. It was easy to pick out the servants and those who were there to wait on the rich by the dullness of their clothes and frowns on their faces as they watched us filter in. Some of them jeered at us, but it was the royalty who were taking the most delight in the death match about to unfold before them.

"Death to the Shadowfire Assassin!" someone yelled from the stands, and more screams to the same effect followed.

Tristen gave a regal wave to the audience as if he was being greeted by loyal subjects—not a crowd that wished him dead.

We were led to stand on marks and face the audience, and I was one of the last. The coliseum floor was nothing but dirt, and at the center about twenty footspans in front of us was a pile of weapons. Past that was a second pile, this one placed on a hill of dirt and more weapons—further away from the first and harder to reach. Atop that second massive pile of weapons, I could see the glint of a sword with a blue blade embedded nearly up to the hilt in a glimmering stone on that hill. It caught my eye, as if calling to me.

The Bluesteel Blade.

Something in my blood sung at the sight of the blade. It felt like a piece of me was embedded in the blade, and I knew in that instant that I *wanted it.*

There was movement in the crowd. I turned to the dais at the center of the crowd where King West of Luminaria and his court sat. King West rose and the spectators hushed into an eerie silence.

"Welcome to the hundred and twelfth Ash Trials," his voice boomed, some sort of lesser magic amplifying it to every corner of the stadium. "Today, we begin the process of rebirth, selecting a champion to fearlessly fight at our front lines to earn this second chance. The Isle of Embermere will test our prisoners and select only one who is of the mettle and strength to be able to shoulder this responsibility and win the gift of absolution of their sins, burning the past to ashes to make way for a brighter future where the Kingdom of Luminaria can be whole once more, and we can restore order alongside our allied Kingdoms of Septerra."

The crowd roared as the island seemed to shift in response. He was every part a regal ruler, even in his aristocratic softness.

"Let the games begin in ten..." the King began to count.

Cassandra murmured something under her breath, and all of our bands dropped to the dirt ground beneath us. A spell to drop our iron bands—which released everyone's magic. I tried to move, but I felt glued in place, only able to swivel my head. The others were frozen as well, all of us caught in place likely by another spell that would fully release us at the end of King West's countdown.

"Nine..."

Cassandra, Callum, and the rest of the guards left through the way we had entered, a grate of metal bars falling behind them as they exited through the tunnel. Callum tossed one more glance my way— I saw his fear for me moments before he disappeared.

"Eight..."

Did he really believe I could survive this? Did I?

"Seven..."

I craned my neck, trying to get a better view of all seventy contestants. I caught Tristen's gaze from where he stood on the other side of the arena.

Gods, his eyes...

"Six..."

But as he stared me down, I felt a sensation on my mind's door. Like... a *knocking*. As if a presence was trying to get in.

"Five..."

He's a reader, a mindweavyr. I remembered Rachelle's words as Tristen stared me down with that ferocious intensity. As if he was trying to decipher me, unravel me. A predator trying to read its prey's next move.

"Four..."

If he was trying to scramble my brains, it wasn't working. I stared him down with a glare. I slammed the gates shut to my mind—so hard that Tristen's eyes went wide.

"Three..."

How did I know how to do that? I wondered. I found myself grinning at Tristen's stunned expression.

"Two..."

I had exactly two seconds to gloat. Callum had said I needed to get a weapon. I fixed my gaze on the pile of weapons in front of me, tensing and preparing to sprint.

"One..."

The moment my feet could move, a huge body tackled me to the ground.

I cried out in pain as Ajax was on top of me, easily pinning me down with his arms. He brought both of my wrists over my head, pinning them to the cold earth with one hand while his other caressed my cheek.

"I won't even need my magic to kill you, girl. Not even your Commander can save you now," he sneered.

"He doesn't need to save me," I said, but my voice wavered. This was my first real test—whether or not I could survive on my own.

I tried to headbutt Ajax, but he pulled away with a *tsking* sound and a sneer on his lips. "Is that really the best you got?"

Before I could respond, a rumbling started emanating from the ground below the coliseum, drowning out even the shouts of the crowd.

Out of the corner of my vision, I saw prisoners begin to engage in battle with each other, many going for the pile of weapons that were closest to us. A flash of shadowfire sparked from across the arena as Tristen easily kept six prisoners from cornering him.

But as the shaking continued, a horrible *crack* sounded—again and again—as the ground split in the coliseum. I couldn't see much from where Ajax had me pinned, but it looked like dark tunnels were being ripped open in the ground all around us.

Ajax swiveled his head to see what was going on, and I managed to yank one of my hands free, smashing my palm upward, slamming into the underside of his jaw with all my might. The blow might have broken the nose of any other prisoner—but it only served to make Ajax angry, my palm glancing off of his face as if I were a mere fly trying to punch a tiger.

"You want death? I'll give you death."

Both his hands went to my neck, choking me. I moved quick, unsheathing the dagger Callum had given me, embedding it into Ajax's exposed bicep just as his hands closed around my neck, cutting off my oxygen.

He released me slightly, looking down at the dagger. Then, his lips curled into a smile. "You think your butter knife can hurt me?" But the effect of the paralyzing elixir was fast. His hands slackened on my neck, his jaw dropping as he started to lose control of his limbs. "What the fuck?"

His body went limp, crashing on top of me. I emitted a cry of pain as I used up the rest of my strength to roll out from under him, stumbling to my feet as my body still screamed from the exertion of the past twenty-four hours.

I'm in no shape to fight today, I realized. Inconvenient timing—it might cost me my life. Suddenly, my thoughts were interrupted by a sickening *crunch* that came from behind me.

I turned, and my eyes went wide.

Before me, a horned demon with beady red eyes chewed on the half-alive body of a prisoner with the casualness of livestock chewing its cud. It was the size of three or four men, towering over me and walking on two feet while hands that ended in sharp claws cradled its prey. It was hairless, covered in black bony muscle and scales.

But as its eyes fixed on me, my breath caught in my throat. The scaly thing quirked its horned head to the right and spit out what was left of the prisoner, its dark black saliva dripping on the ground before me. It took a step closer.

"*No no no no no,*" I whispered, my heart beating as I scrambled backward—and felt my foot snag on another prisoner's body, who had died clutching a blade.

A *blade*.

It was a shortsword, small but polished and sharp. I felt that barely-there intuition once more.

GRAB IT!

I did, and as the demon launched itself at me, pushing off its strong legs as it jumped for me—moving so fast it seemed to just appear in front of me—I thrust the blade upward, pushing it with a thick crunch through its chest—

—and the demon's beady eyes went wide as it slumped back. I yanked the blade from the demon's heart and it dripped with black blood. I immediately dropped the blade, horror filling my veins.

"Am I The Lord Killer, then?" I whispered, trembling. I had so easily killed that thing, known exactly how to position my blade so it lanced its heart. My memory was silent, my intuition giving me nothing more to work with. Not even a flash of something that could shed light into the unending darkness of my mind.

I felt like I was being dragged underwater, going into some sort of shock as the screeching demons continued to turn those around me into their lunch. More demons were clawing their way out of the holes in the ground, as if they were emerging from the underworld itself.

"*Come to me,*" a voice said, crystal clear in my mind. I looked up and saw it again—as if it were calling to me from across the arena.

The Bluesteel Blade.

"*Yes,*" the voice whispered. "*I'm yours.*"

But adrenaline kicked into gear again as I saw yet another demon prowling around the edge of the ring—its gaze landing right on me.

I sucked in a breath, trying to stay calm even as I felt my mind fraying under the pressure of the situation, screams of dying prisoners and the slash of steel filling the coliseum around me. Twenty or so prisoners had already been killed, their bodies littering the ground.

Would I join the dead? Or find a way to stay with the living?

Then, without warning, the demon sprinted toward me—but it wasn't just sprinting, it was jumping through space—moving so quickly that it seemed to be teleporting. Vanishing and reappearing feet at a time, blinking in and out of existence at such a rapid pace that it was in front of me before I could breathe, before I could react, its front claws arced downward.

I took a half-step back, but it was a second too late as I felt a sharp pain across my side accompanied by a warmth of blood cascading down my body, slash marks marring my arms and legs. I stumbled, trying to stay standing as the tang of blood nearly made me vomit.

Help me. I begged my intuition. But it was silent, and tears welled in my eyes as the demon raised its claws once more, this time aiming to disembowel me.

No. Not like this. Please.

I braced myself, dropping into some semblance of a fighting stance and raising my fists as if that would do anything other than allow me to die with some dignity.

But as the demon started to slash downward, a flash of red crossed my vision. And then, the demon was falling...

...and being mauled by a red-furred lioness.

When had a lioness entered the ring?

A lioness that dug for its blackened heart, shaking it loose and squeezing it like a dog toy. The lioness turned to me, and an instant later, it shifted back into... *Rachelle.*

"You stupid girl, get yourself a godsdamn weapon!" Rachelle shouted, striding to me and shaking my shoulders. "You're my only friend and you're not allowed to die, do you hear me?"

"You're a shifter," I said, still in shock.

Rachelle smiled, wiping off the black demon's blood with the back of her arm and tossing her red curls with a grin. "Damn straight. Now *move*."

I didn't have to be told twice, running to the still untouched second pile of weapons on the side of the coliseum closer to the King's dais and all of the nobles—a bit further from the fray of the fighting. There were daggers, weighted spikes on chains, longswords, shortswords, throwing knives—

—but once again, I felt my heart seem to skip a beat as my gaze latched onto the shine of the Bluesteel Blade.

It wasn't in the pile of weapons but instead embedded in a round stone at the very top of the hill of weapons. I would have to crawl across all of the sharp weapons piled on the rocky outcropping to get to it.

"You have good taste, but it's mine," a smooth voice said beside me.

I turned to see Tristen beside me, no worse for wear except for some blood on his clothes—blood that clearly didn't belong to him.

I looked up again at the sword in the stone. It felt as if it was calling for me. "You'll have to race me for it," I said, and then I was off sprinting, scrambling up over the massive pile of weapons.

I didn't know what came over me, just that I knew I *had* to have that sword. I darted over the rocks and steel, my feet nimble despite the shifting rocks and weapons below them, but Tristen was like a shadow, right behind me with every leap.

The two of us landed across from each other, the sword in the stone between us.

"Don't," he warned, but the playfulness was gone from his voice.

"Why? Is this poisoned, too?" I quipped.

"No, but it might as well be," Tristen said. "Let me have it."

"All right. It's yours," I said, pretending to relax my stance.

Tristen seemed relieved, the tension ebbing from his body for a moment—but that half-second head start was all that I needed.

I was about to grab the blade when Tristen's voice shot through me.

"Stop. Step back from the sword," he said, but his voice was layered with something old. Ancient. Commanding. My body, mid leap, simply just... stopped. Obeying his command completely as it took a step back from the blade—and I was completely unable to stop myself from following his command.

Tristen was using his mindweavying to compel me.

I glared at him, anger rising to a boiling point within me. "Let. Me. Fucking. Go," I growled.

He took a step closer to the blade, his expression lethal. "Didn't you learn not to take something that doesn't belong to you?"

"*Oh, but it does,*" the Bluesteel Blade whispered to me, louder now that I was within arm's reach of it.

"Let me go," I said again to Tristen, hating how my body wasn't under my own control. I must have had an edge of desperation in my voice, because I saw him falter.

Did the Shadowfire Assassin care how I felt?

But a roar of a demon snapped his attention away from me as he turned, and I felt his mindweavying power lift.

In the moment he was distracted, I lunged for the blade. Tristen turned back to me, but it was too late.

I watched his expression turn to horror as I darted to the sword, my hands wrapping around its sturdy hilt. As my feet reached the stone, I pulled.

The sword didn't budge at first. But with great effort, I kept pulling, and felt it move. The heat of the hilt started to increase, and it went from hot to sizzling. I screamed as it started to eat through the flesh of my hands, but it was too late. I couldn't drop the blade now— I could only continue to pull. I shoved all my strength into yanking that blade from the stone, the agonizing pain shooting through me as blood ran down the blade—*my* blood—as I fought through the dizzying agony to claim what I felt in my bones belonged to *me*.

"*Yes, claim me,*" the blade whispered. "*I am yours—if you can keep me.*"

As the steel slid from the stone, the holes in the ground floor of the coliseum started to close up, stitching the ground back together—sealing the demons within the earth back into their hellish prison. It was as if the island had *wanted* this to happen. Wanted someone to pull the sword from the stone, as if the Bluesteel Blade was a hero's reward.

But as all the remaining demons slowly swiveled their heads toward me, I saw that the reward came with a cost. All of their eyes locked on me, and they started crawling and blinking toward where Tristen and I stood at the top of the hill of weapons.

"Put your back to me," Tristen commanded. "I'll help you fight them off."

"Why?" I demanded, eyeing the sword he drew from a pile beside us and wondering if he was going to do the demons' job for them and embed that blade into my back before they got to us.

"Would you prefer to die?" Tristen demanded, but the demons were seconds away. I had no choice. I gave Tristen my back—even as I knew Callum would give me hell for doing so—and I felt him growl out a warning behind me. "Focus, *Sael*," he said.

And just as they had done before, the demons seemed to teleport, but to my mortal eye they were just moving too quickly to be fully perceived. They converged on me—too fast. I lifted the heavy sword, screaming with the effort. The sword was leaden and hot. The hilt continued to burn my skin and blood spiraled down my arms in warm rivulets.

I swung the sword at the first demon that came at me, but it was reduced to ashes as I felt heat at my back and a blast of cold shadow-fire as Tristen sent a ball of blue green flame at the screeching demons, giving me space to breathe and once more lift the heavy sword. Its Bluesteel glinted in the sun.

"Are you all right?" I felt his voice by my ear as we continued to fight back-to-back.

"No!" I shouted back at him, trying to ignore the pain throbbing through my limbs and that too-hot hilt.

"I warned you not to grab the sword," he said, something edging his voice. Was he... *concerned?*

I didn't have time to respond, having to heave the heavy sword at another demon—and I realized as I cut it in half that it was the final one.

The Stone Coliseum settled in a moment of silence. I heaved lungfuls of air into my fried body as I scanned the remaining prisoners before the crowd exploded into hollers of applause and wild cheers.

That's when I staggered, dropping the blade with a clatter. A wave of dizzy nausea descended on me. I blacked out before I hit the ground.

8

I awoke in a healer's tent. Near me, I heard a high-pitch cry of the wounded. A stern-faced healer had her hands above me. They glowed as I felt my flesh knit together, and I realized after a few moments that the screams in the tent were my own.

Then, the glowing and the warmth was gone, and I teetered on the edge of consciousness. I felt the healer wrapping my hands in bandages, and I barely held on as I heard a familiar voice.

"She's alive?" a man's voice asked.

"She is. Bandages need to stay on just for a bit longer while the flesh heals, but they can be taken off in a half an hour or so. That sword cut deeper than any magic I've seen. I'll leave you with her," the healer replied, finishing bandaging my hands.

My fuzzy vision clarified and I saw Callum standing above me. "Callum," I whispered, feeling weak from all the pain and blood loss I'd endured.

He crouched next to my bed, his expression hard. "I'm glad you're okay. Why did you go for the sword?"

I flinched. Why had I fought so hard for the damn thing?

Because you needed it. It called for you.

But I wasn't going to say that out loud. "I don't know," I said. "I survived, though. Thank you for the dagger."

Callum looked at me, frustrated. "I'm glad my dagger helped. But how about you trust my advice in the next one?"

The next one. Fuck. That was right. This had only been the first trial. Which meant... there were *five* more after this.

"Commander," a voice said from behind him. "Are we good to escort her back to her cell? We have to head back to the palace to prepare for the ball soon."

"No, I'll escort her," Callum said to the guard. "You are excused."

The guard left us alone in the tent, and my vision cleared enough for me to sit up. "Ball?" I asked.

Callum nodded. "It's honorary for all of the survivors of the first trial to be invited to the Saltspire Palace for a ball as celebration of the beginning of the trials. It's happening tomorrow."

A *ball*? Maybe that past version of me was some sort of fair maiden who loved frilly dresses and dancing with princes, but *this* version of me was a survivalist, I decided.

"Do I have to go?"

Callum quirked a smile. "Can you walk? I'll take you back."

"I think so," I said, slowly pushing myself up off the bed. Callum held me steady, but the healers had done their job. I was a little woozy, but my strength was coming back.

Callum put a hand on the small of my back and led me out of the tent, which was set up outside of the coliseum. It was quiet now, all of the audience and contestants now dispersed.

"The Saffron I knew loved to dance," he said as we walked back to Ashguard on that narrow dirt path.

I felt my exhaustion hit me at once. "Dancing hasn't been a top priority of late."

"I'm... I'm glad you survived," he said, his strong demeanor of Commander Callum Wells slipping a bit as I heard the pain in his voice as he continued to lead me back to the prison.

"How am I supposed to get through five more of those?" I asked, trying to keep my voice light. But my body already felt so beaten. So tired.

"Just take it one step at a time, okay?" he said, and I nodded in reply.

We walked in silence for awhile through the winding dirt path that disappeared through the patches of forest. As the sun was setting, the forest seemed darker. More sinister. I felt as if something was watching me from the dark corners of the forest... but I averted my eyes, not sure if I wanted my intuition proved right.

"Here, this way." Callum led me down an unfamiliar staircase that entered the silo that was Ashguard. I followed him, and the downward slopping tunnel split off to a hallway that led to another hidden stone staircase.

"Where are we going?" I asked, holding onto his strong arm as he helped me navigate the narrow staircases.

"I was thinking you could come back and use my bathing chambers," he said. "The other guards in my wing have left to prepare for the ball tomorrow."

Tomorrow. Which meant... "It isn't interfering if I... spend the night with you?"

"As far as I'm aware, it makes no difference where you sleep. And as I said, most of the other guards have been relieved from their duties here in Ashguard until tomorrow. But if you prefer to stay in your cell..." He paused on the staircase, giving me time to decide as he watched me in the flickering torch light.

"No," I said, biting my lip, and Callum's eyes trailed to my mouth. I swore I could see his gaze heating, just slightly. "I want to spend tonight with you."

"Good," he said. "We just need to make it past Cassandra and her priestesses without being seen. We'll need to move fast and quiet."

He pulled me down the stairs, and we hurried down flight after flight. I marveled at all of the hidden ways there were to navigate this sprawling underground prison—Ashguard felt endless as we made our way down stone halls.

We reached one of the top floors. "I'm just down the hall," Callum said, then froze, pulling me to his side as voices echoed from down the hallway.

"Someone's coming," I whispered.

"In here," Callum said, and then pulled me into a room off the hallway.

The room looked like a meditation room, with cushions on the floor in a circular pattern, a bowl on a pedestal in the center. At the far end of the room, a roaring fire had been built. Callum and I waited and listened at the door.

"Are they coming this way?" I breathed.

"Yes," he said, but maintained his calm. "In here."

Callum led me to a closet on the far side of the room, and I stepped inside. He pulled me down by my waist, holding me against his muscled frame as the voices in the hallway grew louder. There were narrow slats in the closet door, and through the cracks I could see the entire room as the door to the hallway opened.

I watched as two guards entered, holding Otto, the old man, by his arms. They threw him onto the ground, and he started shaking.

"Leave us," that feminine voice said, and Cassandra stepped into the room. The guards turned on their heels, leaving Cassandra alone with Otto.

Otto started hyperventilating and shaking. He tried to back up, attempting to get away from her. His back hit the pedestal at the center of the room, and he was forced to look up at her.

"Oh, Otto," she sighed. "What am I to do with you?"

He laughed, his voice shattering into several different voices. His body seemed to not be his own, and it was shaking and jerking—just like I had seen him do so many times before at roll call or in the dining hall. "I tell you the truth!"

She tossed the hood of her cloak back before sinking into a crouch next to Otto. "I told you when you arrived here that each false prophecy would cost you a year of your life. Have I lied to you yet?"

Suddenly, her hands were on him, and the man let out a high-pitched scream. I sucked in a gasp—but Callum quickly covered my mouth with his strong hand and held me to him as I looked on in horror.

As Cassandra gripped Otto's face in her hands, the folds of his face grew more dramatic, the wrinkles grooving deeper into his flesh.

She was aging him with her magic.

Cassandra let go of his head unceremoniously and it cracked back, hitting the pedestal. Otto let out a low moan, his body still trembling with slight convulsions. She kicked his limp body with her blue satin shoe.

"Give me the truth, seer."

"As you command," he rasped out. Then, his body stilled. Like a puppet on strings, his back arched, and he sat up straight, his eyes glassy and glowing with a strange light. He began to speak in not just his voice, but a voice of something else. An ancient voice. "The one who takes has come to claim what belongs to them. There will be no stopping them. They will sip from the well of the gods and be fed by power beyond their own. They will fight, and they will win—but at great cost."

"Yes, but do you speak of the *Siphon*?" Cassandra demanded, impatient.

Otto just blinked. "The Siphon will rise."

"When? Are they here among the prisoners now?"

Otto let out a gasp and fell back on the floor, breathing hard.

"Useless," Cassandra muttered. She went to the door, yanking it open. "Get him out of here. Then head to the palace to begin preparations for the ball." The guards came in, dragging Otto to his feet.

Cassandra exited the room, the guards following behind, Otto in tow.

The door closed, and Callum released my mouth. His body was so close to mine as he reached over and opened the closet door, his hand on my lower back as he led me back into the meditation room.

"Is it safe?" I whispered, my heart racing as he pressed his ear to the door that led to the hallway.

"Yes," he said after a beat, and opened the door for us to hurry out.

Each step in that hallway had me fearing for what might await us, but luckily, the nightmares of the prison did not follow.

~

CALLUM'S QUARTERS WERE LUXURIOUS, even though they were sparse with not much in the way of personal effects. A fire was roaring in the hearth, making the room smell warm and inviting. Thick carpets lined the floors, but what caught my eye was the massive four-poster bed by the fire. It was piled with furs and pillows, and looked so deeply inviting. There wasn't much else in the space except for a small sitting area and a rack full of additional weapons, swords, and daggers of different sizes and curved edges.

"Nice place you've got here," I said, trying to keep my tone light after what I had just seen with Cassandra.

"My bathing chamber is through this way," he said. "Let me draw you a bath."

He disappeared, and I sat down on a small bench and removed my boots. I was still covered in blood and grime from the trial, and I felt out-of-place in his spacious quarters.

Callum returned to the bedchambers. "Are you okay? After what we just saw?"

"Cassandra has the power to age others like that?"

Callum grimaced. "She does. It's why the King keeps her here. No prisoners would dare cross her."

"That explains the total silence every time she speaks in front of everyone."

"They definitely fear her more than me," Callum said, trying to keep his tone light.

I looked up at Callum, taking in his broad shoulders, his strong frame—and the softness in his expression. My curiosity finally got the best of me and I stood, crossing to him. "What were we exactly... before?"

Callum hesitated, and then reached down, taking my hands in his. "We were as good as betrothed. Our families were just waiting for me to finally get the nerve to ask you to marry me, but it was expected we'd end up together."

I blushed. So my body's reaction to him was based on our history, then. "What... happened? You said I was taken? By whom?"

Darkness immediately shut down Callum's face as he looked away from me. "You were taken hostage by the rebels. Taken by... Tristen, the Shadowfire Assassin."

The floor felt like it dropped out beneath me, and I stumbled, Callum looping an arm around my waist so I stayed upright. "Tristen took me?" I asked.

"Yes," he grit out. "He took you from me. The rebels of Stormgard came and claimed what they said they needed to win the war. They torched the homes of those who didn't agree with their methods, didn't immediately give them what they wanted. When I ran back from the militia's camp to find you... you were gone. Others saw him drag you away."

My blood ran cold. "What did... what did he do with me?"

Callum's jaw tightened. "I don't know. That was the last I saw of you, but I searched every day to find you. I sacrificed everything to try and bring you home. I need you to know that. I wouldn't let that bastard steal you away from me forever."

I tried to process all that he was telling me. *Tristen* had taken me? And Callum... he had been the one who had loved me? *Truly* loved me? The new information hurt my head.

Callum reached to brush a strand of hair out of my face, and I flinched out of instinct, still wound up from the adrenaline of the day and the first trial. Callum let his hand fall.

"Sorry," I said. "It's just... it's so much."

Sadness glimmered in Callum's eyes. "It's okay. I... I just want you to know I don't... expect anything from you. Whatever happened to your memories... I know what we were then doesn't mean we might be anything now." But his voice broke at that last sentence, and he cleared his throat. "But I do have one thing to offer you: a hot bath."

My eyes shot up to him. "You have me, Callum." I knew in that moment I would have paid any cost to be immersed in hot water after all I'd experienced that day. I would have razed armies for a nice bath.

He laughed at my joking tone. "You were always easily seduced by a hot body of water."

"Anyone who isn't is a true monster," I said.

Callum smiled down at me, and that smile was like a ray of sunshine in that dark dungeon. I let his gaze wash over me, even as my thoughts warred inside my head. Then, he led me to the bathing chamber.

"Enjoy," he said, closing the door and leaving me alone with a warm clawfoot tub steaming with hot water.

I quickly shucked my ruined clothes and dipped beneath the hot surface of the water. My aching muscles relaxed with the release as I held back a moan, submerging myself into heated water that lapped at my battered body.

On the wood table beside the bath were vials of different perfumes and soaps. I reached for oils of pressed flowers, opting for the one that smelled of lavender. They were so small they must have been precious—but they were all laid out for me, as Callum had laid himself bare with the truth of our shared past.

As good as betrothed.

That would explain the comfort I felt around Callum, then. And why he had risked his standing as Commander to try and keep me safe.

But my thoughts kept drifting to Tristen. He had taken me in my past life. Kidnapped me. Wrenched me away from Callum, from my home. Somehow, it felt at odds with the man who had stepped in to save me in the first trial. But had Tristen really saved me for *my* sake? Branding me as The Lord Killer had prevented me from getting mercy from the King—but that mercy had led to a crucifixion of the prisoner who had begged and won it.

I felt uneasy about the whole situation. But Tristen had said himself he wasn't to be trusted. Even though he had saved Rachelle and kept his promise, maybe he was keeping those of us alive who would be an easy kill for him later.

My head spun, and I dipped below the surface of the bath, holding my breath. Begging the water to cleanse me from my chaotic thoughts.

I kept myself under the surface of the water until my lungs were screaming for air. I leaned into the pain to let myself forget the past twenty-four hours, and I tried to keep the encroaching darkness at bay.

I emerged from the water with a gasp. I felt my breath accelerate, the water splashing over the side of the tub as panic overwhelmed me.

The doors to the bathing chamber opened, Callum standing there with a towel. "Saffron? Are you okay?"

I took a few deep breaths, sucking in the air. "Yes," I said, breathless. "I'm just..." Suddenly, I started shivering, despite still being immersed in the warm water. My body betraying my broken mental state.

"Saffron," Callum said softly, walking to me. He knelt next to the bathtub, his gaze on my eyes as he reached out and clasped one of the hands I was gripping the edge of the tub with. Both of his hands held it tight, and he leaned over and kissed my wet skin. "Breathe. You're safe."

My breathing quickened, but I pulled it together. I couldn't let myself get too close to breaking. I stood, and Callum stood with me, steadying me as I stepped out of the tub and onto the soft rug. He didn't say a word as he wrapped me in a towel.

What else had been stolen from Callum and I? I wound my arms around his neck, my head resting on his broad chest as hot water dripped down my warm body. I didn't want him to see how much I had been shaken by everything that had transpired so far.

I can't let him see me fall apart.

"Thank you," I whispered. Not just thanking him for what he was doing now—but also for the kindness I suspected lay in our history. A history I so desperately wanted to read, that was so cruelly stolen from us. A love story buried in the ashes of my mind.

Callum pulled away slightly so he could look down at me, trying to read my expression. Suddenly, the towel wrapped around me felt like such a flimsy barrier as his gaze took its time roving over my expression. My lips. Down to the swells of my breasts, barely covered by the towel.

I met his heavy-lidded gaze, caught the question in the way he looked at me. But his hands didn't move from where they lay at my back, holding me to him.

"What do you want, Saffron?" he said, his voice gruff as if it was an effort to ask.

My heart skipped a beat as my lips parted, ready to answer when—

A *knock* sounded at the door. Callum froze.

"Stay here. Don't be seen," he said, slipping out of the bathing chamber, closing the door behind him to keep me hidden as he went to greet whoever was knocking.

I pressed myself against the wall of the bathing chamber, listening through the crack in the door as he opened the outer door to the hallway.

"Yes?" he asked.

"Cassandra is requesting your presence," a polite female voice responded.

"Now?" Callum asked.

"Yes, now," the female voice responded, still polite but sounding a bit annoyed.

"Okay. Give me a minute and I'll get ready."

The door closed, and Callum slipped back inside the bathing chamber. "I'll be back as soon as I can. Stay here and don't answer the door for anyone," Callum said. He lingered, as if not wanting to be torn away from me.

"Go," I urged, not wanting the woman at the door to be suspicious. We were playing a dangerous game when it came to sneaking behind Cassandra's back, and I didn't want Callum to pay the price.

He nodded, but before leaving, he left a quick kiss on my forehead. He donned one of his uniform jackets—he clearly had more than the one he had given me yesterday—and strapped a dagger to his belt before disappearing from his bedchamber.

I waited for a moment until I heard his steps disappear down the stone hallway. I slipped into the bedchamber and saw the clean clothes Callum had set out for me on the bed. I sat down on his bed, running my hands over the fur blankets that covered it. A luxury compared to the cot I had been sleeping on each night.

That's when I saw something on the side table. A single blue ribbon, like a woman would wear in their hair. I reached out and touched it, feeling its silky texture. Then, as if on impulse, I started to braid my wet hair, fixing it into a plait that ran down my low back. I tied it off with the ribbon. It felt right. Felt like it was mine.

I waited for a few moments longer, but Callum didn't come back. My body felt so heavy, the exhaustion pressing me down into the bed. I slipped under the covers, feeling the luxury of the silk bedsheets and the heavy furs that kept the cold out.

I'd wait up for him. Make sure he was safe. Then, I would ask him about our past. About our love story. I'd...

Sleep took me instead.

9

———————

I awoke with a start, at first not sure of where I was. But then I felt the warmth of the furs, and smelled something spicy, mouthwatering...

I sat up on my elbows and saw Callum sliding a hot plate of breakfast onto the side table next to the bed. He was wearing the same thing he had worn yesterday, with dark circles under his eyes.

"Morning," he said, his grin lighting up the room. "I brought breakfast from the guard's mess. And I promise *this*," he held up a steaming mug, "isn't poisoned."

"You rogue," I said, my eyes widened as the smell of darkspice tea hit me. I fully sat up, reaching for the mug as Callum sat on the bed next to me.

"I know how much you love your hot drinks. Careful, don't burn your tongue a second time," he said, but I had already taken the hot mug into both hands and was taking greedy sips. Burning my mouth was the least of my worries as the hot liquid warmed me from head to toe.

"Have you been up all night?" I asked as I watched him run his hand through his hair, his eyes dancing as I kept sipping the tea and wincing at the heat of it.

He shrugged. "I had some things to take care of. Commander duties don't always end at a convenient time. But I'm glad you got comfortable. Did you sleep well?"

"I did," I said, the sheets slipping down my chest a bit, and I caught his eyes widen as I stilled, forgetting that I was naked in his bed—something he realized in that moment as the furs slipped down to bare some of my cleavage. His gaze had a hunger in it, his green eyes taking me in.

"Saffron..." he said, his voice strangled as if he was trying to hold himself back.

I set down the stone mug of tea on the side table. His eyes tracked every movement.

I leaned over, reaching for one of his hands that was gripping the side of the bed. I took his hand in mine, bringing it to my lips, and kissed it.

He reached over, tilting my chin up with his free hand as his gaze locked with mine.

"I want you," he breathed, and I saw the pure male lust in his eyes.

But before I could say anything, breathe anything, footsteps and noises sounded in the hall.

Callum shot up off the bed, hands already going to his weapons, which had been discarded at a table by a dresser, but the footsteps passed.

"The other guards are coming back," he said, turning to me. "Eat your breakfast and get ready. I'll need to escort you to the ball soon."

He was already strapping on his sword, adjusting his uniform. But before he turned to leave, he looked back at me with that gaze full of longing. "We're not done," he said, his rough voice full of promise.

I shivered as he left the room, but not from the cold.

～

AFTER I SCARFED down the hot breakfast of fluffy eggs and salty bacon, my gaze snagged on a small piece of parchment that rested on a folded length of fabric. I walked over and read the note—for *tonight*—and unfurled the dress underneath. It was a pale pink color, with a shimmering interlaced mesh overlay of glittering diamonds. The silk and diamonds brought such a shine to the dress that it almost looked like it was stolen from the final rays of a sunset. *Beautiful.* I slipped it on and went to the mirror by Callum's rack of weapons.

As I stepped in front of the mirror, my eyes widened. Not only did the dress look like it was made of pure magic itself, but it complemented my fair skin and white blonde hair. It glittered in the warm light of the hearth, the petaled skirts unfolding around me, the delicate chain of diamonds shining at my neck. I was a dewy rose, plucked at full bloom. And I felt... pretty. Still a weak, helpless maiden in a tournament to the death with a bunch of overpowered magic wielders—but at least I was no longer dirty, no longer shaking on my cell floor in that tattered wedding dress.

Even though my reflection was still unfamiliar as I had no memory of what I looked like before this, I felt a thrill knowing Callum would see me wearing this dress. I pulled over a chair by the mirror, sitting down as I did my hair. I swept my newly washed blonde hair into a messy bun, braiding strands to wrap over the crown of my head to keep my long hair contained.

Who had taught me to do my hair like this? My mother? A best friend, perhaps? As I sat in front of a floor-length mirror in Callum's bedchamber, I felt my heart ache. I wanted so badly to understand where all of my skills came from. Both the bloodthirsty and the mundane. I wanted to meet the invisible people whose hands had molded me into the woman who was looking back at me in the mirror.

The door of the bedchamber opened, and my heart rate sped up —and then began to beat fast for an entirely different reason as Callum walked in, his brown-blond hair mussed slightly as he took me in.

"Stunning," Callum breathed as I stood.

I blushed, my pale skin turning pink just like the dress I wore.

"It's decent," I joked, turning back to the mirror to admire the gown once more.

He took a step toward me, and then stopped, as if reeling in his restraint. "Would you do me the honor of being my date to the ball?" he asked, that crooked, boyish smile on his face.

I turned to him. This warrior who had fought for me in another life. "Aren't we supposed to be discreet?"

"I don't fucking care anymore," Callum said. "I don't want anyone else to touch you."

"When were you planning to touch me, then?" I challenged.

He took another step toward me, taking my hand in his. He kissed it, his eyes never leaving mine. "As soon as I can," he said, and his eyes promised everything I wanted from him.

But it was time to leave, and he walked to the door, opening it and looking out to ensure there were no prying eyes, and then led me through the narrow passages of Ashguard.

∼

JUST LIKE BEFORE, we rose to the surface on that elevator at the bottom of the silo.

Unlike before, it was just the two of us and a few stray guards who trailed us as we rose to the sunny surface and started down that dirt path. But this time, we walked past the Stone Coliseum, following the path through another dense thicket of trees.

"Where are the others?" I asked.

"They're being escorted separately. The King has a flair for the dramatic. He likes to show off. Your official escorts are behind you." He inclined his head toward two guards that kept their distance behind us. "And I will be forced to hand you off to them when we get closer to the palace. But I wanted to walk you as far as I can."

"What should I know about the King?"

Callum's gaze swept over the forest path in front of us, as if searching for listening ears. His voice was low, quiet enough that the guards behind us couldn't hear what he shared with me. "King West wants one thing—to take back the land that once belonged to Luminaria. These trials? They're all meant to feed his front lines with warriors desperate to fight for their freedom."

"What happened to the past winners of The Ash Trials?" I asked.

Callum tensed. "They were sent to the front lines and never seen again."

My heart picked up its pace. "Never?"

"The front lines of Luminaria is a ruthless place to be. The winners of The Ash Trials have their freedom if they can survive their servitude to King West. But I haven't known a single winner to walk free. The rebels make sure of that."

"What do the rebels want?"

"The rebels who make up the Stormgard Kingdom want chaos. Destruction. And full control over the mortal lands and Luminaria. Their ruling family was known to be bloodthirsty. The King and Queen of Stormgard were vicious warriors turned rulers, and the prince—the sole heir to the throne—hasn't been seen since both the King and Queen were assassinated, their backward laws stating that only he can take the throne when he marries a suitable bride to be his Queen and decides to ascend to his duty. Their laws state that there will be no more royalty unless he returns. But he's speculated to be even more of a monster than they were."

Monster. There was that word again. That word I so often levied against myself, describing what I might have been—what I might still yet become.

There were more questions I wanted to ask—so much more I wanted to know—but I felt Callum's warm, steady hand on the small of my back.

"Here it is," Callum murmured in my ear, and the thicket of trees gave way to a meadow that sloped upward—the path climbing up to the Saltspire Palace.

The Saltspire Palace loomed like a permanent sunrise on the furthest eastern tip of the island, jutting out on a cliff far above the sea. The golds, reds, and oranges of the palace were formed from the way the light filtered through the prism of salt blocks that made up the palace—to keep the Isle of Embermere from cannibalizing it, I remembered being told by Rachelle. Manmade structures didn't last long on the island, and even the Stone Coliseum had to be rebuilt each year for the trials. But the palace? It was made of such exotic shimmering salts that it survived year after year.

"It's beautiful," I said, my heart leaping at the view. Unlike the drab prison or the sturdy stone coliseum, the Saltspire Palace looked elegant. As if it existed just for beauty's sake. Its spires reached up into the sky, curving to pointed tips as if trying to pierce the blue afternoon sky.

"You are," Callum said, and his eyes were drinking me up as I turned to him. "Be careful in there."

I frowned. "Careful of what?"

Callum hesitated. "Just stay aware. I have to meet with Cassandra and King West to discuss the upcoming events, but I'll come find you. Later."

The two guards stepped to my side.

"Your prisoner," Callum said, giving the guards a hard look that promised death should anything happen to me.

The guards bowed, and one of them reached a hand for me, but I stepped back.

"I can handle walking on my own, thanks," I said, leveling a glare at the guard.

I caught Callum's gaze before he turned away, a ghost of a smile on his lips before he cut off down a separate path.

One of the guards motioned for me to go first, and I started walking toward the looming Saltspire Palace, wondering what the ball had in store for me.

10

The interior of the Saltspire Palace was somehow more stunning than the exterior. The pink-hued salt acted like stained glass, but because the entire palace was made of it, every surface seemed to glow with the warm light of the sun. The rays dripped like honey across a nearly translucent dance floor. The ballroom was round and couples spun across it, almost seeming to float with the way the light played on it.

King West was sitting on his throne on the dais, speaking to a few other nobility that surrounded him. Along the far wall, massive surfaces were adorned with tantalizing food, the tables low so that the guests sat on colorful floor pillows to eat. Musicians played sparkling music with notes that bubbled like champagne. Even the chandeliers were made of salt, glowing flames tossing flickering lighting across the hall as the sun began to set.

It was all so romantic, so lush, so *comfortable.*

This was where the King and his court were staying while us prisoners suffered in Ashguard?

It stoked a fire within me. One that cooled only slightly when I remembered that we were prisoners—on death row. Did ruthless killers like Tristen or Ajax deserve comfort? Deserve this?

Did I deserve this?

Conflict warred within me, and I didn't even notice as a man stepped up beside me.

"I'll accept a dance as a thank you," a voice purred in my ear.

I whipped my head to see Tristen standing beside me, a smirk on his lips and his dark hair barely tamed. My heart jumped as I took in his finely cut attire. All black—it cast him in a darkness that just emphasized his natural beauty. His innate power.

"A thank you for what?" I asked, leveling a glare at him as he circled me, taking in my dress.

"For helping you slay all those demons and saving your life," he said smoothly.

"You need a thank you for killing the things that would have surely killed you as well?" I said coldly.

"Come now, wouldn't want others to stare at us," Tristen said, his fingertips brushing down my forearm to my hand, tugging me to the dance floor.

I kept my feet firmly planted, staring him down. "A dance... in exchange for an answer to a question."

Tristen grinned. "There she is," he growled, and prowled toward me. "I accept your bargain, *Sael*."

There it was, that odd word again—but I didn't want to waste my question on deciphering Tristen. He led me onto the dance floor where royalty danced, wearing colors I suspected were from different kingdoms. I spied the rest of the prisoners lurking by the food, not daring to set foot on the dance floor as the royal guards nervously watched them.

"You look like a vision," Tristen said, sliding one arm behind my lower back, the other to my hand as we joined the other couples on the dance floor. I tried not to feel the fluttering in my stomach at his soft touch on my bare skin.

"In this vision, I'm planning your death," I said, scowling at him.

But that made Tristen grin, and he winked at me. "I'd expect nothing less."

The music picked up, and Tristen spun me into a fast-paced waltz, a dance so fast it was dizzying. But his grace made the quick pace and the fast spins feel effortless—even as I stumbled, his strong hand flat on my back helped steady me. I felt his body shift as his strong arms guided me. I wasn't just dancing with him, I was floating through the ballroom in his embrace. My steps became sure, as if his confidence gave me confidence.

I was breathless as the song moved to one with a slower pace, and the couples swaying in time with a more simple dance. Tristen pulled me close.

"Your question?" he asked, looking down at me with amusement and curiosity.

I smiled sweetly, looping both of my arms around his neck. I felt his hands slip down the sides of my gown to rest on my hips. "Yes. I had an interesting conversation today. Where I heard about how you *kidnapped* me from my village in Riverleaf during a rebel skirmish."

Tristen slowed, but didn't stop our dancing. His expression was unreadable. "That wasn't a question."

"I'll put it more bluntly, then. Why did you steal me from my village? From Callum?"

Tristen narrowed his eyes. "Who the hell is Callum?"

I blinked. "Callum. Callum Wells. The Commander—"

Tristen nodded, as if remembering. "Ah. Yes. He was in your village?" A darkness flashed across Tristen's face. "What has he told you about your past?"

"You promised me an answer. Not more questions, *Assassin*," I said.

The song shifted, and Tristen smoothly slipped a hand on my back, the other to my right hand as we began the steps of another intricate dance. "Keep your face neutral. Best to not let the others see us fighting."

I glared. "Why?"

"Don't you want them to think you have my protection in the trials?"

"Answer. My. Gods. Damned. Question," I snarled.

He sighed, and I gasped as he dropped me into a sudden dip, his lips by my ear. "I can't."

I jerked to pull away from him, but he merely pulled me up and into another spin that had others staring at the way my petaled dress shone in the light of the dying afternoon. He dropped me once more into a dramatic dip before I could catch my breath, and as the song ended I was seething, daggers in my eyes.

"We had a deal," I said, feeling foolish for trying to make a bargain with such a ruthless enemy.

"And I had a deal before our deal. So I can't tell you."

"Deal with whom?" I demanded.

A shadow passed over Tristen's face as we resumed our dance.

"Nothing... nothing I've ever—" Suddenly, Tristen pulled back, choking.

I stared, and he stumbled to the side of the dance floor, coughing.

"Tristen?" I asked.

His coughing stopped, but when he withdrew his hand, I saw that it was covered in blood. *Blood*.

What had just happened? In my peripheral vision, I caught a glimpse of Callum arriving, his chest puffing up when he saw who I was standing with. But then his gaze shifted to something behind me —and his eyes widened.

"Let's keep the bleeding to the trials, shall we? Blood is hard to get out of salt. I'm sure you'll understand."

That cold, regal voice was unmistakable.

"King West," I said, turning to see the King standing behind me. He was decked out in finery, his clothes a shimmering gold that reflected the flickering light of the candles shining through the salt chandeliers. The sun was teasing at a sunset, the rays of golden light glimmering on his bronzed skin.

"I'm rather impressed by your performance at the trials so far, Saffron," he said to me. "To think, you were trying to remove yourself from the competition just a day ago."

"I didn't have much of a choice," I said, unable to hold back my glare at Tristen, who was now watching the King with barely concealed hatred.

"A dance?" King West asked, holding out a hand to me.

Turning down the King would be foolish, so I summoned what little court etiquette I had access to, and curtseyed. "I'd be honored, Your Majesty," I said, and took his hand as he led me on the dance floor. I snuck a glance at Callum to catch the horror in his gaze.

King West was a much more demanding lead than Tristen. When Tristen had danced with me, his strong lead moved in time with me, bending to my body while giving me enough tension in his hold on me to keep me moving fluidly with him. West had none of Tristen's smoothness and was dominating in the way he forced me around the dance floor in time to his steps.

I silently thanked the gods when the song slowed, giving me a reprieve. The other couples on the dance floor all gave us a wide berth, and the King fixed his dark black gaze on me as we swayed, our steps in time to a much slower tune.

"Why are you here?" he asked.

I frowned. "You invited me."

He laughed, and the sound caught me off guard. "No. Why are you in my prison? And don't say it's because you're The Lord Killer. I just got word today that that particular murderer is still very much at large, with another noble slain last night. So, I'll ask again. Why are you here?"

I blinked. So I wasn't The Lord Killer. It truly had been a lie by Tristen. Was it... relief that flooded me? "I... I don't know. Is that not information you have access to?"

"I hear from my guards and my spies what crime each has committed, but mostly through gossip if I have not sent a prisoner to Ashguard myself. The ledger of crimes and punishment are kept by the Order of the Serafim, as they have been for centuries. The Order are the ones who work with the island's magic. They bind the prisoners to their fates here commensurate to their crimes. But no one can see the ledgers they keep. I can sentence prisoners to Ashguard—

but if you ended up here without my choosing, then there was another force that brought you here."

"I don't know, Your Majesty."

His eyes narrowed. "What do you mean you don't know?"

I didn't want to reveal too much, but I couldn't risk a lie. "I woke up without... without any memory of who I am."

The song began to end, and the King eyed me. "You're very interesting, Saffron. Maybe you even have a chance to emerge as the victor. It's been so long since we had a Warrior Queen."

My stomach dropped. But I didn't have a chance to say anything as the King let me go as the song ended.

"I'll enjoy watching you," he said, and then he was whisked away by a flurry of courtiers fighting for his attention.

I stood stock still on the dance floor. Another song was struck up by the musicians, but I had to force myself to move off the dance floor.

Warrior Queen.

I had been wrong to see winning The Ash Trials as a chance at earning my freedom, even if that included years in servitude at the front lines. But if King West saw me as a potential queen?

Nausea rose in my stomach as I slipped through the crowd, trying not to run as I gripped my flowing skirts and dashed out of the ballroom and down the spiral stairs. I hurried past courtiers, down an empty corridor.

I found myself at one of the lower levels, reaching where the palace opened up to the gardens, wrapped in round hedges that overlooked the sea. Large white columns framed the view of the greenery, the columns smooth as marble even though they were made of sanded salt.

I gripped a railing on one of the spacious balconies, my breath coming fast—so fast.

What *was* I fighting for? Survival? Or to trade one cell for another?

Shudders ricocheted through my body, the shaking uncontrollable as my breaths came out short.

Something within me was fighting to break free. Something nameless and raw. Something—

"Saffron?"

I turned, finding Callum watching me, concern written on his face.

"Are you okay?" he asked, approaching me with care. His hands went to my hips, and the warmth of him stilled my shaking. "What do you need?" he murmured, standing close to me. So close.

I shoved the fear and whatever the thing fighting to break free from my mind was. I stuffed it all down into a tiny box, locking it away.

As Callum's strong hands brushed the sides of my arms, his warm eyes gazed into mine as the sun's setting rays dusted him in gold. I raised my head, and reached up to weave my arms around his neck.

"You," I whispered, the raw need in my voice. "I need you."

Callum didn't hesitate. His rough hands cradled my face, tilting my chin upward to meet his lips. At first it was a tender kiss, a kiss I imagined a young lover would give to their first crush. But as I wound my fingers in his hair, tugging him to me, the heat burned as his lips moved more hungrily against my own.

And then he was hoisting me up on the railing, my back pressed against one of those salt pillars as Callum's lips trailed from my mouth to my neck, to my shoulder. I tipped my head back, fire trailing in the wake of his kisses.

"Saffron," he murmured against my skin.

His hands roamed my body, sliding up my sides and leaving goosebumps in their wake.

More. I needed more.

My breath hitched as his fingertips brushed underneath my gown, sending electricity tingling up my spine.

But as his lips crashed back onto mine, there was another sensation creeping up my spine. It was warm and tingly, and wholly new. It was heady, intoxicating, and I felt my body *drink* it in, buzzing with a kind of high...

A giggle sounded from somewhere inside the palace and Callum pulled away from me.

"We have to get back," he said, dragging his gaze up my body to meet my eyes, even as they kept drifting down to my lips, which felt so warm and slightly swollen from the way he had claimed my mouth.

I didn't want to leave his arms. I couldn't get enough of his sweetness as my body desired to continue drinking him in. "No," I whispered, pulling him back in for a heady kiss. I wanted to just stay here in his strong arms as his hands explored my body...

"Saffron," he moaned on my lips, and the sound sent a shiver down to my core. "The toast is starting soon. I need to get you back."

But his voice was rough and heavy with want. My breath came out with a shudder as he slowly lifted me up off of the railing and set me down on the floor.

"I'll meet you in there," he said. "Just to keep—"

"I know," I said, not needing him to explain. Cassandra's wrath alone was a good enough reason for us to be careful about being seen together too much.

He nodded, turning to go, but paused at the entryway to the garden. He pulled his hand over his mouth and jaw, drinking me in. "You're gorgeous," he said with that boyish grin of his, and then turned away.

I waited a few moments after he was gone before I straightened my dress and started weaving through the Saltspire Palace, back up to the ballroom. I pushed through the ballroom doors, blending into a busier-than-ever crowd as, at last, all the prisoners had arrived. They looked out-of-place and uncomfortable in their loaned finery.

I stopped by a high table that held long-stemmed champagne flutes and grapes. I picked a few grapes, popping them into my mouth as I surveyed the room.

"Get into a fight with a salt wall?" that silky voice asked. Tristen appeared beside me, and he reached over to brush off some salt from the back of my dress.

"Touch me again and you die," I whirled, glaring daggers at him.

He leaned his head on a closed fist that balanced on top of a high top table, his gaze flickering up to where Callum was standing across the room. "I'm guessing that rule doesn't apply to that guard of yours, does it?" My eyes flashed as Tristen smirked. "What was his name? Oh, right. *Callum.*" Tristen savored my squirm. "Feeling nervous, princess?"

"I'm not a princess," I spat back, still wrestling with what the King had said to me. I wouldn't be anyone's *anything*—I would be the one to pick my own crown. Not someone else. And certainly not Tristen.

"Stop bickering, you're making a scene," Rachelle said, sidling up to us. She looked downright regal in a dress of emerald green. Her eyes flashed at Tristen. "You're a rogue and a bastard. You're lucky I didn't claw out your throat in the first trial."

He shrugged. "I'd like to see you try, kitty cat."

Rachelle bared her teeth at him, hissing.

"What were you saying about not bickering?" I asked with a raised eyebrow.

Rachelle turned to me and grinned, slinging an arm around my shoulders. "Lucille would've liked you, y'know. I wish you could have met her."

I leaned into Rachelle, a warmth growing in my chest. Before this prison, had I known friends like Rachelle? I would have to ask Callum. Ask him who else filled my life and my happy days of being just a simple maiden baking bread before Tristen ripped me from my village.

Before I could dwell on my past, King West stood from his throne, commanding the room.

"Let us raise a glass to the contestants who are here tonight as our guests of honor. A toast to their bravery as they transcend each trial and become worthy of claiming the title of the hero who will save Luminaria and the fate of all of the kingdoms on Septerra. To you," King West said, inclining his head toward us contestants, sweeping his gaze across all of us until his eyes landed on me, his stare weighing too heavy as he raised his glass.

Waiters handed everyone champagne flutes, and we raised our glasses as well.

"Illumia be with you," he said, and the entire ballroom echoed the words back as he took his first sip and they followed suit.

I tipped the glass back... but didn't let the liquid breach my lips. The tea incident was still burned into my memory, and I didn't trust the liquid in the glass. As I lowered my glass, I turned to Rachelle— only to find my friend falling to the floor.

The breath caught in my throat as Tristen's legs gave out from under him, his body falling heavy on the ground on the other side of me.

The sound of breaking glass was all around me, as contestant after contestant fell with their glass.

No no no no.

My mind shouted in fear. I had been right—something had been slipped into our drinks. But as I crouched next to Rachelle to check her pulse, I saw that her chest was still rising and falling. Not dead. Not poisoned. Merely... unconscious.

"Please, wake up. Wake up," I begged Rachelle, shaking her limp body.

Footsteps sounded in the quiet ballroom. I hadn't noticed the hush that had fallen, hadn't noticed how none of the King's court or any of his guards were afflicted. It was just the prisoners. As my gaze rose, I saw King West standing in front of me with a sneer on his lips.

"You do not toast to your King?"

"I—" I started.

"DRINK!" he roared, and I sprung to my feet, shaking my head and backing away.

"I won't—" I caught sight of Callum standing at the foot of the dais, his face pale as he slightly shook his head. I had said the wrong thing.

But King West was already motioning to someone behind him. A man who was crouched over a swirling wooden cane, wearing a black cape with a hood.

"Sophos," he said. "Make her."

The man looked up at me with eggshell white eyes—that were missing pupils. He was blind, but those sightless orbs still seemed to pierce my soul. He raised a hand, and I sucked in a breath as I felt an intruding presence in my mind. *Mindweavyr.* This man was trying to use compulsion on me.

I wildly felt for my mental shields, but I was too rattled.

"Drink," Sophos intoned, his voice frail, but the command echoed in my mind with that ancient power. As if a god had echoed the command, forcing my body into submission.

"No!" I shouted, but my body wasn't listening. My hand reached for the glass I had left on the high table. I forced it not to grasp the cup. Tried to slam down those shields.

Sophos trembled, and I realized I was holding him off. He didn't have nearly as much power as Tristen had, maybe I could—

"*Drink*," Sophos said again, and this time, the compulsion slipped through the cracks in my mental shields.

With a trembling hand and a cry of defeat, I lifted the champagne flute to my lips.

And drank. The liquid tasted strange, earthy. If the land could bleed, it would taste like this. Grainy, almost medicinal.

The last thing I saw before total darkness was the cruel smile on the King's lips as he watched me fall, all of the eyes of his court on me as I was lost to oblivion.

11

I n the darkness, there was nothing but screaming.

I awoke on a cold floor with a pounding headache. The room I was in was all smooth obsidian—just slightly translucent so that some of the faraway moonlight shone through. As I struggled to my feet, I clung to the walls—

—but I nearly slipped, the material so smooth it flowed like water underneath my fingertips.

Another *scream* split through the air. I lifted my head in the direction of the sound, which had come on the other side of the large wooden door. The same kind of door I had seen in the palace.

Palace. I was in a palace.

The last moments of consciousness flooded my mind. I had been in the Saltspire Palace—and after one drink of that drugged champagne I was—

Here. *In the second trial.*

I didn't need my intuition to know that. To know why only us prisoners were drugged. Taken into a slumber to wherever... here was.

I looked down at myself—I was still wearing the sparkling dress. *Great.* I cursed myself for not asking Callum for his dagger to hide underneath my skirts. I was once again unarmed and at the mercy of those around me.

Once again a defenseless maiden.

I tried to steady myself by looking around the room. I was in a small bedchamber. Just a bed and a small sofa. Nothing to fight with, nothing to wield.

THUMP!

I jumped to my feet as something hard hit the door. Someone was trying to break in. I dropped into a fighting stance, when—

—the door splintered into a thousand pieces, and the twins, Priscilla and Felicity, came rolling in, all sharp screams and punches. One of the twins was shoving her hands into her sister's throat, trying to choke the air out of her. But she wasn't just trying to choke her. The two twins were smoking... flames licking off their bodies. Writhing and screaming at each other. Going for throats. Going for the kill.

Fire sprites.

That's what they were, without their magic leashed. As I dodged their flaming bodies, the twin who was pinned tossed her sister off, her flaming body setting fire to the tapestry behind the bed. As smoke started to fill the room, one twin—who I recognized a Priscilla —turned a blazing gaze toward me.

"Kill them, Saffron," Priscilla forced out through gasping breaths.

"Why are you trying to kill your sister?" I asked. The twins were much more bloodthirsty than I had thought.

Priscilla shifted her gaze to her twin, who was starting to pull herself off the now burning bed. "Don't let them live."

And then she pounced. With a feral scream, the fire sprite went at the throat of the other.

I took no time running out of the room, choking on the black smoke as my eyes stung and my lungs burned. I slammed the door behind me, taking in gasping breaths as I looked up. I was in a spire of some sort. The way the tower grew narrower above me made me think of the spires on the Saltspire Palace. It felt so similar. Identical, but in a dark and twisted way.

I need to get out of here. Especially if that fire spreads.

I decided to go down the steps, and I began to hurry down them. It was unusually quiet in the spiral staircase now that the screams had stopped. Had the others already separated? I had been the last to drink the drugged champagne. Maybe they had gotten a headstart.

"Priscilla!" a voice screamed from above me. I leaned over the banister to see Felicity—the other fire sprite twin—covered in blood, running down to the spiral staircase to the burning room I had just exited.

Wait... hadn't I just seen Felicity and Priscilla battling in that room? How did Felicity get all the way up there?

Something was wrong here.

I hurried faster down the stairs. I was halfway down the spiral staircase when suddenly a wave of darkness swept across the stairs—

—and I yelped, stumbling down a few steps.

"Careful, now. It would be an awfully bad tumble if you fell from here," a voice rumbled through the dark.

I whirled to see Tristen in front of me, his hands in his pockets.

"Get away from me," I said, feeling the roiling of his power. It hit me so hard—the raw, unleashed force of it.

"I'm only here to help you. You were headed downstairs?" He held out the crook of his arm to me. "Wouldn't want you to slip."

I glared. "I can handle stairs myself."

"Suit yourself," he said with a shrug.

I descended the stairs in silence, my eyes fixed on Tristen's back as he glided down the steps in front of me. I lost focus as my gaze, like a magnet, fell on the back of his neck, the curve where his dark strands kissed the nape of his neck. His hair was like a brushstroke against olive skin, muscles shifting beneath his inky black shirt with each steady rhythm of his descending footsteps. My pupils widened to drink him in, greedy for every detail. Then, I tilted my head, remembering the feel of a small mole on the back of his neck when my fingertips had brushed his skin when we were dancing. It was missing now—or had I just imagined it?

Get it together, Saffron, I chided myself.

"Do you know where we are? What else is in this palace?"

"Hmmm?" Tristen replied.

"Here. In this palace. What have you encountered so far? I'm guessing this is a trial if we're all here but none of the King's court is. Do you know what the objective is?" Surely he hadn't gotten a concussion in his fall to the floor after being drugged.

"Oh. I think it's probably some sort of battle royale."

"Again?" I asked.

But Tristen just stared at me as if he wasn't fully processing my words. "You look so lovely in the moonlight, Saffron. Has anyone told you that?"

I froze. I had stopped on a step where the milky moonlight dripped through a window in the tower, stroking my face like a lover.

"I don't know," I confessed, truth falling from my lips before I could stop it. Tristen had stolen me from my village. Why was he talking to me like this? And why did my body seem to sing when he looked at me in that way?

Tristen rose to the step I stood on. So close to me. He reached out to brush a strand of hair from my face as my pulse quickened. "You can know this. Know me."

My heart hammered as he leaned closer. *Why wasn't I pulling away?*

"SAFFRON!" a shout came from an alcove above me, and suddenly a man was hurtling down from the floor above, knocking down Tristen.

"No!" I shouted, but the hooded figure slammed Tristen into the wall, grabbing for Tristen's other hand—

—*a hand that had been clutching a knife behind his back, poised to strike me down.*

The cloaked figure took the knife, raising it above Tristen.

But Tristen ducked, the cloaked figure slashing through air with the knife. The figure swiveled, his back against the wall as Tristen descended a step.

"If you wanted a fight to the death, you could have just asked," Tristen goaded.

No.

I couldn't let this man kill Tristen. As much as the Assassin infuriated me, he had also saved my life. I had to try to help him.

I kicked the back of the hooded figure, who stumbled down a step in surprise. Tristen lunged at him again, kneeing the hooded figure in his stomach. The hooded figure gasped, but dropped down and grabbed Tristen's ankle, yanking it and pulling Tristen off-balance.

Tristen's eyes went wide, and he fell—

—tumbling down a set of those hard stone steps, landing with a crack as his body was stopped by one of the stone walls that bordered the staircase.

"Tristen!" I called, but he held up a hand from where he laid on the stone landing, blood trickling from his head.

"Stay there," he said, his voice hoarse. "Get to safety."

The hooded figure advanced down the staircase, holding up the dagger Tristen had held...

...and wasted no time *plunging it into Tristen's chest.*

Straight into his heart.

"NO!" I screamed, something hurt and angry slicing through my blood. I watched in horror as Tristen's eyes glazed over as blood poured from his chest.

I couldn't stop my traitorous feet as I closed the distance between us, shoving the hooded figure aside so I could get to Tristen.

Tristen's eyes met mine as he wheezed. "It's a shame it had to end like this. Right, Saffron?" Then, his face twisted in pain... and then smoothed as his head lolled on the obsidian wall. His final breath escaped his lips as his eyes closed—and I felt my heart still in my chest.

Tristen was dead.

He was my enemy. I should be *thanking* that hooded stranger for removing him from the trials. So why did I feel nothing but terror? And... sadness? I twisted my feelings into anger, my head snapping up to the man with the cape who still had his back to me.

"You fucking monster!" Revenge pulsed deep in my blood, a kind of wrath that felt at the same time both foreign and familiar.

Without thinking, I whirled, grabbing the killer's black hood, pulling it back—

—to reveal *Tristen*. Alive and smirking in front of me.

"Mourning my death, Saffron?"

I scrambled back, gripping the balustrade as I stared at him.

"How... You...?" I looked at the dead Tristen on the ground. He looked identical to the one standing in front of me... but there was something different pulsing in his power. The Tristen in front of me felt more... whole. I couldn't put it into words, but somehow I knew the one standing in front of me—*alive*—was the real Tristen.

Then, the body on the floor—Tristen's double—started to shift and crack, turning to wood. As the body groaned and splintered into wood pieces, it began resembling a fallen tree bark, and no longer looked like him. I stared, feeling like my mind was splintering along with the image.

"Creepy how the island does that," Tristen remarked.

"Does what?" I breathed.

"The gods gave too much of their power to this place," Tristen muttered, and then looked me in the eye. "To win this second trial, you must do two things. First, survive. And second? Kill your double," he said.

Kill your double. So it hadn't been the twins fighting—it had been one of their doppelgangers, conjured by The Ash Trials. By the island itself.

An explosion rocked the tower, and Tristen looked up, bored. "Seems like some of the others have already met theirs." His gaze shifted back to me. "Let's get moving. We have to hunt down the second most beautiful person here."

"And who is that?" I asked.

"Your double," he said with a roguish grin.

I glared at him as we started down the stairs. "How do you even know that I'm the real me?"

He grinned. "A fake Saffron would have merely laughed at my death."

I scowled. "I would have laughed, but I was merely too shocked."

"Do you normally shout '*no!*' and prepare to take your revenge right before you laugh?"

I shot him daggers with my eyes, but he suddenly stilled.

"In here," he said, and pulled me into an alcove at one of the landings beside the stairs. He pressed my body against the stone, angling himself in front of me.

The look of terror I saw on his face made me oblige, his strong hands pulling me into the shadow of a curved corner of darkness.

"Don't make a sound," he whispered.

I felt it before I saw it.

Something large. Not in size, but in power. In *potential* power. Something icy and horrifying. I felt a whimper rise and die in my throat. Stifled by a horrible chill, a slithering coldness.

Then, it passed right by our alcove. Something cloaked in slithering shadows, hissing like snakes. Red, beady eyes sweeping back and forth. Searching for something. For some*one*.

The train of darkness around the figure halted for a moment, sniffing the air. I stiffened, my body flattening further against the stone behind me.

The figure kicked back its head and *roared*. In the wake of the earth-shattering roar was a rotting smell. Death, decay, suffering. All of it so foul it filled my nose, stuffing me with a sensation so rancid it took every ounce of my self-restraint not to double over and vomit on the floor in front of us.

The roar caused all of the snakes that made up the pacing beast to rattle and hiss as it paused. Listening.

And then, it moved on. Descending deeper into the depths of the tower.

I counted my breaths. Praying my legs wouldn't give out beneath me.

Tristen let his hand drop, and my eyes flew to him, but his expression had eased back to that bored, arrogant mask he so easily wore.

"You told me all we would have to do in this trial was kill our doubles," I ground out through gritted teeth at him.

Tristen shrugged. "That *is* someone's double."

I stilled. "*Whose* double?"

"I've read about trials like this in the past. The Isle of Embermere senses the power of each contestant. To keep things... *fair*... it mirrors the power of the strongest contestant—and then some. The rest of us have to face ourselves, sure, but the most powerful of us? They have to go beyond. Become *more*. Withdraw the power hidden so deep within the well of themselves that it could potentially kill them."

I let out a breath of relief. I was powerless, so that creature wouldn't be my problem. *Thank the gods*—finally, something was going my way in this trial.

As I ducked out of the alcove and Tristen and I descended the stairs once again, I shot a sly glance at him. "So you're *not* the most powerful person in these trials?"

Tristen raised an eyebrow. "Don't get any ideas. I'm the *second* most powerful person on this godsforsaken island. Maybe in all of Luminaria and Stormgard, too."

I rolled my eyes. The ego on this man was atrocious. "So who do you think gets the honor? Of being the most powerful?" My mind flipped through all of the contestants. Rachelle could shift—something I hadn't seen the others do. My heart fell at the thought of Rachelle going up against that nightmare. If luck would have it, Ajax would be the one getting ripped apart by that thing.

But Tristen hadn't replied.

"Tristen?" I asked, but before I could turn back to search his expression, an animalistic growl ripped through the tower. That noise was familiar. Unmistakable.

"It's Rachelle," I breathed. I sprinted down the last few steps of the tower to reach the ground floor. For some reason, Tristen was slowing behind me. Had he really tired from the fight with his double? That didn't quite make sense.

"She's in the throne room," Tristen bit out as if he was trying to hold something back, and as I crept into the next hallway, the aching familiarity of the palace made sense as the hallway opened up into a larger room of staircases and the grand entryway before the closed doors of the throne room.

"It's a mirror of the Saltspire Palace," I breathed.

Tristen nodded, but his face was still tight. "And to think it was *you* who said the island had no imagination."

A screeching growl cut through the air—one that was filled with agony.

"This way," I said, motioning to the throne room, but behind me—

—Tristen was starting to dissolve.

"Tristen?" I cried.

He looked down at the particles of himself as they started to disappear. "I've slayed my double. I've resisted as long as I could, but my trial is over. Yours is just beginning."

A slice of panic went through me. I would be powerless without his help, as much as I didn't want to admit needing him. I had survived this far, but what if my luck ran out? I was powerless, a hollow amongst wielders with astonishing powers—and their doubles.

As if reading my face, he shook his head. A wholly undecipherable expression chased his frown. "It's an honor. Take it as such."

"What's an honor?" I demanded, but he was gone, spirited away with his cryptic words.

I turned back to the throne room doors as Rachelle let out another horrible howl. Beside the closed throne room doors stood a suit of armor with...

...a sword. No, not just a sword. The Bluesteel Blade I had stolen from the stone in the first trial. It was there... waiting for me.

"Hello, old friend," I said to the blade as I strode across that big empty hall, ignoring the shadows dancing in the flickering light. "Stalking me? I'll allow it. But only if you promise to get me out of this alive."

"*I go where you go,*" the blade responded.

I stopped at the suit of armor, and reached for the blade. As I grabbed the hilt, it didn't burn me this time. No, instead, it warmed to a comfortable temperature. I blew out a breath, trying to dissipate the adrenaline building in my blood as I held up the Bluesteel Blade. Maybe it would be what I needed to get out of here alive.

I strode to meet the huge oak throne room doors, pausing for a moment with my hand resting against the smooth black wood of them.

Rachelle fought for me in the first trial. So had Tristen. So had Callum. It was time for me to start showing up for the people I cared about—to be the one doing the saving, and not always needing to be saved.

It was time.

With that, I threw open the throne room doors, ready to start repaying my debts.

12

It was so much worse than I could have expected.

Two red-maned lionesses were chained at the foot of the throne, unable to move more than a few feet away, the short leashes keeping them trapped as they growled and bared their teeth. Both of the lionesses bore deep red gashes and other injuries. Laughing prisoners—all of Ajax's cronies—surrounded them with bloody swords.

There was not just one Ajax lounging on the obsidian throne—but a second one leaning against a pillar nearby, with an identical grin, eye patch, and short dagger—dripping with crimson.

All the heads in the throne room turned to me as I strode in.

"Ah, Saffron," Ajax said, cocking his head from the throne. "I've caught your pet, it seems. Not that she or her double put up any real fight."

Both lionesses turned and growled at Ajax—both of them, at least, on the same page that he was the enemy.

I stepped to the center of the throne room, clutching my sword as the other prisoners began to circle me.

"Let Rachelle—*both* of her—go."

Ajax clucked his tongue. "That's not how this works." He turned to his cronies. "Kill her."

A swing of metal caught the light above me, and I barely dodged the oncoming blade after each prisoner stepped out of the circle to make a run at me. They were laughing as their blades nicked my skin, tore at my body as if it were made of paper. I bobbed and weaved out of their paths, just barely faster than their lazy attempts to cut at me —but my heavy sword slowed me down. I didn't dare let it fall from my grip.

Finally, my blade made purchase with a clang, sending one of Ajax's cronies stumbling backward.

He was a slimy snake of a man. He smiled at me, and then spit something in my direction—and where his spit landed, the floor sizzled and burned. His saliva was *acid*. "I want a taste of you," he said with a toothy grin.

I lashed out, slicing my sword through the air in a wild slash, but he just backed off slightly, grinning wildly as he continued to circle me. *I couldn't let him get close to me.*

Another prisoner with a dagger slashed at me, and I was too slow this time. One of the Rachelles roared as I stumbled back. I felt warmth on my arm, and I looked down.

The dagger had cut deep—deeper than I had expected. One look at the blood and I felt woozy, the pain of the slice rushing back to me as my adrenaline ebbed.

The Saffron I knew couldn't hurt a fly. Callum's words echoed in my head.

How stupid was I to go running into a throne room full of Ajax and the rest of his brutal cadre who killed for sport? With no power, no plan, no help?

Shame sliced through me. I would die here—and my double, wherever it was, would giggle with glee as I lost this trial—and my life.

Stupid, stupid girl.

Tears stung hot but I forced myself to stand tall and proud and looked up to Ajax as he lounged on the throne.

"Fight me yourself, Ajax," I challenged.

"And when I win?" he asked.

"Then you'll have what you've wanted this whole time. Would be a shame to let all of your fun go to a bunch of copies and lowlifes. But if I win, I want Rachelle and her double to be released. So, how about it? Come down here and fight me yourself. That is... unless you're afraid of me."

All of Ajax's men turned toward him. The threat was well-placed, aimed right at his male ego. If I was going to die in this throne room, the hell if it would be in vain. I'd die attempting to free my friend, not bleeding out slowly from a thousand cuts.

Slowly, Ajax pushed himself off the throne. He walked past his double—who was oddly silent and still—not making a move to try and kill the Real Ajax. The Real Ajax tossed his dagger from hand to hand, raking his eyes down my body.

"I'll enjoy flaying you apart. Piece by piece."

His circle of prisoners snickered, stepping back and widening the area below the dais for our fight.

Rachelle snapped her lioness-sharp teeth at Ajax and growled as he walked past her—and I knew from the way that the Rachelle on the left put up more of a fight, that that was indeed the real Rachelle. The other one merely stared at what was going on with vacant eyes, occasionally straining against her chains. Unless Rachelle had truly given up hope...

I took in a steadying breath as Ajax started circling me.

"It's an insult to the rest of us that you've even made it this far."

"Says the man who can't even kill his double," I taunted.

"I haven't killed him because I'm here to play," Ajax said, and then lunged at me.

I dodged, swinging the heavy blade with as much agility as I could muster. I held him off, my muscles screaming and more of my hot blood tumbling out of my wounds as I whirled.

Ajax fought like a brute, with punishing, horrible strikes. Again, and again, I parried, dodged. Some past training was ingrained in my instincts, allowing me to hold him off. But I still felt like my body was moving through molasses, my mind dragging my feet through steps it was too slow to execute.

Suddenly, I felt a searing pain through my thigh, and I screamed, stumbling back. Ajax grinned—he had struck low, and the tip of his blade had caught my leg, tearing it open.

I stuck my blade down into the ground, using it as a crutch.

"You're done for," Ajax said, circling me as I tried to keep the black spots from crowding too much of my vision. "It's time to start begging for mercy. Or else I'll just kill you more slowly."

I let my shoulders slump. Let myself seem like I was about to pass out. It wasn't completely an act. Not really. As Ajax tipped back his head and laughed, his cadre of bloodthirsty prisoners joining in at laughing at my breaking body, I bolted.

Not at Ajax. But toward what I suspected was Rachelle's double.

The chained lioness didn't even give me a second look. It merely raised a head as I lunged toward it, driving my sword through its eye.

Please be Rachelle's double. Please. I prayed to all of the gods in all of the realms.

The whole throne room went silent as the lioness with my sword through its eye let out a dying whine, and slumped over.

Everyone's gaze went to the other chained lioness, stunned at what I had just done. I didn't waste a second of their shock, raising my blade once more to sever the chain that kept who I hoped was the real Rachelle leashed to the throne.

And then suddenly, strong hands hauled me back, and I realized Ajax's double had grabbed me from behind, my sword clattering to the ground.

"You idiot!" the Real Ajax screamed at me. But my vision was going hazy as I clung to consciousness, blood still pouring from my wounds. It was amazing how much I had lost—I should be dry as a husk, and I knew I didn't have much left to lose before my veins ran dry.

But as I turned to watch the unchained lioness beside the throne shift back into a human woman, those familiar green eyes looked up at me in disbelief. "Saffron," she said in shock. "How did you know?"

I gave her an easy grin as I tried not to sway. "Lucky guess. Be safe. Tell Tristen thanks for me."

"What are all you doing? Get those chains back on her!" the Real Ajax screamed.

But Rachelle had already grabbed for a fallen sword, fighting against the onslaught of prisoners. I saw how exhausted she was, how hard Rachelle fought as they rushed at her—

—but then one of them roared with anguish as she sliced through him, spinning away...

...and just as Tristen had done, Rachelle started to vanish, dissolving into thin air.

"Saffron!" she yelled.

"Goodbye, Rachelle," I said. "Now we're almost even."

Rachelle's face was drawn in fear and sadness as she blinked from the throne room. I felt tears prick my eyes. The look Rachelle had given me—I knew, deep down, that I had picked correctly. That I had killed Rachelle's double, saved my friend, and repaid at least one life debt.

As all of the heads in the throne room swiveled back to me, I held my head high, even as Ajax's double tightened his grip on me.

"You fucking bitch, you lost me my pet!" Ajax said, turning on me. He tossed his dagger aside. "I will drain you dry and suffocate you on your own blood."

"I've still won," I said, glaring at Ajax. Even as fear sliced through my heart, I refused to give him the pleasure of seeing me break. "Rachelle will see to your end, even if I'm not the one to deal your death blow."

Ajax's eyes flashed. "Your friend will die like the rest of them. But as for you? This kill is for my brother. I know you were there when they murdered him." His dark eyes glinted and he stepped up, raising his arms as his pupils rimmed with red.

Blood Magic.

As he jerked his hand up, I felt all of the blood in my body *yank*. It sang for him, and he whispered words—like a violent prayer in a language I didn't recognize—as a sneer decorated his lips.

Every cell in my body wanted to fight free of myself. Yearning to leave me. The blood hurried to rush free and join him. And I watched in horror as the blood from my wounds started emptying from my veins, floating in the air toward Ajax.

I couldn't stop the cry that escaped from me as my heart stuttered on the blood that refused to flow into it.

This was going to be a horrible, brutal death.

I kept my eyes hard, staring death down as I fought against his magic. Still, my mortal heart began to fail.

But something faltered in his eyes. The smirk disappeared—

—and that's when I felt it.

I fell out of his power, and I was gasping and wheezing on the stone floor just as the eternal coldness swept into the ballroom.

All of the candles went out as that evil creature that I had seen on the staircase entered the room. It was darkness and night and the overwhelming chokehold of a nightmare. It was horror and devastation and suffering all in one creature.

"I've come for you, my dear double," it said. And as the words left its black lips, the shadows receded.

And the face that stared out at me—

—was my own.

13

The other prisoners scrambled for the edges of the throne room. Even Ajax couldn't get away from the creature fast enough.

"I'm—I'm not—you can't be," I stammered.

My double just cocked its head, grinning as her blonde curls—identical to mine—tumbled down a shoulder. She even wore the same dress as me, but there was something evil in her eyes. The snakes and the slithering shadows still followed her like a whispering fog.

"What's the matter, Saffron?" My double continued to make her way across the throne room to me, where I struggled to stay upright. "Don't tell me you're surprised to see me?"

I stumbled back, gripping the edge of the throne. One of Ajax's men, who had been standing by the throne, wet himself and whimpered, running to hide behind a stone column.

My double turned and frowned. With a flick of her wrist, the column *exploded*. The man shrieked, covered in blood. My double rolled her eyes. She raised her hand, summoning a jeweled dagger from her shadows—and tossed it across the room, slicing him through his throat and cutting off his gurgled scream.

I did my best to stand upright by the throne, trying to keep my double from seeing my weakness. "You're only supposed to challenge the most powerful. You've picked wrong. I have no power."

A slow smile crept across my double's face, and she didn't slow her pace as she reached the stone steps and began climbing the dais toward me. Slow, measured, *terrifying* steps. "Oh, dear Saffron. Is that what you believe?"

The creature's rancid smell flooded my nostrils, and this time I couldn't help it—I doubled over and hurled my guts up at the feet of the throne.

"Haven't you learned by now? Your fear will destroy you and everyone you love," my double chided, leaning down as she finally reached me, her icy hand reaching out to caress my cheek and push away some of the blood-stained locks of hair out of my face as I panted. "Why do you believe what everyone tells you? Didn't he tell you to trust no one?"

"It's a bad habit," I choked out.

I tried to pull myself to my feet, but my double just grabbed the back of my dress and threw me across the room. I cried out as I tumbled across the cold obsidian floor at the center of the throne room. A squelch of blood ripped from my wound at my thigh, and my whole body felt heavy.

Up. I had to get up again.

"Did you really think you could win these trials?" my double taunted, once again strolling back to me. "The Isle of Embermere created The Ash Trials to produce *heroes*. Those who can conquer their fear long enough to win battles and wars."

I raised my head, placing my hands beneath me. I pushed, but couldn't lift myself. I *had* to get up. Had to get to my feet. I wouldn't die on the floor, not like this. I scanned the room and saw that my sword was discarded on one of the steps leading up to the throne, its pointed end facing me, but it was so far away...

"I'm not weak," I said, coughing on some blood in my mouth that I turned to spit out.

Suddenly, my double appeared in front of me, grabbing my jaw with a strong hand. Her glittering blue eyes—*my* eyes, but these were so filled with malice—pierced my soul. She yanked me to a kneeling position, and my traitorous body let out a whimper of pain.

"You're not going to win. Give up now and I'll make your death quick."

Out from one murderer's hands and into another. Once again, I was facing my death. Once again, I was facing the depths of my weakness. Rachelle wasn't coming to save me. Callum wasn't coming to save me. Even Tristen with his stupid smirk wasn't coming to save me.

But I refused to let my death be one of weakness.

"You're pathetic," my double said, sneering down at me.

"Go to hell," I said.

In that moment, my rage boiled something within me. Something that was beginning to overflow. It started as a whisper beneath my skin, a flutter of molecules rearranging themselves like stars finding new constellations. Then came the pull, deep in my marrow, as if every atom of my being suddenly remembered a dance it was meant to perform. My body buzzed with an ancient undercurrent, a power older than memory surging through pathways I never knew existed.

Time fractured. The energy within me coiled tight, compressing against my bones until my fingers trembled with the weight of it. I raised my arms—not in surrender, but in recognition of something burning through my blood that demanded to be set free.

For a split second, I saw everything with impossible clarity. Dust particles stood suspended in space. The pulse of my own frightened heart painted patterns behind my eyes.

Then the power broke through, erupting through my body, not like an explosion, but like the first breath after nearly drowning.

Out from my crossed arms, a blast of bright blue light exploded into the throne room.

A shield.

Callum's shield.

A shrieking noise sounded and was cut short—and as my ability to hold myself up flowed out of me, I fell to the ground.

I raised my head to see that my double had been impaled on my forgotten sword. Right through its heart. Callum's shield had tossed my double right in the pathway of the Bluesteel Blade, ensuring her death.

Oh, thank God. Callum had come to save me. My vision continued to blur and eddy around me, and I felt myself being pulled back to reality, pieces of myself splintering like I had seen happen to Tristen and Rachelle.

But as I looked around the throne room, each shocked face was a mirror reflecting back something I wasn't able see, the truth assembling in my mind like pieces of broken glass being glued back together.

Callum was not here.

I had wielded his shield... without him.

The darkness pulled me under as I was whisked away from the second trial—I had won, but I couldn't understand how it had happened.

PART II

THE SIPHON

14

pplause. They were clapping.

So cold. I felt so—

Wait. I *felt*. That meant that I was alive.

I sat up, gasping, clutching my throat, my body. I was greeted by clapping royals and courtiers. They were watching me unsteadily climb to my feet, and everything was unchanged from when I had passed out, save for the darkened sky visible outside of the windows and the glow of torches now tossing light around the room.

I looked down, and my dress was pristine. Untouched. I touched my body, feeling for the gashes...

...that weren't there.

Callum approached me, relief in his features. "Saffron Vale, you have survived the second trial," he said. "May I escort you back?"

I looked around in shock. Rachelle and Tristen weren't there, but there were still other prisoners convulsing on the floor... including Ajax.

"What—" I started.

"We can discuss any questions you have on the way back," Callum said, interrupting me.

As Callum offered me his arm, I took it, but I couldn't wrench my gaze from the unconscious prisoners still on the floor of the ballroom. There were a few who were so clearly dead—blood having pooled from their eyes and mouth—and servants were currently dragging a few bodies out of the throne room. My stomach felt sick, but it did another turn as I caught several royals exchanging gold coins as they watched me leave.

They were *betting* on us. On who would win.

As Callum led me out, I caught the gaze of a woman in white robes with dark skin. She was adorned with jewels—clearly one of the royalty—but she seemed separate from the rest of the group. She watched me with odd gray eyes that stood out against her dark complexion. Her beauty was that of a panther—silent yet deadly—and her gaze followed me until Callum and I left the throne room.

The doors closed behind us, and we were alone.

Callum pulled me into a narrow hallway, and suddenly, I was wrapped up in his strong arms.

"Callum," I breathed, but I couldn't stop the sobs that started wracking my body as he held me. I clutched at his arms that were corded in muscle. He held me until my shaking subsided.

Slowly, I raised my head and gazed up at him. With a gentle gesture, he reached down and brushed away the hair from my face.

"You can't be seen with me like this," I said, suddenly looking down the empty hallway as if we were moments away from being discovered.

Callum chuckled. "It was definitely *not* your double that made it back if you're worried for my safety."

I glared and elbowed him, and he put his hands up. "Don't fight me—this isn't a trial. You're safe," he said.

My expression went soft as I took in his words.

You're safe.

"It was all so real," I said.

"The liquid you drank came from the island itself. It's a kind of hallucinogen that brings everyone into the Mirror Realm together. Not much is known about the Mirror Realm—but if you die there, you die here."

I felt my throat bob. "How many others came back? Rachelle? Tristen?"

Callum narrowed his eyes. "Rachelle is alive. Along with something like thirty others so far, but there are still more trapped within the Mirror Realm. And yes, the *Assassin* lived."

"He helped me. Again."

Anger flashed across Callum's face. "I don't know how many times you need to hear this, but maybe this time it will sink in. *You. Can't. Trust. Him.* You almost died. You know how scared I was? Seeing you convulse on the floor, knowing you were being destroyed in your mind? I wished I was in there with you. Wished I could be the one protecting you."

I mulled his words over. "You weren't, though. In the trial?"

Callum's eyebrow raised. "No. Why?"

"Because... your shield saved me."

Callum frowned. "What do you mean?"

I hesitated. "I... I was about to lose. Against my double. And I reached within myself... and called your shield."

"You're a shielder?" Callum asked, and suddenly was pulling me down the hallway. "Let's get outside. I want you to show me."

"I don't know how I—"

But Callum was already hurrying down the vast hall of the Saltspire Palace, and I rushed after him, the ghosts of my injuries still playing tricks on me as I winced and felt wisps of pain of what had been sustained in the Mirror Realm.

Callum led me out a side entrance to the palace, to a small pocket garden wreathed in hedges to hide us from prying eyes.

"Try," Callum insisted, facing me. "Bring up your shield."

I hesitated. I slid to the ground, kneeling. I raised both hands over me in a crossed position, just like I'd seen him do—just like *I'd* done in the second trial.

...but felt nothing.

I blew out a breath, lowering my arms. "It's not there."

Callum held out a hand and pulled me up back to standing. "Are you *sure* you wielded a shield power? That one of the other prisoners didn't help you?"

I thought back to those final moments of the second trial. My memory was so fuzzy. My blood loss had made me so dizzy...

"Maybe it was," I admitted, but even as I said it, it felt wrong. That burst of power... it had come from within me.

But Callum was already nodding. "I know being powerless is... tough. But you've made it this far. You're holding your own. I'm proud of you."

He brought me to him, and I tried to find comfort in his embrace, but a nagging feeling kept my thoughts racing.

The question I had asked myself when I first arrived here came to me once more.

Who am I?

15

R oll call that morning showed exactly how brutal the past trial had been. Thirty-six prisoners remained, and everyone looked worse for the wear. Rachelle had bags under her eyes, but her face still lit up when she saw me, and she gave me an excited little wave, nearly bouncing up and down as if she was trying not to run over and hug me. I smiled at her, and continued scanning the group. Ajax had survived as well, but he stood unnaturally still, not meeting my gaze. And Tristen? He was gone. He had survived the last trial, I knew it. So why wasn't he here?

Standing next to me was one of the two willowy fire spirit twins—Priscilla. Her other twin, Felicity, was noticeably absent. As one of the guards did the roll call, I saw the remaining fire sprite blink back tears when her sister wasn't called.

"Don't feel too bad for her," Rachelle said as she caught up with me as we left the silo and headed to the dining hall. "Her and her sister used to work with a notorious pirate band that used sea serpents to destroy merchant ships. They were the greediest and most violent of the bunch, setting ships on fire using their powers while they screeched with laughter at the gold they'd stolen," Rachelle shivered. "Fire sprites are the worst."

"And if I were an evil pirate lord in my past life?"

Rachelle threw an arm around me. "Then I'd ask you when you were taking me on your ship, my pirate lady."

"Your morals are questionable, Rachelle," I said as I rolled my eyes.

Rachelle let her arm drop from my shoulders, and she turned to me, suddenly serious. "Thank you for saving me."

"Of course. We're in this to the end. And even then... we'll find a way to keep fighting so the two of us can make it out of here. Together."

Rachelle smiled, but there was something sad in her gaze. "'Til the end, my friend."

There had to be a way for us to emerge together. Otherwise... could I kill Rachelle? I didn't think so. Not with the way Rachelle danced through the food line at the mess hall, picking out some sort of oat-based dish with raisins and topped with nuts as she flashed her smile at the workers before bounding away to our usual table in the corner.

I still wasn't sure what kind of person I had been—or who I was becoming. But I didn't think cold-blooded murderer was on that list —even if we were in a perpetual fight to the death in these trials.

As I set down my plate on the table, I did another scan of the mess hall. Still no sign of Tristen.

"Tristen... he made it out yesterday, didn't he?" I asked.

Rachelle stopped midway through shoveling food in her mouth to appraise me. "Yep. He was out before me. Why?"

"He's not here."

"Probably because he was ordered on lockdown after killing three more guards."

My eyes went wide. Suddenly, I whipped around, looking for Callum—and then exhaled when I caught the Commander at the far end of the hall, discussing something with a few guards.

"Don't worry, your golden-haired warrior is safe from Tristen... at least, he has been so far," Rachelle said. "Shield wielders, y'know? Some powerful magic."

Callum's shield flashed into my mind. "Can someone... use another's magic?" I asked Rachelle.

Rachelle raised an eyebrow. "What do you mean?"

"So nobody can access someone else's magic? That's not a thing?"

Rachelle froze mid-bite, and slowly set down her fork. "Saffron, did something happen in the second trial after I was disappeared from the Mirror Realm?"

I fidgeted under her gaze. "That's what I'm trying to figure out. I was fighting the monster, who ended up being my double—"

"What the fuck? *That* was your double? Saffron, if that creature was your double... that means you have the most power out of all of us in Ashguard."

"I know, which doesn't make sense. But when I fought my double... I used a shield—*Callum's* shield—to fight it off. It impaled on the sword—"

Rachelle held up a hand. "Stop. Stop right there."

My eyes went wide. "Why?"

Rachelle looked around, suddenly nervous. "We can't talk here. Library. Right after breakfast during training time."

As soon as it was time for training, Rachelle snatched my hand and led me down a hallway that passed by the tunnel that sloped up to the outdoor training grounds. We headed down more smooth stone hallways until we reached a wooden door.

Inside lay a huge library, rows and rows of books stacked up to the ceiling with sliding ladders and candles burning softly.

"This was here the whole time?" I breathed, stepping into the cavernous library.

Rachelle sighed. "Yes. For our training, we can either visit the library or the training grounds. The fact that no one else is in here shows you where most of the prisoner's priorities lie." Rachelle moved quickly down a few stacks, and pulled out a few volumes.

She motioned for me to sit, and piled the books in front of me at a large table.

"I take it you haven't heard of the prophecy?"

"Do I *look* like I remember some prophecy?" I asked, picking up another book.

Rachelle flicked my nose. "You look like someone I would *not* like to see splattered across the ground in the next trial." Rachelle dropped another stack of books on the table, and I choked on the cloud of dust in its wake.

"Wow, how kind of you."

Rachelle fell into a seat beside me and cracked open one of the books.

"The prophecy. Here. Read it," Rachelle said, opening to a page in the ancient book. The pages were yellowed and felt smooth like silk, and frayed at the edges as if the book itself had seen the rise and fall of empires.

I read the swirling gold calligraphy on the page Rachelle had open before me:

"While ancient chains on Embermere hold,
A Siphon's heir shall balance the bonds of old.
When twisted shadows dare to falsify,
A true-born's light shall rise to once more defy.
Seven winds shall blow from shore to shore,
Till the kingdoms unite, forevermore."

I shot Rachelle a look. "Is that supposed to mean something?"

Rachelle shrugged. "Are prophecies supposed to mean something, or are they just poetic nonsense? That's the question. But to the King of Luminaria, he'd pay any price to find the Siphon."

"Siphon?"

Rachelle picked up a candle at the edge of the table. "See this flame? It can only burn because it has borrowed the wick, and it feeds off the air. Our magic is the same."

"Right. I figured as much—your magic has a cost," I said.

"Uh-huh. But a very rare type of magic can pull from other magic." Rachelle took another candle that was unlit, bringing it side-by-side with the first candle. Then, she used the first candle to light the second.

I frowned. "So a Siphon can just replicate powers?"

"Yep. It's powerful—and rare. This type of magic is only passed down through a bloodline—hence the line 'Siphon's heir.'"

"So which families have the Siphon power?"

Rachelle shrugged. "No one knows. According to legend, a Siphon's power is only revealed in The Ash Trials, and there hasn't been another Siphon in at least a hundred years."

"What's so special about The Ash Trials that it would affect a power like that?"

Rachelle shrugged. "Who the hell knows? Maybe someone with the Siphon ability needs it to be activated somehow, and the soil here is so charged with magic that it reveals power in a way that nowhere else in Septerra can. That's convenient, of course, because the Kingdom of Luminaria controls this island. And anyone with Siphon magic—that is, magic that pulls from the well of another's power—is claimed by King West. Either as a pawn or a slave."

A truth that felt dark and old slithered down my spine. "Luminaria has slaves?"

Rachelle's eyes darkened. "Not outright. But the Order of the Serafim claim that the prophecy calls for one who wields the power of the Siphon in order to unite the kingdoms. That's their interpretation, anyway. Anyone with these powers are to be turned over to the King—and anyone harboring a Siphon risks death."

My throat went dry, and I pushed aside the books. "How does a Siphon duplicate someone's powers?"

"Through touch," Rachelle said. "Did you touch Callum before the second trial?"

Images flashed through my mind—of Callum and me, his lips claiming mine, my fingers roaming his body—and my face heated in response.

Rachelle leaned back. "Gods, Saffron. You're fighting for your life in deadly trials and you've *already* fallen for a handsome but definitely off-limits Commander of the King's army?"

I swallowed. "Of the King's *army*? Isn't Callum just Commander of the Guard?"

Rachelle gave me a withering look. "No, dear Saffy. The apple of your eye runs the whole damn army of Luminaria."

I froze. "He didn't tell me that."

"Seems like there isn't very much time for *conversation* between the two of you."

"We talk all the time."

Rachelle rolled her eyes, but then turned solemn. "How do you even know he really knew you from your past? He could be lying to you—taking advantage of your lack of memories."

A chill rolled through me. Rachelle was right—I had no way of confirming that Callum was who he said he was. But I didn't want to let my thoughts go there. "I believe him," I said, but now there was a note of doubt in my voice.

"Whether you believe him or not, you should still try and hone your power so you can use it in the trials to protect yourself," Rachelle said as she rolled up the sleeve of tunic, her clothes a dark blue hue that complimented her tanned skin. "Try and absorb my magic."

I recoiled. "No. If I am... what the prophecy says I am, won't confirming it put me in more danger?"

Rachelle's eyes flashed. "Hate to break it to you, but you're already in considerable danger. Might as well have some powers to keep you safe and understand how they work. You just have to keep them hidden at all costs—and kill anyone who doesn't keep your secret."

"Oh, is that all?" I asked.

"I promised you answers, not to make things easier on you," Rachelle replied with a shrug.

I mulled it over. If I did have this strange power—and it hadn't been just a wayward shield sent by another prisoner—then wouldn't it be better for me to know?

Rachelle inclined her head to her bare arm. "Touch me. Unless you think your Commander will get jealous."

I rolled my eyes. "He's not *my* Commander."

Rachelle snorted. "I think he might feel differently."

I placed my hands on Rachelle's warm arm and closed my eyes. I tried to recall the sensation I had felt with Callum. It was a *pulling*, a drawing sensation, something that had been crawling and begging right underneath my skin.

But I felt nothing. I withdrew my hands from Rachelle, and shook my head. "I don't feel it."

Rachelle rolled down her other sleeve. "Who knows, maybe these dampening bands keep you from absorbing anything—but my magic is still there, just lessened. You should still be able to access it because Siphon magic supposedly works different than the rest of ours. Try again."

I placed both of my hands on Rachelle's arms. I closed my eyes.

"Power originates at our heart crystals, Saffron. Think of it flowing from me to you."

I pictured it, the core of Rachelle's power at her heart. Imagined it flowing underneath her skin, transferring to me. I felt those loops at the edge of my mind, trying to hook my attention through them. My mind was grasping at them, pulling a little, but they weren't as accessible as when I had been wrapped up with Callum.

"Saffron... you're glowing."

I opened my eyes in shock and looked down. Sure enough, my skin had a light glow to it. I pulled my hands away, and Rachelle looked at me in awe.

"Try and shift," Rachelle demanded.

"What?"

"Try and shift into something."

"I-I can't," I said. The light on my skin dimmed and then disappeared.

Rachelle frowned. "We'll try again later. Should we go get some training in?"

"Yes. Let's go," I said, and got to my feet.

"Oh and Saffron?" Rachelle said as we headed to leave. "In the next trials... you have to keep this from the King. No one can know besides us. Not even your Commander. You don't want to test his allegiance to you—or his King. He might not choose you."

"I won't tell anyone," I said. Rachelle nodded, satisfied, and I followed her out of the library.

One secret heavier than I had been when we had entered.

16

Rachelle and I trained until dusk started to beckon, the sun dipping behind the horizon and painting our training grounds in its dying rays.

Rachelle drilled me on different movements, tossing me different weapons that she broke off the nearby tree that seemed to produce endless wooden maces, axes, and other methods of killing. After hundreds of drills, my muscles screamed and my body cried out for rest, but Rachelle just took my practice weapon from me and demanded we practice hand-to-hand combat drills again.

Rachelle had saved my life, but it was days like today that I felt like she'd be the death of me.

"So, the next trial," I asked as I threw a punch at the tree we used for sparring, my hands wrapped in bandages, which helped absorbed the blow of my punch as I moved through fighting combinations.

"Harder," Rachelle pushed me, watching my form.

"Yes, it'll be harder."

"No, *you* need to hit harder," Rachelle said with a grin. "But the next trial usually takes place at the Order of the Serafim's temple. It's located up in the mountains past The Foggy Forest. From what I've heard, we go to honor Goddess Orsi, and there's a puzzle to be solved.

But I don't know much more than that—and the Isle of Embermere could change any aspect of the trial at any time."

"What does the Order of the Serafim do exactly?"

"I don't know. They guard an Oracle who lives at their temple here, but it's all rumors."

We were sweaty and exhausted when Rachelle was ready to call it a day. All the rest of the prisoners had already retreated to their cells.

"Done?" Rachelle asked me.

"I think I'm going to stay and finish up some fighting combinations and then stretch," I said, still feeling my muscles screaming. Even though I had been healed from the injuries of the last trial, my body still felt battered.

"Okay. Be careful," Rachelle said, and as she left to find her way back to her cell, I realized that there were no guards left in the training grounds. Just as they had been in previous days, the guards were becoming more and more sparse.

Leaving us up to our own devices.

I suddenly felt the emptiness of the outdoor training ring as I re-wrapped my hands, scanning the grounds before I faced the punching tree again, its soft bark perfect for practicing fighting combinations.

I got in a few hits before I felt eyes on the back of my body, but as I whirled—there was no one. Nothing.

I sucked in a deep breath before turning back to the punching bag.

I'm alone, I reassured myself.

I jumped into a hard combination of kicks and punches. Trying to fight my invisible enemies. Trying not to relive the horrific moments of when my double had tried to kill me and steal my face.

"There she is, daughter of the sun and the moon," a voice hissed from behind me.

I whirled, seeing Otto staggering toward me from the mouth of the cave that led into Ashguard. I gasped as I took in his leathery skin and wiry grey hair. He had aged ten years since I had seen him at the last roll call. Which meant—

Cassandra. She was still draining him.

Otto took another precarious step, then tumbled to the ground of the mossy training grounds.

"Otto!" I ran to his side, and he groaned as his joints popped and cracked as I rolled him onto his back.

His hazy eyes found mine, and then his pupils suddenly dilated. His hands shot out to grab mine with a surprisingly strong grip as he held my gaze with intensity. "All of your paths lead to ruin. All except *one.*"

"What do you mean?" I asked.

"You must make yourself worthy. You won't be able to leave this island with what you want most until you win the final trial."

My blood ran cold. "I don't know if I can win," I said.

But Otto just gripped me harder. "You must. If you don't... none of us stand a chance against the gods when they finally are able to rise."

"Rise? What do you mean?" I asked, but Otto started coughing, his grip falling out of mine before he rolled to his side.

He was coughing up blood.

I whirled, looking for guards. "Help! Please help him!"

But Otto just shook his head as he rolled onto his back once more, his lips glistening with blood. "It is my time to go. The fates are beckoning. But you can still choose life."

"No," I said, clutching his hands in mine. "You don't deserve this—"

"We all get what we deserve in the end," Otto murmured, his breathing growing ragged. "The fates make sure of it."

Then, his head went limp, and his eyes became unfocused as his breathing slowed to a stop.

My tears fell soft and silent like the first drops of rain. I hadn't known him—not really. But I had seen Cassandra's cruelty, had seen her drain the life out of him like she likely did to so many others.

I would pick whichever path that would end in her death—fates be damned.

～

GUARDS CAME to take Otto's body away soon after, Callum with them. As the rest of the guards disappeared in the belly of Ashguard with Otto on a stretcher, I sat on the grass and unwound the fighting bandages from my hands, needing to feel the ground underneath my bare hands as I tried to keep my anger and sadness from boiling over.

"Are you okay?" Callum asked as he sat down beside me, a lantern beside him as the light of the day began to fully dim into evening.

"I'll be more okay when I get revenge on *her*," I muttered.

"What if I said I could get your mind off all that?"

"Then I'd say I'm curious and I want to hear more," I replied, lifting my gaze to meet his.

Callum's eyes danced and he held out his hand. "Come. I want you to see something."

I took his hand, letting him help me to my feet. He started leading me to the edge of the training ring, where the thorny rosebushes were.

"Careful, they'll—" I started. But Callum turned to me, withdrawing something gleaming from his pocket. *An Illumia Crystal.*

"Watch," he said, and held up the crystal to the thorny rosebush. It shrunk away from the crystal, creating a pathway for us to walk through. A free pass for him to wander the island without harm.

"Is this a prison break?" I asked with a raised eyebrow.

"Of sorts," he said with a smile that lit up his entire face.

"Has any prisoner stolen an Illumia Crystal and successfully escaped the trials? Asking for a friend," I said as I followed him through the forest.

Callum sighed. "Don't think you'd be safe and sound back on the mainland by now if I knew how to do that? You'd need at least one fast-moving ship to make it off this island, but Luminaria and its allies maintain a massive naval presence in the Cimmerian Sea. No one gets close to Embermere during the trials without their ships intercepting them. So even if you *did* somehow seize a sea worthy vessel, you'd need to keep it hidden from the King until the day of your escape attempt. Because it would be an *attempt*," he said.

"Sounds like you know a thing or two about the King's forces," I said. "When were you going to tell me that you not only commanded the King's guard—but his entire army?"

Callum looked back at me, his lips twitching into a smile as he held his lantern aloft. "It's not polite to brag."

"It's not polite to keep me in the dark, either," I said, unable to help my irritation.

Callum paused, lowering his lantern. "You're right. It isn't. So how about I illuminate another secret I've been keeping from you these past few days?"

Another secret? I felt my own weight a bit heavier on me, but I just nodded.

Callum led us deeper into the forest, his lantern light bouncing off towering trees that seemed to sway to some invisible rhythm of the night.

"Watch your step," Callum said as we crossed over thick tree roots, pushing through branches until we reached a clearing in the forest.

As we stepped into the small meadow, ahead of us sat the most charming cottage I could have ever imagined. It was cream colored with brown trim and bright flowerboxes overflowing with well-maintained flowers, and a rounded wooden door and two open windows. It was a small cottage—probably just a single room by the looks of it from the outside—and as we approached, smoke piped cheerily from the small chimney, a fire roaring inside that seemed to warm even the chilly clearing itself.

But what pulled me forward was an open window—where fresh baked bread sat waiting on the sill, an aroma of rosemary and other fine herbs swirling in the air.

"What is this?" I whispered, something tickling the back of my mind as the scents of the cottage wafted toward us.

Callum watched me, his expression open and vulnerable in a way I hadn't seen before. "I've been working on it every since you arrived. It's a replica of the bakery you ran with your mother. I thought seeing it might help you remember Riverleaf and our past together."

I looked up at him. In the glow of the light that spilled from the cottage, I could see the ripple of his muscles below his guard uniform, but his hard exterior had softened. He was searching my eyes to see how his act of kindness would be received. But before I could form words, Callum took my hand, leading me to the front door.

"Here, let's go inside," Callum said, a boyish grin lighting up his face as we approached the cottage. He opened the door, pulling me inside.

The cottage was warm and the smell of the crackling fire and freshly baked bread continued to swell over me in waves. Inside, it was simply decorated with just a sitting area, a large wooden table in the kitchen, and some small wooden counters. I shed my boots at the door, not wanting to bring any of the outdoors with me into the cozy space. But as I shucked my boots and socks by the entry and ventured further inside, I saw that there was not just one loaf of bread on the sill, but so many different types of sweet rolls and pastries that had been baked alongside other gorgeous loaves baked with things like olives, sundried tomatoes, and walnuts and cranberries. The counters were overflowing with stunning baked goods that took my breath away.

Callum showed me around the small space as I followed him in awe. "This is the desk where your mother would record order slips while you baked. You were always here, by the window, where you could look out while you rolled out the dough. Your roller was always to your right and your bowl of water to the left. I tried my best to replicate the oven but it was hard to get it quite right. It was made with old brick with materials from the village where your mother grew up. I couldn't find anything like it here, but I did my best to get the coloring right. I hope... I hope it feels familiar to you."

He paused, watching me as I walked around the space, taking it all in. I knew in that moment Callum was entrusting me with a piece of himself that I knew he didn't share with others—perhaps not with anyone. As I took in a place that indeed had a lingering familiarity, I was overwhelmed by his gesture.

"You did this—built this—all for me?" I asked, still in shock.

"Yeah... I mean—" he ran his hand through the gold-brown locks of his hair, "I'd do anything for you."

"This is... incredible," I said. How could I have doubted this man? Even with what Rachelle had said in the library, even with him being the King's right hand man in the war they were waging against Stormgard rebels—he was and had always been *my* Callum.

"I had a little help from a few of my men who were happy to have a break from Ashguard. But the bread? Yes, I baked all of it. I've heard that sense memory can be a powerful thing. Here—" he said, going to cut a piece of the rosemary sourdough loaf from the sill, placing it on a porcelain plate and slathering it with a small pad of butter, "—tell me what you think."

I took the small plate from him, my heart overflowing with the immense kindness of it all. I took a bite of the warm bread—and nearly melted. I closed my eyes, savoring the taste of rosemary, the slight saltiness of flaky sea salt, and the soft interior of the perfectly baked bread.

Callum leaned against the sturdy wooden table at the center of the kitchen, watching me in anticipation.

I finished chewing the bite, setting down the plate.

"So?" he asked, watching me as I finished the piece of bread, washing it down with a clay mug filled water. He waited patiently, his gaze hopeful.

I lifted my eyes to him, stepping closer to him as he encircled my hips with his strong arms. "It tastes like home," I murmured, and then leaned up to kiss him. I pulled away, just slightly—"*you* taste like home."

His rough hands lightly traced up my bare arms, sending shivers reverberating through every inch of my body as he moved his mouth to my ear. "I'll do anything to keep you safe, Saffron. *Anything.*"

His words lit a fire in me, and our lips crashed together once more. I brought my arms around his shoulders and then up further, twining my fingers in his hair. Our kiss became more heated, and I warmed at his touch. My body buzzed with sensation as his fingertips skated underneath the simple white tunic shirt I had worn into the training grounds. His fingers brushed the underside of my breasts as I shivered.

I needed *so much more* than just a kiss this time.

Callum seemed to understand, and he lifted me up like I weighed nothing and pulled me onto the table, and in the process knocked over an open bag of flour onto the ground, which burst into a huge cloud of white powder. I giggled as we were both covered in the white dust, but a glint entered Callum's eyes as he pulled away from me, starting to draw circles in the flour that coated my skin.

"You've made a mess," he said, his tone promising something sinful as his gaze raked over my body.

"What are you going to do about it?" I challenged, sensing the dark, animalistic side beneath his carefully pressed commander's uniform. I wanted him unleashed upon me.

He took a step back, leaning against the nearby counter and crossing his arms. "Undress," he commanded.

My lips twisted into a grin. "Is that an order?"

"It is."

I slipped off the table, standing before him. As I lifted my tunic shirt over my head, I felt his ravenous eyes take in every inch of my exposed skin. I unbuttoned my breeches, letting them fall at my feet with my underthings. I stepped out of my discarded clothes, my bare feet feeling the warmth of the wood floor. I went to the wrap at my breasts, but before I could begin to unwind it, Callum had crossed the small distance between us, like he could no longer keep a part of himself caged.

"Let me," he demanded, and I felt an edge of hunger in his voice as his calloused hands went to the strip of linen. He began unwinding it, his lips finding the juncture where my neck met my shoulder, pressing kisses as his strong fingers stripped me bare.

"You're everything I've ever wanted," he whispered as the last shred of my clothes hit the floor, his eyes roving over every inch of me.

"I want to see you," I pleaded, tugging at the hemline of his shirt. He reached down, pulling it off, his movements surging with purpose as the heat continued to build and coil between us. As the fabric revealed his toned abs, I felt my breath catch. He tossed the remaining scraps of his clothes aside, but couldn't stay parted from me for too long, and there was nothing separating us now. His lips crashed back onto mine, and I felt the hardness of him through his pants as every inch of his body melded with mine.

I felt the vibrating need between both of us, something feral and hungry. A primal need clawing its way to the surface as skin slid against skin, my body begging for what it was due.

Callum's fingers traced the lines of my body, down my breasts, down past my stomach, meeting the apex of my thighs where heat pooled between them.

"Fuck, Saffron, you're already so ready for me, aren't you?" his voice rumbled in my ear, and I felt my hips buck involuntarily as his hand cupped my core.

"Callum," I breathed, feeling drunk off his touch and wanting more.

He didn't keep me waiting, and a needy, mewling sound escaped my lips as he slipped a finger inside of me. I kept my arms wound around his neck as he started to move, my core dripping for him as he worked me.

Callum's thumb swept over that sensitive bundle of flesh and I arched into him. "Glad to see you're as impatient as I am," he said, and I melted into him even more.

He added a second finger, a delicious feeling of being stretched shuddering through me as his electric touch threatened to undo me. I fell back on the table, and he towered over me.

"Just like that," he said, kissing his way down my heaving chest as he pulled moans from my body, playing me like an expert musician with those strong, talented hands.

Once again, I felt that sensation. Of my body drinking from some invisible well. Pulling something into me, as if I were tucking a secret into my soul.

I was so lost in his kiss, his touch—

—I barely heard the door as it splintered to pieces with a *crash*.

The haze of lust cleared in an instant. Callum was off of me and turning to who had just entered the cottage.

Not *who*, I realized—

—but *what*.

The creature unfolded its twisted mass through the cottage's doorway. It was a humanoid mass of roots and wood with glowing eyes and a twisted face with sharp teeth—what I would imagine a demon made from the heart of the forest might look like. Its core pulsed with sickly yellow light as fungal clusters beat in its makeshift ribcage, while dozens of writhing roots scraped against the floorboards.

Callum lunged for his sword, unsheathing it and standing between me and the thing as the twelve-foot horror began its hypnotic swaying dance, root-limbs weaving patterns that made my vision swim. The sweet smell of disturbed earth filled the cabin as the creature's root tendrils began breaking through the floorboards, the sound of splintering wood mixing with an ethereal chiming that seemed to come from the beast itself. I saw the floorboards that were splintering were coming straight toward Callum, and I saw the root slip out and snake for him before he did.

"CALLUM!" I screamed, but it was too late. The thick root snatched Callum's ankle, holding him up and tossing him against the far wall of the cottage where he landed with a dull *thud*.

Callum groaned in pain. I had to *do something*. I looked around for a weapon, but there was nothing.

The thing stalked toward Callum, and it raised one of its root arms—

—which sharpened into a sword made of glittering obsidian rock. Its earthen sword hovered over Callum, his own sword out of reach. His arms were pinned down by its roots, and he was unable to call upon his shield.

He's not going to make it.

Fear shot through me. I was going to watch Callum die—right here in the cottage he had constructed to help me remember who I was. He had fought and broken rules and endangered himself for me.

I couldn't let him die.

The feeling was innate, just as much a part of me as it had been in the second trial.

As if on instinct, I dropped to a single knee, my arms rising above me in a cross.

The power blasted out from me, originating at my heart and racing through the air. The particles shimmered and shot out, a glittering barrier passing over Callum and yanking the creature from where it stood, blowing it straight through the opposite cottage wall.

The dust settled, and the glowing continued to pulse as Callum stared at me, his jaw slack as he stumbled to his feet, unharmed.

I was once again wielding a shield. *Callum's* shield. Protecting him when he couldn't.

He approached me slowly, his eyes wide with disbelief. "Lower your arms, Saffron."

But I was still breathing heavy, in shock as the shield shimmered above me.

"Lower them," he said again, a steady command, but I felt frozen.

Rachelle had told me to keep this a secret. And Callum now had seen it—would he be forced to go to the King? My mind whirred as my secret was on full display, and I was turning over the consequences in my mind.

Callum advanced toward me as the shield continued to glitter above us.

"You can't let anyone else see," he said—no, he *begged*. Only at his frightened words did I yield, Callum's shield—*my* shield—vanishing.

But even as the magic dropped and Callum swept me up in his arms, I saw the flash of fear on his face.

What had I done?

17

W e dressed and hurried back to Ashguard, the creature having fled after being blasted away by my stolen power. Callum was silent the entire trek back, deep in thought.

When we finally returned, he opened my cell wordlessly and we both slipped inside.

A moment passed as we both stood facing each other.

"What was that thing?" I asked, my mouth still dry from the encounter with the creature born of leaves and nightmares.

"It's a Root Dancer," Callum said, still looking shaken. "It likes to force its branches into its victims, replacing their blood vessels with wood. It wears flesh like a costume until the body fully decays."

I shivered. "Your Illumia Crystal..."

"Doesn't work on monsters who are commanded by the gods."

"That monster was sent by a god?"

Callum shook his head. "I don't know for sure. The gods have all sorts of creatures that are meant to protect their sacred burial grounds."

"There's a god buried near here?"

Callum grimaced. "Yes. Six gods are buried on this island, having been contained by our ancestors. But you don't have to worry about them right now—do you know what you just did?"

I blew out a breath. *Here we go.* "I know about the prophecy, Callum. Am I... am I the Siphon?"

Callum lunged for me, his hand covering my mouth as his eyes glittered with fear. "Don't say it. No one can hear you. No one can know."

I wrenched his hand off my mouth. "I need to know what I'm capable of in order to stay alive in the trials, Callum."

Callum winced. "You can't be the Siphon."

"Why? Because you think I'm still a hollow?"

"Because I just got you back!" Callum yelled.

I blinked at his sudden anger.

"I'm sorry. I—I'm so sorry, Saffron." He took in a shuddering breath. "When he... when Tristen took you from me that day, I made a vow to find you. To protect you. And I can't protect you if you're the Siphon. The King will steal you away. Make you his... and I'll have to *watch*." At the thought, his jaw flexed so hard it could have bent metal.

My memory flashed back to the dance I had with the King. His mention of looking for his Warrior Queen. The gilded cage that still lay yawning open before me even if I did win. But I shook my head. I was not defenseless—even less so now.

"You don't have to worry about that. I won't let him. I have a say in this, too."

But Callum shook his head. "The King and Cassandra will kill anyone who tries to keep you from them. I'm not powerful enough to fight them. I'll lose you if they find out. And that can't happen. Because you're mine."

"How am I supposed to be yours, Callum?" I asked, softly. "How am I even supposed to make it out of these trials alive, especially if I can't use this power?"

His eyes looked sad as he gazed at me, as if he was trying to figure out the same thing. "I'll fight until my dying breath to ensure your survival. I swear it."

I pursed my lips. "If I win, I belong to the King, even if he doesn't know about my powers. If I lose, I belong to a grave. Shouldn't I try and learn what I'm capable of?"

Callum grabbed my hands. "No. You can't use your power. You can't train it or tell anyone else what you can do. Doing so will ensure your death sentence. Do you understand me?"

"I have nothing to go back to," I said, the truth of it ringing in my ears. "Only a future to win."

$\sim$

THE NEXT DAY, Rachelle stole me away to the library once more. I filled her in on what had happened the night before.

Rachelle had a thoughtful expression on her face. "You were out with Callum... and you were able to call upon the shield when you two were attacked?"

"Yes."

Rachelle's expression hardened. "He reports to the King, Saffron."

"He's loyal to me," I said. "He's shown me he's willing to risk treason again and again."

Rachelle frowned. "You're sure?"

"Yes. He's gone against the King for me on several occasions already. I trust him."

Rachelle sighed. "Gods, Saffron. What part of 'keep this a secret' did you not understand?"

I shrugged, but Rachelle just rolled her eyes at me. "And you touched him? Before using the shield, even with your bands on?"

My face heated at the memory of his skin on mine, and I tried to shake it off to keep my clarity. "I did."

Rachelle grinned, a flicker of her mischievous side coming back as her anger subsided. "And...?"

I looked away from my friend, my face flushing. "And... he kissed me. Again."

Rachelle's eyes danced. "One of the last times he kissed you—that didn't happen to be right before the second trial, was it?"

I bit my lip. "It was."

"I knew it!" Rachelle crowed, the candles flickering around us in our dim corner of the cavernous library. Rachelle sighed, putting her face on her propped up fist. "How sweet. Is he good in bed?"

"I didn't say we slept together!"

I swatted at my friend, but Rachelle pulled back with a smirk. "It's only a matter of time, dear Saffy. How long were you touching him before you wielded his shield last night?"

"Seconds. Minutes, maybe," I said.

"Time flies, eh?" Rachelle teased.

"Get on with your point," I growled.

Rachelle leaned closer to me, her pale blue eyes sparkling. Rachelle's soft hands went to roll up the sleeves of my tunic. "So I have two experiments we should try. The first—time spent with bare skin on skin."

My hands curled around Rachelle's forearms as our bare skin touched, our cool metal bands the only interruption of skin-to-skin contact.

"And the second?" I asked, suddenly a bit breathless as I caught Rachelle's light lilac scent.

A wicked smile flashed across Rachelle's face. "Play along with my game, Saffron. I'm trying to save your life here."

And with that, Rachelle leaned in and kissed me. The surprise that shot through me melted as my friend gently cupped my face, pulling away slightly to search my eyes, her smile still wide. When I didn't pull away, Rachelle kissed me once more, a smile still on her lips as she dipped her head to kiss my neck, and I yelped as Rachelle bit a sensitive spot on my neck.

"Tell Callum you like that," she said sweetly, leaning in to kiss me once more. I wasn't sure if I had kissed another woman—or someone as lovely as Rachelle—in my past life, but I was surprised at how natural it felt.

But once more, that molten sensation underneath my skin started to move. Started to flow from Rachelle to me, and I finally felt that loop of power and *pulled* it toward me.

Rachelle pulled away, her eyes wide.

"You're glowing again," she said.

I felt like I was in a haze. I looked down at myself, and realized that yes, I was glowing like the orange of the flickering candles around us.

"Shift," Rachelle commanded. "Try it. Shift."

I looked at her, eyes wide, unsure how to will that kind of transformation. "How?"

Rachelle reached out and brushed a hand through my hair. "Reach within. And pull out the form you want to be in. It's like flipping a switch. Or turning a door handle. Reach out. And *pull*."

My eyes fluttered closed. I wanted to be something proud. Dangerous. My blood turned molten as I stumbled back from my chair, rising from the table.

My body fell to the ground, my bones and muscles groaning and stretching...

...until I cried out with a yowl.

I raised my gaze to Rachelle, who stood with a self-satisfied expression. "Look," she said, pointing at an antique floor-length mirror on the wall behind us.

And I prowled—on all fours, I realized—to the mirror. Looking back at me was a majestic—and terrifying—creature.

I was a panther. A thing to be feared in the woods—just what I had wished to be.

But as I gazed at my reflection, turning my dark black head and watching the panther in the reflection do the same, the glow returned. My vision went slanted and the stretching feeling came over me. I tumbled out of the form of the panther, breathing heavily as I gasped in front of the mirror, drawing lungfuls of breath back in my human form as I cradled myself on the floor.

"Saffron..."

I looked up to see a shocked Callum in the doorway.

Rachelle had already risen and walked to my side. "You saw nothing, Commander."

His eyes hardened. "And neither did you, *prisoner*."

Rachelle helped me to my feet, and I struggled to stay upright. "No fighting," I said. "Nobody's going to tell anyone."

Callum opened his mouth, and then closed it, his jaw tight with tension as he glared at Rachelle. But the sounds of footsteps interrupted us.

"We have to go," Callum ground out.

"The third trial?" I asked as my heart skipped a beat. It was too soon. I wasn't ready yet. Not until I could figure out the depths of the power I possessed and how to wield it to my advantage.

"No," Callum said, his expression grim. "The King has summoned all of the *contestants* to his throne room."

A shiver slipped down my spine.

18

I struggled to walk across the forest path from Ashguard to the Saltspire Palace. Shifting back to being a human from the panther form had left me feeling boneless and sweaty. And knowing we were headed to see the King? My nerves were fried.

Callum didn't walk by my side. He strode silently at the front of the line of prisoners, speaking to no one. Was he angry with me? Worried? All I knew for sure was that the rush of that power had been intoxicating—even if it was putting my life at risk to try and wield it.

The only person missing from the line of prisoners was Tristen. I still hadn't seen him since the second trial. Was he injured? Rachelle had said he had killed more guards. Was he truly so bloodthirsty that he continued to fall prey to his violent nature?

Soon, we were cresting the bend of the dirt trail that gave way to the soft salt path that crunched gently underneath our feet as we passed the sentries of the palace and continued through the gates. The afternoon sun was hidden behind billowing clouds. A soft sea breeze tickled my lips as the scent of salts from the palace and the sea met my senses.

We were once again brought through the main hall of swooping staircases and to the looming doors of the throne room. A hush fell over the prisoners as we we were led through those huge doors.

Inside the throne room, beaten and bloody in the center—was Tristen. The Shadowfire Assassin, his clothes torn and gashes ripped open on his body as he stood, surrounded by guards with swords at the ready. But he still held himself with a haughty confidence. His shoulders back and his head held high as he leveled a death glare at the King.

Tristen's gaze whipped around as we were ushered around him in the semicircle. His eyes met mine and I couldn't tear my gaze away. He gave me a wolfish smirk, blood dotting the edge of his lips.

"I see you've brought me an audience," Tristen said, turning back to the King. "How kind."

Underneath the King stood a line of guards, and I noticed now that they were holding three men. The three men all wore leather fighting gear, and bore bloody injuries almost as gruesome as Tristen's.

At their feet—at Tristen's feet—lay Sophos, the King's mindweavyr who had forced me to drink the elixir before the second trial. Sophos was clearly dead by the looks of the blood on him. Had Tristen killed him?

"Contestants," King West bellowed, ignoring Tristen. "The Isle of Embermere seeks to protect its inhabitants. And protect, it does. These three rebel soldiers were caught trying to dock on the island—in what we pieced together was a rescue attempt to recover the Shadowfire Assassin. They came in here and killed my mindweavyr, crippling our abilities to demand answers from them."

Mutters filled the throne room, some of the courtiers and the King's guards sliding sideways gazes toward Tristen and the three men.

But Tristen just cocked his head. "If I didn't want to be here, you wouldn't be able to stop me from leaving," he said, low and deadly.

The King leaned forward with an amused grin on his face. "Big talk for an Assassin who has been rotting away in Ashguard. Not so strong now that you got caught, are you?"

Tristen shrugged. "I have my reasons for being here."

The King's eyes narrowed. He looked up at the contestants. "The arrogance of Stormgard's rebel forces knows no bounds. This is what we're fighting against. Those who don't blink at claiming the lives of our people, who seek to slaughter us and send bloodthirsty killers after us and into all of the kingdoms. Luminaria will not be safe until we have eradicated this rebel threat."

Cheers broke out in the throne room and I felt my heart jump into my throat. What had we been brought here to witness, exactly? I searched for Callum, but his gaze was stony, focused only on the King.

"Even as a King leading a war, I can show mercy," King West said as the throne room hushed. "Tristen, oh *Shadowfire Assassin*, I have a simple offer for you. Tell me why these rebels are here and what they're after, what their plans are. I'll even remove your iron bands so you can break into their minds if you need to dig a little for the truth. In giving over their plans, I'll set you free. You'll receive a full pardon and can live out the rest of your life comfortably in exchange for this information. And you can even walk away from these trials—a sure death sentence for everyone in this room save one."

Freedom. The King was offering Tristen freedom. Would he take it?

But Tristen just looked bored. Calm. As if he was a placid body of water, untouched by the King's words. Smooth and steady.

Tristen brushed his gaze over the rebels in front of him, one of whom he gave a small incline of his head, lowering his eyes as if in... apology?

Was he about to give up his friends?

Tristen rolled his shoulders back and stared down the King. "I decline your offer. I am exactly where I am meant to be."

The throne room roared in chaos, courtiers hurling their shouts at him.

"*Rebel scum!*"

"*Murderer!*"

"*Kill him!*"

I stared at Tristen, and those stunning obsidian eyes slid to mine once more. Drinking me in. He was still his handsome self, but he looked so... exhausted. As if he had been tortured for days on end. I wondered how much of his aloof nature was an act. There was so much blood on him...

The throne doors flew open. I scented the electric zing of magic in the air as I felt the mystical breeze that had blown open the doors. Then, the dark power coming from behind me nearly threw me to my knees. Not just in its power—which rivaled Tristen's—but in the ugly heaviness of it.

Every eye in the throne room turned to her. *Cassandra.* She was vibrating with power, and three of her hooded acolytes followed her, their eyes replaced by glowing orbs. It was as if they had been caught mid-ritual, and Cassandra and her priestesses were being imbued with a power that carried a heaviness to it.

Cassandra walked to the front of the throne room as the crowd parted for her. She stopped in front of Tristen, her lips parting into a smile that looked too soft. Too sweet.

"Oh, Tristen. Why can you never simply behave?"

Tristen's eyes were blazing, and I saw his hand twitch as if it were going for a dagger that was not sheathed on his belt.

"Cassandra," he spat out. "Still bowing to the King's orders, I see."

Cassandra ignored him, turning to the rest of us. "Illumia be with you all," Cassandra said, her voice lilting over the echoing room.

"*Illumia be with you,*" the chamber murmured back.

"Justice, Cassandra," King West said. "That's what we've called you away from your full moon ritual for today. These are three of Stormgard Rebels. We only need one to question."

"Don't you dare," Tristen said, his voice low and deadly. "You touch them and I'll see that you die ten times over before the light claims you."

Cassandra's gaze lit up at Tristen's threats. "Such violence. But the rules are the rules. No one sets foot on this island if they aren't invited. It's not the gods' will."

Several guards crept up behind Tristen, and I realized what was happening. The rebels bowed their heads, just as Tristen was grabbed by the guards. He cried out, shouting for them to stop.

Cassandra lifted her arms and tipped her head back to the sky beyond the vaulted ceiling of the throne room. She started whispering words that I could feel in my bones. Ancient, heavy words. Words that were imbued with threads of magic.

Suddenly, a lightning bolt shot from above, and there were screams and the smell of burning flesh as a *crack* of thunder boomed through the massive throne room.

Tristen's voice was rough and angry, cursing out Cassandra, and the guards held him back as he strained to lunge for her and tear her apart.

Behind her, two of the rebels were nothing more than piles of ash.

"Take the rabid dog back to his cell," King West said, and it took five more guards to haul Tristen away. He turned back to address us. "Let this be a warning to the rest of you—your fate is decided if you defy the rules of these trials."

I clutched the edges of my breeches, my palms sweaty and my heart pounding.

Cassandra turned to address us prisoners. "See you all at the next trial. It will be a delight to host you." She curtseyed and then walked out the way she came, the crowd in the throne room giving her and her acolytes even more berth than before.

My mouth went dry. I turned and spotted Callum, but his eyes were far away. Stony. He was unseeing, as if he were in battle with his interior demons.

This was the King he served? Whose armies he led?

Maybe I was missing something. Maybe my blank slate of a mind had failed to grasp something basic. But everything felt *wrong*. I needed answers. Different ones. I needed to know what the rebels were planning—to know Tristen's secrets.

As the guards started to funnel us back to their cells, I stumbled in front of Callum, and he snapped out of his reverie to grab me.

"T-thank you," I murmured, sliding my hand down his body.

"Keep it steady," Callum said softly, a gaze flicking up to where the King was discussing something low and urgent with his advisors as the third surviving rebel was hauled away to the bowels of the palace.

I just nodded, playing the part of the dumb maiden as I followed the rest of the prisoners out of the throne room.

Callum didn't even notice that his keys were missing.

19

I waited until the evening shift guards had slowed their circles around my cell block before I stuffed my flat pillow underneath my threadbare sheets to create a lumpy look in case the guards raised a lantern to see if I was asleep in my cell. But I doubted that the guards would even look. They probably assumed everyone would behave tonight after the show in the throne room.

As I unlocked my cell door with the keys I had stolen from Callum, I wasn't afraid as much as I was driven by my search for answers. I was guilty—just a little bit—but I needed to know what side I should be on—and the implications that came with Callum serving the King. I needed to understand what the rebels fought for —and whose side Tristen was really on, or if he truly was just a vicious monster.

I darted down stone hallways, heading into the belly of the prison. Most of the prisoners were asleep already, but I kept silent and to the shadows just in case someone looked up to see what was going on in the hall.

I knew I was headed in the right direction when the hallways sloped upward, and I wove my way around back entrances and narrow staircases to creep past quiet cells where the other prisoners snored softly.

After twenty minutes of dodging guards and climbing up the secret passageways that Callum had showed me when we had been sneaking around the prison before, I finally found myself at the top of Ashguard—at the floor that housed the most dangerous prisoners.

Except, there was only one cell that was occupied. As I crept closer, I found Tristen sitting on the floor of his cell, leaning against the back wall.

He had no cot. No blankets. Never mind that it was freezing, he lounged against the back wall as if he wasn't affected even as I saw his face tinged slightly pink with the chill. Yet he lounged as if he wasn't bothered by the scuttling sound of rats and insects that littered the damp cell floor.

As I approached his cell, he raised his head of dark hair, disheveled and unkept. His eyes widened slightly at the sight of me, but he chased the expression away with his signature half-smile. He cocked his head.

"To what do I owe the pleasure of such a beautiful guest stopping by my humble abode?"

I froze, trying to hang onto my courage. "I... I have some questions."

"What makes you think I will answer them?" His injuries still glinted in the moonlight. Just as I'd suspected, the guards hadn't bothered to call a healer.

"A bargain," I said. "I'll clean your wounds in exchange for information on what the rebels want, what you're up to—and anything else that could help me in the next trial."

Tristen's eyes lit up. "Oh, so she's a clever thing. Yet so eager to enter into another bargain with me when I didn't fulfill our last?"

"I want a blood bargain," the words sputtered out from me before I fully knew them. *Blood bargain.* Somehow, I knew what it was. It emerged from the recess of my mind as Tristen rose in his cell.

"A blood bargain? How do you know about that?" His voice was low. Dangerous.

"I remembered," I said, the only explanation I had for it. Indeed, it had risen to my mind, unbidden, my intuition giving me only whispers of my past knowledge.

He studied me. "A blood bargain binds to your life. If you fail to fulfill your end, the bargain demands payment. It comes to collect its debt in the form of your life, taken from you as you die screaming."

I shuddered but kept my expression blank. "Yes. That's what I want."

He cocked his head. "You know that in order for this blood bargain to work, you have to unleash my power so I can call it forth." He lifted his hands, holding up his iron bound hands. "You'll have to take these off me," he challenged, goading me to enter. When I hesitated, he smirked. "Afraid?"

"You wish," I said.

"You don't know what I wish," he said, his voice low and deep like an ocean's current.

I took in this lethal killer in front of me. Even beaten and bloody and locked up, he couldn't be contained. His handsome face belied an inner strength that radiated outward—and I knew in his cold resolve that everyone who hurt him would one day pay.

"Don't make me regret this," I warned. I went through Callum's key ring, trying a few on the cell door until I found the key that opened Tristen's cell. As I stepped inside, I quickly closed it behind me.

"Now these," Tristen said, holding up his iron bands. I noticed a tiny keyhole in the side that faced away from him, easy to miss at first when they had been placed upon us.

I settled in front of him and tried to smother a gasp at how tightly his bands had bit into his flesh. I saw deep red gashes underneath the bands that sliced deep.

"They did this to you. Why?" I breathed.

Tristen just shrugged, but I caught a small wince as he did so. "The King and his men thought I would break. I proved them wrong. Now set me free and then we'll make our little blood bargain."

It made sense. So I cradled his wrists, feeling his warm skin beneath the cold iron. With my other hand, I slipped the rusty key into his iron bands and turned. One after the other, I removed all four bands—he had an extra two at both ankles unlike most of the rest of the prisoners, his power unable to be contained with anything less.

As the last iron band fell to the floor, he sighed in relief, and I felt the rippling of his power wash over me once more as I slid the key ring into the pocket of my pants. It was heady, that feeling of his power. It buzzed within me like a low rumble.

"Why does yours feel like that?" I said as he dipped his head back, filling his lungs as if he had been holding his breath the entire time the iron bands were leashing his power.

"My what?" he said, glancing at me with a half-smile. He flicked a hand, and the dark cell was then illuminated by a floating orb of his blue-green shadowfire, which made his eyes dance in its glow.

"Your magic," I said, entranced by the shadowfire, watching the unnatural cold flames fight with each other as they tossed light around the cell. "It feels like..."

"Like what, Saffron?" he challenged in a teasing tone. His wounds were starting to heal, his skin knitting together in a way that didn't look too pleasant. My eyes widened at that—he had healing powers on top of his shadows and mindweavying? *Who is this man?*

"Your magic is overwhelming," I said, not meeting his gaze. Lost in the thrum of his power, even more strong as I sat next to him on the cold, hard floor of stone.

"It's not my magic that's overwhelming you, *Sael*," he said, smirking.

"You're right—it's the immensity of your male ego."

"Most women compliment me on my... *immensity*."

I narrowed my eyes. "Our bargain. I need answers."

He moved in front of me, so fast I could barely track him. He captured my chin in between his thumb and forefinger, tilting me to look up at him. "You have all the answers you need."

His face was inches away from me, those deep obsidian eyes drinking me in. I felt my pulse quicken, something low in my stomach tighten as his touch on my skin heated something within me. Something that buzzed and hummed, drinking from his skin on mine.

"What do you mean?" I murmured, my gaze dropping to his lips for just a second before I wrenched them back up to his eyes.

His answering smile was feline. "Thinking about something you want but can't have?"

I yanked my face out of his grip, and reached for his left hand, shoving it in his face, his wedding band glimmering in the shadow-fire. "I'm thinking of how your wife feels about you flirting with other women."

But that dig only served to make his smile grow wider. "I think she'd approve."

I went to throw a punch at him, but he was suddenly rising to his feet. He was lightning fast—before I could blink, he had the cell door open and had slipped outside his cell—

—locking me in.

I whirled, feeling for the ring of keys I had just put in my pocket.

"Looking for these?" Tristen held up Callum's dangling keys with a grin.

"You bastard!" I yelled, lunging for the keys from between the bars of his cell, but Tristen just shook his head as he held them out of reach. "I told you not to trust me, didn't I?"

"What about our blood bargain?"

He shrugged. "I'll be back. I just have to visit a friend. Then I'm all yours. Until then... enjoy my home."

"You'll pay for this!" I yelled, but he winked and strolled away as I growled in frustration, stomping around his cell. All I heard was a low male laugh and the sounds of footsteps fading down the stairs of the dungeon as he disappeared from view.

I swore under my breath, planning all the ways I would get my vengeance. If Callum found me here, he would go out of his mind and probably do something stupid.

How could I be so gullible? If I wasn't powerless—

I froze. I *wasn't* powerless. Not completely. Focusing my attention on the lock, I closed my eyes. Emptied my mind. Tried to pull from the tiny ripple of power I had drawn from him when I had touched his skin. It wasn't much, just a lick of an ember I had stolen when I had brushed his wrists to remove the cuffs and then he had touched my skin...

...I raised my hands, calling it forth, begging it to rise, to *burn*...

Nothing.

Had I touched him long enough to pull at his power? I tried again, focusing my energy onto the lock of the cell door, thinking about his shadowfire.

Cold power flared at my palms, and my eyes flickered open. A slow screech sounded as the door opened, the lock frozen and shattered as though it had been blasted open by his shadowfire. Not much—I hadn't touched him for very long—but *enough*.

I darted out of the cell and bounded up the stairs.

The Assassin would pay for crossing *me*.

~

I SLIPPED BEHIND Tristen as he melted through shadows and made his way through stone passageways. If I hadn't walked these winding corridors several times before with Callum, it would have been hard to trail the Assassin. He wasn't just a man, he was the whisper between the wind. He seemed to not just walk, but to float over the stone steps, his footfalls barely registering a sound as if his shadows cushioned the sound of him.

I kept just far enough behind Tristen that I was out of earshot. As guards and their nightly patrol passed by, I slipped into alcoves and pressed myself against the cold stone, holding my breath as they passed. Then, I darted up a secret stone staircase to catch up to Tristen as he slipped through one of the final stairways that led up to a hatch that spilled out into the forest above.

As I climbed the last set of stairs, I saw the closed flat metal doors above me.

Those wouldn't be soundless or easy to push open. I'd have to assume Tristen had already moved on to where he was headed next, not lingering by the doors to hear me.

I hesitated. Should I wait for longer? If I did... I would be at the risk of losing him in the forest. And I needed to know what was so important for him to storm off in the middle of the night and lock me away to go and do.

No, I'd need to do this. *Now.*

So, without another moment's pause, I heaved the heavy door open, and kept it pressed open for long enough to slither out, but it still made a low *clang* as I closed it—

—and suddenly, strong hands were dragging me up, and I felt myself pushed flat against a tree with a knife at my throat.

"Weren't you taught not to sneak up on the things that go bump in the night?"

It was so quick, the gasp hadn't even left my throat as my eyes adjusted to the man in front of me, holding that glittering knife. When I recognized Tristen, I narrowed my eyes.

"I've forgotten everything I've been taught, so no, *Assassin*," I shot back.

"I love how you make my reputation sound like a dirty word," he said, scraping his knife lightly against my neck, and even in the dark I could see his eyes drift to my lips.

"Keep dreaming," I said, knowing exactly where his mind had gone.

"Do you have some revenge fantasy for people who lock you up in cells?" he asked.

I frowned, suddenly remembering who was likely locked up in the dungeon beneath the Saltspire Palace. "You're going to free your rebel friend, aren't you?"

Tristen lowered the knife, but kept his body pressed against me. I was all too aware of all the places his hard body met mine, the way he was searching my face as if trying to read between the lines of every expression I made.

"How did you get out of that cell?" he asked.

"I have my ways."

"What do those ways entail?" he said, eyes narrowing.

"Why should I tell you?"

"Because I'm deciding between letting you come with me or finding another cell to throw you in. Your answer will decide that," Tristen said.

Callum and Rachelle's words rang in my head, and I couldn't let Tristen know about my powers. Especially because it seemed like trustworthiness was not a quality he possessed.

"Lockpicking was evidently something I learned in my past. Maybe at the bakery," I said with a sweet smile.

He stepped back, letting me go as if the answer had satisfied him. The emptiness between us suddenly felt vast, too large.

"My blood bargain," I demanded.

"If you come with me, you'll get some of your answers without having to put your pretty little life on the line."

I glared, but decided this was going to be the best I was going to get out of him. "You lied to me."

He shrugged. "And you think your Commander doesn't?"

"He helps me, unlike you." Tristen turned and started walking, and I followed. "Where are we going?"

Tristen pulled me to the shade of the forest trees. "We stick to the shadows. The palace's dungeons can be entered through the back gardens."

I looked around, watching the trees sway toward us. "The island—"

"If a branch comes to strangle us I'll rip out its roots and burn it in my eternal flame," Tristen said, tossing a lazy glare at the darkness. "Hear that?" The island seemed to quiet in response.

"So we *are* going to save your friend," I said. "Even though you're hurt?"

Tristen's expression glinted as he pulled me through the dark by my arm. "I'm alive. And, thanks to you, with my full power. I won't be hurt for long."

Suddenly, Tristen pulled me down behind a bush. I was about to protest, but his hand clamped down around my mouth. I glared daggers at him, but then I heard them.

Guards.

"*...my bet is on the big mean one surviving. He's got this crazy stare in his eye since he came back from the second trial. Looking like he can fuck some people up.*"

"*Well, I'm putting my silver on the Assassin.*"

"*No way. Everyone in that arena wants his head on a platter. And if he survives? Who's to say that the King won't just send him out on a suicide mission to the frontlines? There's no way that the King would trust him.*"

The voices disappeared down another path, passing the bush.

"Wishing you could bet on my death right about now?" Tristen asked with a smug smile as I watched them go.

I ripped his hand off my mouth. "I don't need to *bet* on it if I just kill you myself."

"I would expect nothing less from you," he said. Was that... *pride* in his voice? "This way," Tristen said, motioning for me to follow as we darted across the exposed path and into another line of trees.

"That's the spirit. We are in a giant death match, after all," Tristen muttered.

"You thought I forgot?" I asked, sarcastic.

"You do seem to have a selective memory."

"Even though I don't have all my memories, I wasn't born yesterday."

"I'd hope not with everything you've been doing with Callum."

"I'm not—"

Tristen turned away. "You can't lie to me. I *smell* him on you."

"Smell...?"

He tossed me a withering look. "Some of us wielders have... advanced senses of smell. And you have the scent of another all over you." His expression turned playful. "Although, if you'd like to regale me about how you and Rachelle ended tangled up together—"

"Prick," I said, stomping away from him, but he caught me, pulling me away from the path we're following.

"This way, princess," he said, nodding to a narrow dirt strip of land that zig-zagged in between some tall bushes.

I huffed, following him deeper into the foliage. "I'm not a princess."

"How would you kno—"

I whirled on him, yanking him back to face me. "No jokes about my lost memories," I said, and his eyes widened at the anger in my tone. "I already hear every day how I'm just some defenseless *hollow* without any power or substantial strength. I don't need to be reminded that I don't even have the basics of my humanity intact, either."

A cloud crossed over the moon, shrouding us in deeper darkness.

"Maybe the past isn't for you to remember," Tristen said, his voice low.

"That isn't for you to decide," I ground out, my teeth clenching. What did he know about me, anyways?

"Maybe your mind is protecting you. Maybe it's better this way."

"Better this way?" I froze. "Do you even know what it's like?"

"I didn't mean—"

"I wake up to nightmares of a giant void swallowing me whole. Being in that dark cell makes me claustrophobic because it's what the inside of my head feels like every day. I have *nothing*. Nothing to give me familiarity or warmth or comfort or strength. I have my words and whispers of skills I once learned—but I don't remember my parents. My friends. What my childhood was like. Or—" my voice cracked. "Who I was standing at the altar with when I was supposed to be married."

Tristen's eyes softened. "I'm sorry."

"For what? Making fun of me or stealing me away from my village? Away from Callum?"

Tristen's expression darkened, but he said nothing. Gave me *nothing*.

"Aren't you going to explain yourself?"

A flash of sadness crept across his eyes, but it was chased away by a coldness. "I don't have answers I can give you."

"You're lucky I want answers more than I want to kill you," I shot back. I turned from him, storming down the path as we crept closer to the palace. What did I expect from the legendary Shadowfire Assassin? The one who slaughtered families and helped to stoke the fire of the rebel-led war?

I didn't know what side I was on yet, but his did not look particularly appealing.

We didn't speak until we finally reached the outer wall of the palace.

"Here," Tristen led me through the gardens. Past the tall hedges and night-blooming roses. The beauty of the palace was nearly unmatched. But even amongst the stunning foliage, I found my eyes falling on Tristen. That infuriating, smug Assassin who was a thorn in my side at every turn—but he was hard to look away from. Maybe it was his rippling power or the way the moonlight poured onto his skin. Or the feline way he crept across the landscape, surefooted and strong. Maybe it was the tendril of shadows that seemed to caress me and keep me hidden beside him.

So many things about him were dangerous, and I had a hard time staying away—despite my better judgment and the warnings of everyone else. Maybe I had lost my common sense with my memories.

"Here," Tristen said, stopping at a grate half-hidden beside flower beds. He removed the metal grate, revealing nothing but endless darkness below. "It's a straight drop down, but I'll go first and then I'll catch you. You just have to pull it closed before you let go. Okay?"

"You can't be serious."

"Or, you can wait here," Tristen said with a shrug.

I considered it, but heard the far-off sounds of guards walking this way.

"Fine. I'll follow," I told him, my heart pounding. I needed answers—but I also absolutely *could not* let Callum or his guards see me sneaking around in the dark with Tristen. I looked around, scanning the darkness for the guards as their voices grew closer.

Tristen made the connection. "Am I your little secret?"

"Shut up and go!" I said, punching his arm.

"If you insist." Tristen lowered himself with a lithe grace, hanging from the side of the open hole in the ground, and then let himself fall down. I peered down into the darkness, but couldn't see him—I only heard a soft echo of his feet hitting the ground far, far below.

"Drop down, Saffron. I've got you," he called up at me.

Footsteps sounded on the far side of the garden—more guards.

I grabbed the grate, and my body fell through the hole, dangling into the dark abyss as I clutched onto the slats on the metal grate, yanking them back into place above me.

"Let go," I heard Tristen's voice command me.

And so I did, falling in darkness, tumbling until I landed in his strong arms, wrapped with muscle.

I felt his hot breath tickle my ear. "I told you I'd catch you, didn't I?"

"That's at least one promise you've kept to me so far," I mumbled and twisted out of his arms. Trying not to let myself feel the comfort of his strength too much.

My eyes adjusted to the dark. "Where are we?"

Tristen snapped his fingers and a small ball of his shadowfire floated before us, its flickering light illuminating a dark hallway filled with barrels and bottles.

"Wine cellar. Can't let the poor King and his court go without their celebratory booze. This way," Tristen continued down another hallway, and we descended deeper.

The air grew colder as we climbed staircases deeper underneath the Saltspire Palace. "Why aren't there guards here?"

Tristen shrugged. "The King gets cocky. Thinks there's nowhere for us to run if we escape."

"Is there?" I asked. "A way to escape?"

Tristen quirked a dark brow at my line of questioning. "Let me guess—your commander told you that any escape attempt would be futile?"

I wanted to interrogate him more on that, but we arrived at a small block of cells, and the furthest one was occupied. At the sounds of our arrival, a lanky man with long silver hair jumped to his feet. He had dark eyes like a raven, and birdlike grace. He looked the same age as Tristen, but had a killing grace and bandaged fingertips that made me take him for an archer, not a warrior.

"Aldric!" Tristen said, striding to the prisoner's cell. "Good to see you still in one piece."

"Tristen! How—?"

Tristen already had the ring of keys out. "You have to get the hell off this island and tell the others to stay away for now. I have everything under control."

Aldric's eyes slid to me. "Saffron..." he murmured.

I went still as I took in the rebel soldier. "How do you know my name?"

Aldric looked confused, but Tristen merely shot a glance at me over his shoulder as he finished unlocking the cell door, swinging it open. "It's hard to forget a pretty face."

I glared at Tristen, but Aldric was already throwing his arms around Tristen. "I'm glad that witch didn't touch you." Aldric pulled away and looked at me. "And you—thank you for risking your life to help him. Gods know that Tristen can be such an ass that it's easier to let him stew in his own problem soup rather than help him, so thank you for putting up with him long enough to spring me out. I owe you one."

My cheeks heated at the praise. "You deserve better than Cassandra and King West's wrath," I said, remembering the way Cassandra had drained Otto of his youth, how she had killed those other two rebels without warning in the throne room.

Aldric shifted his gaze to Tristen. "When are you coming back?"

"Are things that bad?" Tristen asked.

The rebel winced. "Worse. The King... it's a bloodbath. We need..." The rebel looked at me again, struggling to get out his words. "We need things to get back to the way they were as soon as possible if we have a shot at holding them off. That's why we came—"

"I told you *not* to come," Tristen seethed. "This is my battle to fight. We have contingencies in place if things don't turn out the way I planned—"

"Those contingencies will lose the war for us. You know what needs to be done for us to right Stormgard."

"Wait for my signal," Tristen said. "Only after then we will be in the position to fix this. Tell the others. *Wait for my signal.*"

Aldric hesitated, but then bowed his head. "Understood," he said. He raised his head, looking around. "The best route to the beach?"

"Same as we discussed," Tristen said.

"Good luck," Aldric said, "to both of you." Then, he turned on his heel and disappeared down a tunnel that seemed to dive even deeper into the dungeon.

"Wait!" I called after the rebel, but he was already gone. I turned back to Tristen, advancing toward him. "How did he know my name, Tristen? *How?*"

Tristen looked hurt. "I'm sorry, I can't—"

"Get away from her."

I turned and saw Callum and a whole host of guards flanking him.

Tristen subtly moved his body in front of mine, and placed his hands in his pockets. So casual, even as shadows curled at the edges of his body, tinging in him a warring mix of darkness and a faint glow of the ember of his powers.

"Ah, finally doing your job, I see," Tristen said. "Or did you only notice I was gone because you couldn't find her? Can't go a day without trying to put your hands on her, right? I understand the urge."

Some of the other guards snickered, and Callum shot them a look, the laughter dying on their lips.

"Get him," Callum commanded. The guards stepped out, but Tristen shook his head.

"Stay right there," he said, his voice echoing with that other-worldly power that I knew was a compulsion. The guards shouted, but remained stuck to where they stood.

Callum, to his credit, didn't flinch. "Come here, Saffron," Callum said to me, knowing that I was still free to move. I started toward Callum, but a bolt of shadows shot out, and Tristen once again shifted so he was between Callum and I, keeping me behind him.

Tristen clucked his tongue. "Not so fast, Commander. I have some questions for you." And with that, Tristen fixed his gaze on Callum, who let out a shout and fell to his knees.

Callum was scratching at his head—Tristen was using his mindweavying abilities on him. I felt sick, remembering how it had felt for King West's mindweavyr to compel me.

"Stop!" I cried, throwing myself against Tristen's back, pounding him with my fists—but he stood steady, his eyes glassy as he flipped through Callum's memories.

But I saw Tristen's powers waver, as if he couldn't hold both Callum's mind and the guards in thrall at the same time. His power over the guards disappeared, and they yelled as they charged forward.

They were upon him almost instantly, but they were thrown back by Tristen's shield of shadows. His other hand summoned a bright flare of shadowfire, keeping them at bay. His power... it was immense. I felt the waves of it all over my body, my mind. It was heady. Strong —but flickering under the weight of having to exert so much over so many people at once.

Suddenly, Tristen unhooked from Callum's mind—

—and his gaze dropped to me, eyes wide in alarm.

"What?" I whispered, my throat dry as Tristen turned back to Callum—

"YOU BASTARD!" Tristen shouted, and every single shadow in the room lunged at Callum, going to tear him limb from limb—

—but then Callum's shield *blasted* Tristen back, and Tristen was thrown against the cell bars like a ragdoll. Tristen landed on the ground, coughing out blood as he pinned Callum with his gaze, hatred roiling there in his obsidian eyes.

Callum grabbed my arm, yanking me behind him.

"You are going to pay for what you've done," Callum said to Tristen, his voice cold as ice as he stared the Shadowfire Assassin down.

Tristen pulled himself up, staggering a step toward us. Pure fury burned in his gaze, his eyes fixed on Callum.

"You," Tristen breathed. *"You're a fucking traitor."*

I felt my skin grow cold as bloodlust shone in Tristen's gaze.

"You dare fill her head so full of lies?" Tristen roared, and even Callum's guards took a few steps back. "You dare to touch her? To pretend to protect her after *what you've done to her?*"

I took in Tristen, the wild fury in his eyes. I had never seen him unruffled, not when he was in the coliseum fighting demons, not when he was fighting his own double. "What did you see?" I demanded. I needed to know. Needed to see what he saw.

Tristen opened his mouth, but then he was suddenly choking. He struggled against some unseen force, turning away from us as he gagged on his own blood, leaning against the cell door.

"Cuff him," Callum commanded, and the guards shook out of their stupor and surrounded Tristen, the iron bands in their hands binding to his wrists and ankles as they swarmed him. Whatever force had Tristen coughing up blood had disoriented him long enough to be imprisoned once more, his powers dampened with a heady *whoosh* like all of the air in the dungeon had disappeared at once.

"What did you see, Tristen?" I begged again as the guards started to drag Tristen to the far corridor.

"He saw nothing, Saffron," Callum said. "He's a monster who wants nothing but destruction."

Tristen fixed his gaze on me. Something glinted there—something devilish. Tristen slackened in the guards hold, starting to fall to the floor as they cried out in surprise.

But as their hold loosened, Tristen twisted out of their grip. He went to the closest guard's sword, unsheathing it. With a whisper of steel, he slashed with the sword—

—turning and *lunging at me with the blade.*

I screamed, twisting away from his oncoming strike. But before the steel could slice through my flesh, Callum tossed up his shield, falling to his knees beside me as he held up his shield. His arms crossed above him as he channeled the magic through his heart crystal, keeping me safe from Tristen's blade.

Tristen had just tried to attack me. Why?

But then Tristen's deadly gaze lowered to where Callum kneeled in front of me, holding the shield. "You're shielding a prisoner, Callum. A prisoner I'm trying to kill."

"Stay away from her," Callum breathed.

"You are not her guard. You are the King's guard. And you are interfering with the trials," Tristen said, pressing his sword against it. "Not to mention..." Tristen reached into his pocket with his other hand and held up Callum's key ring. "I have your keys. It's treasonous to give a prisoner your keys, isn't it?"

The other guards gasped.

Callum held his shield strong. "I didn't give you my keys."

"No, but you gave them to her, and she gave them to me."

Callum swiveled his head to me, and I saw devastation flash through his eyes. "Saffron..."

"I needed answers," I begged, but I saw in Callum's expression that the damage had been done.

Tristen pressed his sword against Callum's shield once more, which still encircled me in a blue glowing bubble. "Drop this shield. Or else the Isle of Embermere will enforce its rules. You will choose to submit to its punishment if you keep shielding her."

"*I will not let you touch her!*" Callum yelled, his shield pulsing.

I saw what was happening—saw how Tristen was goading Callum.

"Let down your shield, Callum! Tristen won't hurt me," I said, but Callum wasn't listening to me. Wasn't hearing me.

"You're a coward. A stupid coward at that," Tristen said, bouncing his sword off Callum's shield once more. "You're interfering with The Ash Trials!" Tristen roared as he slashed at it again.

"DROP YOUR SHIELD, CALLUM!" I screamed, but he didn't listen.

Callum was making his choice.

A *rumbling* started to grow beneath our feet. I struggled to stay standing as Callum kept his shield up, his arms crossed above him. The Isle of Embermere started to answer in kind, magic threading through the air.

Callum cried out as his shield splintered, shattering into thousands of threads of magic. Then, the island's own magic—smoke-like tendrils tinged a deep green—flew right to him on a roaring wind that now filled the prison cell. I was thrown back by the intensity of it, my clothes and hair whipping around me.

"Callum!" I yelled, but my voice was muffled by the roaring sound.

Callum screamed in pain as he held out his left arm. The colors began binding to it, everyone else in the room clinging onto any surface we could as the earthquake began to subside.

As it did, I dared to lift my head. Callum raised his left arm...

...to reveal the mark of The Ash Trials inked on his trembling flesh.

20

Callum was taken away. So were Tristen and I. Tristen was still shaking with rage over whatever he had seen in Callum's mind. I felt like I wanted to scream and shake everyone's secrets loose, but I was in the dark. I was sick of it.

As I was thrown back into my cell, the guards were stonefaced as I shouted after them to bring me to Tristen, to bring me to answers, to tell me what would become of Callum—but my cries went unanswered by the dark.

I paced the length of my cell, my body sizzling with anger.

What had Tristen seen in Callum's mind?

What had become of Callum?

And why, godsdammit, could no one fill me in on the details of my past?

I must have been pacing the better part of the night, because by the time the guards had shown up at my cell and thrust a bundle of clothes and boots at me, I knew it was time.

The third trial.

Luckily, the guards had disappeared for enough time for me to change into what they had handed me. The tunic was simple, cut at my waist and flowing softly around my body. The pants were tight-fitting and lined with leather. The clothes were paired with the black riding boots I slipped into, and I hoped that my past included being able to ride a horse without falling off. That would be an embarrassing way to die in a trial.

The clothes came with a pouch that I attached to my waist with a belt. It was empty, save one gold coin. What the coin was for, I wasn't sure, but I kept it in the pouch just in case. A cloak had been delivered as well, black and lined with fur. Looks like our journey would be cold.

As I was led into the silo floor by the guards for roll call, Cassandra was already waiting for us.

As we arrived in the semicircle, another guard calling our names one by one, I saw the last prisoner get hauled out to join us.

Callum.

Two guards held onto him, fury sparkling in his eyes as he now wore iron bands on his wrists and ankles—marking him, like Tristen, as one of the more powerful magic wielders.

Tristen, standing closest to where Callum was to join the semicircle, raised an eyebrow. "Looks like someone didn't get his beauty sleep."

Callum shook off the guards holding him with impressive strength, took two strides toward Tristen, and decked him in the face.

Tristen staggered backward, and a hush settled over the prisoners as I held my breath.

Tristen recovered quickly, straightening up to reveal a red mark on his jaw. He leaned away from the line of prisoners, spitting out some blood on the floor. Then, he turned back to Callum with a dark glare.

"I'd like to see you actually try and kill me in the trials, *Commander*," Tristen taunted. "Or did you lose your precious title for involving yourself in matters that didn't concern you?"

"Why wait for the trials? Let's settle this right now," Callum said, his expression promising death.

"My pleasure," Tristen said.

"Boys," Cassandra's voice lilted over us. "You really want to keep the rest of us waiting?"

Callum stiffened, but backed down from Tristen. "Soon," he promised.

Tristen just shrugged. "I'll be waiting."

Cassandra watched as Callum got in line, a smirk twisting at her lips as if she reveled in seeing Callum's demotion. "As you all know, Commander Callum Wells has joined your ranks for the remainder of the trials."

Murmurs swept down the line of prisoners, a few deep chuckles and cheers confirming that more than one prisoner would like the opportunity to put the Commander in the ground. My blood ran cold at the target that was growing on his back.

Cassandra continued, the prisoners going quiet once more. "Today, you will begin a pilgrimage to the Temple of Orsi—the temple I reside in when I'm not ensuring order here in Ashguard. It will take you two moons to arrive, and myself and my priestesses who serve the Order of the Serafim will greet you at the temple to take you to the Oracle. The trial is straightforward. If you survive the journey, follow the rules and arrive when called to answer the Oracle's question—you'll get to ask a question of your own. Then, you'll be permitted to return here and await the next trial."

"That's all?" Rachelle challenged, her eyes narrowed. The rest of us held our breaths at Rachelle's outburst.

But a sly smile crept across Cassandra's full mouth. "The only road to the Temple of Orsi is through The Foggy Forest, of course."

A hushed silence fell over the prisoners once more.

"Each of you have received a map in your saddlebags along with basic supplies and a gold piece as an offering for our goddess. Horses have been prepared for your journey. No guards will be accompanying you, as the third trial is already underway. May Illumia be with you," Cassandra said and turned away.

"*May Illumia be with you,*" murmurs repeated back to her, but it was clear whatever was in The Foggy Forest had everyone rattled.

As Cassandra disappeared down a hallway at the far end of the silo, she snapped her fingers and at once all of our magic-dampening bands dropped—unleashing our powers yet again as the third trial officially began. The guards followed her, leaving us alone on the platform as it started to rise to the surface.

Callum turned to Tristen, his eyes flaring with an urge to fight, but in a few strides, I slipped myself between the two men, facing Callum.

"*Stop!* Stop this," I said, pushing Callum back. Surprised, he yielded a few steps.

His eyes flickered down to me. "He's done this—"

"What did he see in your mind, Callum?" I said. But it wasn't a question. It was a *demand*.

Callum's eyes flickered back up to Tristen. "He's trying to drive a wedge between us. Don't you see that?"

"What did he see?" I seethed.

"Why are you questioning me, Saffron? After all I've done for you? All I've sacrificed? I chose to enter these trials. Chose to lay down my life for you. I did this all for you," Callum said, his voice softening. "Don't you see that? I'm here to protect you."

"Don't you realize what you've just done?" I said, my heart breaking even as Callum's calloused hands gently cupped my face. "*You're in The Ash Trials.* Only one of us can survive. Which means you destroyed the one shot we had at a future together."

"Tristen would have killed you if I hadn't made my choice."

My breath hitched, and I fought back tears. "He wouldn't have. I told you to let down your shield last night, but you didn't listen. You betrayed me. You betrayed *us*."

"Then it will be an honor to die by your side," Callum said, solemn.

His words *gutted* me. I stared at him, the certainty in his face. I felt my heart twist further, but my anger still burned. "I don't want you to die. I want you to tell me the truth."

Callum stared at me, searching my expression. "I need you to trust me."

Again, that phrase. But I didn't want to offer up blind trust. I was already in the dark, already lacking any bearing of who I was. I wanted answers.

As the platform reached the surface of the island, the prisoners around us jumped into action. Beyond the platform's edge, a group of horses awaited us with full saddlebags of what I assumed were supplies for the trip ahead. The rest of the prisoners scattered, racing to claim a mare—and get as much distance from their bloodthirsty fellow contestants as possible on the road to the temple.

Callum grabbed my arm. "Saffron. Do you trust me?" he asked again.

"You shouldn't be here," I said.

"What do you want me to say? Because I'll say it," Callum said, holding me in place on the platform as the rest of the group started mounting their horses. "I'm here for *you*."

But how could that be true when his anger had gotten the best of him last night? Tristen had goaded him and he had taken the bait.

Before I could reply, Tristen strolled back over to us, holding the reins of two mares. One was white as snow, the other as dark as night.

"Looks like it's the three of us left, and only two horses. Want to ride with me, Saffron?" Tristen's smooth voice asked, holding out the reins of a stallion with a shiny black coat. I hadn't even heard Tristen step away to get the horses.

Tristen held his hand out for me. His posture was cool, unruffled. As if Callum's boiling rage and my simmering frustration hadn't affected him.

"If you can't tell me what Tristen saw in your mind, then I need some space," I told Callum.

Callum just shook his head.

So I took Tristen's hand.

"Don't," Callum seethed, but I was already walking with Tristen over to his horse.

"Come find me when you're ready to explain some things," I said, and I felt Callum's eyes bore holes into every place where Tristen's hands were on me as Tristen reached around my waist and effortlessly hoisted me atop the black horse.

"See you later, *Commander*," Tristen said, winking at Callum, and slung himself behind me on the horse.

As we rode away, I caught Callum clenching and unclenching his fists, murder in his eyes.

∾

I MADE one grave miscalculation when I agreed to ride with Tristen to spite Callum. Tristen's body was *so close* to mine. As the dark mare trotted in between the towering trees down the twisting forest path, I was aware of every inch of his strong body that pressed into me as his arms cradled the reins in front of me, his arms lightly draped over my thighs. I tried to remain upright, keeping my back straight to maintain a respectable distance from this confusing, arrogant, and despicably handsome man—but, as my muscles ached, I slowly found myself leaning back into him, trying not to note his distinct pine and spice scent and how good his arms felt around me.

"Enjoying the ride?" Tristen said, and I could feel the rumble of his voice through his chest as his lips were just so close to my ear.

But his wedding band gleamed gold on his left hand. "So what does your wife think of you being here, flirting with me like this?"

Tristen chuckled. "Her jealousy rivals the bloodlust of the realm's most vicious armies."

"What is she like?"

Tristen was quiet, and I pivoted slightly on the horse to see his expression. He was deep in thought, a faraway look in his eyes. Then, he looked down at me and smiled—not a smirk, but instead a beaming smile that took my breath away.

"She is my reason for being," he said quietly. "There have been several moments in my life when I nearly lost every part of myself. But then I met her. She became as vital to me as the air I breathe. She isn't my world. She's my *universe*. Stars bow to her courage, and she has made innumerable sacrifices for those she cares about. Her kindness is a sea that sweeps away the wreckage that others bring to our shores. I would be nothing without her."

The words washed over me, and it was my turn to be silent. The way he spoke of her—it was clear he worshipped her. A piece of me felt... bitter about it.

Was I jealous?

Oh, come on—I couldn't be. Tristen had proven to me that he couldn't be trusted, and he was already deeply in love with this mysterious woman who was waiting for him on the other side of the trials.

That is, if he was the one who won.

If *I* won, then she would become a widow. That is, if I could even kill Tristen—it seemed unlikely, though not impossible.

I wouldn't think about it—*couldn't* think about outliving Tristen and Callum and Rachelle. Without them, I would be alone again in the darkness of the world, with just the void to keep me company.

One step at a time.

"You're quiet," Tristen mused. "I'd expect you'd be more at my throat today."

"I'm just glad you and Callum are too far away to try and kill each other," I said.

"It was his fault he chose to enter the trials. He signed his own death warrant."

"There can truly be only one winner?"

"That's what the Isle of Embermere has fated in all of the past Ash Trials, yes." Tristen's voice was soft.

I felt a pang in my heart. "I don't accept it."

"Oh?"

"There must be a way to change things," I said, a boldness simmering within me. After days of straight fear and emptiness, this feeling was... new.

"There she is," Tristen said.

It was my turn to twist and give Tristen a questioning glance. "Oh?" I asked, echoing him.

Tristen smiled at me, but shifted his gaze to the forest in front of us. The sunny day had given way to clouds, and even as morning bled into afternoon, it looked like it could be a cold fall night headed our way.

"I lied. About you being The Lord Killer," he offered.

"I figured as much," I grumbled.

"You're actually much worse than that death dealer," he said, but there was an edge of teasing in his voice.

I reached behind me for the hilt at his belt and whirled to him, placing the dagger at his throat. "Say that again, I dare you."

He chuckled, his eyes heating. "Careful, princess. You'll give me the wrong idea if you keep reaching for what's near my belt."

I glared at him. I turned forward once more, but still held his dagger, sliding it back into its sheath. "I'm keeping this as payment."

"Might be helpful to have in this next trial," he said.

"What do you know?" As we rode deeper into the woods, I felt as if the air had stilled, and I waited for his response.

"The Order of the Serafim. Has the King's... *pet* told you about them yet?"

I rolled my eyes. "*Callum* is not the King's pet."

"Of course he wouldn't want you to think that."

"If you two want to whip 'em out and measure, I'm sure there's a ruler in one of these saddlebags," I said haughtily.

Tristen reached down and tilted my chin to bring my gaze up to meet his.

"Do I look like a man concerned about something like that?" His voice was sinful and hot. "I assure you, women have never had a problem with me in that area before."

I shivered, but not from the cold. Tristen noticed from the low chuckle I felt rumbling in his chest and I glared at the forest ahead.

"Tell me about the Order," I snapped.

"Well, since you asked nicely," he said with humor in his voice. "Everything known about the Order of the Serafim is just a rumor, as they're shrouded in mystery. The priestesses live here on the island all year—and they are the only ones who are undisturbed by the island and its power. Their Oracle isn't human, though, so don't take the riddle lightly. The cost of answering it wrong will likely be your life—or worse."

"What can be worse than death?"

"Just answer the riddle correctly and you won't find out."

"Great," I said, trying to keep my tone light, but my stomach twisted. The afternoon began to grow darker as the clouds passed over the sun. I found myself leaning a bit further back into Tristen, craving his warmth. A shred of comfort. "Aren't you tired of all this death?"

"More than you could ever understand," he said. I fell silent as we rode deeper into the woods.

21

We were forced to set up camp when the sky grew dark overhead. All of us prisoners picked the same open valley, but everyone set up their tents in a mirror of the mess hall—all the cliques bunched their tents together, creating a clear delineation of who was aligned with who. As we rode in, I took note of the different alliances as we slowed to a stop by an empty area of camp.

When Tristen helped me down off our horse, I saw Callum standing by an outcropping of trees, waiting.

"Don't pick a fight with him," I said to Tristen over my shoulder as I strode to Callum.

"Me? I would never," Tristen said, but I could hear the smirk in his voice as I headed to greet Callum.

As I reached him, Callum stepped forward and swept me up in his arms.

"I'm sorry," he said.

"Just... no more entering deadly trials on my behalf, okay?" I pulled away, frowning.

"Trust me, knowing you were riding with him was crueler than any trial could be."

"I'm not trying to hurt you."

"I know," Callum said, and we started walking deeper into the camp together, the flickering of campfires beckoning us closer with the smell of burning wood.

A snarl ripped through the dark forest just as Rachelle leaped from her gorgeous lioness form into her human one. She still had blood on her lips, and she grinned at Callum and I as she shifted.

"It feels so good to hunt in the wild," she said, wiping the blood from her face with the back of her forearm. "And a good reminder that any of these contestants could become dinner if they cross me." She waggled an eyebrow at Callum.

"He's not a meal," I teased.

Callum looked warily at Rachelle. "Hello, shifter."

Rachelle looked him up and down. "The King's Royal Commander-turned-contestant. How'd *his majesty* take it?"

Callum's face darkened. "The island's rule supersedes the King's rule, as the island's will is that of the gods."

Rachelle flipped curls of her red hair over her shoulder. "Well, I've heard the rules state that dashing gentlemen should be the ones to set up a lady's tent. Will you do the honor and set up the one Saffron and I will be sharing tonight? I left the saddlebags with the tent over there," Rachelle pointed to the edge of camp.

Callum sketched a bow. "Of course." He gave my hand a squeeze before walking away, eyeing some of the other prisoners watching us as Rachelle and I settled on a log by one of the fires.

"So, we're sharing a tent?" I asked—secretly grateful she had claimed me. There was so much... baggage between Callum and I—especially now that I knew he was keeping his own secrets from me.

Rachelle waggled her eyebrows. "Unless you and the Commander had plans tonight. But I did see you ride in with tall, dark, and unstable over there, so...?"

"I'd be delighted to share a tent with you," I said. But then something prickly crawled up the back of my mind. "But I... I was also thinking about tomorrow."

"Oh? Going to stay up late practicing riddles?" Rachelle teased. "I've heard this trial is notoriously difficult. The Oracle doesn't go easy on us. She wants us to be worthy for what's ahead."

"There is something I could do. To ensure I could get the answer. Or, rather, *read* it. And then maybe find a way to share it with you and some of the others."

Rachelle's gaze snapped to mine. "Read... you don't mean?"

I bit my lip. "Having the powers of a mindweavyr would prove rather useful tomorrow. And I can't trust that Tristen would use them to help us, so..."

Rachelle's mouth dropped. "You want to copy his powers."

"I don't want to. Gods, I just want us to survive this trial," I said.

"You'd have to get close enough to him for a long enough period of time to have his powers still be useful by tomorrow's trial. Which means... that's a lot of skin-to-skin contact."

I winced. "I—I just can't see you get hurt. Any of you. Now that Callum's in the ring, too, I just..."

"You know we're all going to die, right? Only one of us is walking out of here," Rachelle said softly.

I met my friend's gaze, seeing the pain there that was reflected in my own. "I'm not ready to lose you. Everyone I know and care for in the world is in these trials. If you die... a piece of me will die with you. I'm not—I'm not ready—" I sucked in a breath and fought my tears off.

Rachelle just quirked out her pinky, holding it out to me. "Friends to the end?" she asked.

Understanding, I twined my pinky with hers, and we shook. "Friends to the end," I echoed.

The embers and crackling flame of the campfire lit up Rachelle's red hair and freckles, giving her an ethereal glow as she let my pinky go.

"Callum won't like you spending time with him. It might break him."

I thought back to our interrupted evening in the cottage. How

Callum had constructed a piece of my past—just to try and help me. "And Tristen is married, if you weren't aware. So I don't know if I can even get close enough to... absorb enough of his power. But I have to at least try—for Callum's sake, just as much as yours and mine. None of us will fail this next trial—I can't let us. I'll fight with every scrap of power I have. Or can... *borrow*."

"Callum should still think you're sharing a tent with me. However you decide to get close to Tristen tonight to try and borrow his power, Callum shouldn't know. And... be careful. Some of the others have their hearts set on taking out the biggest threat before the next trial begins. You don't want to be in that crossfire."

I nodded, and Rachelle reached into her pack and pulled out some small tins of dried meats, cheeses, and apricots. I huddled close as Rachelle and I ate our small meal, talking and scoping out our competition huddled all around us. It was almost normal. Almost.

～

CALLUM CAME over as the others had finished their meals and were starting to turn in for bed.

"Your tent is all set up," he said with a bow. "There's a stream nearby if either of you would like me to escort you there for a dip."

"I'm good, thanks," Rachelle said. "Saffron will have to enjoy my scent au naturale as we tangle in the sheets tonight. Right, Saffy?" Rachelle said, jokingly running a hand down my arm as if she were my lover.

I laughed, pushing Rachelle's arm away. "Well, I'm going to bathe," I stood, hooking an arm around Callum's. "Show me the way."

He beamed down at me, and I swore the boyish excitement on his face lit up by the lantern he held underneath the vast night sky.

"This way, milady," he said with mock formality, leading me deeper into the forest as we walked arm in arm.

As we walked, a branch cracked and I froze. Callum paused with me, scanning the forest, but then he tugged me onward.

"It's not the sounds you have to fear in the forest," Callum said. "You should fear when all of the creatures in the forest fall quiet."

It wasn't quiet I heard next—instead, a *zip* of metal flying through air whispered past my ears.

I turned just in time to see a wobbling dagger embedded in a tree at my back.

Callum had his sword out and was pushing me behind him just as one of Ajax's cronies stepped out from the dark. The man had a tattooed snake that climbed its way up out of his shirt, up his neck, and across his face—the black ink rippling with the curl of his menacing smirk. I remembered his name from roll call—Viktor Lynch. He crept toward us, as if he was ready to turn into that creature tattooed on his face at any second.

"You missed," Callum said.

Viktor's grin just widened. "Did I?"

Suddenly, I heard a burning and creaking noise. I whirled just in time to see the dagger—which I realized had been coated in some sort of acid—had put a hole in the tree and it was now falling toward us—toward *me*.

"*Saffron!*" Callum pushed me out of the path of the falling tree, and he barely had time to stumble back before it fell in front of him.

I yelped as I landed against something, and then felt cold steel around my throat as Viktor pulled me to his chest. The hand that wasn't keeping the dagger poised at my throat was wrapped around my midsection, holding me to his lanky body. I went to try and pull at Viktor's powers, but none of my skin was touching his. His clothes covered every part of him that touched me—even his blade was the only part of him at my exposed skin.

I wasn't going to be able to use my Siphon powers to get us out of this. And from what I'd seen of Callum's shield? He could cover a radius—but couldn't be so precise that he could shield me and not Viktor.

"Let her go and I'll consider letting you live," Callum said, stalking around the fallen tree, his sword outstretched as he approached us.

Viktor *tsked* at Callum. "That is close enough, *Commander*. But you weren't a commander when we first met, were you?"

"I meet many soldiers. I don't remember every face."

"You're right. But I knew you when you weren't commanding armies—just a militia in a small neutral village."

Callum froze, his eyes roving over my captor's features. "*Viktor*. I didn't think... It can't be... You died in Riverleaf. No one from your unit made it out alive."

"I was guarding the armory that was hidden in the hills. Y'know, the one that both Luminaria and the rebels weren't even supposed to know existed? '*This is a very important job, Viktor. This is what will keep Riverleaf safe, Viktor.*' You were my hero," Viktor spat out, his anger boiling as he mocked Callum. "Tell me, how did everyone die in the militia—everyone except people who were fighting by *your* side? Not only that, but you were sworn right in as *Commander* to one of the enemies at our borders. Isn't it funny how the timing of that worked out?" Viktor jerked me as he grew heated, and I held back a cry as his blade prickled the skin at my neck.

"Careful," Callum warned. "I don't give a fuck if you call me a traitor, but if you hurt her, your next breath will be your last."

Viktor looked down at me, his wild eyes flashing. "You have many enemies in these games, Callum. If you survive this, they'll be delighted to know that getting to you is as easy as cornering your favorite plaything." His tongue slithered out, threatening to melt my cheek. "Would you still love her even if she was unrecognizable to you? If her pretty face was as marred as your soul?"

"Stand. Down," Callum growled, taking a step closer.

Viktor laughed, the cruel sound making the snake tattoo on his face and neck undulate as if it was preparing for its next meal. "It's time for you to join your fallen friends, Commander Wells."

Callum lunged just as Viktor, in one swift motion, withdrew another dagger with his free hand—and *licked the blade with his tongue.*

It dripped with saliva, but also with something that sizzled. As he held the second blade aloft, a drop of his acid saliva landed on my arm.

I couldn't stop the scream that tore out of me as the acid burned my forearm. I shook it off before it could go too deep, but my nostrils were filled with the smell of burning flesh—*my* flesh.

Callum skidded to a stop in front of us just as Viktor threw the dagger—but Callum threw up his shield just in time for the dagger to glance off it.

Viktor pulled me back another step into the forest. "I can kill her by dagger or even with just a kiss," Viktor taunted, tracing his mouth over the column of my neck. I wanted to shirk away from his vile touch, but his dagger was still keeping me unable to move lest I sever my own neck. "Lower your shield and your sword, or she'll drop like the tree did."

Callum lowered his shield.

"No!" I yelled, but Callum was already setting down his sword.

"That's it," Viktor hissed. "Too bad, she dies anyways."

Before I could blink, Callum took a handful of soil and tossed it at Viktor's face, the dust blinding him.

Viktor stumbled, and it was enough for me to twist free of his grip.

"GET DOWN!" Callum bellowed, and I hit the earth just as Callum's shield shot out, blasting Viktor back against a tree. Viktor slumped forward, groaning as Callum lowered his shield and went to me.

Callum kneeled by my side, his fingertips brushing my neck. "You're okay," he said, as if reassuring himself just as much as me.

I nodded. "Thanks to you," I managed to force out as adrenaline continued to roar through my blood.

"I know how to fight dirty, one could say." Callum kissed the top of my head, going for his sword on the ground. Then, he walked to Viktor, who was already trying to scramble away from him.

"Have mercy on your fellow militia man, please," Viktor begged.

"Any chance at mercy disappeared when you laid your hands on her," Callum said, and with a swing of his sword, Viktor's head rolled off into the ground, blood pooling as the snake tattoo became forever separated.

Callum cleaned his sword on a nearby patch of grass before sheathing it and walking over to me, holding out a hand.

"Let's go get washed off," Callum said.

"Okay," I said, taking his hand. "But tell me about what he was saying back there about what happened in Riverleaf."

Callum stiffened. "I had a choice that day to go and rally with the additional troops of Riverleaf and those of a neighboring village, or to stay and try to find you."

My mouth went dry. "What did you choose?"

"I went after you."

"And they all died? The men who were left in the Riverleaf militia."

"I never found out," Callum confessed.

Something didn't sit right with me, but I didn't know what else to ask. My stomach churned as I followed Callum through the rest of the dark forest. Was I just missing too much context from my past life to make sense of all that had happened?

We kept walking, but I chose to set aside my spiraling thoughts as the sound of running water reached my ears.

As soon as we broke through the treeline and reached the bubbling brook, I nearly stumbled. Flying above the slow-moving stream was a sky of fireflies. They flitted from the long blades of grass surrounding the water, flickering like the stars in the night sky above us.

"Pretty beautiful for an island trying to kill all of us, isn't it?" Callum asked, his voice warming as the adrenaline from the fight finally started to ebb.

I nodded, taking another step forward into the sea of fireflies. I yelped as a few of them landed on me, a giggle slipping from my lips as they tickled my skin as they jumped off me and took to the wind.

I turned back to Callum, and he was watching me with an expression so full of emotion my heart skipped a beat.

"What?" I asked, but he sucked in a breath, just taking a single step toward me.

"Hearing you laugh..." He smiled to himself, scrubbing a hand over his mouth and his stubbled chin as he drank me in. "It undoes me. Tears me apart."

"Why?" I asked, the word bobbing like a lump in my throat.

Callum stared at me for a moment, but then his words started rushing out like a dam had broken. "Because I love you with all my being, Saffron. I love you to the moon and the stars and to the gods who put them them there. It's been you—it's always been you. I've sacrificed everything in my life for you. I left home. I lost my friends. Lost the soldiers who fought beside me in Riverleaf. I did everything I could just to be sure you're okay. I'd sacrifice the world for you and everyone in it if I knew you'd be safe."

"Callum..." I said, my head swimming. I felt the whiplash of my poor heart, unable to stay steady as it rode the waves of everything that had happened—everything that was happening.

Callum took another step toward me, his eyes searching mine. "And that still isn't enough for you? I don't know what else to give for the person I'm supposed to spend the rest of my life with. Today, I was chained to a reality where you were held by a man more vile than all the demons in hell. I'm trying to respect you and your process, but it's tearing me apart inside. I am a man with nothing but the clothes on my back, sentenced to death for the woman I gave it all up for. Tell me it's not for nothing. But even if it is... I'll fight for you until my dying day, even if I'm not what you want. Just know it was all for you."

Every word felt like a weight, dragging me under the surface, pulling me to the depths of my soul. Especially knowing what I would have to do tonight to try and secure our victory in the next trial —my emotions were too tangled for me to even begin to unspool how I felt and what Callum truly meant by his words.

"Callum?"

"Yes?" he said, hope flashing in his eyes.

"Tell me this another day. Please."

I saw that glimmer die in his eyes, and with it—a piece of me. "If you wish."

He set down his lantern by the shore, and then turned and walked back to camp, leaving me standing cold and alone by the bubbling brook.

The water washed the tears from my face as I tried to scrub the guilt and pain from my skin.

It didn't come off.

22

After I bathed, I headed back to the tent I was to share with Rachelle.

As I slipped inside, Rachelle sat up, tenting her hands and watching me eagerly from where I sat atop my bedroll, combing my drying hair.

"Oh, don't look so excited," I said as I reached into my pack for a white shift dress that I had packed away in the saddlebags. As we advanced deeper into the trials, our wardrobe had expanded slightly —riding clothes, more sets of breeches and tunics, and this shift dress I had found in the saddlebags. "You were the one who warned me to stay away from him, remember?"

"The warning still stands," Rachelle said as I slid off the day's clothes, sliding into my shift dress that fell too thin on my body, the cold night air tickling my skin. "But it looks like you're determined, and I can't blame you."

"I am," I said, and hiked up my dress to strap the borrowed dagger I had taken from Tristen, sheath and all, during the day's ride.

"Powerful wielders are known to be great in bed, so I can't wait to hear all the details," Rachelle crooned.

"Goodnight, Rachelle," I said, and Rachelle winked at me just as I stuck my head outside the tent. I slipped into a pair of satin slippers that had also been impractically packed in my saddlebags.

The campsite was empty, the last embers of the campfires dying as night settled.

I had marked the tent that Tristen had picked. It was the furthest outside of the group, deepest into the woods. It was—thankfully— out of sight and earshot of most of the camp. I didn't allow myself to think too deeply about what I was going to attempt—Callum's confession had left me raw and vulnerable, but I tried to harden every soft part of my soul.

Remember, you're doing this to give you and your friends an edge. You need Tristen's power to see the answer to the riddle in the Oracle's mind. This is just warfare—nothing else.

The reminder didn't lessen my nervousness, and I felt sweat prickle on my palms.

I kept to the perimeter of the camp, noting every rustle in the forest. As I approached the lone tent situated halfway up the hill— better to see the other contestants or any threats coming, I supposed —I heard a low tune carried over the wind. Someone was whistling a song so wonderful and deep.

As I emerged into the small clearing, I spotted Tristen sitting on a tree stump, moonlight glinting off a blade he sharpened as he whis- tled the tune. The sound jostled something in my mind as I stepped closer.

His eyes ticked up to me just as I stepped into the clearing. He relaxed, sheathing the knife and looking up at me. He had changed from his riding gear into a white linen shirt that was unbuttoned, exposing the planes of his chiseled chest. His black hair glimmered underneath the stars, tousled and as unruly as ever.

"To what do I owe the honor?" he asked, and his gaze skated down my form, taking in the dress that bared my legs, my shoulders, barely a nightgown in its sheerness as it rippled in the breeze.

"I still have questions you never answered," I said, and inclined my head to his tent. "Shall we?"

He raised an eyebrow, but in a fluid motion simply rose to his feet, holding open the tent flap for me. "Come in," he said, and I did.

The inside of his tent felt warm and inviting—a few small candles flickered—and I realized the flickering was not a normal flame, but the mesmerizing blue-gold flame of his shadowfire.

"They won't burn the tent down, if that's what you're thinking," he said as he kicked off his shoes and sprawled onto the bedroll. His sleeping area was neatly set up, with blankets cushioning the floor and the warm blue Shadowfire casting him in an ethereal glow.

"Don't think I'm that concerned about your well-being," I said as I stepped out of my slippers and sat next to him on the bedroll, trying not to be overwhelmed by the closeness to him in such a small space.

"Right. You just have..." his eyes danced, "questions. Questions that couldn't wait until morning." He leaned into my space, a wicked grin on his face. "I wonder... does Callum know you're here asking your... questions?"

I glared at him—then immediately softened my face. I was supposed to be seducing him, not angering him. I turned my expression sweet even as the words I uttered next made me sick. "Callum isn't my keeper."

"That's right," Tristen said. "No one could keep you if you didn't choose it. You're like a lick of flame. Deadly and beholden to no one." He leaned in, trailing his fingertips up my bare arm. "I can't wait to see when you finally let go and *burn*."

My heart sped up. His presence had caught me off guard. He spoke of me as if he knew me. Not the scared girl trying to survive in these trials but... a version of me that was strong. Powerful.

Focus. I had to focus. I *was* powerful. And I'd be even more so with Tristen's abilities going into the next trial—powerful enough to ensure everyone I cared for would live to see another day in this horrible fight to the death. I just needed to take what I needed from him. That's all. My heart hammered in my chest.

I'm doing this for Rachelle. For Callum. For me.

Tristen pulled back slightly and cocked his head at me. "You're nervous."

I reddened. "I'm not. I'm just—"

Tristen reached over and pulled me fully toward him, and I let out a surprised gasp at his casual strength. "Why are you nervous?"

He was so overwhelming. I just needed to let go. Just needed to get out of my head, and do what my body has been begging me to do. I closed my eyes, trying to regain my sense of balance. "I just need to ask—"

"What do you *really* need, Saffron?" Tristen asked.

I opened my eyes, so struck by his dark gaze. The shimmering of his obsidian eyes felt alive and molten in the glowing flicker of his flames. My eyes coasted over his face. Down to his lips.

"You know what I think?" Tristen asked.

"What?" I said, suddenly breathless.

"I think you can't stay away from me. You feel what I feel—something pulling us together." I yelped as he pulled me closer, his mouth inches from my lips. "And you're curious. Aren't you?"

I tried to move backward, get some space to *think*, but I edged too far off the bedroll, my hand catching on my skirts as I tumbled back —and then Tristen was moving, lighting-fast. He caught my head before it hit the ground, pulling me back on the bed, his body atop mine.

My chest rose and fell against his, and I felt overheated by all of the places our bodies touched—and I knew we'd fit well together. On instinct, my right hand went to trace his chest, scraping across the bare skin above his tunic. Why was I hesitating? Why did it feel like I was on the edge of a cliff, about to dive off into something so deep and dark and vast—

"*Sael,*" he breathed, his lips tracing my neck, feather light and questioning.

"Kiss me," I breathed.

He hesitated, all of his flirtatious joking gone now. Why was he pausing? Was he thinking about how he was about to betray his wife in the same way I was worried about what this might do to Callum if he found out? I was tempting him, and by the way his breathing hitched and his eyes drank me in, I knew he was fighting the last shreds of his restraint. I would doom us both to hell for doing this, but I couldn't back out now.

But why, despite all of my guilt, did a part of me long for him to cross this line with me?

"Please," I begged.

In an instant, his lips were on mine as if my plea had cut through his willpower in one slice. It wasn't a delicate kiss. It was a crashing union, and I was abuzz with the scent of him, with the thrum of his power as it vibrated through my body. I wove my fingers into his hair, pulling him into me. He obliged, his body molding to mine, not an inch of space separating us as his strong hands slid over my bare thighs, hitching the dress up.

As he claimed my mouth with his lips, I opened my magic to him. Just a little at first: drinking from his powers. *Just a sip.* But that sip filled my body with tingles, slamming me with warmth and pooling my body with fire—*his* shadowfire. His shadow wielding. His mindweavying.

More.

I opened my magic even further. As his power flooded into me, I arched my back, breaking the kiss as a gasp slid from my lips.

Tristen's lips ghosted to my neck, his strong hands slipping up my bare torso underneath the dress, skating across the underside of my breasts, and I needed more—my body *burning* for him.

I reached for the hem of his tunic, pulling his shirt up and off him, needing to feel his bare skin on mine. As he tossed his shirt across the tent, I sucked in a breath at his strong body, rippling with muscle. He was built like a lithe warrior of the night, the planes of his chest wrapped with muscle. But what I saw there caused me to pause, to bank the fire raging inside me.

Across his chest, his torso, were vine-like scars. They were tinted blue-green, almost like a tattoo had left them. But I could still see where the thin chains had burned at him, where they had torn his flesh, the injuries reminiscent of a kind of chain that also had sharp barbs.

"Who did this to you?" I breathed, thinking about those days after the second trial he had been imprisoned for killing guards, supposedly. Was this...?

"These are old scars," he said, taking my hand and kissing the back of it. Then, he looked up at me. "King West knew better than to leave a mark when he tortured me."

I shivered, my lust abating. "So these were from a job?"

Tristen watched my expression as he spoke. "No. These are reminders of when I failed."

"How?"

Tristen settled cross-legged next to me on the cot, pushing the dark hair out of his face. He took a breath, and then looked at me with those obsidian eyes. Those eyes that now looked so sad. So haunted. "These were from the night my parents were murdered in front of me."

I gasped, my hand fluttering to my face. "When?"

"A long time ago. They aimed to kill me, too, but they didn't finish the job."

I shuddered, trying to imagine Tristen wrapped in magical chains and having to watch his parents' lives end in front of him. "Is that why you became an assassin? For revenge?"

His eyes flashed. "Yes, and no. I became what I am today because it's my duty to defend those who can't defend themselves. The only way I could help Stormgard stave off Luminaria was by doing what no one else wanted to do. Pick up a blade and master a set of dark arts that would allow me to use my power for the people I care about."

I tried to reconcile the man sitting shirtless beside me with the stories I'd been told. Of a ruthless assassin who killed children, who set villages on fire, who took me from my life in Riverleaf.

Tristen kidnapped you. He ruined your past life. He would do it again.

"So what does that make me?" I asked. "Wasn't I defenseless when you stole me away?"

Tristen stilled. "I never did anything you didn't want, Saffron."

His words ran right through me. It sounded like the truth. Felt like it, even. But if he was telling the truth, that meant Callum was hiding something.

Callum. Rachelle.

I was here to help them. I was here to try and gain an edge in the next trial.

I reached over, caressing his chest with my fingertips. I felt him still under my touch as my fingertips trailed downward. When I met his gaze again, his dark eyes were ablaze.

"What if I want you?" I didn't give him a chance to reply, leaning in to recapture his lips. In a moment, our flame sparked once more, and I felt my body responding to him.

I reached to the strap of my dress, starting to pull it down—

—but Tristen's hand shot out to grab mine, stopping me. I looked up at him in surprise as he pulled away to study me, but I still saw desire roiling in his gaze.

"Are you sure?" he asked. Tristen's muscled chest rose and fell, his mussed hair and dark eyes burning into me, just as I was still burning with the taste of his magic.

"Yes," I breathed.

His hands dipped under the ties of my dress, sliding the material to the floor as it gathered like moonlight at my feet.

He pulled me on top of him, and I straddled him on the cot as his hands pulled me to him and his lips moved against mine. Demanding. Claiming. I opened my magic wider, bringing in more of his shadowfire, drinking it in as I felt my body alight.

And then it happened.

I dropped into darkness like water tumbling over a steep drop.

Drip.

Drip.

D

r

i

p.

The ripple in my mind echoed, and suddenly I was seeing through my own eyes.

My past self's eyes.

I was kneading bread inside a small bakery, the morning light coating my workspace like watercolor staining a page. Callum's face appeared by the open window, his face so much less unburdened, just a bit younger than the Callum I knew him as. I couldn't hear what he was saying, but he was teasing me, and I felt a warmth bloom in my chest.

Then, something stole his attention. He turned, backed away. Held out a hand for me to stay there. *Stay inside!*

But I couldn't. Children were running. Running away from some threat.

I ran outside, Callum already turning to try to corral some of the villagers to go, pointing down the road.

There, walking down the dirt road to my village, swirling in shadows, was a god of destruction and fear. His shadows stretched high, higher—blocking out the sun as he made his approach.

Tristen Greywood. The Shadowfire Assassin. And his eyes promised endings and death.

His eyes locked on mine, and the memory slipped away—faster and faster and

f

a

s

t

e

r—

"Saffron?" Tristen asked, studying me with concern.

"I remember you," I said with a gasp. But before I could fully digest what I'd seen, I turned my head, listening.

There was no sound coming from outside of our tent.

You should fear when all of the creatures in the forest fall quiet.

"Down!" Tristen said, pushing me off to the side, extinguishing all of the shadowfire in the tent just as a spear made from ice lanced through the tent, shredding it open in its wake. The faint cracking of wood—footsteps in the forest—sounded from outside the tent.

Tristen pulled me out of the tent, and we ran for the edge of the dark forest, a man's laughter sounding from the treeline. I shivered in the cold as we turned.

Ajax and three of his crew emerged in the moonlight, steps away from Tristen's ruined tent. Something was thrumming under my skin. A call to war. A call to *fight*.

Tristen stepped into their path, blocking their view of me.

As Ajax's beady eyes glittered under the moonlight, I didn't see any of the sneering bravado underneath his exterior.

"Ajax is... different," I said to Tristen, trying to keep my voice down. "Do you see it?"

"I do," Tristen whispered to me, keeping his eyes on Ajax as the hulking man took another step forward.

"We meet again," Ajax said, but his voice was once again the monotone emptiness.

Tristen quirked his head. "You're not like the last time we met."

"Neither are you. And it will be your undoing," Ajax said, and then a slow grin spread across his face. Off in some fundamental way, as if he was commanding the muscles in his face for the first time. "Kill him."

The prisoners beside Tristen shot out at him, but Tristen wasted a moment to shove me further back, out of harm's way.

When he turned back to the caster wielding ice, Tristen's shadow-fire grew at his palms...

...and then winked out.

I saw surprise flash across Tristen's face, but he kept his composure as his magic disappeared. He rolled out of the way of another ice spear, stealing a sword from one of the nearest guards in a fluid move —before he spun and duck and sliced through some rather important tendons of one of the oaf-like prisoners who lumbered at him. The muscle in the man's leg shot up like a rubber band, balling and making him go limp. The man screamed and then fell to his knees— but not before raising his cutlass and slashing a terrible gash in Tristen's side on his way down.

Tristen hissed in pain, staggering just a step before whirling and blocking a downward strike from the ice wielder who had changed his spear into a razor-sharp frozen sword.

As the blood leaked from his body, I realized that... Tristen was losing. Ajax and one of his cronies remained, but he was badly injured.

I had done more than just replicate his power. I saw Tristen grasp for his power again and again—and by the way it simmered out, by the feeling of heat screaming in my veins, I knew—

I hadn't just borrowed Tristen's power.

I had stolen it.

"Go! *Run!*" Tristen roared at me over his shoulder, blood sliding down his body from the slashes across his flesh—healing too slowly.

"Yes. Leave him to me," Ajax said. But then he did something horrible. Ajax lifted his eye patch and winked at me with his ruined eye—*a ruined eye that was now just a pit of swirling, inhuman darkness.*

This wasn't Ajax who had survived the second trial.

It was his double.

23

"Saffron. Go. Now," Tristen growled at me as he parried and fought with the ice wielder. His movements were swift, lethal, but I saw the slightest twinge of pain as the blood gushed from his torn side.

That thrumming in my veins pounded louder. I took a step toward the clearing. Toward the fight.

No more, something said softly inside of me. *No more of this.*

Across the fight in front of them, I could see Ajax watching me. Waiting. Seeing what I would do as his final remaining fighter ripped and tore into the Shadowfire Assassin, still so strong even when he was powerless.

Even though he was my enemy... or, whatever he was to me, he didn't deserve this. Even though he had ruined my past, he had guarded my future. I wouldn't forgive him, maybe not ever, but I would give him something in this clearing.

My blood sang as I took another step closer, Tristen's eyes flickering to me in wariness, in fear—not for himself, but for me.

No more. No. More. NO MORE!

The soft voice broke into a scream, and then *I* was screaming, my blood boiling, overheating, and I let my yell coat the clearing, coat it in *fire*—

—because I was fire, cold and cruel, yet flickering brightly all the same. All at once I burned from the inside out. Burned at the nothingness. Burned at the void. Burned at the injustice, the unfairness of it all. Burned at the secrets. Burned at the pain. Burned at my human weaknesses.

And I became the burning. Willed it as it seared the ice wielder where he stood, anguish stolen from his lips as I burned him from the inside out until he was a pile of frozen ash. Even as several of Ajax's other cronies ran from the forest as well, I burned them, too. I burned the injured one who still had bloodlust in his eyes, his mouth agape in shock as he fell to glittering dust beside their comrade. The shadowfire built and tore at them like real fire, but the way it burned with an intense cold that seemed to freeze as it eviscerated was captivating to watch.

Tristen slowly turned to me, his eyes wide in awe as he beheld me. That's when I realized that I was burning, too. Such a roaring fire surrounded me, *consumed* me, and it was so cold. So heavy. As suffocating as the darkness, but in a different way. It was so immense— that cold, that burning.

I let out a gasp, and the strange cold disappeared along with all of the strength in my body. My muscles could not hold me up any longer, and I stumbled, but Tristen had already moved to me, had already caught my heaving body. I caught eyes with Ajax's double across the clearing. He—no, *it*—pinned me with a hard glare, and then turned transparent, disappearing before my eyes.

I felt my body go boneless, and Tristen laid me down on the moss, so gently. "Rest," he whispered, and the darkness claimed me. "I've got you."

24

I awoke to the soft glow of the morning sun warming the tent.
Tent. *Wait.*

As my vision came into focus, I saw that the tent had been roughly repaired, some twine made from branches keeping it together.

Images from last night started flashing back into my mind, but I couldn't handle them. Not this early. I nuzzled my face in the layers that surrounded me, searching for more comfort instead of facing the bite of the creeping chill of dawn—and the reality of what had happened. At what I'd done. As my mind reached a higher state of consciousness, I realized that I was wrapped in a pile of blankets and a cloak that smelled of that smoky spice and sweet pine scent. *His* scent.

"Good morning, little thief," that smug male voice said. I lifted my head, my blonde hair in disarray around my face. Tristen was lounging across the small tent from me, and he was grinning.

"What happened?" I asked, propping myself up on my elbows.

"You stole my powers last night. Took you long enough to use them, too. Tell me: did you come into my tent last night to steal my power, or was that just an unfortunate accident?"

"You're a bastard," I said, shoving off his cloak, trying to get away from the overwhelming smell of him in the tent—but I froze before ripping off the final layer of blankets, realizing I was naked underneath. As I looked up to level a glare at him, he was already throwing me a bundle of clothing.

"Well, *this* bastard got your clothes from Rachelle," he said. "Shadowfire loves to burn through clothing if you can't control it, which you can't do. Yet."

Yet? I shook my head, trying to make sense of the fact that he wasn't... angry with me. I picked up my riding clothes from yesterday. Somehow they had been cleaned and dried and warmed... and they smelled of campfire.

"You... you cleaned them?" I asked.

He shrugged. "Rachelle brought them early this morning. I thought you'd want something clean to wear."

Such a thoughtful kindness. It stole my breath for a moment—but only for a moment. Kindness from a kidnapper didn't count.

"The others must have heard what happened last night," I said, my mouth going dry. Had Callum heard...?

Tristen shook his head. "When you heard the forest go silent last night? That was one of the prisoner's powers, to create a sound barrier. You killed him, luckily, so we don't have to worry about that nuisance anymore."

I let out a breath, relieved. Then, I caught myself. "I killed them," I whispered.

Tristen studied me. "Does that bother you?"

"Not as much as it probably should," I said, my eyes flickering up to Tristen. "Unless I wasn't a stranger to killing in my past?"

Tristen's expression gave nothing away. "You killed them in self-defense. Plus, I think the gods would forgive you considering we're in these trials for their benefit. Your past self would understand, also."

"Speaking of my past," I said, trying to sound casual, but my voice betrayed me by sounding shaken. "I remembered you. Last night. I had a flash of a memory."

"What did you remember?" His expression was hard, stony. Unreadable.

"You... you showed up in my town. In Riverleaf. To take me away. From my village. From Callum. From my... my mother," I choked on that last word. Trying to conjure the face of a woman I so desperately wanted to know. But no matter how much I wanted to see her, her image would not come to my mind.

Tristen's dark eyes flickered. "I have nothing more I can give you about your past." With that, he rose. Tristen nodded at a few tin containers on the floor by the bedroll. "Breakfast," he said, and then he was gone.

I watched him go, the flap of the tent closing behind him. I felt shattered in some way. Maybe it was the residual feeling of wielding his power in a blaze of uncontrolled fury last night. Maybe it was the coldness in his final response to me. Maybe it was the scent of him and campfire on my cloak and riding clothes as I shrugged them on in the tent.

Even with my first memory returned, I felt emptier than ever.

～

I MADE a show of going down to the water and returning to camp as if I had just bathed and dressed for the morning—and hadn't just spent the night in Tristen's tent. Callum was waiting for me by the time I had reached Rachelle's tent.

"There you are," Callum said. "Want a ride?" His tone and quirk of a smile was suggestive, but then he threw a thumb over his shoulder to indicate his saddled horse.

"I'd like that," I said with a smile. Callum's answering grin was so bright it hurt a bit. I felt a slither of guilt as he helped me pack the saddlebags and hoisted me onto his white horse.

He hugged me close as we rode through the cool morning, the others on the path in front of us as we brought up the back of the pack.

"How far until the temple?" I asked.

"Maybe a few hours, give or take the conditions of the trail," he said. "We just need to make it through The Foggy Forest."

"The Foggy Forest?"

"Just a dense stretch of fog and trees that look like withered witches' hands. We'll be fine," Callum said, but it was a little too quickly for my liking. "Are you ready for the third trial?" Callum asked, changing the subject.

"Yes," I said—a lie. My plan had failed last night. I hadn't realized that absorbing Tristen's powers would take them from him. Then again, it wasn't like I had tested what I was capable of. I had probably taken Rachelle's and Callum's powers, too, they just hadn't been in need of them after I had pulled their power from them. I would have to win in this next trial with my wits alone. No extra power would save me or my friends.

"You're quiet today," Callum noted.

I fixed my eyes ahead on the trail. About a mile ahead of us was Ajax and what was left of his cronies, climbing a steep mountain that lay between them and the temple. "I don't think it was Ajax who emerged from that last trial."

"What do you mean?"

"I think it was his double."

Callum laughed. "That's not possible."

I bristled. "I know I'm right. Ajax has his other eye intact underneath the eye patch. But it's... different now."

Callum tensed. "Did you run into Ajax last night?"

"Just briefly. But he's different. Be careful around him," I warned.

"I think *I'm* supposed to be warning *you* about being careful."

"I can look after myself," I shot back.

"I didn't say you couldn't. Are you needing to let some anger out? Because I can help with that, you know," he said, a teasing edge to his voice.

I massaged my fingers into my temples, suddenly feeling the weight of my exhaustion. "I'm sorry. I just... I just have a headache."

"It's okay to be nervous. We'll get through this," Callum said, and he squeezed my arm, pulling me closer to his strong chest. Callum was steady, never changing in his affection for me. Not like Tristen, who seemed to be warm one moment and cold and brooding the next.

I let Callum hold me against his body as we continued to ride, even as my mind drifted to the man who had his lips against mine the night before. The *married* man at that. Guilt clawed its way even deeper into my chest.

25

The tendrils of clouds began beckoning for us as we reached the edge of The Foggy Forest that awaited us at the top of the mountain we had been steadily climbing.

"What is this?" I asked as the clouds of The Foggy Forest wrapped us in their grip. The fog wasn't like normal fog. It clung to us like a swamp.

"The realm is thinnest here," Callum said. "It's said that this fog here magical properties."

"What kind of magical properties?" I asked, wishing I had grilled him on it earlier as our horse bucked and whinnied in fear as the fog climbed higher and higher. It had risen up to the chest of our horse, and was still creeping up like a rising tide. The prisoners riding on the narrow path ahead of us were getting harder and harder to see.

"It will try to convince us to stay," Callum said, his jaw tight.

"Stay where?"

"Here. In the fog. Whatever you do, don't get off this horse, Saffron."

I gripped the saddle, and Callum tightened his hold on me. I cleared my head. I wanted to press Callum for answers, but I knew that it was better to stay focused. I kept my attention on the steadying climb of our horse's footsteps against the ground. Callum's strong body against mine, holding me tight. But the fog was starting to look more and more strange. As it floated by, I swore I could see... *faces.* Stretching and elongating into expressions that looked like they were mid-scream with hollow eyes—only to be turned into ragged whisps by the next errant breeze.

The fog crept higher until it blinded our horse and I choked back my fear. It was like that feeling of drowning in complete nothingness that often haunted me at night when I couldn't sleep. Sensory deprivation so absolute that I was no longer tethered to reality, to myself.

"Hold tight, Saffron," Callum said.

The fog consumed us.

I reached blindly for Callum's hand, clutching it as he held the reins steady in the other.

"Don't let me go," I begged, my fear rising in my chest as more faces seemed to continue to appear around me—but this time, the faces seemed to grow hands, reaching for me.

"I've got you," he said, but I felt my panic hammering my heart, causing me to suck in gasping breaths of air. "*Breathe.*"

I did, trying not to grow too frenzied by the cage of floating white I found myself in. I raised a hand in front of my face—and sucked in a gasp when I realized I couldn't see it, not unless I brought my hand mere inches in front of my face. I cowered back into Callum, my body trembling as I was faced with the void of nothing.

A void so like the emptiness of where my memories should have been.

Then, I heard it.

"Saffron. Don't be worried, sweetheart," a calm, clear voice cut through the fog. A woman's voice. But not any woman—

"*Mother,*" I sobbed, and in that moment, I knew it to be true. "Where are you?"

"*I am here, by the whispering wood. Come find me, daughter. Follow my voice.*"

I felt Callum's strong arms caging me into the saddle, but it was as if I were in a trance. I rocked back against him just as the horse let out a terrified whinny as it bucked at something none of us could see.

The fog was so dense it wasn't so hard for me to slither underneath Callum's grip as he tried to get his horse under control. I ducked underneath the reins and twisted out of the saddle as Callum yelled for me, but I dropped to the ground of the forest floor, determined.

My mother was here.

I found myself walking toward the voice, even though I couldn't see anything.

"Mother!" I called out again, stumbling through the white fog. Pain ripped from me in great, heaving sobs as I threw myself at the white.

"Here. I am right up ahead. Come home to me, daughter."

As I walked, a great witch's tree extended from the fog. The tree had spindly arms that grabbed for me as if it was trying to snatch me. Then, I saw other trees, bare and twisted like the mangled hand of evil crones. They emerged from the fog like ancient gods. Watching. Clawing for me... Or did they? I couldn't tell if the trees were just swaying, or trying to swipe at me.

I tripped on one of the roots, skinning my arm as I landed in the dirt. The plants below my skinned arm seemed to absorb my blood, as if they were parched plants in the desert tasting water for the first time in months.

"Hurry, daughter. I'm just up ahead. Run to me."

So I stumbled to my feet and *ran*. Tears were streaming down my cheeks, and I was sobbing. Sobbing for a woman who I didn't fully remember. Another void within the larger one that was threatening to consume me whole. I couldn't bear the way the emptiness cleaved at my heart.

I chased after a breeze edged with the scent of freshly baked bread. The smell fit within the grooves of moments long since left blank. I felt a tug to something that began materializing in front of me.

That's when I saw the bakery. It looked almost like what Callum had built for me in the meadow, but this was different. I saw her—my mother—standing in the doorway. Gesturing for me to come in.

For me to come *home*.

"Come inside, Saffron. It's so dreadful out today," she said.

"Mom," I sobbed, and I threw myself step over step toward where an invisible thread was pulling me, until—

—strong arms caught me, and suddenly my feet were dangling.

"*Saffron!*" a familiar male voice called for me.

I cried out, and then realized my eyes were closed. When I opened them, I looked down—and the fog parted to reveal that I was dangling above a massive cliffside, right under my swinging feet. The fog had just started to dissipate, and I shuddered as my mind cleared. I had been just about to run off that cliff. I had ran toward—

"Mother!" I cried out, looking around, but as I whirled to the owner of those strong hands, I turned and saw Callum as he set me back down.

"That's not your mother, Saffron. It's just the fog," Callum said, pulling me into him.

My whole body trembled as the voice came through the fog once more, except this time it sounded monstrous, like the cry of the dead or the groaning sound of a tree about to break in a storm.

"*Come home, Saffron,*" the eerie voice called out, but this time I heard it for what it was.

"No," I said, not wanting it to be true. But Callum's head suddenly swiveled, and I felt him go still against me. "What is it?"

"Stay here," he said, unsheathing his sword.

"Callum..." I said, but I followed him in the fog, not letting it swallow him up in front of me as he stalked in another direction.

That's when I heard it—the same ruined voice, as if nails scraping on metal could form words.

"*You were supposed to protect usssssssssssss,*" the voice said with a slithering sound, the syllables getting lost in the floating fog. "You were our leader..."

"I didn't think I was making the wrong choice!" Callum suddenly called out in reply, and the pain in his voice had me stumbling a step as I tried to keep up with him. "Everything was falling apart. What was I supposed to do?"

"Callum, stop!" I cried, realizing he was being held captive in the same way I had just been.

But he just started walking faster, nearly picking up into a run.

"*You made the selfish choice. And we suffered for it!*" the voice creaked.

"I did what I thought was right!" Callum shouted, his voice echoing in the soupy swell of the endless fog that threatened to sweep us away.

This was all wrong—just like what the forest wanted.

"STOP!" I screamed at Callum, and I broke into a run to try and catch him. But he was now running. Too fast—I wouldn't be able to catch him. I had to stop him before something happened—"This isn't real, Callum. You're in The Foggy Forest!"

But Callum was deaf to my attempts to slow him down.

Finally, I pulled out the last card I could think of to try and snap him out of it.

"HELP ME!" I screamed, the shrill sound of my terror cutting through even the thickest of the fog trying to separate us. "CALLUM, I NEED YOU!"

Suddenly, Callum stopped...

...and swayed.

As I caught up with him, I saw why. One foot was on solid ground —the other was hovering above a pit covered in spears at the bottom.

He slowly pivoted to face me, stepping away from what had been certain doom a minute ago.

"Saffron," he said, and I saw him become lucid once more. He fell on his knees before me, and he leaned his head against me as I twined my fingers in his hair. "You saved me."

"As did you," I reminded him, and I felt him take a shuddering breath underneath my touch. We had both been tempted by our pasts—and had both fallen prey to our desires and guilt. We would only survive The Foggy Forest together. Apart? We would have met our deaths screaming.

Callum seemed to remember where we were, as he stood and took my hand. "We have to get out of here."

"Let's go," I said. I was eager to be rid of this place.

A deep rumbling sound filled the forest—underscoring my unease.

"Run!" Callum called and yanked me ahead.

We were sprinting side-by-side, and I was about to demand what we were running from—when I saw it. Those gigantic sleeping trees that stretched and grasped like the gnarled hands of sleeping witches? They were now moving. And reaching toward Callum and I, swiping for our bodies.

Callum dodged the trees, pulling me with him as great thick branches swung at us. I ran faster, trying to keep up with Callum as he sprinted down a hill, and I followed. Great clumps of earth were thrown our way as I skidded down a hill as roots sprung out from underneath me.

I saw it before Callum did. "Duck!" I yelled, pushing Callum to the ground just as a branch swiped the air above our heads, sending us rolling down the hill.

Breathless, I found myself tangled in Callum at the bottom of a grassy slope—with the rumbling now in the distance.

"Are you okay?" he asked, brushing my hair out of my face and looking for injuries with a concerned look.

"Are *you* okay?" I threw his question right back at him.

Callum's gaze darkened as I felt him pull me closer to him, our bodies intertwined. "I'll never turn down a roll in the hay with you."

"Let's get moving," I said, and untangled myself from Callum.

As we rose, I heard another yell cut through the fog.

A flash of blue-green light through the fog had me moving toward who I knew was on the other side, but I felt Callum pull me back.

"Saffron, this way—"

I hesitated long enough to hear a pained battle cry from Tristen— and an earth-shattering roar that seemed to hurl back at him.

"He needs our help," I said.

Callum's eyes darkened. "It's his problem."

"He saved me last night when Ajax came after me," I said in a rush, Callum's eyes going wide. "Don't you think that's a debt you ought to repay?"

Hurt flashed across Callum's face, and I knew it was a low blow knowing how he had just lost himself to the guilt of those whom he couldn't save just moments ago.

But to his credit, Callum took my hand and we started running once more—but this time into the direction of the sound of battle.

When we grew closer to the flashes of blue-green shadowfire, the fog became not a still slithering thing, but instead a twisting tornado, caught in a horrible vortex.

At the center of the swirling mist was Tristen, caught in a battle with a hooded creature made of shadows that was three times his size. It shot out at him with spindly arms, oozing toward him like some sort of nightwalker on stilts, tall and made of pure darkness.

Tristen was fast, but the creature's arms were faster. Tristen's shadows lashed out like hundreds of flying whips, but seemed to have no effect on the creature. In fact, the creature seemed to grow stronger from each attack, absorbing the shadows and dodging the shadowfire as if it knew Tristen's power intimately.

"*Let me in, Tristen,*" the creature said in the same croaking voice of the island, but somehow it sounded like it was speaking from the core of the earth. "*Let me in and hand it over. I only want to wear it for awhile.*"

"Stand back," Callum told me, and for once, I listened.

Callum fell to his knees, crossing his arms over his head the way he always had to do in order to summon his shield. But instead of throwing his shield around Tristen, he tossed it around the creature, who turned its hooded head with a slowness that had my skin crawling. But underneath its hood was more vast night—and red eyes staring right at us.

Tristen snapped his head in our direction.

"We can't fight him and escape. Send your shadows to get him out of here!" Callum bellowed.

Tristen didn't need to be told twice. He raised his arms like a conductor of an orchestra of nightmares, and his shadows tensed. Then, he lowered his arms slightly and they all shot out—wrapping around Callum's shield that was keeping the creature contained. Instead of attacking the creature, Tristen's shadows lifted the orb, levitating it as they carried it up, up, up and away, the fog seeming to lift it into the currents of its strange breeze.

Tristen had sweat beading down his face, and Callum's breath was coming in heavy pants as the two men worked.

"Almost... Far enough..." Tristen ground out.

"Any time now," Callum said through gritted teeth.

"Now!" Tristen dropped his arms just as Callum did, the men releasing their grip on their magic.

Callum didn't wait for me to run by his side, and simply scooped me up in his arms as he ran. Tristen didn't give me so much as a glance as he ran by Callum's side, and I almost demanded that Callum put me down—but my legs had gone weak from the horrors I'd seen in the forest, and exhaustion had pressed into me just as the fog had.

So I held my grip around Callum's neck as he ran over branches and discarded swords. Finally, a dirt path was revealed beneath our feet, the thick fog finally lessening.

When we burst out of the wall of fog, I had never been more grateful for the sun and the cloudless sky above me than I was in that moment. Our horses were whinnying and stomping around in the grassy patch of sun—and from the looks of some of the other lost horses, it seemed like there were other prisoners still trapped in The Foggy Forest.

Callum set me down on the ground just as Tristen emerged from the fog steps behind us, his dark hair mussed and his bedroom eyes blazing.

Callum whirled on Tristen, and the two men stood face-to-face.

I scrambled to my feet, waiting for the moment I would surely have to throw myself between them.

But Callum simply looked Tristen in the eye. "Now we're even."

Callum turned and stomped away, frustration rolling off him.

But before he was out of earshot, Tristen's voice rang out in the sun-drenched stretch of land.

"Thank you, Commander."

Callum stiffened, but didn't turn his back. "Don't thank me, Assassin. I'm still plotting your death."

Tristen didn't say anything to that. His gaze just slid to mine, and I held it for a beat before turning and joining Callum by our horse. Callum lifted me up, setting me in the saddle.

We rode away, Tristen still watching us go, his back to the terrible fog still boiling behind him.

26

C allum had fussed over me when he had pulled me back onto his horse. The fog was fading now, and the path was clear as we crested the mountain. I assured Callum that I was fine—but despite the sunny weather, I felt cold, tired. The thick fog still shrouded the edges of my consciousness.

"Here it is," Callum announced as our horse started its descent down the mountain. The last of the fog parted and I saw it.

The Temple of Orsi was perched on a cliff. It was surrounded by greenery and gorgeous gardens, bursting into explosions of color that dripped from every surface. The temple had huge domed structures with imposing gilded pillars. But what was most stunning were the massive waterfalls tumbling out from underneath the temple and down the cliff face below. It gave the temple an illusion of having been built atop a waterfall, and the cliff was so high in elevation that clouds drifted by the marble columns and hanging gardens. What was it like, to live amongst the clouds like that?

"What is this place?" I asked. Nothing in my lost memories could possibly look as beautiful as this—could it?

"Only the most remote temple in all of Septerra," Callum said. "Orsi is the goddess of creation, prosperity, and knowledge. She's a blessing to craftsmen, and the Kingdom of Solhaven have claimed her as their deity."

"Have you been to Solhaven?"

Callum snorted. "As if. They rule an entire continent double the size of what Luminaria and Stormgard split. King West likes to claim they're an ally, but no one really knows what goes on in Solhaven. We only hear rumors of golden fields and prosperous cities, but no one beyond their citizens are allowed within their borders."

"So why have their god's temple here?"

"Cassandra hails from Solhaven," Callum said, his jaw tightening at the mention of the High Sorceress. "Which does not give me hope that their wealthy kingdom came upon their riches from just the benevolence of their land."

We rode for another half hour, winding down the narrow road that bordered the cliff and the steep drop below. Then, we arrived at the drawbridge that was lowered for us and our horses to cross to the temple.

I made the mistake of looking over the side of the drawbridge and I hissed and leaned back into Callum.

He chuckled. "So you throw yourself into rings with demons without any fear, but some measly heights scare you?"

I went pale. "Callum, we are on top of a cliff. No, scratch that. *We are floating on a scrap of wood above a cliff.*"

"Just close your eyes," he said, and I did. "Think of something that makes you happy."

"What are my options?" I asked.

"Shush. Visualize an attractive former-Royal-Commander-turned-contestant who plans on finding new and... *creative* ways of transferring his power to you," he whispered in the shell of my ear before trailing kisses down my neck. One of his hands brushed under the hem of my tunic... slipping under to run his fingertips across my bare skin. "I didn't get to finish what we started."

"Callum," I said, not sure if I truly wanted him to stop. "The others will see."

"Let them. I want them to know that if they try to touch you they'll have to deal with me."

I leaned back into Callum, feeling the trail of his fingers as they made little circles, climbing up the side of my ribcage. My heart stuttered... and then Callum's hand was gone, and with it his leather and citrus scent. I looked up, and the drawbridge was coming to an end. The others were stopping in front of stables with vaulted ceilings and stained glass that let in brightly colored sunshine. Ajax, I noticed, was missing from our group. Maybe The Foggy Forest had eaten him for lunch.

"To be continued," Callum said, and I couldn't help but let out a disappointed noise that made him chuckle.

Callum swung his leg off the horse and promptly reached over to lift me up and off the horse.

Just as he did, a black mare came thundering past us. We looked up to see Tristen push ahead of the rest of the group to get to the stables, smoothly making it off his horse in one motion as he handed off the reins to a stablehand. He turned to the temple, stalking past the confused priestesses who were emerging from the temple to greet us in their ice blue robes.

One of the priestesses continued to our group. She was young, maybe in her twenties, and underneath her hood tumbled a waterfall of raven hair. She bowed slightly to the travelers.

"Welcome to the Temple of Orsi. I am Iris, one of the priestesses here. We are the Order of the Serafim. We invite you to dine with us this afternoon and rest up before your trial this evening. Before I show you to your quarters, I invite you to make an offering at our Sacred Fountain."

All of us contestants followed, and I trailed behind Callum. I observed the rest of the priestesses as they lined up outside of the temple, smiling at us and greeting us as we entered. Each one wore the ice blue hooded robe with billowing long sleeves, a gold circlet with a sapphire stone perched on their foreheads.

The priestess who called herself Iris led us through sprawling indoor gardens and reflection pools, past plush sitting areas with colorful pillows, and down several open air hallways.

Iris paused in a courtyard, allowing us to filter in. Tristen was already at the fountain, waiting. At the center of the courtyard was an ornate stone fountain featuring the goddess Orsi. She wielded a hammer, preparing to strike the rising sun. The crystal blue waters of the fountain danced around her and the piles of books and weapons that surrounded her like a shrine.

"You have been invited here to make an offering to the Goddess Orsi," Iris said, and she held out a gold coin in her palm. We all dug through our things until we held our coins, too.

Iris moved closer to the fountain. "Orsi is one of the six gods who has been relegated to this island after the Divinity War, but her gifts still bless those who make the pilgrimage here. She is the goddess of creation, prosperity, and knowledge. She's been known to bestow the heroes of her choosing with magical artifacts, bonded to their blood-line to give them a chance to change the course of history. But at her fountain, she gives her blessing in the form of future promises. If the water splashes blue, you must continue to acquire knowledge to be worthy of her. If the water runs red, you must kill your way into her favor—likely with an ancient artifact she will bestow upon you, or one that has already been promised to your bloodline. If the water runs black, your death has been promised to her."

Iris paused, allowing us a moment of silence filled only by the gentle gurgle of the fountain. A soft breeze picked up, and I smelled the spicy scent of the hanging gardens. The gods made such violent promises in the most beautiful of places.

"Now, step forward and present your offering," Iris said, and she turned over her palm and let the gold coin drop into the fountain below. The water stayed its translucent blue, and Iris folded her hands in front of her as she looked at us expectantly.

We all stepped up to the fountain and did the same, gold coins falling from outstretched palms.

The moment my coin touched the water, it began to bleed. I wish I could say that I was surprised, but I wasn't. My path was already stained with red. But when I looked over to see where Callum's coin had landed...

...there was nothing but an inky blackness.

"Callum," I whispered, trying to keep the shock from my face.

But Callum just shook his head, his expression serious. "I always knew where my path would eventually lead."

The other prisoners reacted to their coins—most of their waters remained clear, but across the fountain I saw a red swirl curl up from Rachelle's coin. She angled her head to see my color, and grinned.

"Twins!" she called.

My curiosity kept my gaze roving around the circle of the fountain, and I saw Tristen's coin...

...had turned the water *gold*.

Iris had seen it, too. I saw a slight tremble in her hands as she leaned over the fountain, as if questioning her own eyes.

"How...?" she began.

"One of the guards probably gave me a gold painted copper as he lined his pockets," Tristen said with a shrug.

Iris had gone pale, but she just nodded and addressed the rest of us. "The Goddess Orsi thanks you for your offerings, and deems you worthy to stay in her home. Let me show you all to your individual chambers. Come."

Iris' ice blue skirts swished as she walked out of the courtyard, and we followed after her. We headed down more grand hallways with rounded archways and indoor-outdoor spaces where priestesses were studying, praying, or gossiping. The gardens seemed to invade every space. Fruits such as fresh grapes looked juicy on the vine from where they sat in rooms and libraries, the priestesses occasionally going to pick them. Some took great bunches of the grapes, giggling and feeding each other with them while lounging on sofas.

"Can I quit the trials and just become a priestess?" Rachelle asked as she caught up to me.

"I think the Goddess Orsi would be mad we didn't spill blood for her, first," I said.

"Got it. This can be our retirement plan after we win many vicious battles, then," Rachelle said, and then floated away to get a closer look at a set of oil paintings of the goddess as the group slowed to a stop.

Iris paused at the mouth of a long hallway with doors on one side, and artwork on the other.

"Your names are on the doors. Make yourself at home. We will begin serving refreshments in the main hall when the bell chimes. See you then." Iris bowed and then nearly floated away with her effortless grace.

I watched her go before turning and walking down the ornate hallway, scanning the names written in clean calligraphy on pieces of parchment affixed to each door.

"See you in the main hall?" Callum asked, pausing at a door with his name on it.

"I'll meet you there," I said, eager to bathe the smell of horse from my skin. I split off from him until I got to the last door at the end of the hallway with my name on it.

And next to my door—as luck would have it—was Tristen's room.

Great, I grumbled as I slipped inside my room. The thought evaporated as I beheld the grand chambers. There was a huge sitting room, a sprawling bed, and a balcony with an arched window and floor-to-ceiling curtains that billowed in front of the open door.

I parted the gauzy curtains, stepping outside onto the balcony. I stopped, standing frozen in awe. Across from the temple were those jagged peaks covered in fog. But the valley below—so, so far below— was lush and green and broken by veins of sapphire rivers that fed into a sparkling lake. It was breathtaking—quite literally as the sheer drop of the cliff face below me nearly stole the air from my lungs.

"Enjoying the view?" a teasing voice asked.

I whipped my gaze to Tristen, who was lounging on the balcony next to mine. He wasn't looking out, but merely watching me as he leaned against the railing.

"I don't like heights," I said.

He didn't look surprised, and a dark cloud passed over his face. "I'm sure Callum would catch you if you fell."

I pushed my shoulders back. "What problem do you have with him?"

"I've told you. He's hiding things from you."

"And you're not?" I shot back.

"I *can't* tell you things. He *won't*. There's a difference."

I made a move to turn back inside, but his voice stopped me. "He's not on your side, not completely."

"He did save your life, after all."

"Only to threaten me moments later. Or should I assume he is not a man of his word?"

"What about you? Are you a man of your word to your wife?"

"Obviously," Tristen said, and I looked over my shoulder as he gazed out at the view beyond. His eyes slid back to me. "I promise you that Callum will tear you to pieces. Not a matter of if, but when. You won't even see it coming."

Anger slid through me as I whirled on him, leaning over the railing. "Jealousy isn't a good look on you, Tristen."

His obsidian eyes were steady. Level. "You'll know when I'm jealous. That isn't what this is. Callum will destroy you. He already has."

"Funny, he says the same things about you. So tell me, Tristen, who should I believe? Should I ask the Oracle when I win the trial tonight?"

The blood drained a bit from Tristen's face. "You have one precious question you get a true answer to. I pray you use it wisely. Not for my sake, but for your own. See you soon, *princess*." With that, he disappeared back into his room.

I hesitated, my whole body tensed with anger and frustration. I wanted to break down Tristen's cryptic nature and get true, honest answers from him. At least Callum was forthcoming. Callum had been there since the beginning, answering my questions. Helping me.

I sighed, walking back into my room. As I did, a knock sounded at the door. I went to answer it, and a woman in an ice-blue dress entered. It was the same color as the priestesses' robes, but much more simple and she wore no jewelry.

She curtseyed. "Saffron? I'm here to dress you for lunch."

I opened my mouth, about to protest that I didn't need help dressing, but the woman was already breezing into my room. Light flared at her fingertips as she snapped and a splashing sound came from the bathing chamber. She held out a silk robe of that same bright blue to me.

"Here. Go bathe," she instructed. At the idea of washing the grime off me, I nodded in thanks and took the robe. I went to the bathing chamber, eyeing the tub that was now filled with steaming hot water. I was already enjoying this third trial *much* more than the others.

An hour later, I was bathed and clothed, wearing the color I assumed was the only appropriate option in the Temple of Orsi— that turquoise-glacier blue that matched my eyes. My dress was made of flowing tulle skirts, with a slit up the right side showing glimpses of the creamy skin of my thigh beneath. The bodice of the gown was made of glittering diamonds with blue silk ribbons that served as tied straps on my shoulder. The back was open, plunging low over my bare skin. My blonde hair was sectioned into small braids that were intertwined with those same diamonds, and swept into a low chignon above the nape of my neck.

I felt a whisper of the cool afternoon air tease the places where my skin was bare, but it was pleasant. I stared at my reflection in the mirror, turning slightly so the skirts billowed around me like a frothy cloud.

"It's beautiful, thank you—" but as I turned to thank the handmaiden, she was already gone. Somewhere above me, a bell chimed. Summoning us contestants together once more.

~

I STILL HAD one of Tristen's spare daggers, which I had fastened to my upper thigh. It was hidden underneath the massive swells of tulle on the side without the slit in the fabric—one of the few benefits of a dress like this.

I had stepped out of my room—only to stay frozen in the doorway when I heard low voices a few paces away from my room. I closed my door softly behind me, waiting in the alcove of my room's doorway as I recognized Tristen's voice carrying in the cavernous hallway.

"...I won't accept," he said.

"Are you sure?" a lilting female voice asked.

I snuck a glance around the corner of the alcove. Cassandra was standing across from Tristen, her gorgeous eyes flaring the color of her sapphire robes. She was decked in more finery and jewelry than the other priestesses—much more than what she usually wore when she was playing warden in Ashguard.

Cassandra leaned into Tristen, who had his back to me. Cassandra walked her fingers up his chest.

"I think you'd give up a lot for what I'm offering you," Cassandra crooned.

"I don't make bargains with the King's witches," he shot back, but I noticed that his steely resolve had faltered slightly. He didn't withdraw from Cassandra's touch, and I felt a flare of senseless jealousy heat my blood.

Cassandra swept a hand underneath his chin, angling his face down to her. "I answer to no King, *Assassin*. Are you sure you want to turn down my offer? This next trial will be a challenge, even for you." She leaned in closer, and I felt myself holding my breath. "Take my bargain, Tristen. You know it's what you want."

What did he want? I wondered.

Conflict flashed across Tristen's eyes, but it was chased away by certainty. He took Cassandra's wrist, removing it from his face and returning it to her side. "I told you. Unlike some of the others, I refuse to accept any of your *offerings*."

Cassandra's eyes narrowed. "You think you're special?" She took another step closer to him. "Your people will die in this rebellion. And many more as well. You've been leading lambs to slaughter. Why? Because you're a selfish bastard. Always have been, always will be." Cassandra stepped away, schooling her face into that poised calm. "See you at lunch." She drifted away, humming a hymn of some kind to herself.

Tristen stood stock still in the hallway, fury dancing over his features. I just watched him from behind as he took in a ragged breath, scrubbed his hand over his face, and then walked down the hall where she had disappeared.

Questions flitted across my mind, but I stifled them. After a heartbeat, I followed as well, winding down the stone hallways and colorful rooms until I reached where everyone had gathered. This was a cozy throne room that prioritized comfort. Just like our bedchambers, gauzy white curtains flowed across huge arched doorways that led out to a massive veranda, the afternoon light dripping inside and splashing a warm glow about the room. Alcoves were hidden away in so many corners, each filled with so many wine red cushions around low tables.

High Sorceress Cassandra Wraithborn sat perched on a throne at the far end of the room, all of her priestesses lined up by the tables with their hands clasped behind them and pious smiles on their faces as they watched us filter in. As each of us contestants entered, the priestesses broke off, ushering us one-by-one to seats at the main floor table that filled the center of the space.

As I entered, I felt so many heads swivel toward me. Callum took in my dress with wide-eyed wonder. Rachelle gave me a wry smile and a wink. And Tristen... he looked like he had been punched in the gut. He tore his gaze away from me with effort, and I felt heat rise to my cheeks from all of the attention.

Callum motioned for me to come to him, and I joined him at the middle of the table, Rachelle across from me. Tristen sat a few seats down from Rachelle, but he didn't spare me another glance—especially as Callum's hand rested on the small of my bare back.

"You're stunning," Callum whispered in my ear, and I smiled up at him.

Callum wore an outfit fit for a prince. His pale blue uniform felt regal, as if he was a member of the guards of this temple instead. It was very different from the dark black silk shirt and pants that Tristen had been dressed in—as if he had gotten in a fight with whoever had showed up to his room with pastels and he had won, still dressed in his roguish attire that would allow him to slip back into the shadows at any second.

Rachelle was stunning in an ice blue corset dress that showed off her ample curves—to the point where one of the more dapper prisoners beside her looked like he wanted to steal the dress right off her and get at the prize underneath.

Cassandra rose and the hall fell silent as her priestesses dispersed into the crowd, handing glasses of wine served in gold, gem-encrusted goblets atop gold trays. They were the picture of fine elegance as they floated throughout the room.

Iris stopped in front of me with my goblet. I took the glass she held aloft for me, and I sniffed at the sweet-smelling wine. They had taken tea from us—why not wine?

I peeked at the other prisoners, and everyone was doing the same thing, no one daring to take a sip.

"Welcome, contestants of The Ash Trials, to the third trial. And welcome to my home. My priestesses and I reside here, the Temple of Orsi, home of the great Oracle. Before we begin our meal, a toast to your continued success in these trials, and to bringing the forgotten lands back to the light of Luminaria as we banish the Stormgard rebels once and for all in this senseless war."

Everyone raised their glass in a toast... but again, the hesitation to drink.

"If it's poisoned, we're all fuckin' dead anyways," Rachelle said loudly as she knocked back her glass. Everyone else did the same. I hesitated, but followed suit as Cassandra's stare bore into all of us, and it was pretty clear that we had to drink or suffer the consequences.

The sweet wine hit my veins fast, and I felt a heady rush from the alcohol. The sensation was strong, and I was momentarily caught off-balance, despite being seated on a soft floor pillow. I hadn't had wine since waking up in Ashguard. Was I a lightweight in my previous life?

"It's time to eat, our guests. Please, enjoy the feast until the chime of the next bell. Then, we will begin calling out names to see the

Oracle. If you miss your name being called three times, you shall be disqualified. So stay sharp," she said with a giggle.

I watched as she returned to her throne, as if she was offering up herself for the meal. More handmaidens emerged with plates overflowing with spiced meats, steaming mashed potatoes, and exotic fruits both prickly and scaly that I had never seen before. The smell was intoxicating, and I found myself picking from different plates, wanting to sample everything.

I cracked open a scaly fruit, the liquid inside sweet and sticky. I tipped back my head, drinking it in and felt a shudder go through my body as the tangy fruit flooded my senses. It was so... *intense*. Had fruit always tasted this... vibrant?

I felt Callum's thumb brush my lower back again, and I felt sparks of electricity shoot through me. His touch was so... so *much*. It didn't normally feel this heady, though.

I turned to Callum, and he hadn't glanced at the food, his body shifted toward me on those floor pillows. His eyes were ravenous. Like *I* was the meal he wanted to devour.

He swept his thumb back up my spine again and I arched, a soft gasp escaping my lips at the touch.

"What—" I whispered, feeling the heat rise in my veins. But my mind clouded as the question got lost on my lips.

"It's not fair," he said, his eyes darkening with lust. "To see you dressed like this."

My cheeks heated. "You prefer me in a tunic and breeches?"

His fingertips traced up the column of my throat, tipping my chin up. "I prefer seeing your clothes on my floor."

He leaned forward, and I somehow had to fight my instincts and place a hand on his muscled chest.

"I feel... tingly," I whispered, and that cleared the fog in Callum's eyes.

"It's the wine," he said, his eyes widening slightly with realization. "It... it must have been an aphrodisiac."

My eyes went wide, and I swept my gaze over the rest of the prisoners. The priestesses now sat amongst us, mingling. One of the priestesses fed one of the prisoners a grape, gleaming from where she had picked it from a plate. Another led the fire sprite to an alcove on the far side of the room, their hands intertwined. The whole scene moved as if it were in slow motion.

And it was in slow motion that I caught Cassandra drift down to the table, effortlessly slipping herself right next to Tristen.

But Tristen's eyes were on me. On Callum. There was such severity in those eyes. So much intensity.

Callum began drawing his fingertips up my bare back again and I shuddered, gasping and reaching out to clutch his arms as Callum's eyes darkened again. I felt myself losing my grip on my mind. Why were we here, again?

"What—what's happening?" I asked, my stomach fluttering as Callum leaned down to kiss my neck.

"You're so beautiful, Saffron," Callum murmured in between kisses. He trailed his lips to the swell of my breasts, leaving me breathless. "I want you," he whispered on my skin, raking his gaze back up to meet mine.

One moment Callum's lips were on mine—

—the next he was thrown across the room, Tristen stalking toward him.

"Keep your hands off her," Tristen said low and dangerous as the shadows collected around him. Some of the room shifted to watch, but the lust-filled haze was growing stronger as more priestesses pulled prisoners to alcoves of the room, the sounds of moaning starting to fill the cavernous space.

Even though my senses felt so heavy and my skin burned, ached to be touched—I scrambled to my feet, watching as Callum pushed himself up and faced Tristen.

"She's *mine*, Assassin," he said, turning to face Tristen.

The shadows gathered around Tristen, rage glittering in his eyes. "This is a godsdamned trial, you *idiot*! You're not supposed to give in. Not *here*."

Callum lunged at Tristen, but Tristen merely disappeared in a swirl of shadows, appearing on the other side of Callum.

Callum dove for a steak knife on the far edge of the table, and turned and hurled it at Tristen.

This time, Tristen did not dodge. He let the blade catch his arm, let it slice him, and I flinched...

...but Tristen merely looked down and yanked out the blade— and watched as the injury stitched itself back together.

He brought his gaze back up to Callum. "We have met, but I still do not think you know who I am. I am night. I am flame. I am an enemy you don't want to make today."

But Callum's eyes were blazing, and he snatched another knife, starting to advance toward Tristen—

"Stop!" I said, and grabbed his arm. "Please." The hand holding the knife went limp, and Callum looked down at me again, his eyes alight with that feral hunger. The knife clattered to the floor, and Callum was turning to me once more, my head in his hands.

"I can't stay away, Saffron. I need you." His words set off an ache in me, one that felt like an earthquake or a tremor in my veins. I felt so wobbly I wanted to dissolve in a puddle, right then and there.

But then Tristen's strong hands were on me, yanking me out of Callum's grasp.

Callum's eyes went hateful and dark as he once again fixed his gaze on Tristen. But Tristen smoothly set me in an empty alcove behind him, and blocked Callum's path to me.

"If you *need* her to survive what the Oracle has planned, you'll go find some acolyte to fuck to get the potion out of your system," Tristen said in his deadly calm. "It's a test. Don't fail it, you stupid oaf."

Callum's fists went to his sides, his eyes sliding to me.

"You should go, Callum," I said, knowing that if he stayed it would spell trouble for all of us. "I'll be okay. *Go.*"

His jaw tightened, but he turned and strode past the billowing curtains and out into a courtyard beyond my view.

Tristen stood, watching him go. Then, in a slow movement, he turned back to the small alcove I was seated in. My blood was still screaming. I suddenly felt hot.

"Hot. I'm too hot," I said, and found myself pulling at the ties of my dress. I needed it off. Off my body. I yanked at one ribbon and it fell easily. I reached for the other—

"*Stop*," Tristen said, suddenly seated next to me on a floor cushion. His hands—his *trembling* hands—stopped mine from ripping the dress from my body. "You have to resist," he ground out, and it felt as much of a reminder for himself as it was for me.

"I'm so hot," I begged, and indeed my body felt so overheated. I didn't know what to do, feeling that ache and that heat threaten to consume me.

"Stay. Right. Here," he commanded. And then he was gone.

My hands went to the other strap of my dress, and I was unable to stop myself from pulling the silk bow loose, my dress starting to drip down my body. I leaned back, feeling the cool air starting to trail down my bodice as it slipped lower—

"*Gods*, Saffron," Tristen said, and he was suddenly beside me once more. He set a cup down at a low table beside us, and then turned to pull my dress back up, his deft fingers retying the twin bows that kept the dress on my body.

But the heat threatened to end me, and I kicked my legs out of the suffocating layers of my dress, the slit of the fabric allowing my bare flesh to slide free.

Tristen caught one of my legs, frozen as he spotted the dagger strapped to my thigh with the belt I had found earlier.

"You brought a weapon to an orgy? Naughty girl..." he said, his wicked eyes gleaming as his fingertips gripped my leg, keeping me from kicking my way completely free of the fabric on my body.

"I didn't know—*oh*," I said. Tristen had reached into the metal cup and taken out an ice cube that he was now running up my thigh, so slowly.

"You didn't know *what*, exactly?" he asked, dragging that frozen cube of water up my inner thigh. "What you were getting yourself into?"

The cool ice cube threatened to end me, right then and there. I struggled to focus, but as he began drawing lazy circles with the ice cube on my hot flesh, I felt the cool liquid begin to creep back—back to my core underneath the lacy underwear I had been given to wear.

"Tristen," I begged, his name coming out more of a desperate plea than I intended.

"Feeling cooler yet, princess?" he said, watching my hips arc up slightly as my fingertips clawed at the pillows.

"No," I said, reaching out my other leg to kick him—but he caught that one, too.

"Oh, really? Then I'll have to do this one as well." He reached for another ice cube, starting at my ankle. Then, he started sliding the ice cube up... and up. I leaned back against the wall behind me in the alcove as that frozen sensation crept up over my bent knee... the cool water dripping down, down between the apex of my thighs.

"You're wicked," I gasped out, breathless.

He watched me, his eyes playful... but something darker was twisting underneath. A hunger that was leashed, but still bit at its chains to be free.

"I'm trying to make sure you survive," he said. "But I still haven't heard a 'thank you' from you after saving your life so often. Or do I have to settle for you begging me to keep going?"

He crested what was left of the ice cube further up my inner thigh, and I could barely keep from squirming underneath his touch, a low moan leaving my lips. The ache was growing to a full roar, and I reached for him—

—but he simply took both of my hands and pinned them on the low table beside us in the alcove.

"No touching. And not because I don't want you to have a sip of my powers. But because you need to stay focused," he said, his voice low and taut like a bowstring, and I could tell he was struggling to stay focused, too. Around us, the room was growing more frenzied, the priestesses encouraging the rest of the prisoners to participate. To get lost in the bodies around them.

"Focus is so overrated, don't you think?" a sultry voice asked.

I whirled, watching as Cassandra slipped into the alcove beside us. She was Tristen's shadow tonight, it seemed—and I hated it.

Cassandra sat next to me this time, and her floral perfume overtook my senses as she turned to me.

"Such a pretty thing you are, Saffron," she said, running the back of her nails lightly up one of my arms, and the fog fell more heavily over me as her perfume and her touch sent waves through me. "Why don't the three of us play together?"

But Tristen hooked an arm around my waist. In one gentle tug, he pulled me out of arm's reach of Cassandra, bringing me slightly behind him.

"*No*," he said, his eyes blazing.

"Aren't you the picture of restraint, Tristen? Why are you no fun?"

I suddenly felt so tired, and I wound my arms around his neck, my head collapsing against his chest. He was so warm. So comfy. So *nice*. I sighed in contentment.

He wound an arm around my waist, keeping me tucked into him. "We have a trial to win, Cassandra. Go be with your *coven*."

Her eyes flickered with rage, and I lifted my head. I saw what Tristen saw, in that moment. Not a demure, pious woman worthy of a godly duty, but a Sorceress and head of a coven.

We were surrounded by *witches*.

The thought sent a bucket of cold water through me, and I sat up straight.

"Be careful, Tristen," Cassandra said, her eyes flashing. "You've seen what I'm capable of taking from you."

And then she was standing, striding away from us. I watched her go, my eyes wide as I saw this place for what it was. A honey trap.

"What?" Tristen asked, his voice rough as his eyes lingered on my lips.

"They're witches," I voiced. "And everyone here..."

"Is under their spell. The island wants to punish those who choose momentary pleasure over long-term gains." Tristen leaned in closer, his voice silky against my ear. "Not that there's anything wrong with pleasure. But timing is everything."

Suddenly, a chiming of a bell rang out. A priestess emerged from the lust-filled frenzy and stood by a set of huge stone doors at the far side of the hall.

"The Oracle is ready for Ewing Mathers now," she said. And waited, even as no one in the room seemed to be listening. "Ewing Mathers?" Again, she waited, and no one appeared. "Last call for Ewing Mathers. Show yourself for the trial or find yourself as a sacrifice for the Order of the Serafim."

He did not appear.

The priestess just nodded, and folded her hands. Moments later, a disheveled prisoner was dragged in front of her by two other priestesses, his pants falling off his body and his shirt missing. He was clawing at the females, clearly having just been interrupted.

The priestesses pulled him behind the gilded doors, and they shut behind them.

And then the screaming began.

27

I started to rise to my feet. I had to do something—

"Worry about your own fate—not anyone else's," Tristen said, pulling me back down to the floor cushions. "You'll need a clear head for her riddle."

I flickered my eyes over his body. The black silk he had been dressed in showed off his muscular form. The top few buttons of his shirt were left undone, hinting at the way his bronze skin glowed underneath.

I couldn't stop myself as my hands pressed his chest until he was leaning back against the wall of the alcove. I climbed on top of him, my body straddling his. I started to bring my hands to his face, wanting to tangle them in his dark hair once more...

...but Tristen took my hands and, with great effort, pinned them to my sides.

"Clear. Head. *Now*," Tristen said, but I felt him against me. I felt his arousal, long and hard against where my body brushed against his, and the surprise in my eyes must have alerted him to what I felt as I sat in his lap.

"*I* need a clear head?" I asked, a smile creeping on my lips as my traitorous hips ground down against him and he closed his eyes and let out a rumble of a groan.

With great concentration, he picked me up by my waist and placed me beside him, putting more space between us. "*Focus.*"

Another scream behind those closed doors shook me out of the clutches of the aphrodisiac.

"Gods," I whispered, fear slicing through me.

"Hold onto that," Tristen said, shaking his head as if he was trying to clear his own thinking. "But don't let your fear consume you. We're almost through the effects of it."

"Will you be able to use your mindweavying ability to get through this trial?" I asked, curious to hear if my hunch had been right—even if I hadn't been able to take his magic in time.

"No," he said.

"Is there anyone's abilities that could help me in here?" I asked, turning to scan the debauchery going on in the crowd as my head grew clearer and clearer by the minute.

Tristen took my chin in his fingers and turned his gaze back to him. "I don't want to see you trying to seduce anyone else in here."

I raised an eyebrow, looking at him with a knowing smile. "Trying? You seemed more than willing to acquiesce to my requests the other night," I said, my voice lowering as my mind was suddenly flooded with images of the other night.

Tristen glared. "Nice try, princess. But you'll need to do this yourself. The Oracle can block powers. Which is why you'll need to keep your wits about you in this trial. All of this," Tristen gestured at what was going on around us, "is just a distraction. To feed the well of sacrifices for the Order so their witches can use the unfortunate losers for their rituals and drain their life forces."

"The Oracle is ready for Rachelle Deveraux."

My blood turned to ice. *Rachelle.*

I whirled, scanning the writhing bodies for Rachelle. "Where is she?"

I sprung to my feet. Tristen followed as I scanned the long center table. But she wasn't there. I stalked over to an alcove, my mind suddenly clear. I pulled back the curtain that was closed to see a moaning priestess being taken by Ajax's shadow double. He turned and grinned up at me, and I closed the curtain with disgust, walking away.

"Where is she?" I muttered, Tristen still at my side.

We both turned as we heard Rachelle shout, racing around a corner to an antechamber just off the throne room...

...where Rachelle was howling in victory as she smashed her opponent's arm into a table. She was... *arm wrestling.*

I stared at her, and she stood, the man whose arm was across from her was cradling it in pain.

"You owe me three gold pieces," she said with a grin, then turned to me and Tristen. "Having fun?"

"I'm not the one arm wrestling," I said, surprised.

Rachelle sauntered over to us. "How else was I supposed to blow off this godsforsaken steam?"

"The Oracle's guard is calling your name. You need to go, now," I said, grabbing her and dragging her back to those gilded doors.

We stopped in front of the guard, who lowered her notebook, a tad disappointed that Rachelle had shown up after all.

"This way," she intoned, turning on her heel. Rachelle started to follow.

"Wait," I said, and swept up Rachelle in a hug. "Good luck."

"Mmm. You hug nice," she said, still a bit unsteady on her feet like I was. "You can get in line for an arm wrestle one of these days," she said with a wink, and then followed the Oracle's guard and the priestess down the long hallway beyond the gilded doors.

I stood and watched the double doors for a moment, fearing that I would hear Rachelle's screams all too soon. But as I waited... nothing sounded. I sighed, and then caught sight of Callum on the balcony.

"I'll be right back," I said to Tristen, and at his raised eyebrow—"I mean that. I'm more... clear now," I said, and it was true. The aphrodisiac had already begun to subside, but that didn't stop Tristen from standing preternaturally still as he watched me leave the throne room, heading out to the large, sunny veranda.

Callum was white-knuckling the railing of the balcony when I found him, the afternoon sun starting to fall toward the horizon.

"Should have known that all of this beauty was a trap," I said, a joking tone in my voice as I joined him at the railing.

He turned to me, his expression pained. "I'm sorry. I didn't mean to lose control like that. I didn't expect... I'm just sorry." He hung his head, and I stepped toward him, taking his hands.

"It's okay. I was feeling it, too."

He searched my eyes. "It wasn't just the wine, Saffron. I can barely hold myself back around you. I just want you. All of you." His voice came out low, and I could hear the male need in it. It caught me by surprise. I had known Callum had wanted me—but I still felt the guilt biting at me. For what I had experienced with Tristen. For how good he felt.

"I know," I said.

"Our time was cut so short when *he* took you from me. I can't bear to think I might lose you again."

"An island death match isn't the most promising of circumstances," I said with a smile, but the endless sorrow in his eyes cut my joke at its knees. "We'll find a way out. Both of us."

He tugged me close to him, wrapping me in a hug. Then he groaned, pulling away. "You smell too good, Saffron. I can't be close to you right now."

I felt my heart flutter, but before I could respond—

"The Oracle is ready for Saffron Vale," a voice floated outside.

"I have to go," I said.

"You've got this," Callum said, and I could see in his tensed shoulders that he was holding himself back from trying to whisk me away from whatever lay ahead of me.

I turned and breezed back through the open doorway, past the gauzy curtains.

Tristen was waiting, and he just locked eyes with me and nodded. "Keep it simple," he said.

"Do I ever?" I said, tossing him a slight smile over my shoulder as I turned to the Oracle's guard. They turned back to the double doors, leading me to whatever awaited me in the rest of the third trial.

28

I followed the Oracle's guard through a dark hallway, lit with an occasional blue-stained skylight above, casting the passageway in a deep sapphire color. The quiet threatened to crush me under the heaviness of it. It was so silent I almost felt as if I had lost my sense of hearing altogether like the attack in the clearing.

Then, the Oracle's guard stopped at a large metal door.

"May Illumia light your way," the guard said, and opened the door for me, gesturing that I enter. As I did, he closed the door behind me, shutting me into the cavernous room.

Unlike the other colorful rooms of the Temple of Orsi, this room was entirely dark, with one single flame burning atop a raised platform that was at the center of the room, surrounded on all sides by shallow stairs. The room itself was also framed by a dark reflecting pool, one that I could hear better than see in the dark. The walls and floors were painted a matte black, giving it the feel of being a silent black box.

Atop the raised platform were a pair of glowing red eyes.

"Approach, human," a female voice purred at me, the sheer immensity of her summons nearly shaking the room with how loud it was.

It took all my concentration to steady my shaking legs as I climbed the short flight of steps and reached the top of the platform. On top of that platform and next to that flickering torch was the Oracle.

She was a creature ripped from nightmares. A beautiful, feline sphinx with the head of a woman, and a feminine body that turned into lion-like paws. But it was her wings that were truly magnificent and horrendous all at once. They rested statue-still behind her, and as I stood before her, those glowing red eyes took me in.

"You did not give into your baser instincts, I see," she said.

I forced my voice to stay steady. "I had help."

"Ah, yes. I smell him on you." She prowled forward, and every cell in my body screamed at me to *run*. "What a *special* one he is. But you are special, too, are you not?"

"I don't know what you mean," I said. Did the Oracle answer directly to the King? If she knew about my powers, would she tell him that there was a chance that I could be the Siphon from the prophecy?

"Cool your raging thoughts, *girl*," she warned. "I can hear them in your heart and it is unbecoming of someone with your future to be so afraid."

"I am not afraid," I said.

"Little liar," she taunted, circling me. "I can smell your fear on you, too. So wipe it from your mind and let's begin. Solve my riddle and gain an answer to your most pressing question. Listen close, fearful one, as this is my riddle for you:

Through crystal seas and starlit skies,
I travel far yet never rise.
In stillness I show truth most clear,
Yet you'll find me in every tear.
When truth itself begins to fade,
I remain unchanged, yet unafraid.
What am I?"

I sucked in a breath, trying to sharpen my muddy mind. But I came up blank. The sphinx continued to circle me, and repeated the riddle again, slowly.

As panic started to rise up within me, I thought bitterly of how unfair this was. I, the only contestant without a memory, had to dredge up an answer to this creature's ancient riddle?

I felt the asphyxiating void of my mind vibrate as if in laughter, as if it, too, was enjoying my terror.

"If you don't answer, you become my lunch," the sphinx purred at me, circling closer. "The others left me feeling hungry, still."

Crystal seas... starlit skies... travel far...

I was going to die in this room.

My fists balled the fabric of my dress as my panic continued to beat my chest like a war drum. I whispered the words of the riddle to myself again and again and again—

Suddenly, claws shot out from the dark. I cried out at the impact, my side flaring in pain as the creature sliced through skin in one swipe.

I stumbled back a few steps to the edge of the raised platform, my hand gripping my side as those red eyes drilled into my soul.

"I grow weary of those who succumb to their terror. Your time is almost up, girl," the sphinx announced.

"I need more time," I gasped, feeling hot blood drip down the side of the claw marks that had pierced flesh through the sparkling bodice of my gown.

"Greedy, greedy—as your kind always is. You're not special enough to get what you did not earn. Tell me. WHAT IS YOUR ANSWER?" The booming voice shook the entirety of the temple, cracking some of the stone in the dark room.

"I don't know!" I yelled, unable to lie. Unable to stall.

The sphinx lunged at me again, but I rolled out of the way. It missed me—barely—but I hadn't seen the edge of the platform in the dark, and I went tumbling down the shallow stone steps and landed with a *thud* on the ground, a final roll putting me in the reflection pool that framed the square room. My entire body ached from the impact.

The cool water soaked my gown, and as I pushed myself up. In the flickering torchlight I could see the waters were not blue or clear...

...they were stained red with blood. And not just my blood, either.

I gasped, splashing furiously as I pushed myself to make a move out of the water, but the sphinx bounded for me, its wings outstretched like a god of death, and I was cornered in the pool of water as it slowly stilled around me, the sphinx stalking close.

"Time's up," she said, lifting that paw with those razor sharp claws.

I caught a glimpse of my reflection as the water in the reflecting pool stilled. The world slowed, and I saw the fear twist my face. Saw how it contorted my features. Saw how it consumed me. Saw how—

Reflection. *Wait*—

Tristen's words rang in my head. *Keep it simple.*

"REFLECTION!" I screamed, bringing my hands above my head to shield myself from the blow of the sphinx... a blow that did not come. "Reflection," I gasped again. "That's the answer to the riddle."

When there was no reply—and no killing blow—I lowered my hands. The sphinx seemed to sigh, its beady red eyes flashing at me in the darkness.

"Looks like you're getting somewhere, human. Join me on the platform to receive your answer."

As I hauled myself out of the bloody water and followed the sphinx back to the platform, water and blood dripped from me and onto the dark floor. Everything in my mind narrowed in on the real question I knew I needed answered.

The question that would begin my path to set myself free from the void.

The sphinx curled up at the foot of the flickering flame like a housecat in front of a hearth. "You passed your third trial. What do you wish to know? Ask carefully as you only get one question. I know much, but questions of the future are not set in stone, and are still to be written by the fates."

"I do not wish to know of my future," I said. "I wish to know of my past."

"Ask away, daughter of the sun and the moon."

I sucked in my breath, holding my tongue from asking about *that* title—trying to stay focused. "What happened to my memories?"

The sphinx grinned. A truly feline gesture. "You ask a question with an answer that will only bring you pain."

"Tell me," I said, keeping my head held high. I would know. I would find out what happened so that I could reverse the damage. So I could be reunited with all that I had lost. So I could stop the void from closing in on me.

The sphinx lowered her gaze to me, reveling in the words she spoke. "Your memory was erased by one of the rare few who have the ability to take them away. But you know this man, for he is here in the trials. Here, he goes by Tristen Greywood. The Shadowfire Assassin."

29

The handmaidens intercepted me as I left the Oracle's chamber through the opposite doors. I was shaking. Shaking with absolute, undiluted *rage*. They asked if I was all right, asked if they could get me anything as they led me back to my room. I said no and sent them away.

Then, I went to my balcony, slipped over the railing and onto the balcony next door, and easily pushed open the unlocked balcony door into *his* suite.

I turned one of the chairs to face the door, the sky darkening as evening descended.

I collapsed into the chair, still bloody.

And waited.

With every breath, my blood boiled.

The words rang in my head over and over again.

Your memory was erased.

Your memory was erased.

Your memory was erased.

The sphinx had given me the truth, and Callum had been right. Rachelle had been right.

Tristen had been, and would always be, my sworn enemy.

I forced my trembling hands to grip the arms of the chair I was sitting in. Forced myself to inhale, exhale. I had learned the truth about who Tristen was—and what he had done to me.

When the door handle clicked open, I was already standing with my dagger unsheathed—*Tristen's* dagger.

Tristen saw me and stilled. His silk suit was unwrinkled, unblemished. He took me in, his eyes wide at the blood and water that marred my dress.

"You're hurt—"

"You stole them!" I shouted, trembling. "You stole them from me and you pretended like I was your ally. Like I could trust you!"

"What did the Oracle tell you?"

"Give them back!" I said, creeping closer to him with my dagger held aloft. He let the door close behind him, but held his ground. "My memories. Give. Them. Back."

His eyes flashed with a kaleidescope of emotions. "I can't."

I pressed the knife to his throat, pushing him back against the closed door. "Give them *back*, Tristen."

"Kill me, if you wish. You'd make everyone's life a lot easier, maybe even yours. You'd have to continue without my aid, but... I know that you *think* Callum is helping you."

"Callum didn't take my memories," I said, drawing a line of blood from the skin at his neck.

"No, but he's taken much worse. One day you'll find out."

My resolve wavered at his calm. His stillness. My anger kept cresting on the shores of his quiet responses.

"Why did you take them?" I asked, trying to keep my voice from wavering.

"I can't tell you," he said. "But if I was put in the same position, I would do it again."

The words shot through me like fire. I lowered my blade, and then slapped him. He didn't react, just slowly turned his face back to me. "*There* are your claws. I was afraid they would never come out to play."

"Play?" I seethed. "That's what you think this is? Play time?"

Tristen's humor disappeared. He reached a hand out to me. "Saffron—"

I stepped back, disgusted by his touch. "You don't get to touch me anymore, Tristen. Callum was right. You've already ruined my life. Why did I think we could be different?" I laughed, the sound hollow.

"You thought about *us*?" Tristen asked, his wild eyes taking me in.

"There is no *us*," I said, shuddering as my reality continued to hit me in waves.

"You're bleeding," Tristen said, taking another step toward me. "You need a healer, let me help—"

"NO!" I shouted, and he flinched as if I'd hit him. "Stop pretending that you're helping me!"

"The Oracle didn't tell you everything—"

"I don't care. Get out of my way," I said, going to the door. I was unable to be here any longer, unable to see the devastation on his face.

Tristen hesitated, watching me. I was feeling weak, feeling like my feet were about to give out on me. But I couldn't do it here. Couldn't bear to let Tristen pretend to help me once more.

"Get. Out. Of. My. Way," I said, pointing the dagger at him.

A muscle feathered in his jaw, but he opened his door for me. With all of the energy I could muster, I walked out into the hallway and went to my room.

I slumped on my bed, not caring that I was still covered in blood, my torn dress looking something hideous on me as the moonlight streamed into the room.

I was ready to slip into darkness and let sleep take me when I saw it.

The Bluesteel Blade, glinting blue in the light of the moon, and leaning up against the door.

The same door I had just closed.

I sat up, staring at the blade. I hadn't seen it since it had sliced through my double in the second trial. And now it was here.

"What are you doing here?" I asked.

It merely shimmered in the moonlight, waiting. It didn't seem like it was in a speaking mood tonight.

I rose from the bed, striding toward it. I reached out a hand toward it—

—and grasped air.

It was gone, but there was a slight creaking noise as the door had been opened slightly.

What...?

I pushed open the door, looking out into the large hallway outside all of our rooms.

There, as if daring me to go after it, lay the Bluesteel Blade next to a marble sculpture of the goddess Orsi, holding a book in one hand and the blade in the other.

Frustrated, I walked down the hallway, going for the blade. After all, it could be useful should we have to journey back through The Foggy Forest once more.

But as I reached the statue, the blade disappeared. *Again.*

A small *clang* made me whip my head to where the blade had now appeared at the foot of a staircase leading up to a tower. I cast a glance around the cavernous hallways to make sure no one was around, and I continued to follow the blade.

Somehow, I knew that the blade had something to show me. Whatever magic it was imbued with, it had protected me in the battle against my double and deemed me worthy when I pulled it from the stone in the first trial. If it was leading me somewhere, I would follow.

I had reached a narrow hallway at the top of the tower when voices drifted from the other end. I ducked into one of the open door-ways, spotting the Bluesteel Blade leaning against a wall of tapestries depicting ancient battles. I darted across the open room, which was some sort of study, and slipped behind one of the tapestries. They were heavy and dark—perfect to keep me hidden, but still allowed me to see through the fluttering curtains pooling beside the tapestries, hanging from the cavernous ceiling of the large room.

No sooner had I hid behind the tapestry than the blade disap-peared and three pairs of footsteps funneled into the room.

From my vantage point behind the tapestry and next to the fluttering curtain, I could make out Cassandra holding a velvet bag that seemed stuffed with heavy objects. She dropped it down on the desk in front of her with a heavy *thump*, settling in the plush armchair behind the desk as two priestesses stood on the other side. One of them I recognized as Iris.

"Here's the report from Solhaven," Iris said, handing Cassandra a folded piece of parchment.

Cassandra broke the wax seal with a pop, and scanned what was etched within the letter. Then, she tossed it aside. "No progress. The plague continues to ravage our lands, with no end in sight. Do you two know what that means?"

Both women nodded, but Cassandra spoke as if they were merely ornamental in this conversation.

"It means that our work here remains more vital than ever. If we're to heal our people, we must continue to do the gods' bidding. If we don't, we doom the lives of everyone who resides in the Kingdom of Solhaven, leaving our once glorious lands ravaged forever by this terrible disease."

Cassandra wrenched back a flowing sleeve of her robes, and it took every ounce of my restraint to hold in a gasp. Her arm was covered in festering wounds, so numerous that her skin resembled a mottled cheetah print of sickness.

This must be the plague she was speaking of.

"Our work here will continue until a cure is found. Let us begin," Cassandra said, and leaned back in her chair.

As she did, the two priestesses kneeled on either side of her chair as Cassandra reached for the velvet bag and overturned it on the desk in front of her. Out spilled dozens of heart crystals—those magical sources of power I had only seen once in person when the man in Ashguard had killed himself before the first trial.

I had a sinking suspicion who those crystals had belonged to.

What happened next, however, turned my blood to ice in my veins.

Cassandra tilted her head back, but as she did so, she *unhinged her jaw*, her gaping maw something horrible and monstrous looking. The priestesses seemed mostly unfazed by this, and I only saw a slight tremble in their delicate fingers as they took the heart crystals and placed them in her mouth. They had placed nearly a dozen in her mouth before she closed her mouth and dry swallowed all of them.

This can't be real, I thought. But the nightmare continued, and I watched as the priestesses placed the last of the heart crystals on her tongue, and she swallowed them with one final gulp.

The priestesses rose, returning to the front of the desk as Cassandra's eyes flickered shut. A glow enveloped her, and her skin bubbled with magic as the welts were smoothed out and replaced by her supple, youthful skin once more. Even her face seemed to soften and become younger. She sighed as the glow subsided, a smile returning to her full lips.

"Anything else?"

"O-one last thing," Iris stumbled. "Lady Melisandre requests an audience. She's waiting at your mirror. It's about Tristen Greywood."

Cassandra stood. "I tire of her whining, and court business for that manner. It is time for me to retire for the evening."

The priestesses bowed, exiting the room, closing the wooden door behind them. Cassandra rose as well, and she seemed to vibrate with a different energy than she had before as the heart crystals she had consumed began to shift the very fibers of her being. She left the room, taking her cursed energy with her as the door closed once more.

I waited until all of their footsteps had disappeared until I dared enter the empty study. I paused by the desk, running my fingers over the velvet bag that had once held the kernels of power sacrificed by the prisoners who had lost their lives in this trial.

I shuddered and started toward the door when the mirror in the corner caught my gaze. It looked like any other mirror, but with gold wreaths gilding its frame. It stood a bit taller than I did, and was mounted on a golden stand. But as I faced it and took a step forward, I realized that it wasn't tossing back my reflection. Instead, something inky swirled in its depths.

I couldn't stop myself from reaching out with a hand and brushing its surface, which was oddly hot to the touch. I withdrew my hand quickly, but the swirling gave way to the image of a woman.

She was standing in a lush bedroom, and she was wearing a fine gown of sapphire and gold trim. Her dark brown hair glowed in the light of the candelabra, falling in thick curls to frame her heart-shaped face and amber eyes.

She quirked her head. "You're not Cassandra."

"I'm Saffron Vale," I said. "Who are you?"

She took me in, a flash of something crossing her face and then disappearing. A small smile crept across her lips. "I'm Lady Melisandre Greywood. Tristen's wife."

30

Tristen's *wife.*

I gaped at the woman in the mirror, taking in her sheer beauty and stately posture. Of course this would be Tristen's wife—someone with deadly poise and otherworldy beauty. But there was one more thing about her appearance that I noticed that I had glossed over before. She was wearing a delicate crown of golden leaves atop her head.

"You're a... Queen?" I asked, my mind racing. "Which would make Tristen..."

"The sole heir to the Stormgard throne, and the only one who can help us win this war," she said. "I called to ask Cassandra's favor, to see if there was anything she could do to ensure his victory. She may work for Luminaria, but I was hoping she'd see... reason. Do you work for her?"

"No," I said. "I'm a contestant in the trials. And Cassandra won't help you—trust me on that one."

Realization bloomed in her eyes. "I take it you've seen what Luminaria is capable of?"

"I have."

"So you know they must be stopped. At all costs."

"I'm still making up my own mind," I said, and it was true. How was I supposed to truly understand the politics of the revolution that Stormgard had undertaken to become its own kingdom when I had no memory of either side? I was only able to see what was unfolding in front of me and make my decisions based on what I believed was true.

"You have to let him win," Lady Melisandre said, her voice urgent. "Tristen left behind his people to join The Ash Trials. He's noble, but we will perish without him leading us to victory. His survival is paramount for Stormgard ensuring that Luminaria's reign of terror ends."

I shook my head, my anger simmering once more. "*Your husband* saw fit to rob me of all my memories. So as far as I'm concerned, he's not fit to lead—let alone ensure good conquers evil."

A cruel smirk curled across Lady Melisandre's blood-red lips. "If he did that to you, then you must have deserved it."

"I don't give a fuck what you think, Lady. Now excuse me while I go bury a dagger in your betrothed's back."

I turned on my heel and stormed out of the room, Lady Melisandre's peals of cold laughter following me as I snuck back down to my room.

By the time I had closed the door of my bedchambers behind me, I was breathing heavily and the wound in my side had reopened and was bleeding once more.

I collapsed on my bed, unable to rid myself of my tattered dress as exhaustion pulled me under.

There were more snakes lying in wait in these trials than I could have ever anticipated.

31

————

Dawn was just breaking when I woke. Outside my window, I could see the light blue rays of the morning sun. I started to sit up, and pain lanced through me. I hissed, and looked down to see bandages wrapped around my midsection.

A figure stirred by my bedside, and I saw Callum asleep on an uncomfortable looking chair. Dark circles were underneath his eyes, but he was otherwise unscathed. He had made it through the trial.

I struggled to sit up, feeling the bruises that I had gotten from landing on the hard stone yesterday. A whimper escaped my lips as I tried to breathe through the pain that had been masked by adrenaline yesterday.

"Saffron," Callum said, and he was awake, jumping to his feet and coming to me, his blond hair disheveled by sleep.

"We made it," I whispered. "We're still alive."

He pulled me into a hug, and I clenched my teeth at the pain from my bruises but held him back all the same. "We did," he said.

He released me, and his eyes scanned over my body. "I couldn't find you last night. I heard you were injured and I was running around trying to find you after I got out of the Oracle's chambers. You were gone when I first came to your room, so it took me time to get back here again and take care of your injuries. Where were you?"

"Couldn't sleep," I lied. "How did you make it through the trial?"

Callum shrugged. "I used my shield to hold out against the sphinx until I could think of the answer. But it was a hard one. I'm glad you made it."

"I almost didn't. What did you ask the sphinx?"

Callum's eyes darkened. "I wanted to know who was going to win the trials."

My hand shot out for his, my stomach churning. "Who? Who does?"

Callum grimaced. "She told me that the fates haven't decided yet. But that fate isn't on my side."

"Callum," I said, but he just gave me a sad smile.

"I knew I was taking a risk by entering these trials. If the fates have it out for me? Good. Because I'd rather have them wish me ill than turn their attention to you."

My heart cracked at that, and I reached a hand to caress Callum's face. "I will fight the fates for you," I swore.

He leaned down, capturing my lips in a kiss. He pulled back, tears shining on his face. "My wish since you were taken from me was to see you again. And I got that. Whatever the gods take for being able to hold you again is fine by me. I will pay my debts."

My breath hitched. *No.* I didn't want him to start talking like this. To accept defeat when we still had so long to go. "The Oracle told me something, too."

Callum's eyes widened. "What did she say?"

"You were right—about Tristen. He was never my ally. He was the one who stole my memories."

Callum rose to his feet, anger clouding his expression. "That bastard—kidnapping you wasn't enough? He had to take those from you, also? I'll kill him."

He looked serious enough to follow through on his threat, but I grabbed his hand, pulling him back down to sit on the bed by my side. "No, Callum. No more killing. I know who he really is. Now, we can focus on what really matters. Us getting out of here. *Together*."

Callum nodded, but the fury was still simmering in his gaze.

A knock sounded at the door and he tensed. I held my breath as Callum went to answer it—one of his daggers held behind his back—but as soon as he did, a flash of red hair bounded through the room and tackled me.

I let out a pained giggle as Rachelle hugged me, my bruises screaming.

"YOU'RE ALIVE!" Rachelle shrieked, squeezing me.

"Not... for... long..." I gasped out as she tightened her grip on me.

She pulled back, beaming. "I knew you'd make it, Saffy baby. Three trials down? Three more to go!" Rachelle punched her fist in the air in triumph.

I laughed at her pure joy. "You're not injured either? Is everyone just better at riddles than me?"

Rachelle tented her fingers, mock seriousness in her expression as she gazed at me. "I cheated."

"How?" Callum asked, joining us.

Rachelle flipped curls of her red hair over her shoulder. "I asked the Oracle for the question first, before the riddle."

"That's allowed?" I asked in awe.

Rachelle grinned. "It sure is. So I asked for the answer to the riddle as my one question."

"Brilliant," I said, impressed by her.

"Sorry I didn't think of it earlier," Rachelle said, seeing my bandages. "It dawned on me right as I entered the room. And, of course, they kept us from going back to talk to y'all while you were waiting to be called. I was going to try to use my shifting powers, but the sphinx had dampening magic, just like I'd been told."

Right, the sphinx had nullifying powers. My eyes shifted to Callum—how had he used *his* magic in the trial?—but there was yet another knock at the door and he went to answer it. He returned moments later with a heaping tray of breakfast, and my mouth watered at the smell of fluffy scrambled eggs and salty bacon.

Rachelle stayed in my room, picking pieces of bacon off my break-fast tray as I ate in bed. We talked about the upcoming trials, who had survived—and who hadn't. Only about fifteen prisoners were left. Callum disappeared and returned with freshly squeezed orange juice for all of us as we talked.

As I listened to Rachelle gossip about the priestesses, I thought that I should feel content. We had made it through the trial, and likely had a momentary reprieve until the next one.

So why did I feel so uneasy?

32

After breakfast, it was time to leave. I changed into a clean set of riding clothes, braiding my blonde hair into a plait that hung down my back. I took a small bag of leftover food with me, and headed out of my room to go and pack it in the saddlebags of Callum's horse.

I walked through the cavernous halls. Priestesses in blue robes drifted in-between the tall pillars, placing fresh flowers in vases or giggling in pairs as they passed by prisoners. They looked so pious, so innocent today—it was as if the previous trial and the... *distraction* they had become was all a far-off memory. Not to mention the horrific sight I had witnessed in Cassandra's study the previous night.

"You could stay here," a female voice said, and I turned.

The High Sorceress Cassandra Wraithborn leaned against a pillar, her arms crossed over her chest, and her shiny brown hair curled over her shoulders like a waterfall of maple syrup.

"I have no interest in that," I said.

One of Cassandra's eyebrows raised. "My priestesses learn how to harness their power here."

I turned to keep walking. "I have no interest in harnessing *that* kind of power."

Suddenly, Cassandra appeared in front of me in a blink, and I yelped, stepping back.

"Oh?" Cassandra breathed, taking a step toward me. I stepped back on reflex. "Is that because you have powers of your own the King doesn't know about?"

Dangerous. "I don't know what you're talking about," I said, trying to school my face into neutrality.

"Really?" Cassandra said, and she began circling me like a shark. "I find it hard to believe that you've made it through so many trials as a powerless *hollow.*"

"Believe whatever you want. I'll still win."

Cassandra threw back her head and laughed. "That's cute. You know, my offer still stands. You can stay here at my temple and the island will forget you're even supposed to be competing in the trials. Why should you fight in these nasty trials? Why not just train in whatever way you please here? I could use someone as... *unique* as you are."

She reached out to run her fingertips across my arm, but I recoiled from her touch.

"She said no," a cool voice of darkness said.

Cassandra's eyes narrowed and she stepped away from me as Tristen emerged from a shadow in the cavernous hallway. "You again," Cassandra said with a frown.

"Get away from her," Tristen said.

Cassandra looked toward me and smiled sweetly. "Can't wait to see how you survive the rest of the trials, Saffron." She turned and swept away, her ice blue robes whispering across the marble floor.

I let out a breath, relieved. I turned to thank Tristen—but the words froze on my tongue as my bitter rage crested once more.

"Glad to see you survived the night," Tristen said, his gaze dropping to the bandages peeking out from under my shirt.

"Is that really what you're concerned with, *Your Majesty*?"

Tristen's eyes hardened. "What are you talking about?"

"Oh, please. I'm tired of your lies. I know you're the heir to the Stormgard throne—not just some legendary assassin. I met your wife, Melisandre—turns out she was trying to cut a deal with Cassandra to help ensure your victory. But I was the one who answered her stupid call through the mirror, so I got the pleasure of her presence instead."

"You don't know the whole story," Tristen said, trying to contain some sort of bitter anger that coated his voice.

"Then are you going to enlighten me?"

"I can't. You know I can't."

I shoved him, and he stumbled backward a step. "I know you're a lying bastard who stole everything I held dear. I can't wait to see you die in these trials, and if you cross me again, it will be at my hand."

Something in Tristen's expression crumbled at my words, and even in my rage, I bit back an instinct to apologize. But he just bowed his head.

"Safe travels back to Ashguard," Tristen said, and he adjusted his dark riding cloak and walked out to the courtyard, leaving me alone in the hallway with my writhing thoughts.

~

THE PRIESTESSES HAD LINED up outside of the Temple of Orsi once more to bid us farewell, but this time their pious smiles looked much more sinister.

Callum helped me onto his white mare, and we led the pack of prisoners over the precarious drawbridge and back up the mountain toward The Foggy Forest.

"Don't get off the horse this time," Callum chided as our horse started to whinny at the encroaching fog.

"I won't," I said, a bit indignant. "Especially now that I know its tricks."

But I still felt Callum hug me tighter to him as that suffocating fog swept over us. I tried not to hold my breath, tried not to let the nothingness consume me.

As our horse clopped along the trail through the white void, I tried to find comfort in Callum's arms. But something was still nagging at me. I couldn't get Tristen's look of devastation out of my head when I had confronted him with what the Oracle had told me.

The Oracle didn't tell you everything.

Was I expecting Tristen to fill in the gaps when he was so tight-lipped about what he knew about my past?

I was brought back to the present as the whispering fog tried to call out to me. I pressed my hands over my ears, and Callum held me close as we got through the fog and reached the trail on the other side.

I sighed in relief as our horse descended into a flat forest clearing, dead grass around us and the fog at our backs. Ahead of us stretched a path that led into a forest without any additional fog. Maybe our journey would be uneventful after all.

The moment the thought echoed in my mind, there was a flash.

Our horse reared, whinnying as it came to a halt—

—in front of a flickering Ajax, who had appeared in front of us.

"Going somewhere?" he asked with a grin.

Callum threw up his shield around us, but Ajax raised his hand, and blasted us off the horse.

I cried as I hit the ground, my bruised body tumbling a few steps away from Callum.

"Are you sure you want to do this?" Callum asked Ajax, who suddenly blinked out of view—

—and then blinked back in front of us. But it wasn't just Ajax standing in front of us—it was him and *three copies of him.*

He was multiplying.

Ajax and his doubles all laughed in unison. Then, the Ajax at the center raised his sword—glowing a horrible red color.

"The Mirror Realm calls. It wants sacrifice for the lives you took," Ajax announced. "You took my subjects, and for that you will pay."

"We're not going back there," I said. "Your stupid Mirror Realm will have to deal with what happened."

Callum lowered his shield and unsheathed his own sword, settling in a fighting stance as he sized up the three copies of Ajax in front of him. "I'd be happy to introduce you to the underworld where you belong, though."

Then, without warning, Callum whirled out to strike a blow at one of Ajax's doubles. He got a clean swipe, and the double went screaming to its death—black blood draining from it as it collapsed to its knees and fell over.

"Bravo," Ajax said, clapping. He then nodded to his other copy. "Now you."

Again, Callum struck out with his sword, but this other double was faster. Swords clanged in the forest clearing, the warrior and Ajax's double parrying and thrusting so fast.

Callum blocked another blow and stepped backward, catching his breath as the double started circling him, Callum's eyes watching him, analyzing for weakness.

Ajax turned to me. "You think your hero is strong enough? Do you think he's worthy of fighting for your life?"

Callum roared and struck hard at Ajax's double—throwing him off guard and tossing him to the ground. With a fierce blow, Callum had Ajax's double pinned on the ground underneath his boot, and jammed his sword through his heart.

Callum yanked his sword out, still dripping that black blood. He turned his wild eyes to Ajax, who was cooly observing the warrior.

"You're next," Callum promised, death in his gaze.

But Ajax just smiled. A strange, toothy smile. "I admire your confidence, *Commander*. But it is misplaced, as you soon shall see."

Then the entire forest grew quiet. The birds stopped chirping. The wind froze.

Callum looked around, hearing the new quiet just as I did. He shifted his gaze back to Ajax, zeroing in on his target...

...until a crack in the woods beyond us had all of us turning...

...to see skinless humanoid creatures with mouths stitched closed emerging toward us. There were a dozen of them coming from the forest, and as they crept closer on halting, uneven steps, I saw that they had huge dark hollows where their eyes should be.

"What are those?" I asked, my mouth dry.

"Void Stalkers," Callum breathed, and his grim expression told me this wasn't good. "Stay out of the shadows, Saffron. They have to fully materialize to attack—and they disappear in direct sunlight."

I stepped out from the long-reaching shadows of the trees around us, but the sun was being threatened by clouds. The sunny patches of the dead meadow were few and far between.

"I see you know of my pets," Ajax said. "Let's get you better acquainted."

One of the Void Stalkers disappeared and reappeared right in front of Callum, in a shadow that had formed next to Ajax. The creature screamed—a horrible, high-pitch keening sound—and it ripped its stitches on its mouth free in a bloody gesture as it unhinged its jaw, as if going to swallow Callum whole. But he stepped backward, dropping low. Callum sliced the thing at its knees and it dropped. Callum wasted no time beheading it, and then immediately lunged toward Ajax—

—who disappeared and reappeared several steps away.

Ajax clicked his tongue. "Them first."

Suddenly, four Void Stalkers jumped in front of Callum, their keening wails so ear piercing as they swiped at him with their long claws at the end of their bony fingers.

I watched, helpless without much of a weapon. I had to do something. Had to come up with a way to help—

Then, out of The Foggy Forest, a black mare galloped out of the fog.

Tristen.

All of us turned—even the Void Stalkers froze as the Shadowfire Assassin dismounted, rage in his eyes. He shifted to me, seeing that I was safely separated from the fray, and then turned to Ajax.

"No more of this," Tristen said with a cold fury. With a flick of his hand, Tristen unleashed his power.

It hit me in that moment as lightning and shadows fell from the sky, striking all of the Void Stalkers and reducing them to piles of ash.

I had not known The Shadowfire Assassin and his true power. Not like this. Even as more Void Stalkers came sprinting out of the forest edges, Tristen kept a look of icy fury on his gaze as a mere shrug of his power struck them dead. Again and again—as waves of the undead rushed at us, Tristen reduced them to *nothing*.

The power rippling off him was so intense, it sent me to my knees.

Tristen was all darkness and shadows, his obsidian eyes glowing as he approached Ajax. "We're done here," Tristen said.

But Ajax just smiled. "Are we?"

And then Ajax multiplied again, flexing that power from the dimension of the second trial with such ease. But he didn't just replicate himself two or three times—but a *hundred* times.

Callum brought up another shield around he and I as the clearing was suddenly flooded with Ajax's replicates.

Tristen wielded his shadowfire now, sending blasts of fireballs through dozens of Ajax's replicates at once, cutting down rows of them where they stood.

But Ajax kept replicating them, flooding Tristen in a sea of the doubles.

Tristen's power looked endless—so much so that the ripples of it left me breathless, even as I was protected from the blasts of the fight within Callum's shield.

However, there was something different about Tristen now. As he fought the endless stream of Ajax's army, I saw that his body was beginning to darken. His shadows were not only lashing out at Ajax, they were crawling up his own body, obscuring his limbs in darkness.

Magic has a cost.

And Tristen was using so, so much of it. Ajax was laughing, enjoying this. Enjoying wearing Tristen down even as Tristen dug deeper into his well of power.

I couldn't stand by to see what the cost was of using this much power. Even though Tristen was my sworn enemy, he was once again in this clearing, fighting for me.

That was enough to shock me out of my trance and I started moving. I darted away from the grasping hands of the Void Stalkers, bobbing and weaving through the chaos as I locked eyes on the sole

Ajax I cared about. The original double who had crossed over instead of the real Ajax during that second trial.

He whirled, realized I was sprinting for him, but he was too late.

I flung my hands out for him, snatching his bare neck and heaving him backward. He fell on me, his doubles running to me now, a blast of shadowfire keeping them and their blades at bay. Ajax struggled as I tightened my hands around his neck.

But I wasn't trying to kill him. I was trying to disable him, and with my hands on his bare skin...

...I reached within that loop of his power, and hooked mine around it. And *pulled.*

I gasped as his dark magic flooded into me, my skin crawling and burning with the sensation. I needed more—his replicas were still in this clearing.

I pulled again, and screamed at the feeling of the burning underneath my skin. It was like lava erupting, his dark power threatening to burn me from the inside.

"Let go!" a male voice called—from so far away—but I couldn't. I couldn't see anything but blackness. My body was eating itself from the inside, the smell of the power so putrid I felt my physical body roll to the side and vomit.

"LET GO, SAFFRON!" Tristen's voice roared.

And I did. My physical body dropped my hands from Ajax's neck, and my vision came flooding back as I rolled out from underneath him.

The clearing was empty.

I had done it. I had drained Ajax's powers, nullifying him.

But his power was now trapped within me, and it was fighting to get loose. My breathing was too erratic, my heartbeat struggling to hold the sheer weight of that terrible power.

I felt Tristen's hands grip my shoulders. "You have to let it out. *Now.*"

A strangled scream left me. I was going to die. I had absorbed all of his power, and it would destroy me from the inside.

"*Now,*" Tristen growled out, low and commanding.

I lifted my eyes to him, his dark obsidian eyes commanding me to *do it.*

So I did. And suddenly, the clearing was dotted with... *me.* But not me. *Versions* of me. Half-wild, bloody, beaten versions of me.

They all stood, silent. As if waiting for orders. I gave them none.

Tristen looked up at them. "Finally, magic put to good use," he remarked, and I could hear the relief in his voice.

I exhaled, and all of my doubles disappeared.

"You made it," Tristen said, and he helped me to my feet as I stood on unsteady legs.

"Let go of her," Callum said, advancing toward us. I was too weak to do anything as Callum hauled me away from Tristen, pulling me into his arms instead. "Stay away from us."

Tristen went still. "Haven't you been keeping track, Callum? Of how often *I* have saved her when you could not?"

"It was Saffron who saved *you*," Callum shot back.

Tristen grinned, but his smile was warm. Proud. "She did."

I slumped in Callum's arms, unable to hold myself up any longer. I felt myself nearing complete burnout, blackness creeping in on the edges of my vision, when a rumbling shook the ground.

Tunnels barreled through the ground, opening up vertically as people started emerging from them as if the island itself had granted them passage and parted the soil for them. Not just any people—King West, his court, the royal guards, and Cassandra herself.

By now, the other prisoners had just started emerging from the fog behind us, converging on the meadow and coming to a stop as King West and his court arrived.

Ajax, his face pale, started to sit up.

I had drained him, but we were both alive. A slow grin spread across his face, and Callum pieced it together just as I had.

Ajax had seen me. Seen what I could do, in an undeniable form.

Callum ran at Ajax with his sword, but Tristen had already speared out his power, sending a blaze of his shadowfire directly at Ajax—

—freezing him where he stood, and crumbling him to ash in front of our eyes.

King West looked down at the pile of dust where Ajax had just been standing. I let a small sigh of relief leave my lungs—my secret was safe.

"Pity. It feels like that particular contestant might have seen something rather... interesting. Would anyone else like to enlighten us about what may have occurred here?" King West said.

A young boy walked out from one of the trees beside us. I recognized him from earlier in the trials—Issac. He was still alive? He was easily the youngest prisoner here.

Had he been watching us fight this whole time?

If he had, he had seen *everything*.

Callum took a step toward Issac, and I saw the intent to kill in his face, even as he seemed conflicted. Was Callum really going to kill the boy?

"No," I said, grabbing Callum's arm. "We can't cross that line."

"He saw," Callum cautioned, but I shook my head.

"He's just a boy."

Tristen was watching Issac as he stepped to the King.

"Careful now," Tristen warned. Issac's wide eyes swung to Tristen and then back to the King like a pendulum.

"I was waiting here like you told me to, Cassandra," Issac said, and my heart sunk.

This wasn't some random attack.

This was a trap. And I had just waltzed into it.

Cassandra smiled at the boy. "What did you see?"

Then, Issac slowly turned to me, and raised a shaking finger.

"It's her. She's the Siphon."

33

There was a moment of silence as Issac's confirmation rang through the meadow.

She's the Siphon.

He had said it just as I knew it to be true. Whether I liked it or not, I was not some maiden or baker's daughter. I was not a hollow.

I was the subject of a prophecy. A powerful being who could steal magic with just a touch.

And the moment that Issac confirmed it, King West looked at me with greed in his eyes. I was no longer a human, but instead a pile of gold in his eyes. Something to be *owned*.

"Take her," King West said with a smile that made me shiver.

Guards ran forward, but Callum's shield shot out around me, and the guards bounced back.

"Planning on joining the revolution, Commander Wells?" King West asked. "Because if you decide to fully cement yourself as a traitor to Luminaria, that's the only group that will have you."

Callum hesitated, taking in the King's armed guards who had also emerged from the tunnels, calculating his odds... and then lowered his shield.

But Tristen was already stalking forward, placing himself in between Callum and I and the King's men. "Are you interfering with the trials?"

King West strolled forward. "Hardly. I'm just picking my favored. And you know what? Since I lost my last mindweavyr, I'll take *you*, too."

Favored. The world struck me and I clung to Callum. "Don't let him take me," I begged.

But King West was already motioning to Callum. "Bring her here, Commander. And all will be well once you finish these trials."

It was a not-so-veiled threat. Callum would cooperate or face the consequences.

Slowly, Callum started walking me forward.

I looked up at him in sheer terror. "Callum—"

"Just keep your head down. Follow what the King tells you to do," Callum said.

Betrayal stung in my eyes, but... what else could we do? We were surrounded by the King's guards, who would be ready to strike us should we step out of line.

Tristen turned, stepping in our way.

"Move," Callum said, his voice cold.

"You think this ends well?" Tristen asked. "You think by not taking a stand now things will get *easier*?"

"*Move*," Callum repeated.

Tristen shifted his gaze to me. The edges of him still looked like they were darkened by shadows. As if all of that use of his power had started to eat away at him.

Even with our history, I couldn't let him burn himself out for me if that's what he was willing to do.

"Don't," I whispered, the words hard to get out. Tristen's eyes hardened, but he just dipped his head in a single nod.

We turned to the King's men, and the guards rushed over with our iron bands outstretched. One of them clamped the bands on me so roughly I cried out, but they ignored me, ripping me from Callum's arms as he watched on. The guards hauled me in front of the King. I tried to stand, but I fell onto my knees, unable to hold myself up any longer.

The guards had gotten Tristen's iron bands on as well—I knew from the stunning loss of that rippling sensation of him in the air—and threw him down on the ground beside me. He stayed on his knees beside me, keeping his head held high.

"The gods have smiled down upon us," King West said as he looked at the two of us with a demure smile.

Tristen bared his teeth like a wild animal at the King.

"Take these two back to the palace," King West said with a wave of his hand, and the guards were pulling us up, dragging us to those earthen tunnels that smelled of soil and sparked with magic.

We were dragged into the depths of the island, and walked in the dark for what felt like minutes. Then, as if the island had dragged us through the dirt faster than our feet could carry us, a light emerged at the end of the tunnel.

The guards pulled us to the light, and we were standing in front of the Saltspire Palace once more.

Our new prison.

PART III

THE FAVORED

34

I was dragged to a windowless room gilded in gold. The four poster bed was covered in nearly a dozen gold-trimmed throw pillows. The sitting area had a golden table etched with intricate designs and gold leaves. Even the plush carpets that blanketed the floor across from the roaring hearth had golden tassels. I was told to bathe in an adjoining chamber, and when I returned to the bedchamber, a slight handmaiden dressed in ice blue entered.

"It's time to get dressed," the female said, and I remembered her from the Temple of Orsi. "King West wishes for you to join him for lunch," the handmaiden continued, and held up a silk dress she had draped over her arm.

My eyes flickered up to her. "Don't you work for Cassandra?"

"I am just a steward on this island, although Cassandra did bring me here to assist you," the handmaiden said, and curtseyed. "My name is Leah."

"Nice to see you again, Leah," I said, careful. Despite her quiet presentation, she was probably privy to many secrets. Or—she might be looking for mine.

I rose, and she handed me the dress and some underthings, and I slipped them on. The dress was a pale pink color with a tight bodice and white capped sleeves that fell off my shoulders, bringing attention to my cleavage. Not something a warrior would wear, but something a King's *favored* might.

The word rippled through me as Leah had me sit in front of a mirror as she combed my blonde hair into an elegant updo. Not only would I have to find a way to win The Ash Trials, I'd have to find a way to escape its "prize."

Again, that fear wound around me like a vice, its jaws threatening to steal the breath from my lungs. It made me want to curl up in this prison of a room and never leave.

"How long have you worked with Cassandra?" I asked, taking in Leah's appearance. She had pale blue eyes and dark hair that looked almost reddish in the light, but I couldn't be sure. She had a small frame, and seemed to be almost swimming in her long servant's dress.

"Too long," she confessed, her eyes flickering up to me. "You know Rachelle, do you not? I saw you helped her in the last trial."

"I did. She's my friend."

"I'm grateful my younger sister has someone she can trust in these trials," Leah said.

My eyes widened. The similarities... "Your hair is dyed."

"It is," Leah said. "I joined the palace staff when I found out what Rachelle had done. My aim was to help her the best I could—but it seems like you've done much for my sister so far."

"She's helped me, too," I said. "What was your life like... before all this?"

Leah gave me a sad smile. "A question for another time, I'm afraid. It's time for us to make our leave," Leah said, holding open the door for me.

I blinked, not realizing she had finished. In the mirror, a pretty version of me blinked back. She had added some color to my cheeks, a coral stain to my lips, and some light shimmer to bring out my bright blue eyes. I looked like a princess, but I needed to act like a warrior.

I rose, following Leah as I stepped out into the hallway—past the guards who stood by my door. I eyed them and their swords.

She led me down a series of hallways that opened up to the larger main stairwell. The morning light crept through the salt blocks the palace was made of with that gorgeous color, as if heating it with a molten pink and orange glow. The railings and stairs were all capped by gold, which glinted in the light. It would be stunning if it weren't yet another prison. It might have well just been a beautific Ashguard, because it would serve the same purpose of trying to suffocate me.

Leah stopped by a towering set of doors. With effort, she pried one open and ushered me in. I stepped inside—or, rather, I stepped *outside*.

The doors led to a gorgeous patio that was on one of the higher levels of the palace. Vines and greenery dripped over the space, framing the view of the ocean beyond the pillars. A salty breeze wafted into the patio. In the center of the patio was a large slab of marble that made up a narrow table with more of those floor pillows. King West sat at the center.

When he saw me, he motioned me to sit at a spot beside him. He was wearing an unbuttoned tunic and no crown, as if he were going for an understated appearance. But his hair was still combed in careful waves, and he still wore rings of what I assumed were family crests as well as the insignia of Luminaria.

"Sit," he said, and I realized I had still been standing and staring.

I made my way around the table to join him, scanning the others at the table who were waiting by untouched baskets of bread, sandwiches, carafes of juice and wine, and still-steaming plates of meat. It was all men at the table, warriors and dignitaries by the looks of them. All men except for one—a woman wearing white robes, who sat across from the King. She had grey eyes and smooth dark skin that glowed in the afternoon light, and I remembered her curious gaze from the ball. Who was she?

But at the end of the table, furthest from the King, sat Tristen. He was dressed in another dark black shirt and pants, his dark hair unruffled, his obsidian eyes staring me down. He was all intensity, and the courtiers and generals who sat next to him seemed to inch away from him, not wanting to be close to the legendary Assassin. I *almost* smiled, had I not recently declared him my new target. Tristen could not and would not be tamed. So why did the King have him here?

I sat next to the King, smoothing my skirts as I arranged myself on a floor pillow beside him.

"Eat," King West said to his court, and they began digging into the food before them. Everyone except Tristen, who watched the King and I with that stony focus. "You must be hungry after this morning."

I nodded, reaching for a bread roll, and then started piling my plate full of what was on the table. Whatever was coming, I needed my energy. "Your palace is quite beautiful."

"That's very kind. You know, I wasn't surprised when my spies sent word to me that you had wielded the Assassin's shadowfire in the forest on the way to the third trial."

Ajax's double must have been spying for the King—which is why Cassandra had interrogated me before I had left the temple after the third trial. I tensed, but tried to keep my movements smooth as I filled my cup with a sweet-smelling juice. "That makes one of us. I barely knew what I was doing," I said mildly.

"That's hard to believe," King West said, studying me.

I turned a smile up at him, trying to channel what I imagined a dumb, vapid woman would look like. "What even *is* a Siphon?"

King West's eyebrow rose. "You don't know?"

I shrugged, eating some of the bread roll and taking a sip of juice before responding. "There's so much I don't know."

I felt a hand running up my arm, and I stiffened mid-sip. King West leaned in, and every instinct in me wanted to run. "I find it hard to believe you didn't run at Ajax without a single weapon just to *put your hands on him* if you didn't know what you were capable of."

I set down my glass, trying not to choke on it. "It was instinct. I barely understand what it is I can do."

The King studied me. Then, he leaned back, and I tried not to let my relief be so evident. "That's why I've brought you here. Each year,

The Ash Trials grants me a choice of picking favored contestants. You can stay here, eat my food, and receive special training and privileges. It is the way that the gods allow me to exert my influence on the outcome. And this year, I've picked you. If you are what I think you are, you have the potential to destroy Stormgard and reunite our fractured kingdoms. Your power is quite intriguing, but it needs to be honed. That's why I've brought *him* here."

The entire room turned to Tristen, who was sitting stone still in front of an empty plate, his eyes still narrowed on the King. He hadn't moved a muscle since I had seen him last, that unnatural stillness reminiscent of a predator stalking its prey. He didn't say a word, something simmering underneath his outer calm.

The King continued, "The Shadowfire Assassin proved his reputation of being one of the most powerful beings in these trials. You will train with him and he will teach you how to wield your power so you can win the trials and end the rebels once and for all."

"Why him?" I asked, my mouth dry. "Callum could—"

"No," the King said, his voice sharp. Then, his gaze slid back to Tristen, a cruel smirk on his lips. "I want him to arm the weapon that destroys his peoples' cause."

The words hit me like a gut punch.

King West was fighting a war. And he would use Tristen and I like pawns on his chessboard.

And there was nothing I could do about it.

35

After a tense lunch, Leah allowed me time to stroll the gardens. I wandered the rows of rosebushes, surprised that the plants hadn't tried to kill me yet here. Maybe they sensed I wasn't trying to escape.

"They will write ballads about you one day, you know," a quiet female voice said.

I turned, and saw the same woman who had been sitting across from me in long white linen robes. Underneath, she wore a flowing linen shirt and pants, with delicate diamonds around her neck. At her chest, she held a pad of parchment paper and a quill.

"I'm Zara Hassan, a traveling scribe," she said, holding out an ink-stained hand.

"Saffron Vale," I said, taking her hand and shaking it. "Dead woman walking."

Zara shook her head. "I've covered The Ash Trials every year and I've never seen a prisoner perform quite like you."

Perform. Ah, so she was just like the other royals who watched the trials like a sport. "I'm glad my *performance* is to your liking, then."

I turned to walk away, but Zara kept pace with me. "I didn't mean it like that. Forgive me, I hail from Frostcrown and I am the only one from my kingdom to attend the trials. Our court is small and often burdened with the weight of our endless winter."

"What do you want from me?" I said, turning on her. I had no patience for court politics—I was exhausted and trying to piece through so much that had happened. Small talk was not in the cards for today.

"I want you to know that you can talk to me if you need anything," Zara said, something strange in her tone. "The King expects me to talk to you so I can write my account of his favored. And I have access to things you may not be able to get to should you need them. I would hate for you to lack something essential for your continued survival."

"You're offering to... help me?"

Zara smiled from underneath her hood. "It is not in Frostcrown's best interest for Luminaria to do everything as it pleases. It feels like you're aligned with us in that way."

Ah, so she was a scribe with an agenda. "Understood. And where can I find you should I need your assistance?"

"You can find me in the East Wing or its library. Good luck with training, Saffron."

Then Zara was floating away as if being carried by a breeze, and I was alone in the gardens once more.

I was starting to amass more allies, and I had a feeling I'd need all of the help I could get.

~

"ABSOLUTELY NOT."

Leah stared me down. She had dressed me in fitted fighting leathers that were flexible enough for me to move in, but had built-in leather armor to give me protection against a wayward blade. I found pockets to hide daggers—but no daggers.

"I will not be in the same room as Tristen without being armed to the teeth," I said. "I plan on killing him if he so much as thinks about betraying me once more."

Leah's scathing look deepened. "No weapons for you. You will only be able to practice with your magic in the warded training room on the roof," she said. "We go there now."

"And if I refuse?"

"I assure you, it will not be you who suffers."

I sighed. "Did a sense of humor skip over you?"

Leah pursed her lips. "Rachelle's humor was born from great trauma."

I bit my lip, remembering Rachelle's past. "I'm sorry, I didn't mean it like that."

Leah waved her hand. "Rachelle left our home far before I did. She knew what dangers awaited her. Now come, we will be late for your training session."

I considered putting up a greater fight, but didn't want to give Leah more trouble.

She led me up through twisting, narrow stairwells until we were on the top floor of the palace, nearly as high as the spires that stretched even further above us.

I stepped out onto the outdoor training ring perched on the roof of one of the towers. It had a soft moss-covered patch of earth that formed a circular sparring ring, similar to the one in Ashguard, but clearly manmade instead of born from the forest. As I stepped onto the ring, my iron bands unclipped and fell to the ground.

I looked around in surprise, but as the wind tossed my braided blonde hair, I saw that Leah had already disappeared back down the stone stairwell.

If I had my magic back, could I...

I started to walk off the sparring ring, but I *bounced* off of some sort of invisible wall. I stared at it, confused...

"It's warded. The spell will disarm your irons, but won't let you storm off and conduct a killing spree. As gratifying as that would be," that male voice said from behind me.

I whirled, and saw Tristen entering the ring from the other side, his irons dropping the moment he passed through the boundary. He kicked them to the side and faced me. "Are you ready, princess?"

I took in a breath, feeling my fury rise—and then bank, slightly. Despite my renewed hatred for him, I couldn't help but notice how he looked—how he held himself. As the wind tossed his black hair, the morning sun bathed his body in golden light. He was wearing tight-fitting fighting leathers, too, and they emphasized his lithe strength, his strong arms bare. His power rippled over me, as if caressing me. It took my breath away, and I was distracted, until—

—Tristen tossed a lazy bolt of shadowfire at me. I dodged—barely—and glared at him. "What was that for?"

"Can't have you *distracted*," he said with a playful smirk. He had known I had been admiring him.

I glared. "I don't want to be trained by you. You stole my memories, my past, everything I was—and I wasn't even granted the privilege of weapons to put you in the ground myself."

Tristen cocked his head. "Then use that."

"Use what?"

"You hate me, so use that. Kill me right here, right now with your bare hands."

I did want to kill him for what he'd done. And if he was going to let me? I'd steal his last breath. My anger boiled, and I lunged at him. He dodged my punch, but I dropped down to sweep his legs. He was already a step ahead of me, sidestepping my attack. I jumped to my feet once more, trying to land a punch.

"That's it. Get in touch with your anger. *Use it*," he said.

He didn't have to tell me twice. I felt the depths of the emptiness of my mind. That suffocating void that was in place of where my memories once were. He was the one who had taken my memories of my childhood, of my parents, of my love story with Callum—

I spun and elbowed Tristen in the jaw, and he stumbled back.

Stunned, I watched him touch the tender spot I had just bruised. I expected him to be angry, to maybe fight back... but he just looked at me with a wide grin. "Yes. You've been training during these trials, I see."

"With Rachelle," I said, panting from the effort.

"Rachelle's good. I'm better. Now, let's do some drills."

It felt good to move my body. I liked the rhythm of the drills that Tristen put me through, honing my combinations of jabs, punches, and kicks. I lost myself in the flow of it, so much so that the constant fear that flooded my mind started to ebb, and I found some kind of... peace. I hadn't realized that the sun was creeping into the sky until we took a break and Tristen tossed me a waterskin.

"Drink," he commanded.

I sat down on the edge of the training ring and drank the cool water he had brought me. My muscles felt thoroughly worked. "I thought we were supposed to be practicing magic."

"That comes next. But magic *is* physical. You still channel it through your body, so if you're not in control of yourself, you can't possibly control your magic."

Tristen took a long swig of his water and tossed it to the side. Then, he started undoing the laces and buckles of the fighting leathers that covered his chest. He tossed the armor to the side, standing bare-chested before me.

"What are you doing?" I managed to get out, my mouth suddenly dry. Tristen was, without a doubt, the most handsome man I had ever seen—even if I resented what his beauty did to my traitorous mind and body. He was built like a warrior, but he moved with a feline grace that felt elegant. But here, shirtless in front of me, his rippling muscles bathed in that warm glow of the sun, he looked like a god— thoughts that I needed to fight. I couldn't keep letting myself indulge in admiring him.

He caught my gaze, and seemed to pick up on the conflict warring there. "Don't let your boyfriend catch you looking at me like that."

I got to my feet, glaring daggers at him. "He's not my boyfriend," I said, but as soon as the words left my mouth, I froze. *What were we, then?*

Tristen's eyebrow rose. "That would make sense. He treats you like something to be controlled rather than an equal."

Oof. The words struck a chord I wasn't willing to hear. "Let's train," I ground out, stalking to the center of the ring.

Tristen took one look at my leather breastplate. "Off," he demanded.

I frowned. "Is practicing magic an innuendo I'm not aware of in this world?"

"You've proven you love listening to no one and just getting yourself and everyone around you into trouble. So how about you just let me train you for once?"

Tristen reached for me, but I backed away. "I think I'll hang onto my clothes."

Tristen growled in frustration. "Do you want to kill me or not, Saffron?"

"Of course I want to fucking kill you!" I screamed. "How many times do I have to remind you what you took from me? How many times do I have to bare my brokenness to try and remind you what a horrible monster you are? I hope you and Melisandre are happy together when I send you back to her in a coffin."

Tristen's expression went stone cold, but he just nodded once. "To do that, you'll need to take off your leathers. You'll need to bare more skin so you can use it as a conduit and see how much you can take from me and wield effectively. Now, can I help you unbuckle these so you can send me to that early grave you're so fond of reminding me of?"

His quiet voice nearly cut me at my knees, and I just nodded, unable to hold the jumble of hate and frustration and other strange emotions that always bubbled up at his nearness.

His hands slipped to the laces on the back of my leathers, expertly undoing them and unbuckling the leather buckles with strong hands that brushed against my bare skin. He circled me, removing the last buckle with a strong pull that brought my back against his bare chest, leaving me standing in front of him in just a strip of fabric that bound my breasts and my leather pants. His skin was so warm, and I could smell the spice of him. It was heady, being so close to him, feeling his bare skin on mine...

He tossed my leathers to the ground, and then pivoted me to face him.

"Now. Take my magic."

I stumbled a little, shaken from how close we were. He grabbed my hands, keeping them placed on his bare chest. "Take it from me."

I tried to concentrate on the currents running underneath his skin, the way his magic reverberated through his blood. But his chest burned underneath my hands, and I felt my heart skip at our closeness.

What was wrong with me?

"This century, please," Tristen said.

I squeezed my eyes shut, concentrating. I tried to find those loops of his power. Tried to focus on them... and then I found them, hooking my magic around them... and started to pull. I took a step closer to him, placing my forehead on his chest. I pulled more magic from him, feeling it fill me...

Then, Tristen pulled my hands off him, backing up. I immediately felt the loss of his body, his power, his magic as he put distance between us.

I looked up at him, wide-eyed, but he was serious, focused. "Now use it."

I felt his power underneath my skin, felt it coursing through my veins. I willed it to my hands, feeling my palms grow cold with shadowfire... and then it just sputtered out. I felt the *whoosh* of his power flow through me, and I stumbled back, hitting the barrier as my body went boneless under the strain.

"I can't," I whispered.

Tristen walked over to me. "I saw sparks. But you didn't control it. You let it go before you could channel it."

"It just... slipped away," I said.

Tristen shook his head. "You have to be able to control it at will. That's the only way you'll be able to fight back against the King. Because even if you do succeed in killing me and winning this thing, you'll have to see to his demise, too. Or else you'll just be his prize at the end of all this. Do you want that?"

"Of course not!"

"Then fight! Absorb my power and throw it back at me."

I put my hands on his bare chest again, but it was as if the hooks of my power were blunt. I was so exhausted after everything that had happened that I just... couldn't.

"Let's take another water break," Tristen said, but I heard the concern in his voice as my thoughts drifted.

What a prize the King had claimed for himself.

36

I had somehow made it off the roof, barely comprehending that I
had to place my iron bands back on before I could stumble out
of the training ring and back down the hallways before Leah
intersected me and guided me back to my rooms. Two guards were
stationed at my door—likely to keep me in rather than keep threats
out.

After bathing, I found a simple tunic and dark leggings in the
dresser. I dressed and then opened the door, turning to the guards.

"I want to go to the library. The one in the East Wing," I said. Zara
had mentioned a library in the Saltspire Palace—and whether I
would be allowed to visit. But it was a seemingly innocent request,
and one I'd hope they wouldn't think twice about.

They exchanged looks, and then the tall thin one stepped forward
and led me down a series of hallways.

The Saltspire Library was just as stunning as the rest of the
palace. It was a quiet, cavernous room that was completely empty
when I entered. Towering bookshelves were accessible by golden
rolling ladders, and I could smell the familiar scent of aging tomes
from where I entered.

But after I piled my arms high with those dusty books, I found myself trying not to drop them all as I turned a corner and found the reading room.

The reading room—if you could call it something as humble as a mere *room*—looked out onto the sea. I was in one of the lower levels of the palace, so I could see the way the azure waves hit the rocky shore, spraying the gardens below with its salty spray. The reading area itself was a sloping pit in the center of the room with cozy couches that almost looked like one large bed. Salt lamps scattered across side tables lit the space with that warm light, and I melted into the comfort of it, picking a spot with a view of the ocean from those panoramic windows.

Then, I started to read. The books I picked were about the gods, about how heart crystals reflected magic, and what magic could be wielded beyond what was gifted in those heart crystals through spells and ancient rituals. I read about how King West had sentenced rebels to death in Luminaria in order to reestablish his dominance.

I read for hours, but knowledge didn't set me free. I couldn't find the clarity I was looking for, didn't receive the answer to my question of *why me?* in the thick volumes of history and guides for magic wielders.

Instead, I found myself gazing off into the sea beyond the huge windows, my thoughts drifting like the tides.

"Find anything interesting?"I looked up as Zara landed on a cushion across from me.

"No," I admitted. "Just historical texts, but they all conveniently leave out any history of past victors, or anything else regarding the outcome of the past Ash Trials."

"You see the importance of my role, then. So much of these games have been lost to history. Almost as if we forget why they're put on each year."

"And why are they?" I asked, realizing I wasn't sure of the answer.

Zara gave me a serene smile. "Over a hundred years ago, the gods were captured and lulled into imprisonment on this island. Six gods for the six kingdoms of Septerra. But King West's late father didn't believe in leaving the gods imprisoned. Instead, he believed they should return to the kingdoms that worship them, and that humans should once again fight for their favor. This was the basis of the beginnings of the revolution that would eventually split Luminaria in half, the western side of the continent becoming Stormgard as the rebels gained territory."

"But that still doesn't explain why these games are played."

"You're right," Zara said. "Luminaria runs these games to restore the power to the Queen of the gods—Illumia, the goddess of light and order. They believe if they give the Queen her freedom to roam the earth once more, then they will rule over all of the other gods— and the rest of the lands. But the gods were imprisoned and sucked dry of most of their power by a Siphon, who made sure the gods were too weak to leave this island. She gave her life to absorb their powers, and was destroyed by them. But she succeeded in keeping them trapped."

"If a Siphon imprisoned them, why would they think a Siphon could help change the tide of the war? Is it because of the prophecy?"

"Yes. The prophecy can be interpreted as saying that a Siphon would be able to affect the tide of the war, but it was not described *how*. The Ash Trials are like an ancient sacrifice, run by disciples of Orsi who try and raise the sleeping gods after each victor is crowned, hoping that the fallen prisoners will feed the soil and the drained gods with their sacrifice."

"Is it working?" I asked, afraid of the answer.

Something flashed in Zara's eyes. "Every monster that slips out from the underground prison that holds the gods is proof that they're growing in power. And if they manage to escape from the bonds that imprison them, only the Brightborne and the foretold Siphon will be able to put them back."

"What's a Brightborne?"

"A human touched by a drop of a god's magic. They're faster, stronger, and live longer thanks to that god's touch—but they also bear the burden of the god's power they are gifted with."

I bit my lip, drawing blood. Something felt very wrong about what was happening here. The Ash Trials were deadly already, but hearing what they may be preparing to unleash... somehow, the threats seemed to loom larger, like growing shadows.

I was about to ask Zara for more, but footsteps had us turning as Leah entered the library.

"King West requests your presence at dinner. He wishes for you to demonstrate your power to the court."

I took a steadying breath as I sat up. My servitude had begun.

37

The dress that Leah put me in was a dusty gold, with so many sheer panels around the bodice it was almost as if I wasn't wearing much at all. The bodice looked like it was an ornate spider's web, turning into an embellishment that hid my breasts. The skirts were sheer with long slits, the golden hue of the tulle providing some semblance of coverage. Leah let my curls fall around my face, gathering some strands into tiny braids that snuck back behind my head. As a finishing touch, she wove gold-plated butterflies in my hair. I was just as much a gilded ornament as anything else in this palace.

I swiveled to her on my chair in front of the mirror as she placed the final butterfly. "Do you know how he means to test my powers?" I asked.

Leah's face revealed nothing as she toyed with my hair, putting the final touches on her creation. "It's best if you just do what the King says. The island does not care if he kills its contestants."

"What about you, Leah? When are you planning to make your stand against him?"

I caught a sad expression flit across Leah's face. So heavy and dead, just like the gold butterflies in my hair.

"It's time to go," Leah said.

~

THE THRONE ROOM was adorned for a party, and it was even more full of courtiers and emissaries from foreign kingdoms wearing different colors and insignias. Everyone was seated, and Leah led me to my place next to the King. The low tables were overflowing with food, and I spotted Cassandra floating around the outer rim of the throne room, hanging onto the arm of a different handsome prince or high born royal every single time I looked up. I tossed glares her way because I had nothing better to do—even as food was passed around in front of me, I had no appetite.

King West was engrossed in a conversation to my right that I didn't bother to tune into. I didn't care for politics, not when survival was my only aim.

I scanned the room, searching for Tristen, but he was nowhere to be found.

King West turned back to me, the crown a little lopsided on his head as he sloshed his wine around in a golden goblet.

"How are you finding my palace, Saffron?"

"It's beautiful," I said blandly, not meeting his eyes. Where *was* Tristen?

"And your training partner? Is he teaching you everything you need to win?"

I snapped my gaze back to King West. He wore a knowing smirk.

"To think that he was the best you had to train me is quite sad. I worry for your kingdom," I replied.

"You worry? Are you not looking forward to helping us turn the tide in this war?" King West asked, reaching over to caress a hand down my back.

It took every shred of self control for me not to gag at the touch, and I backtracked. "It would be an honor to serve your armies," I said, playing dumb.

"Ah yes, my armies. One of many areas where you can *serve* me," he said, his other hand going to a bowl of grapes. He popped one in his mouth, still raking his gaze over me.

I plastered a cool expression on my face, giving him no indication of the rage that was beginning to boil underneath my skin.

"But in the meantime, I hope you don't mind helping us with a little something." King West took a small spoon, tapping it on the side of the goblet as my stomach dropped. "Guests, please sit."

Everyone took a seat at the low table. Even Cassandra took her place several seats down from us.

"It's wonderful to host you all at the Saltspire Palace, even on the precipice of total war. But the gods have blessed Luminaria and our allies, and they have given us a way to end this unnecessary bloodshed. They have given us the Siphon." Gasps echoed around the room as King West took my hand and kissed it. "She will be ours to wield in future battles, draining the rebel forces dry and keeping us in power as we regain control of the continent. But the reason that I called you here today was not just to join us in the final stages of The Ash Trials, but also to witness her power. We have a unique moment right now. We have with us tonight one of the key leaders in the rebel movement. The Shadowfire Assassin."

There was a hush as the second set of doors on the other end of the throne room opened, and guards shoved Tristen in. He was disheveled, bound in those heavy iron bands, and spattered with blood as if he had been trying to fight his way out.

He caught my gaze, and immediately straightened up and bowed in my direction.

"Princess," he said with a smile.

I let out a breath as he shifted into a stroll, defiantly staring down all the royals who had gathered at the low table.

"You know, this furniture is growing on me. I love looking down at all of the cowards in this war," Tristen said with a smug smile.

The King's lips thinned, but he ignored Tristen and turned back to his guests. "You've probably known from your own dealings with the Shadowfire Assassin that his mindweavying abilities are unparalleled. Gifts that our new Siphon can borrow and use for the benefit of Luminaria and all of our allies."

All gazes shifted back to me. I felt the color drain from my face.

King West gestured for me to go. "It's time, Saffron. Take Tristen's powers and go into his mind. Tell us what you see. Where are Stormgard's forces hiding their troops? How can we take them down?"

I stared at King West. "I can't—"

"You will," King West said, and suddenly guards were hauling me up, propelling me to the center of the room.

They tossed me in front of Tristen, and I took a breath as I stood in front of him, straightening. How was I supposed to do this?

"Do what you need to," Tristen said, and his expression was resigned. No one else in this throne room even knew that Tristen wasn't just a famed assassin, but was also the sole heir to the throne. I could reveal that and see to his death, but the way that Tristen seemed so... *defeated* just hurt what remained of my soft heart. Even if I wanted nothing to do with him, he deserved better than death by the King's hand.

"Any time now," the King called out, annoyed.

"Hey," Tristen said, catching my gaze again with those steady obsidian eyes. "Do it."

The tense guards around us made it clear I had no choice. King West would not grant any sort of mercy if I embarrassed him in front of the rulers of his lands and those beyond his borders.

I stepped in front of Tristen, and his hands went to my waist as if we were dancing. I reached out, placing my hands on Tristen's bare forearms.

I squeezed my eyes shut, trying to remember the sensation from my training, from the times on the island I had called upon my power. At first, I felt nothing. But then, as I dug deeper, I felt those same loops of power. I hooked my power around them, yanking them to me. I was faster this time—I could yank a few loops at a time, bringing the string to me more quickly as if I were a cat playing with a ball of yarn. I let it unspool, flowing into me—

—I stepped back with a gasp, and the whole room was watching me, silent. I hadn't pulled much of Tristen's power, just enough to be able to use it to look into his mind.

Tristen just stood in front of me, silent. That unnerved me more than anything. Tristen was usually armed with a witty comment or a flippant remark, but now he was stone still and quiet. Just watching me, seeing what choices I would make when his life was truly on the line—and the lives of all of his people. He was their King, their Assassin, and I had the fate of everything he held dear in my hands.

"Look into his mind, Siphon," King West commanded.

But I ignored him. I would do this because I had to, because survival was the aim right now. But I would be lying if I wasn't just a little bit curious what Tristen was hiding in his mind.

Tristen leaned close, his voice by my ear. "I'm ready for you," he said, but it wasn't flirtatious. It was an offer laid bare.

The words knocked the breath out of me, but I showed no reaction as I brought my hands to both sides of his face.

"Show me some truth," I said, a command that would feel strong to a room full of Luminarians who were hungering for information about the war. But my demand was for something deeper from Tristen. He had kept fighting to win my trust. Now, I wanted him to prove that he deserved it.

"I can't *show* you anything. You'll have to see it for yourself," Tristen said in that low voice that caressed a deep part of me.

And then I dove into his memory with a

s

p

l

a

s

h.

38

Mindweavying felt like diving in a pool of images that sparked with each touch like static electricity. I was so overwhelmed with the sheer immensity of the memories surrounding me that I decided to focus on the image I had seen in the tent.

The image of Tristen walking down the street to my village, his entire presence promising death.

As soon as I did, the memory flowed around me—this time from his perspective. I saw as he laid eyes on me. Not the version of me now who was constantly covered in blood and injured, but a version of me with rosy cheeks and a fullness to my figure. My eyes went wide in the memory as I ducked back into the bakery.

A *boom* shuddered through the village, and suddenly Tristen turned his head. Shadows surrounded him as I saw soldiers running to buildings, holding torches.

They weren't just any soldiers, however.

They wore Luminaria's gold and white colors, and I felt Tristen's horror as they spread out, holding torches aloft to thatched wooden rooftops that went up in flames immediately.

"GET OUT NOW!" Tristen called. "Everyone needs to evacuate!"

Tristen was sprinting, his shadows spearing out for the soldiers just as his shadowfire enveloped the rooftops, freezing the fire. The damage was already done, however, and the houses still caved in, even if he was able to stop the flames from burning. He sent his shadows to try and protect those inside, but he was draining fast.

A sword flung out at him, and Tristen dodged the blade—barely. But his shadows were climbing up his arms, and I felt his control slipping.

Control. That's something that echoed through his mind. Control of his power? Why? What was so important about maintaining control?

The memory began to blur, and I felt myself being pulled from it as Tristen cut down another Luminaria soldier as more swarmed in.

One thing had been made clear to me in his memory.

Luminaria had been the one to torch Riverleaf to the ground. And they'd do it again and again if it meant they got what they wanted.

I fell out of his memories with a

f

l

a

s

h.

I opened my eyes, my hands still on both sides of Tristen's face. I was out of his memories, back in the ballroom.

Tristen's thoughts rang through my weakening connection with his mind. *Tell the King that the rebels are stationed on the Northeastern border. They're gathering in the foothills for their next attack. It's what he wants to hear. But you won't have any innocent lives on your conscience.*

I stepped back, dropping my hands as I stared at him.

"So? What did you see?" King West said.

I looked around, feeling disoriented. The entire throne room was watching me. Waiting for me to reveal the contents of Tristen's mind.

Focusing on the King, I told him what Tristen had fed me mind-to-mind. "I saw the rebels. They're gathering near the Northeastern border. They're gathering in the foothills for their next attack."

Murmurs broke out in the throne room. King West clapped his hands together once, silencing the room. "See? It's just as I told you. The Siphon will usher in a new era of peace and prosperity, and bring the end to these bloody skirmishes once and for all. Let us drink to our reunited lands. Illumia be with us all!"

The room raised their glasses, and the toast was made. I was still in a daze as Leah arrived at my side, pulling me back to my seat by the King.

Food and drinks were shoved before me, ambassadors clapping me on the back, congratulating me as if I had already won The Ash Trials. As if I'd already given them everything. Zara sat across from the King and I, quietly scribbling on her parchment as if capturing a grand tale.

I wanted them all dead.

~

I SLIPPED OUT of the dinner as soon as I could, returning to my room. The throne room was filled with so much mirth and drinking that no one seemed to care, and even the guard who escorted me back seemed to think I was so thoroughly owned by the crown that there was nothing I could do to alter my fate.

When the door of my room closed behind me and I was at last alone, I fell to my bed and wept for those in my village who had lost their lives in the senseless brutality wrought by Luminaria.

~

THE NEXT MORNING, Leah dressed me in fighting leathers and brought with her a tray of breakfast. I did what I could to force down a hard-boiled egg as she braided my hair. She said nothing about my silence or the dark circles that had formed underneath my eyes, and merely motioned for me to follow her.

"Come. He's waiting for you."

He was. He was pacing the training ring by the time Leah had deposited me on the roof, and he stopped as he caught sight of me. I entered the ring, my iron bands falling to my feet.

"You look awful," he said, meaning it as a jab but I heard the twinge of concern.

I took three steps toward him and threw a punch.

He dodged. "So that's how you want it this morning?" he asked, his smooth voice knowing.

It was.

I threw every piece of myself into our sparring. I threw my anger into every jab, every kick, every spin as I fought until I was doubled over, my breath heaving and sweat dripping off my bow.

I looked up at him. "Why?"

"Why did Luminaria attack a defenseless neutral village? Or why didn't I tell you?"

"Both."

Tristen shook his head. "You know I can't say a word."

"Why?"

"Try again."

I shook my head. "You're keeping things from me."

"Why?" he challenged.

I narrowed my eyes. "I don't know."

"Not good enough, Saffron."

"I don't care about being good enough for you," I shot back.

He shrugged. "Fine. Then be good enough for *you*."

I rolled my eyes, but it was exhausting to keep my anger refueled.

As the morning sun drifted over the horizon, it illuminated Tristen and his broad shoulders. The golden light glinted off his dark hair as the waves curled over his face, framing those deep obsidian eyes.

"It's time," Tristen said, starting to shed his fighting leathers, baring his chest. "You should learn how to control my magic. Not just siphon it off and use a piece of it—but truly channel it from the source of my power and learn how to truly control and dominate it. And that requires focus. Breathwork. Attention."

As if on cue, tendrils of shadows crawled to him.

Tristen reached for my hand and pulled me up to stand in front of him. He made quick work of my leathers, too, and my body heated as his sure hands brushed across my skin, unbuckling and unlacing my armor, leaving me bare except for the band around my breasts and my leather pants.

I reached for his chest, but he grabbed my wrists, stopping me. "You're starting to get stronger, so it will be easier for you to take my magic."

"Isn't that a good thing?" I asked, annoyed.

"Do you know who gave me my magic?"

"Is this some quiz? Because I'm not in the mood," I said.

He sighed, and let my wrists drop. "No. I was given my shadowfire and mindweavying abilities by Nocterin, the mad god."

"Aren't all gods mad, in some way?" I asked, remembering some of the stories I'd read in the library.

"You could say that. The older ones are less tethered to the suffering they are capable of inflicting upon the creatures of this realm. The younger ones are more... curious. But the six major gods —the ones with real power that all kingdoms in Septerra worship— are all buried here."

I glared at him, trying to keep my legs from going wobbly at the way his voice stirred something in me. "I didn't sign up for a history lesson, *professor*."

"A mad god bestows power that can go wrong, fast. If you let it control you, it could destroy you. It takes and takes until you become nothing."

I remembered the way Tristen had started to become overtaken by his own shadows when he had used up his power. "Has that happened to you? Were you close to losing control when your shadows started to consume you?"

Tristen's gaze hardened. "I have *always* been in control."

The words shook me. "Okay. So I just have to... what, focus?"

"Yes. You have to keep a firm grasp on any borrowed power. The stronger the power, the more it will try and take from you. I'll be here to help you, but you need to tread carefully."

I shuddered as I thought about how Ajax's power had torn through me. "Ajax's power…"

"Was still nothing compared to my full power."

I quirked my head at him. "Aren't you at full power now?"

Tristen's face was unreadable. "I have enough of my power for you to practice. You just need to focus on not losing control."

I started to put my hands on him, but he shook his head slightly. "Before you start, I want you to breathe."

"I think I've been doing that just fine on my own, thanks."

"You need to slow your breathing. Understand how to calm the deepest recesses of your mind with just a few seconds. Ready?"

I sighed, but nodded my head in agreement. "Sure."

"Inhale through your nose. Then purse your lips, and exhale slowly through your mouth, as if you had just tasted something sour."

I followed his instruction, limiting my exhalation to a small trickle of air through my puckered lips.

"Good. Again."

Tristen made me practice the breathing exercise two more times before he was satisfied.

"If you start to feel your control slipping, you can return to this. Okay?"

Was he really that afraid of me falling prey to his power? I had felt an insistent buzzing when I just pulled a sip of power from him in the throne room. Was this about to be much different?

I placed my hands on his chest and focused. But, as my palms pressed into his warm body, I couldn't feel those loops of power. My head felt fuzzy and tired from lack of sleep.

Come on.

I tried to focus, but felt so scattered. So… weak. I tried to see the strands of his power, but the haze of my mind was so heavy.

"Just relax into it," Tristen said. I felt him place his hands on my back, his strong arms encircling me. The comforting touch settled me, and I tried again. This time, I saw the threads, the loops in which

I could hook onto his power. I wrapped my power around them and pulled.

This time, there was no trickle of power that entered me.

It was a *deluge*.

Tristen's power roared through me. I knew I should turn it off, should unhook my power from his. But I couldn't. It felt too good to bring his power to my body, to feel it join with mine.

I felt a giggle bubble up to my lips. Suddenly, I dropped my head back, laughing.

Why was I laughing?

"Release the thread," Tristen commanded.

Shadows wrapped all around me, and I thought how funny it was that death was hiding in every corner. Why did we ever think we could evade it, when it awaited us in so many dark places?

"*Give yourself to me, oh special one,*" a strange voice echoed through my mind. It was deep and echoed with fragments of other voices as if it were not one sound, but many sounds all at once. How strange it was that I wanted to agree with the voice, wanted to give it what it desired.

"Release it *now*."

I laughed harder, the sound of it so high-pitched and strange. But I couldn't stop. Couldn't—

"SAFFRON!"

Suddenly, my hands were ripped from Tristen's chest, and I was tossed to the ground. The connection was severed, but the power was still there, and my hands shot out to my sides, and shadows jumped out from them like snakes. Slithering all around the ground, all over me—

I became enveloped in that slithering dark, and I started to *scream*.

I tried to claw at my eyes, tried to pull the shadows out, but hands clamped down on mine. I screamed and growled and felt that choking darkness swallow me whole.

And then... it began to subside. The shadows began to thin. I opened my eyes, and saw Tristen straddling me, his face filled with concern.

"What happened?" I asked.

"You lost control," Tristen said simply. He raked his gaze over me as if checking whether or not shadows were still leaking from me, and then rolled off me, but stayed close.

I sat up, my arms trembling. I tried to stop the shaking, even hugging them around myself. But then my legs started trembling. And then my body. And my breath became more shallow—

I looked up at Tristen, not sure if I would ask him for... I don't know, help? Something? By the time I brought my fearful gaze to him he had already moved closer, pulling me into his lap as he wrapped his arms around me.

"Breathe, Saffron."

I tried to breathe, but a choking sob came in its place. And to my horror, I started crying in his arms. The fear that had taken me, had shook me loose, coursed through my body. That ugly truth that death awaited us all—so close, *too* close—had shaken me more than I could ever admit. Tristen held me through all of it.

Then, I started doing the breathwork he had just taught me. A deep inhale through my nose. A slow exhale through my lips. Over and over again as I calmed the parts of myself that had never known peace.

Minutes later, my sobs turned to hiccuping breaths. I was finally able to suck in lungfuls of air. Slowly, I turned my face to him, trying to do some damage control. "I—I didn't sleep well last night."

He reached down, gently brushing a tear off my face. "This work is hard. You're learning not just to control your power, but also to control the flow of energy from the person or deity you're channeling from. It's not just their energy, either. It's the descendants of power that came before them, the previous magic holders in their ancestral line, and the gods who gifted them that power. All of those forces are alive in every drop of magic that is in their blood. You borrow that, and you borrow all of the baggage that comes with it. It's a wild, unpredictable source, and the only thing you can do is prepare and give yourself what you need to become more resilient."

A knot formed in my chest. "Why should I do all of this?"

Tristen stiffened. "What are you saying?"

"What am I fighting for? To be King West's plaything? His Warrior Queen? Why continue through three more trials at all if what's ahead will just be even more difficult?"

Tristen leveled his gaze at me. "You do not belong to him. You write your own fate. You take all of the power in the world and use it as the ink to wet your quill and write the story of your life in a way that serves you. Not him. Not anyone else. And definitely not some godsforsaken prophecy. Spill the blood of your captors until rivers run red if you have to. Just *never. Stop. Fighting.* Do you understand me?"

I nodded, but a question bloomed in my mind. "What are you fighting for, Tristen?"

Tristen's gaze crumbled—but then reformed into something stone cold. "I'm fighting for an impossible shot at the thing I want more than life itself."

39

A storm was coming, and because of that, food was being restricted in Ashguard. The island was preparing for something, it seemed. I overheard the servants chatter that the prisoners weren't receiving their normal rations of food at the prison over breakfast in the palace—where we had plenty of food.

After I was escorted back to my chambers, I decided I was tired of being holed up in Saltspire while my friends starved in the prison.

The servants and guards were distracted, boarding up windows and running around to stoke fires in all of the royals' rooms to keep them warm, tending to those who had traveled to the Saltspire Palace from allied kingdoms across the seas. They were too busy to see me, the King's favored and the supposed Siphon from the prophecy, as I ducked through the halls and out through the servants' hallways.

There was enough chaos to allow me to slip out unnoticed into the windy afternoon, the sky darkened with clouds heavy, full of unshed rain. I darted along the treeline with a pack I had filled with cloaks, blankets, and all of the food I could take from the kitchens.

I hid in a bush as the King's guard walked by, eager to return to the palace and swap out for another patrol as the temperatures dropped.

So eager that they barely pretended to scan the path ahead and behind them.

I made my way to the metal doors that protruded from the dirt that led down into Ashguard. The guards were gone, and I was hidden under cloud cover as the afternoon began to turn to an early night.

As I placed a hand on the cool metal handle to wrench open the doors, I heard a rustle in the forest behind me.

I froze, slowly turning my gaze to the dark trees and bushes behind me.

Nothing. Or, nothing that was willing to show itself.

I took a breath and yanked open the door, dropping inside the stairwell and closing it as quietly as I could.

⁓

THE CHILL of the prison cut through my bones as I descended into the heart of Ashguard. After being away for a few days, I had forgotten how the dank, musty smell of the prison reeked of despair and loneliness.

I had an idea of where Rachelle's cell was, and when I reached the fourth floor of the silo, I began to weave through the dark cells, guessing that with the strength of her power, she wasn't on the lower levels. With so many already killed in the trials so far, the cell blocks were mostly empty.

I had covered most of the wing that I knew Rachelle to be in when I heard a soft sobbing in one of the cells to my left. I slowed to a stop, peering through the dark lit by a single torch. There, crying in her cell, was the fire sprite, Priscilla. She rocked back and forth on the stone floor of her cell.

I took a step toward the cell, and she raised her tear-stained face.

"Here," I said, reaching into my pack and handing her one of the cloaks followed by a loaf of soft bread and fresh apples from the palace.

She took the cloak, draping it over herself, and ripped off a piece of bread, shoving it into her mouth. "Why?" she asked, her mouth full.

"I..." I searched for a reason. Why was I feeding my competition? But I couldn't really come up with a reason other than... "I wanted to."

The fire sprite gulped down the bread she was chewing and reached out a slender hand through the bars. "I'm Priscilla."

"Saffron," I said, shaking her hand. I had known her name, but maybe she had written me off before learning mine.

"I remember you from the earlier trials," she said.

"I do, too," I said softly. "Where's your sister?" I asked, looking around to the other cells around her.

Priscilla wiped away some of her tears. "When we both got captured, I knew only one of us would make it. I just had hoped it would have been her. So I wouldn't have to be left carrying the loss."

Her twin sister. The two fire sprites had been inseparable until the second trial, when only Priscilla had returned.

"I'm sorry for your loss."

Priscilla smiled sadly. "I'm sorry for all of our losses. The fourth trial is soon, right?"

My breath caught in my throat. I knew it was coming, I just didn't know when. "Yes. I'm here to visit Rachelle and Callum. Do you know where they're being held?"

"Yes," Priscilla said, and gave me directions to both of their cells.

I thanked Priscilla and rose, feeling so weary and heavy. I was so tired of death, of the fighting that tried to turn us against each other.

I wouldn't let it. Not until my dying breath in this arena.

I finally made it to Rachelle's cell. Before I could even approach, I heard her humming some sort of sea shanty, and when I arrived, I saw her stretching into a backbend. She swiveled her head, seeing me and jumping to her feet with an incredible agility.

"Saffron!" she said, jumping to the bars. "You're here." She wrinkled her nose. "Why?"

I laughed, and handed her a heavy wool cloak and a paper bag of food. "The palace had pastries—"

"NO!" Rachelle gasped, and snatched the bag out of my hands so hard she almost tore it. "You didn't!"

I smiled as she shoved a tart in her mouth and her eyes rolled back in her head. "Better than sex." But as the dim, flickering torch light hit her face, I saw that she had a black eye.

"Rachelle, your eye," I said, stepping forward to her cell.

She tossed her hair. "Don't worry, I won."

"Are the prisoners fighting?"

She shrugged, a little too nonchalant in her dismissal. "Everyone's getting antsy as we start to get closer to the end, that's all."

Guilt twisted in my gut. "I should be down here with you—"

"No," Rachelle said, her tone hard. "You've got too much to worry about."

"I met Leah," I said softly, keeping my voice down.

Rachelle's eyes widened. "Leah's... here?"

"You didn't know?"

Rachelle's bottom lip trembled slightly. "She shouldn't be here. She should be back with our people. Back at sea."

"At sea?"

Rachelle wiped a stray tear on the back of her arm. "I didn't tell you the whole truth before. I'm from the Kingdom of Tidereign. I gave up a life of living in underwater palaces for land the moment I realized that I was a shifter and I could grow legs."

I stared at her. "You don't normally have legs?"

"I normally have a tail, actually," she said. "But the legs are my most used form, so I can keep them even with these on." Rachelle held up her iron bands. "My power, just like yours, can divert the iron cuffs just enough. But Leah... she would only be here to try and help me. Keep her safe, okay? And far away from the fighting?"

"I will," I promised.

Rachelle nodded. "She was never supposed to be dragged into all of this."

"None of us should have been," I said, sighing, and then stilled at the sound of guards' footsteps. Rachelle and I tensed, waiting for them to grow closer...

...but the footsteps and the voices passed the hallway adjacent to the one I was in, and they faded.

"I've got to go find Callum," I whispered, tossing the pack over my shoulder.

"Stay safe," Rachelle said. "He should be two blocks over." I nodded as I darted down the hallway, waiting at every hallway intersection to listen for guards.

I slipped past the second cell block to find Callum pacing in his cell.

"Callum," I said, and I ran to the bars.

His face lit up, so boyish and youthful as he looked me. "You're alive."

"I am. I brought things for you." I handed him the bag of food and the extra cloak I had packed just in case.

He took them, setting them down on his cot before turning to me and taking my hands through the bars. "I have something for you as well."

I felt him place a small round object in my right palm. I took it, and withdrew my other hand to pry it open.

Inside the case was a single white pill.

"You should have a choice in what happens to you," Callum said softly as horror dripped through my veins.

"This is..."

"A fast-acting poison pill. Now that the King knows what you are, there's no telling what ways he'll seek to use you and your powers. I wanted you to have a choice."

I shivered, the poison pill seeming to sear into my flesh as I closed the case and pocketed it in my cloak with a shivering hand. My mouth was so dry I couldn't force out a *thank you.*

"Is everything okay up there?" he asked

I swallowed, remembering the other reason why I had come to see him. "The King had me take Tristen's powers and search his mind for information about the rebels. And in his memory, I saw the day that Riverleaf was attacked. It looked like it was Luminaria forces who torched our village, not the rebels."

Callum's expression was unreadable. "Of course he made it look like that. Because it wasn't the King's men, it was rebels *dressed* like the Luminaria army."

But the pieces didn't add up. "In his memory, Tristen was fighting to *save* the villagers. The Luminaria men were attacking him. If they were rebels, wouldn't they have recognized Tristen as the Shadowfire Assassin and helped him?"

Callum gripped the bars of his cell with white knuckles. "He's poisoning your mind, Saffron. You can't let him win."

"Win what?" I asked. "What exactly awaits the winner at the end of all this?"

Callum hung his head. "I don't know."

~

MY HEAD SPUN as I wove through the forest's edge as the winds whipped around me. I snuck through the garden entry to the palace, the large windows already boarded up in preparation for the coming storm.

Guards were placing sandbags at some of the doors, moving furniture, and ordering the handmaids around. It wasn't hard for me to slip through the servants' hallways and wind the way I came back up to my room, which had been left laughably unguarded.

I slipped inside my room, closing the door behind me.

"Have a nice date?"

I whirled to see Tristen lounging on my bed, one head propped up by his elbow.

I flushed. "What are you doing here?"

"You left. I was curious where you went."

"I went to visit Rachelle," I said, crossing to the hooks by the fireplace, going to hang up my now empty bag.

"No one else?"

"No," I said. Tristen raised an eyebrow. Annoyed, I hung up my cloak with a flourish, but in doing so, the small container I had stashed in my cloak pocket went skittering across the floor.

Before I could blink, Tristen was on his feet, crouching down to pick it up.

I stepped toward him, but he grew angry, cold. "What is this?"

He opened it, and my heart skipped a beat.

"Callum wanted to give me a choice," I said.

Tristen's face turned icy. "Death is not a choice, Saffron. You are no powerless maiden. You do not bake bread for villagers. You *fight*. You fight for your people. You fight for the good of the continent. You fight for the good of our world. You *do not* choose death for yourself."

Before I could protest, he tossed it in the fire, and it went up in a quick puff of smoke and crackle of fire.

"Get out," I said through gritted teeth.

Tristen stepped closer to me. "Now that your *easy way out* has been eliminated, are you sure you don't want to hear what I know about the next trial?"

I sighed, and sat at the small loveseat at the foot of the bed, crossing my arms. "Fine."

Tristen settled beside me. He faced me as one arm rested on the top of the couch, and there wasn't much space between us. I felt a pull within me to move closer to him, but I resisted it. "How much do you know about mermaids?"

I stilled, thinking about Rachelle and her and Leah's secret of their lineage. "A little," I said. I hadn't read much about them in the library, only that they had once ruled a great underwater kingdom. "Some of them are shifters?"

"That's right. But most of them are monstrous creatures of the deep. They're territorial and can rip apart any being with their sharp teeth. They covet a variety of shiny, beautiful things, and love to make deals that will result in being able to chew on your eyeballs."

"They sound like nice company."

"Good, because the fourth trial starts tonight. And you need to figure out whose power you're about to steal, because you can't swim and I can almost guarantee you this trial is underwater."

My blood ran cold. Beyond the stone walls of my room, I could hear the howling of the wind as the storm continued to grow in intensity. "The trial is tonight?"

"Yes. I overheard the King talking to his advisors, mentioning that there were sightings of the mer-people on the shores. They must be involved somehow—my guess is that the island summoned them to be the arbiters of this next trial—especially if this storm is any indication of an upheaval in the seas."

"What do I need to know about them?"

"The Cimmerian Sea is known for its creatures who covet what does not belong to them. They will try to make a bargain with you. Don't take it."

"But I can't swim. You're sure?"

"I am. If there's anyone who has powers that might help you—"

"I can think of someone," I replied. If Leah was Rachelle's sister…

"You should take this." Tristen handed me a single iron spike, sharpened at the tip. "Some of the creatures of the deep can't be killed with a blade. The iron will help. You have my dagger still?"

"No, the guards took it from me."

Tristen pulled out another dagger from his boot and handed it to me with its sheath.

"Are you sure?" I asked.

"I have plenty where that came from," he said, but his eyes were humorless, his jokes flat.

"Of course you do," I said, curious just how many weapons he had managed to keep hidden on him.

Voices and the sound of boots sounded in the hall. "You should go," I said. Just as the words left my mouth, the door opened and Leah slipped in, holding a small golden shell.

Tristen raised an eyebrow, but Leah just stared him down in her deadpan way. "You can stay and keep secrets, or you can leave," she said.

Tristen leaned back, crossing an arm. "I can keep a secret. And Saffron can, too."

Leah's gaze swung to me. I sighed. "He can stay."

Leah stepped forward, holding the small golden shell to me. It was ridged and textured yet smooth to the touch. I turned it around in my palm, feeling its cool weight.

"If you need help from my people, open this shell underwater and think of the message you wish to send through the tides."

I took it from her. "Thank you. Rachelle told me—about where you come from. Do you miss it?"

Leah's expression softened. "I look forward to returning home with my sister when I'm able to save her from these trials."

"Thank you," I said, holding up the shell.

But Leah was already holding up another small bag I hadn't seen her bring into the room. "I also have this, which you should put on now to make sure it fits."

She withdrew a shimmering black bodysuit, made of some sort of stretchy black material that had a slight iridescent glow as if it were made from scales.

"This will help keep your core body temperature as close to normal as possible when you're underwater."

"It's stunning," I said, taking it from her and feeling the durable yet silky texture of the thing.

Leah nodded to the small divider, and I ducked behind it to change. Moments later, I stepped out wearing the bodysuit.

Tristen's eyes flickered in surprise—and then shifted into something a bit more coveting as he took in what I was wearing. "Impressive," he said with a whistle, his voice low and rough.

"It is," I said as I stepped in front of the mirror, Leah fussing over me and checking the fit. The bodysuit clung to all of the right places of my body, highlighting my feminine curves. It was dark but shone just slightly, tossing a rainbow glow onto my face that reached my bright blue eyes. Wearing it made me feel as warm as if I were standing right next to a roaring fire.

"How does it feel?" Leah asked.

"It's perfect."

"Agreed," Tristen said, stepping forward, barely able to keep his eyes off of me. "Leah, you mentioned you were a shifter? There's one more thing Saffron could borrow from you."

∾

THE GUARDS CAME for me half an hour later. The fourth trial was here, and I was fully decked out in my bodysuit and a pair of skintight boots, with some hidden daggers strapped to my body in clever pockets and sheaths that had been fastened into the suit.

Before the first three trials, I had felt cold terror. Now, all I felt was a blunt uneasiness. A small improvement marked by more time spent training. Or were my emotions reduced to this numbness after the constant threat of death? I wasn't sure, but I tried to keep my mind clear as I was led out of the palace, past the gardens, and up a steep hill to a cliff overlooking the rocky ocean below.

The other prisoners were already gathered, some of them shaking and cold in the wind as the eye of the storm approached. There were less than ten of us left, our numbers severely whittled down after the last trial and the encounters with The Foggy Forest.

I smiled as I saw Callum, Rachelle, and the fire sprite, Priscilla, wearing the cloaks I had snuck out for them.

King West stood flanked by several royal guards, wearing thick furs as a fire wielder kneeled by his side, keeping the King warm with continuous burning fire from his hands. Behind King West stood his court, also dressed in warm furs.

I was the last to arrive, and I stood next to Rachelle. Her eyes glittered as she took in the King and his court. A promise of death in them.

King West just looked on at us, and addressed his court.

"We are here to bear witness not only to the competitors who still remain, but also to see the word of the gods be fulfilled. Step forward, my favored, and be recognized as the one who will fulfill the prophecy."

Murmurs rippled as I realized I was the one he was talking about.

Eyes pivoted to me, and I took a tiny step forward, trying to keep my head high as King West's court watched me.

King West grinned. "May Illumia be with you," he said to all of us —but his gaze was only on me.

Then, an unnatural, magic-scented gust of wind struck us, lifting each of us off our feet as our iron bands dropped to the ground.

In one powerful gust, we were blown off the side of the cliff and toward the roaring ocean waves and sharp rocks below.

40

My body was tossed over the ocean, and for one terrifying moment, I was held in suspension over the azure waters, the other prisoners beside me. Callum yelled and tried to grab for something. Rachelle had already shifted into the form of a hawk, and was flapping her wings but was still stuck in place. Tristen had a stoic look on his face, but his gaze watched me as I felt the wind slowly tilt me over the edge of the cliff.

Then, the wind dropped me.

A scream ripped through my throat as I barreled down to the rocks below. Then, the magic yanked on me—just for a moment to slow my fall—and I hit the cold ocean waves with such force the air was chased from my lungs. I shuddered as the current pulled me under, every inch of my body had felt like I had been battered by a fight.

Air. I needed air.

I opened my mouth but water rushed in. I looked up at the surface, knowing I needed to get my head above water, *fast—*

—but my body just froze up, and my limbs were fighting against me.

Shift. I had to shift.

I had borrowed Leah's powers just for this, but for some reason I couldn't convert her power into a form like Rachelle had taught me.

SHIFT! NOW! I screamed at myself, but it was no help. My focus was being shattered by the panic that overtook me.

I wish I knew the names of all the gods so I could curse each one of them as the pressure began building in my lungs. The other prisoners were nowhere near me—everyone had been scattered to the current and waves—and I felt myself sinking deeper into the dark blue abyss below.

I wished I could do something as simple as keep myself above water, but Tristen had been right—I hadn't possessed the ability to do so. My past self had cultivated so many skills to keep me alive by fighting and surviving—but somehow she had neglected to learn how to *swim*. The irony was nearly as cold as the frozen tide pulling me under. The realization hit me as I sunk deeper. I would drown here, and not even make it to the fourth trial.

I was minutes from death. Maybe less, as my lungs began to burn. I reached into my pocket for the golden shell that Leah had given me, and I cracked it open, my mind going to its panicked plea.

HELP ME!

A shadow darted into my vision as the current seemed to accelerate, dragging me deeper to my watery grave as the light above began to dim, the surface growing further and further away.

I felt the pressure on my chest growing unbearable. It was time. I would have to suck in water in place of air. I would—

Suddenly, a creature appeared in front of me. He looked like a man, with pale blue eyes the color of the tide—and the same color as Rachelle and Leah's eyes. He was bare-chested and seemed to be built like a cresting wave. But below his navel were green scales that covered his lower half, ending in a powerful tail of the same green.

A merman.

He reached out, cupping my face in his hands as my panic rose. He smiled, and I could see his razor-sharp teeth. Was he about to eat me?

"I see you have been gifted a shell to call for us. Clearly one of our

own cares for you, so I'll grant you a kinder bargain than the rest of the contestants shall receive. I'll save you in exchange for knowledge of your greatest fear," his voice rang in my head. *"Nod if you agree to this bargain."*

Black spots had started to appear around my vision, and despite what little I knew about avoiding bargains with mer-creatures, I knew I had no choice.

I nodded.

Then, his lips were on mine, and air—such beautiful, precious air!—flooded my lungs at the same time I felt an odd pulling sensation at my neck. I pulled away from his kiss and gasped—throwing my head back as oxygen flooded my system. But how? The merman smirked at me as I stared at him, wide-eyed.

I closed my mouth, my hand going to it. But I was breathing. Underwater. My fingers traced down to my neck. Instead of smooth skin, I had... *gills.* They opened and closed in time to my breathing, small air bubbles emerging from them as I stared in shock at the merman.

"This way," his voice rang in my mind.

Then, he was dragging me *down down down*—deeper into the dark ocean. It grew colder, but I still remained fairly warm in the bodysuit that was clearly built for these temperatures. The merman's tail pushed us deeper with each powerful movement, and I wondered how deep we would truly go.

The darkness of the deep ocean suddenly parted, and as we arrived at an outcropping of underwater boulders, the merman paused. Below, a bright green glow illuminated a massive structure that sat on the ocean floor.

It was a huge underwater castle, and it looked as if it was made of bone-white material that had glittering pearls adorning it. The green glow seemed to be emanating from orbs surrounding it on a circle in the ocean floor.

My heart skipped a beat as I took in the shadows circling the oceanic palace. They undulated like snakes, bobbing up and down in hypnotic waves. *Sea serpents.* Massive ones, at that, easily the length of ten or twelve grown men. About four of them made lazy circles around the structure, as if they were guardians of this place.

The merman tilted my head back to face him, and I felt him speak in my mind once more.

"Inside the castle are ten enchanted pearls. Bring me back just one of them and you will be free of this trial."

Despite being surrounded by water, I felt my mouth grow dry. I had my dagger, but how would I fare against these massive sea serpents? Or anything else that awaited me in that glowing castle?

But there was no choice. I had to do this.

I nodded, and the merman released me.

I took a deep breath of sea water, and awkwardly began paddling my way toward the glowing castle, trying to teach my body the movements it had never learned. I kept to the shadows, following the edge of the sea cliff I was on down to the ocean floor. Maybe if I moved slow and kept myself close to the sea floor, I would evade the sea serpents circling above.

I reached the edge of the underwater palace, finally getting the hang of reaching my arms out and cupping my hands to propel myself through the sea. Above me, the sea serpents continued their slow swim around the perimeter. I found myself holding my breath as I passed underneath them—stilling for just a moment as one of them swished its tail... but then continued on its slow patrol of the waters around the castle.

I spotted a set of doors at the base of the castle, and with the way that the glow seemed to concentrate there, I figured that's where I needed to go. I continued to swim, trying to keep my movements small as to not attract the attention of the sea serpents above.

But a cloud of darkness shot through the ocean in front of me. I stopped, backpedaling through the water as three prisoners cornered me. I didn't remember their names, but as they unsheathed their daggers, I recalled that they used to run with Ajax before he had been killed.

Revenge then—or trying to ensure I didn't make it to the next stage of these trials. I unsheathed my dagger, unsure of how my skills would fare underwater when my past self hadn't even learned how to swim.

One of the bulkier prisoners didn't waste a second, which is how I knew he was here to ensure my death.

He struck out with his own dagger, and I barely twisted out of the way in time—my own blade shooting out and making purchase on his flesh as the current shifted as he darted past me. But as droplets of my blood floated up in the ocean around me, I looked down and realized his blade had still caught the edge of my forearm.

I swiveled to face him, caught in-between him and the other two prisoners. The one who had attacked me was bleeding, too, the current carrying his droplets of blood up, up, up to the tides above.

The prisoners were no longer facing me.

Instead, they all shifted as the dozens of sea serpents above us stopped circling the castle.

And began swimming with incredible speed in the direction of us —and our blood.

They had scented us.

It took me a second to process this—but before I could do anything, I was rammed by a fast-swimming creature.

I screamed—the sound muffled underwater—and raised my knife to strike. But before I could, the thing that had hit me tossed me across the sea floor, and I got a better look at it.

It wasn't a shark. It was a barracuda. Not any barracuda—a barracuda with startling pale blue eyes. *Rachelle's* pale blue eyes. The creature winked at me, and pivoted back to the doors, tossing her tail as if she was trying to point at it.

I had to get to the doors. I started swimming, but turned to see where the prisoners who had attacked me were.

The sea serpents had arrived. Even in the oppressive silence of the sea, I could hear the screaming of the prisoners who had attacked me as they were mauled by those giant beasts, their beady eyes red with greedy hunger in the feeding frenzy that had broken out. One that I would have been right in the middle of had Rachelle not arrived and tossed me aside. Rachelle had entered the fray now, biting off limbs and embedding her sharp teeth in the flesh of the sea serpents that were upon us.

I kicked harder, paddling toward the doors, the blood trailing me from my wound as I hurried along. As I got closer to the doors, I saw that each one had a name on them. I saw my name etched into the far door.

That was the entrance to the trial, then.

I swam as hard as I could, but in moments, a dark shadow appeared above me.

I twisted, looking up to find a sea serpent twisting down toward me, those rows of razor sharp teeth glimmering in the eerie green glow of the underwater palace.

I raised my dagger, wishing that I had some other power with me—

—but then out of nowhere, Callum appeared, landing atop the sea serpent, stabbing it again and again.

He was here! I felt relief flood through me as the other prisoners arrived, swimming to the doors. Aside from Rachelle, they all had gills—meaning they had all made the same deal that I had with the merman. I wondered if Leah had given them shells, too, knowing they were important to me. I warmed a bit at the thought.

The sea serpent twisted, but Callum kept mauling it with his blade, rendering it useless.

He rolled off the serpent and swam toward me. He pointed to the doors, and I nodded.

I had to go.

I started swimming, casting a glance back at the fray.

A dark whirlpool was descending on the fight, and I knew in an instant the spinning shadow was Tristen.

He had eyes for only one thing. His prey, which, in this moment, happened to be the prisoner who had slashed out at me.

I had reached the door just as Tristen raised his hand and his shadows shot out and strangled the prisoner.

Even in the depths of the sea, the sound of the prisoner's neck cracking seemed to echo on the currents. The sea serpents, sensing a bigger threat, refocused their attention onto Tristen.

I felt panic seize through my body, but then I felt a slimy creature hit me again, propelling me toward the door.

Rachelle.

She glared at me—as only *she* could do whilst in barracuda form —and I knew there was nothing I could do in this fight.

She seemed to understand my panic, and instead of just going through her door, she swiveled around and shot right into the fight, using her small form to dodge the outstretched jaws and twisting forms of the sea serpents. She joined the fray with Tristen, and while the other prisoners used the distraction to flee, I saw Tristen, Rachelle, and Callum fighting the sea serpents side-by-side.

My heart cracked open a bit to see them united against a common enemy. And as Callum turned to motion at me again to go through the door, I finally relented. I prayed to whatever sea god might be listening to keep them safe.

I pushed through the door marked with my name on it and advanced into the depths of the fourth trial.

41

The moment I passed through the underwater palace's door, I was met with gravity and oxygen—my two new best friends.

I gasped as I landed on the stone floor with a slick thud, my gills closing on my neck as my lungs switched gears. I heaved and coughed, getting used to my human lungs again. Apparently, the transition from breathing water to breathing air wasn't so seamless.

After I had finished hacking up my guts, I stood. The hallway I was in was long and had the same green glow that I had seen on the outside of the palace. The glow here emanated from a green fire that emerged from open shells on the walls in the place of where torches should be.

I started to push myself up off the ground when the door behind me opened and a rush of water knocked me off my feet. I slipped, trying not to yell as I slid along the hallway.

Behind me was a small coughing form. Priscilla, I realized.

"What are you doing here?" I asked. "You've entered the wrong door."

She shook her head, coughing up more water as she struggled to get to her feet, and I helped her. "I came here to give you a gift."

I frowned. "What do you mean?"

She smiled, and held out her hands and took mine. "Take my power. You'll need it."

"I can't leave you powerless—"

"I already completed my trial. I made a deal with the merman who chose me to drop me off in front of my door. Take my fire. I know it's not that strong, but you'll need it."

"Why?"

She smiled. "Because you went out of your way to help me, and I know that you're our best chance to end the war that killed off most of my kind even before I ended up in Ashguard. If I can't win, I want you to carry the power of my people forward. Please, I know you are who the prophecy predicted."

I felt my heart swell. There it was again, that prophecy. I didn't know what to think of it—what everyone thought I was capable of— but I didn't dare turn down Priscilla's gift.

"Thank you," I said, and she gave me a small smile. Then, I reached out and grasped her hands, and closed my eyes.

As I reached for Priscilla's power, I felt the threads of them grow a warm hue. They didn't hum with the kind of power that Tristen, Callum, or Rachelle's power did, but it had a kind of lightness to it that felt welcoming. I gently looped my own power around it, and pulled it to me as I felt it hum under my skin.

I opened my eyes and stepped back. "It's done."

"I'll see you on the other side. Good luck."

"Thanks. For everything," I said, and she gave me a small smile before she yanked open the door, a barrier keeping the water at bay. She threw herself across the barrier and into the water on the other side, the current tugging her away.

I turned back toward the hallway and started walking into the darkness. The only sound in the musty dampness was the dripping of water, as if the heaviness of the encroaching ocean was trying to reduce this palace to rubble. Starfish and other creatures made homes in the cracks of the hallways, living in this strange in-between of land and sea. It was almost as if air had been returned to these hallways as a special occasion for the trials.

There were no doors on either side of me, no path to choose. I was just walking forward, being propelled to the destiny this palace had chosen for me.

Then, the hallway began to grow larger and darker, as if it were opening into a larger room I had yet to see. Glowing algae creeped along the walls, seeming to breathe in time with the current outside of the castle.

I heard a scuttling noise—like claws being dragged across stone. I froze, trying to see in the near-dark, but nothing. I kept walking forward, but slowed my steps, unsheathing my dagger to hold it at my side.

Then, it lunged at me. A row of razor-sharp teeth came at me, and I screamed, slashing at the creature that lurched forward at me. It had the face of a piranha and the body of some sort of scaly humanoid and was covered in shell-lined armor as if it were some sort of guard.

My dagger caught the creature it in its shoulder and it stumbled back as blue blood sprayed out. It cocked its head to the right so it could see me out of its right eye. It opened its mouth and let out a horrible scream—and then ran at me again, its hands going for my neck, shiny claws retracting.

I called the power from my fingertips and Priscilla's fire came from me in a second. The creature let out a terrible scream as it was incinerated to ash at my feet.

More scuttling made me scan the darkness, and then two more of those creatures ran at me. I felt the ebbing of Priscilla's fire in my veins already, but I summoned it all at once and decimated the creature on the left in one blazing ball of fire. Then, I turned to the right, ducking low and dodging its claws before my dagger shot at and sliced its legs. It howled as it stumbled, and I wasted no time embedding my dagger in its back. I withdrew it and, as it fell to the ground, I sliced down into its heart. Its claws dropped to the ground, and I wrenched my knife up as blue blood spattered.

The past version of me might not have spent much time learning how to swim, but she at least knew how to fight.

I listened, my heart beating fast in my chest as I stared in the darkness. I still had one last bit of fire in my veins, so I raised a hand and let the last lick of fire slice through the dark—and land in front of a stone door.

I had reached the end of the hallway.

I sighed in relief, but kept my dagger out. Thank the gods for Priscilla and her magic—I shuddered as I considered what would have happened if I had been on my own and without her borrowed power.

I reached the stone door and hesitated. Whatever was behind this door, I would have to face as I was.

I took a deep breath. It would be enough. *I* would be enough.

I pushed open the door, and entered an eerily lit throne room. But my gaze shot immediately to the three figures in chairs at the center of the cavernous room. Tied, gagged, and bound with iron chains were Callum, Tristen, and Rachelle, their eyes watching me with fear.

King West turned to me from where he stood at the foot of a throne.

"Ah, there she is. My favored. Ready to win The Ash Trials?"

42

I stood in front of Tristen, Callum, and Rachelle. They wore iron chains as well as iron bands, and were secured to the chairs they were bound to, King West looming before them with shining eyes.

They had just been outside fighting. How had this happened?

"How are you here?" I asked King West, turning to him. He didn't have a drop of water on him.

"My dear Saffron, I'm here to ensure the victory of my favored on a more... *abbreviated* schedule. Did you not think I would ensure my victor would fulfill her role in the prophecy?"

My stomach dropped as I realized what he meant. I took a step forward. "No."

"No?" the King asked and withdrew a jewel-encrusted dagger that he flipped end-over-end. "So you would leave the world to an eternal battle and continue to let innocents die?"

"Why are you here?" I demanded.

"To protect you and our future," King West said simply, and then turned and hurled the dagger—

—where it embedded right in Rachelle's heart.

No. Panic tore through my body.

I screamed, running to her. I yanked the dagger out, and she let out a choked sound from underneath her gag. Blood ran down her mouth and her head slumped over.

Dead. She was dead.

Anger flashed through me. I whirled on the King, but the dagger flew out of my hand and back to King West.

"Don't you see? The island is trying to make you strong. It is you or them, and it has been the whole time."

"It's not," I said, standing between King West and Callum and Tristen. "I won't let you."

King West just smirked at me. "It's not your choice."

I unsheathed my dagger and ran at King West, but he disappeared... and reappeared behind me.

"No!" I screamed, but two twin daggers appeared in his hands, and he stood above Callum and Tristen, poised to spear their hearts.

He quirked his head. "You seem to have an affinity for these two that goes beyond casual friendship. I'll let one live if you choose which one to sentence to death."

"I can't choose," I said, the horror flooding me as I realized this was the truth.

"Then you'll lose them both."

Before I could scream or rush at him, King West embedded his twin daggers into the hearts of Callum and Tristen.

A cold emptiness crushed me as I ran to them.

No no no no no no no.

Tears were falling down my face as I dropped to my knees in front of them just as King West disappeared and reappeared by his throne.

But as Tristen and Callum spluttered, their eyes fluttering closed in death, I felt my grief shudder through me.

How had this happened? They couldn't be gone. Callum was my best friend. My only true tie to my past life, my childhood, my youth. And Tristen? He may have been... whatever he was, but I wouldn't have been able to get this far without him. Without either of them.

And Rachelle? She had done nothing but be the kind of friend I had hoped for. And her and her sister had looked out for me when I needed their help.

A sob escaped my lips, but I knew I couldn't let myself unravel here. Not yet.

I forced myself to my feet, facing King West.

He held out a green velvet pillow. On it sat two items.

"It's your choice, Saffron. Would you like a way out? Or would you like to help me end this needless suffering and put this war to rest once and for all?"

I took an uneven step toward him, staring at the pillow. I realized that the pillow held the suicide pill Callum had given me... and another unmarked box.

"What is that?" I asked, pointing to the white pill, my hands shaking.

King West grinned. "You always have a choice, Saffron."

Emptiness howled in my heart at that. I was truly and utterly alone in the world now, with no one else to help me escape the prison I'd be in now that King West would wield me as his weapon. My far too brief memory flashed through all of the times Callum, Rachelle, and Tristen helped me. And then, I remembered Tristen's words to me when he had thrown away the poison pill.

You do not choose death for yourself.

The words echoed in my mind. Even though I had lost him, lost Callum and Rachelle, my only allies—my only true friends—I wouldn't choose death. They had fought too hard for me to be here. Fought too hard to try and help me. I wouldn't let their sacrifices be in vain.

With a trembling hand, I picked up the box. It was just a small green box, but then a great green flash emitted from it, and I squeezed my eyes shut. Everything in the room disappeared. The bodies of my friends. King West. Gone. All of it.

I looked around, and saw that the box had been replaced in my hand—and instead was a shining pearl glowing green.

The magic pearl that the merman had requested. I found it.

Did that mean this had all been a part of the trial? A small glimmer of hope formed in my chest as I ran through the throne room, sprinting down the long hallway as I went to the door.

They might still be alive after all.

43

W ater hit my lungs. The gills on my neck re-opened as I threw myself through the door back into the ocean beyond the castle.

I emerged to find bodies of the slain sea serpents on the ocean floor, blood still drifting on the sea currents. I swam past the carnage. A pair of sea blue eyes greeted me as the merman who had offered me my deal drifted in front of me.

"Did you get it?"

I nodded and reached into the pocket of my bodysuit and withdrew the pearl, still glowing that unnerving green.

"You did well," his voice echoed in my mind, and he reached out and touched my neck. My gills closed up, and suddenly I was choking on sea water.

My panicked eyes met his, and he grinned, those razor-sharp teeth smiling at me.

"Good luck."

As I was gagging on the rush of sea water, a strong current ripped me away from the sea floor. I writhed in its grasp, my body struggling without oxygen.

As my lungs burned and the pressure intensified, the current tossed me above water. I spluttered, coughing and hacking as I bobbed above the ocean—

—but then slipped under again, my panic overtaking me.

I struggled, kicking against the current, but it was no use.

As I fell below the waves once more, I tried to make my limbs cooperate and tried to force myself to the surface.

But then strong arms were around me, bringing me above water.

"Breathe, Saffron," Callum said, and I took a coughing breath. He slung me over his shoulder, his muscles rippling as I felt him swimming to shore beneath me.

Callum was alive.

I was alive.

The dual truths shot through me.

"Rachelle... Tristen...?" I asked in between coughs.

"Last time I saw them they were alive," he said, and the panic that had flooded through me in that throne room dissipated.

Callum reached the shallows and he paused, gently bringing me to his bare chest and cradling me in his arms as he carried me to the shore. His body was so warm. I clutched him closer.

He placed me on the sandy shore, tilting me to my side. I coughed out what felt like an endless stream of sea water, and felt him brush back my wet hair from my face as he kneeled beside me on the sand.

"You made it through the fourth trial," he said. "You're almost there, Saffron."

"So close," I said, my throat raw from the sea water.

"C'mon Saffron, we gotta get you warmed up."

It was then that I realized I was shaking as the cool air made my wet bodysuit grow even colder. Callum didn't let me protest as he pulled me into his arms again, carrying me away from the shore and deeper into the treeline. I nestled my face against his warm chest, breathing in the scent of him mixed with seawater.

"You're alive," I whispered, the image of King West stabbing him through the heart still flashing in my mind.

"You think some men with *tails* could kill me?"

I glared up at him. "There were giant sea serpents, too."

He raised an eyebrow. "Do I look like fish food to you?"

I laughed, and his face softened as he pulled me closer to him. "Where are we?"

"We're on the west side of the island, at the tip of Dragon's Tail across from Siren's Rest, from what I can gather. The rock formations look similar to the ones I used to see on the map of the island," Callum said, his tone wary.

"Meaning...?"

"We've got a long walk back to Saltspire Palace—but we can't get going if you freeze to death."

"I'm not going to freeze to death," I muttered, but I was already feeling much warmer in his arms.

"You're right. Because I'm not going to let you," he said, approaching a small clearing that was hidden by the dense foliage of palm trees and rough underbrush. He set me down on some of the palm fronds. "We're going to make camp here tonight. I'll build a fire."

"I'll help," I said, but Callum's strong hand held me down.

"No. You need to rest. But first... you should take off your wet clothes first."

I looked down at the bodysuit, and started to unclasp it, then paused. "I'm wearing leggings underneath this, but I don't have a shirt..."

Callum was already removing his white shirt. "I'll get this dry for you by morning."

"Are you sure?"

"Yes. Let me get a fire going so you'll be warm."

I just nodded, my head suddenly swimming with all of the exertion. As Callum disappeared beyond the palm fronds, I removed the bodysuit, wearing just the cotton leggings and band around my breasts as the night chill teased my wet flesh.

Even with the cold, I somehow slipped into sleep.

~

I AWOKE to a crackling fire and the smell of smoked meats that had my mouth watering. As I blinked the sleep away, scrubbing my face with my hand to try and get my bearings, I realized that Callum had covered me with his now-dry cloak, and I was resting on a mat of braided palm fronds. His tunic shirt was folded underneath my head like a pillow, and smelled of his leather and citrus scent.

Callum glanced over at me from where he was rotating a spit on top of the fire, made from teepeed sticks to create a makeshift cooking area above the flames. He looked every bit a chiseled warrior, the flames dancing off the muscled planes of his bare chest. His brown-blond hair glinted in the flickering flames. His green eyes landed on mine, pools of verdant gems.

He removed the meat and placed it on a large leaf, and settled next to me as I pushed myself up.

"Eat," he said, handing me the leaf.

"Where did you get this?" I asked, taking the leaf from him and picking up the juicy meat with my fingers. I popped a piece in my mouth and stifled a moan as I chewed. I hadn't realized how hungry I was.

"I used to hunt back in Riverleaf," Callum said, his eyes gleaming with amusement as he studied me. "There were some island doves I was able to catch for us tonight."

"With what?"

"I have my ways," he said with a grin, his ego on full display.

I finished eating, taking a swig from my waterskin. "Do you think it's safe for me to wash off in the ocean?"

"It is if you go with me," Callum said, and I saw the heat in his eyes.

"Then let's go," I said, and rose to my feet, just wearing my leggings and the band around my chest.

"I'll race you," he said.

"I hope you like losing," I replied and we took off running.

We sprinted through the palm trees, my bare feet hitting sand as I ran across the moonlight-soaked shore to the sparkling ocean. I pulled off my leggings, laughing in surprise as Callum flung his pants in the breeze and I dodged them, losing precious seconds in our race.

"Cheater!" I called, and I heard him laughing as he hit the water.

"I still won," he called.

I smiled, pausing at the shore to unwrap the last pieces of clothing from my body and standing before the water completely bare.

Callum's eyes went wide. "I've definitely won."

I brushed my hair out of my eyes, suddenly a bit shy as the ocean lapped at my toes.

"Come in," Callum said, and rose out of the ocean to beckon me in. As he stood, I realized he was completely naked, too. I couldn't stop my eyes as they roved over every inch of him, his wet skin shining in the moonlight as if he was covered in diamonds. His torso was wrapped with thick muscle, sharpened and honed by his years of training. The 'v' shape of his muscles ended in something so impressive I... *blushed*. Suddenly, my knees felt a bit weak.

"See something you like?" Callum asked with a very male grin.

I began wading into the water then, and then dove into the current, ignoring his outstretched hand.

"Maybe," I said as I resurfaced.

He turned and swam after me. "Well I see some*one* I like. Very much."

I let him pull me into his strong arms, and I wrapped my legs around him. The water was cool but his body heat kept me from shivering. "Do you now?" I asked.

He lifted a hand to my lips, tracing them with his thumb. "I see the woman I've been waiting for ever since you were taken from me."

I tilted my head. "Waiting?"

He paused, then said, "I knew you would find your way back to me."

I searched his green eyes, wishing I could see all of the memories we had shared together in his gaze.

As we floated in the quiet ocean, I felt my body heat at every place it touched his. His fingers clasped my chin, angling my face to his as his lips met mine.

The kiss was urgent, wanting. I felt his tongue sweep out on the seam of my lips, demanding entrance, and I parted for him, letting him claim my mouth. My right hand curled in his golden hair, pulling him toward me.

He pulled away, and I let out a soft moan, wanting his lips back on mine.

"Saffron..." Callum said, his eyes raking over me with a kind of desire that made my blood heat.

But before he could make due on that desire, a lone coyote's cry pierced the silent night.

I clutched Callum, turning my gaze to the shore as the shadows grew longer in the moonlight. More coyotes joined the first one's call, and even though we couldn't see them, they sounded like they were moving closer.

"We should get back to the fire," Callum said, holding me to him as he began to wade from the water. I must have looked disappointed because he chuckled. "To be continued," he said.

He let me down gently by the shore, and I picked up my clothes on the beach, following him back to the camp.

"I didn't know that there were coyotes on this part of the island," I said.

"There are much worse," Callum said as he pulled on the clothes he had discarded on the beach, wearing only an undershirt he must have had on underneath the tunic shirt he had gifted me. "Which is why I'll be keeping watch while you sleep."

"I can keep watch—"

Callum turned to me, and I stopped as he ran the back of his hand gently down the side of my face, and then cupped my chin. "You need sleep. I can handle it." He leaned down, kissing me in a way that stole my breath away.

He let me go, but I reached up, winding my arms around him. "I can't lose you."

"You won't," he said, his voice firm. "We will find a way to win these trials. Together."

I leaned my forehead against his chest and sighed. I wanted nothing more than to believe him.

44

I had fallen asleep by the crackling fire on the pile of braided palm fronds. I was so tired from the fourth trial that oblivion claimed me faster than normal, my eyelids heavy and the sweet scent of burning firewood quickly lulling me to sleep as Callum kept watch on the other side of the fire, his gaze sweeping the forest around us every so often as he tended to the fire.

When I was roused from my slumber, I realized the distant sound of shouts had awoken me.

I pushed myself up to a sitting position, my borrowed white tunic shirt smelling like embers of the dying fire before me. The morning sunlight was dusting the palm trees in a warm glow. As the yelling got louder, I could make out voices.

Tristen and Callum.

I shot to my feet, tugging on my socks and boots before running to the beach where the sound of the argument was coming from.

"...I've got something you'll want to see," Tristen was saying.

"The only thing I want to see is you walking away from this beach!" Callum yelled back.

I burst through the treeline, and saw Tristen with his shadowfire glowing at his hands, Rachelle prowling beside him. Callum held a sword aloft, preparing for a fight.

All of their heads swiveled to me as I stepped onto the beach. "What's going on?"

"Nothing. Go back to the camp. I'll handle them," Callum said, gripping his sword.

Tristen turned a bored expression to me. "Your warrior thinks we're here to kill him. If that were the case, he wouldn't be breathing."

My feeling of relief of seeing Rachelle and Tristen alive wavered a bit from the implication of them all being here on this beach. "Why are you here, then?"

Tristen watched me, his gaze assessing me. "We finished the fourth trial. And now we're headed into the fifth."

"*What*?" I asked, fear vibrating the marrow of my bones. It was as if I had been doused with cold water, and I was suddenly wide awake. I looked around the stretch of beach we were on. Our area was shielded by palm trees, but just around the bend, the palm trees disintegrated into endless swells of desert and rocky outcroppings with sweeping ocean views.

Tristen made a step toward me, but Callum put himself in Tristen's path. "Don't get near her."

Tristen leveled a death glare at Callum. "Don't tell me what to do."

Callum took another protective step toward me. "I'll tell you whatever I want."

Tristen sighed, and doused the shadowfire at his hands and reached into his pocket. He withdrew a small scroll, gilded in gold, and unfurled it. He began to read. "'Welcome to the Fifth Trial. You must survive and find safe passage through The Eternal Sands, returning to the Stone Coliseum.' I found this on the beach this morning, and Rachelle found one as well with the same message. When we saw your campfire, we decided to do you the *courtesy* of filling you in on what to expect in case you hadn't found one as well."

"What are The Eternal Sands?" I asked.

Callum shifted his gaze past where the trees end. "We have to cross through Dragon's Tail to get there. Both Dragon's Tail and The Eternal Sands are some of the most dangerous stretches of the island."

"Well, we better get going, then," I said, looking at everyone.

"We are not traveling together," Callum said.

Rachelle growled at Callum, flicking her tail in annoyance.

Tristen cocked his head. "You think that's wise?"

"Please," I said, stepping forward and putting a hand on Callum's shoulder. "Our odds are better if we all go together."

Callum sighed. "Fine," he bit out, but then leveled another glare at Tristen. "But I'm calling the shots."

Tristen raised an eyebrow, but quick as a flash Rachelle shifted into her human form. "I'm tired of you two bickering," Rachelle said. "*I'm* in charge."

"Sounds good," I said.

"Good with me," Callum said, sweeping his arm around my waist. Tristen watched, his expression cool and deadly. "We need to collect our things at camp. We'll meet you back here in a few minutes," Callum said, corralling me back to the treeline.

"Make it quick!" Rachelle said, putting her hands on her hips like a mother hen.

"Yes ma'am," I said, tossing her a smile before Callum and I disappeared into the small wooded area beyond the beach.

We headed back to our small camp, and I got a better look at Callum. He had a bit of stubble on his face, but below his eyes were dark circles.

"I should have kept watch for part of the night," I said, realizing he was going into this fifth trial without any sleep.

"I'm fine. I'm used to being tired," he said.

We picked up the rest of our weapons we had left back at camp, and I fumbled a bit with strapping my dagger to my thigh over my skintight leggings.

"Nervous?" he asked.

"Yes and no," I breathed. I was still reeling from the fourth trial and the mind tricks it had played on me, but I felt adrenaline running through my veins in a way that pushed me onward.

Callum studied my face, as if he was memorizing my features. "We can leave on our own," he offered. "We can go now and get a head start."

I frowned, shaking my head. "We need them. They're... my friends."

Concern flashed across Callum's face. "Saffron..."

"I know we're almost at the sixth trial," I breathed, knowing what he'd say. "I just... I can't let them go."

"The Assassin wants you dead," Callum challenged.

"Maybe he does, maybe he doesn't."

"Even if he... *cares* for you in some twisted way, he will always choose his rebellion over you. His kingdom needs him to win these trials—even if it means slitting your throat."

I took in a sharp breath. The truth felt so cold laid bare like that. But it was the truth, wasn't it? I had powers that had helped Tristen survive this far. He was a cunning assassin, renowned for his ability to lie and manipulate. Why would I think he wouldn't try to manipulate me—his competition—and just use me as a stepping stone for him to save Stormgard against the rule of Luminaria and the King's goals?

"We travel together," I said. "Then, we regroup before the sixth trial."

Callum took a step back, but nodded. "I'll go along with this. But if he touches you, he dies."

~

CALLUM and I returned to the beach to meet up with Tristen and Rachelle. Rachelle remained in her lioness form as we started walking down the beach together, an awkward alliance, but one that I hoped would hold. We didn't even get to the where the line of the palm trees ended before I saw Priscilla and two other prisoners packing up their campsite.

"Priscilla!" I called, and ran over to them, grass turning to stale dirt beneath my feet. "You saved me in that last trial—I wouldn't have escaped without your help."

Her eyes shone. "I'm glad you made it out."

"Take a step back," Callum's voice said firmly. Before I could protest and say Priscilla wasn't a threat, I saw that the two prisoners behind Priscilla had their swords out.

The first one I recognized as Issac—the boy whose life I had told Callum to spare even as he had revealed that I was the Siphon. He looked like he hadn't slept in days, and his white tunic and breeches hung loose on his frame as if he'd lost weight.

"*You,*" I spat, whirling on him. "You gave me over to the King."

Issac shrank back. "I h-had no choice. Cassandra said she'd hunt down and kill my little sister if I didn't spy for her."

"But you had no problem handing Saffron's life over?" Callum asked, his eyes blazing with anger.

Issac's lower lip wobbled. "I couldn't risk my sister."

I sighed, my anger fizzling. "Be careful what side you do favors for," I said. "Cassandra is only out here for herself—and she'll discard anyone she doesn't find useful."

Priscilla's eyes jumped between us. "The three of us got the scrolls about the next trial. Are you all headed to The Eternal Sands as well?"

"We are," Tristen said, stepping into the conversation as Rachelle continued to circle all of us, as if trying to assess any potential threats.

The second prisoner behind Priscilla was a quiet man with a mop of brown hair. He cast a wary look to all of us—especially at Rachelle. "Priscilla, do you trust them?"

"I trust Saffron," Priscilla said, then her gaze slid to the rest of us. "I can't say the same about her friends."

Tristen sparked an inferno from his hands, and everyone stepped back. "I'm tired of talking. If you want to fight, let's get it over with already."

"How about we all travel together?" I said. "Who knows what we're about to face next. I meant what I said—we should all make a pact to get to the other side of this trial together and then it's everyone for themselves in the sixth and final trial."

Everyone looked at me like I was speaking tongues.

"Do any of you think you can take whatever is ahead on your own?" I challenged.

The men behind Priscilla studied me. Priscilla turned to them. "She's right. The Assassin will provide great protection for whatever is up ahead. Let's make a pact to fight together until the sixth trial. Agreed?"

Everyone nodded, and Tristen let his fire extinguish. "This way, then."

Tristen turned, and started to lead the way. I followed him, Callum falling into step behind me as Priscilla and her crew finished packing up their campsite, Callum keeping his body in between me and them.

Rachelle shifted back into her human form and threw her arms around me. "Hi Saffron."

"Hi Rachelle," I murmured into her curly red hair. I released her, and we continued walking, staying a few paces behind Tristen. "I'm glad you're unscathed from the last trial."

"Perks of being a shifter. I can be one big bad barracuda and avoid making deals with the pesky mermen. My kind loves to use their bargains to fuck with outsiders."

I might have imagined it, but I thought I saw Tristen stiffen a bit in front of me where he led us down the path beyond the last of the palm trees.

"I would have preferred not to have bargained with them," I said. "They made me give them my worst fear. I saw... I saw you die. All of you."

Rachelle's eyes went wide. "Your worst fear... was seeing us die?"

I tried to keep my voice steady. "I don't know what kind of friends I had before these trials, but I already know that you've changed my life in more ways than one. Thank you for your help—and I promise I'll do everything I can to help you and Leah escape."

Rachelle's eyes were shining with tears. "Friends to the end?"

"Friends to the end," I said, and we joined pinkies. "I know the sixth trial is coming—"

"A wise peacemaker just said we'll figure it out when we get there. So let's just focus on surviving this one first, okay?" She punched me in the arm.

"Okay," I said with a grateful smile.

A few birds squawked above us, and Rachelle licked her lips. "One second, I'm going to get some breakfast."

She shifted into a hawk, flapping powerful wings as she leapt into the sky and then dove after the smaller birds with her razor-sharp teeth. I grimaced and looked away as blood rained from the sky.

Tristen had paused, watching Rachelle as I fell into step beside him as we passed the last line of green.

"Hey," I said, tentative.

"Hey," he said back, and I saw a bit of warmth flicker in his dark obsidian eyes. "I'm glad you got out in one piece from the castle."

"Me too. What did you see inside?"

Tristen paused as if debating whether or not to tell me. Then, he blew out a breath. "I saw you choose Callum over me."

I nearly tripped over my own feet. "What do you mean?"

Tristen didn't meet my gaze, keeping his eyes fixed ahead at the horizon as we climbed the rocky ground that was leading up to a small hill. "I mean what I said."

"You're married."

"I am."

"I'm... missing something."

Tristen looked right at me, a deep unending sadness in his expression. "I am, too."

I tried not to gape at him, tried not to feel the headiness of the emotion rolling off him. What did Tristen mean by that? Had his greatest fear been... losing me? To Callum? Why?

Rachelle cawed from above, continuing to hunt birds with a vengeance. Tristen looked up at her and then back at the rest of the group, Callum and the others trailing behind us.

"Be careful out here," Tristen said quietly, breaking my reverie.

"I think you're the biggest threat in this group," I joked, trying to lighten the mood.

Tristen's gaze was still dark. "He sees you as his now. You still need to be careful."

I knew exactly what *he* Tristen was talking about. "I can make my own decisions."

"Of course you can. I just... I wish I could tell you the truth about him. Because he certainly won't."

My face grew hot. "I could say the same about you."

Tristen started climbing an incline path that was leading up to a small hill with a rocky outcropping. "I've seen into Callum's mind. He's the kind of man who takes what he wants."

"And you?"

Tristen turned back, his face grave. "I fight for those I love." He turned back to the view of the valley below. "And we may be in for quite a fight."

I stepped up beside him, and what I saw stole the breath from my lungs.

Below the outcropping, stretched out for miles in front of us, were thousands of unhatched eggs—each easily the size of a tree. They were embedded in a rocky desert, not a living thing growing in the craggy landscape. At the center of the mass of unhatched eggs was a skeleton. Its bones towered above the eggs, the ribcage easily the size of a hundred men stacked on top of each other. Beside the ribcage were wings made of gleaming ivory bone.

At that moment, I knew exactly what was resting in the wild desert graveyard before us.

A skeleton of a dead dragon.

45

I stood beside Tristen, Callum, Rachelle, Priscilla, and her companions Issac and Henry at the top of the rocky outcropping as we all surveyed the dragon graveyard below us.

"So all the dragons died?" I clarified.

"Yes," Callum said.

"And those eggs... they're dragon eggs, aren't they?"

Rachelle frowned. "I don't know what else could lay eggs that big."

"Rachelle, can you—" I asked.

"Shift into a dragon? Nice try," Rachelle said sarcastically. "The biggest thing I can shift into is a beluga whale, and that's not really going to help us here."

"The Eternal Sands are just on the other side to the east," Callum said, pointing past the massive skeleton of the dragon to where the giant swells of sand dunes began. "We can make it there by nightfall and set up camp for the night on the edge before we get too deep into that territory. But we have to get going now before we lose daylight."

"The dragons won't... *hatch*, will they?" I asked.

Callum shook his head. "We haven't had dragons in these lands for millennia. Only graveyards and petrified dragon eggs. They won't hatch. If they did, that would be a once-in-a-millennia miracle."

Tristen leveled a glare at Callum. "You speak of the mysteries of this world as if you know them."

Callum rolled his eyes. "And *you* do?"

"No. I have the humility to know that there are things that are far more ancient than I on this island."

Callum shrugged. "We'll tread carefully. But it's a graveyard— nothing more. Watch your step and let's make good pace so we can get through this before nightfall."

Callum made a gesture for Tristen to go first.

Tristen raised an eyebrow. "You're not worried, but you still want me to go first?"

"You are the most powerful amongst us, aren't you?" Callum challenged.

Tristen sighed. "And what a burden it is to bear," he said, and strolled down the path that dipped down into the valley below us.

I started to take a step after him, but Callum gripped my forearm. "Let the others go first. Rachelle and I will hang back with you."

Priscilla was already moving to follow Tristen. Issac and Henry followed behind Priscilla, flanking her down the narrow dirt path.

"Thought you weren't worried?" Rachelle asked Callum as the first part of our group walked out of earshot.

"I'm not worried about the dragon eggs. I'm more worried about them," Callum said, inclining his head to the other prisoners. "I'd prefer not to be dragged out of the fifth trial with a dagger in my back. We all know that Issac didn't hesitate to betray us before."

Which is why he had sent Tristen first. A cold fear landed at the pit of my stomach at the thought of Tristen's death, and the image of him being stabbed by King West flashed back in my mind.

"It's okay, Saffron. You're safe with me—both of you," Callum said to Rachelle and I.

Rachelle snorted. "Thanks, Cal, I feel *so* much safer now." Out of spite, Rachelle shifted into a huge black bear twice Callum's size. She huffed in his face, but he only patted her side and started to walk down the rocky path. Rachelle began to roar at him in annoyance, but she hit her furry head on a dead branch of a nearby tree.

I held back a laugh, following my two stubborn friends down the path.

And so we descended into the valley of dead dragons.

～

THE SUN HAD RISEN OVERHEAD as we walked for hours in the dusty graveyard. The dragon eggs created a kind of labyrinth. They were nearly double the height of an average human, and were quite wide. They had a shine to them, even as they were covered by hundreds of years of dust and sediment.

I sipped from my waterskin that was starting to run low. We had no pots to boil water and no streams to refill our supply, so we were all rationing our drinking water as the sun beat down on us. Rachelle had gotten hot in her black bear form, and had shifted back into a human. Less hair seemed preferable under the sun as we walked through the arid desert landscape—a far cry from the cool and humid forests I was used to.

"What happened to them? The dragons?" I asked Callum as we walked.

Callum followed the others as we continued to weave through the massive graveyard. "Luminaria scholars tell the story of a world in chaos, dragons torching villages and leveling continents. They were the creation of the gods, and the gods had to create a hero who would be strong enough to take them down as they couldn't be tamed."

"So the gods care about what happens in these lands?"

Callum laughed. "Maybe before the war."

"War?"

"Rachelle, did you teach Saffron *anything* when you two were holed up in the library together? What were you two doing?"

"The same thing you and Saffron did when you found yourselves alone," Rachelle said as she winked at me.

Callum raised a questioning eyebrow at me and I blushed in response.

"I didn't exactly get any history lessons from either of you," I said.

"The Divinity War was fought between factions of gods over the creation of Brightbornes—mortals who have a drop of a god's power in their blood. Brightbornes can be born or made by a god bestowing a piece of their divinity onto a mortal, but any Brightborne born or created becomes hunted. A few gods were afraid that the gifts bestowed on the Brightbornes would make them too strong, and one day the Brightbornes would overthrow them. That didn't stop a select few of the gods from fraternizing—they were simply infatuated with the humans they took to their beds. Lust, or more rarely, love brought them to intermingle with us."

"What happened?" I breathed.

"In the Divinity War, the Brightbornes and the humans succeeded in putting the gods to sleep."

"That can happen?"

"Gods can't be killed. But they can be left in a state of suspension, near death, that can kill them if they are left that way for long enough. They enlisted a Siphon to help drain the gods to a point where they could be trapped. The gods are buried in coffins made of Starforge Steel—the only metal that can keep them powerless and near death. Starforge Steel can only be found here."

"Where are the gods buried?"

"All over the island. But one of the strongest is housed beneath The Eternal Sands."

My blood ran cold. "That's... that's where we're going."

"Yes, it's the only way for us to get back to the east side of the island," Callum said. "Which is why we shouldn't camp too far in. There are a number of feral beasts that act as protection against would-be graverobbers."

"Who would want to rob the graves of the gods?"

"The small faction of Brightbornes who wish to see them set free," Callum said simply.

"The Brightbornes are still alive?"

"A few, but they are hunted by the gods' monsters. Even beyond the grave, the gods seek to protect themselves against the threat they think the Brightbornes represent. "

"Great," I muttered. "So you think we're walking into a death trap for the fifth trial?"

"When I was able to get a look at the maps of the island, I think I saw a threadwell not too far into Eternal Sands."

"A... threadwell?"

"Yes, it's a vacuum tunnel filled with water directed by a strong current that crosses underground to another part of the island. Each pool leads to one other, and I believe this one's twin is located right next to the Stone Coliseum, so we'll be able to make it back hopefully within one more day of trekking."

"So... we swim through it?"

Callum nodded. "Sort of. The current is magical, and it pulls you underneath and sucks you through to the other end. They're dangerous, though—they're only taken as a last resort. Or by those who are already in a death match."

"That's nice," I said bitterly.

A rumbling under my feet interrupted my questions, and all of us stilled. We stood quiet as the shaking stopped. I craned my head to try and look ahead, but too many dragon's eggs were blocking my vision from where Tristen was leading us.

"What was that?" I murmured to Callum, but he held his fingers to his lips.

Rachelle shifted, taking to the skies in her bird form. She circled, the sun casting her shadow on the dusty earth beneath our boots.

Then, she landed somewhere at the front of our group. She appeared moments later, walking back to us as the front of our group began moving yet again.

"Nothing out of place from the skies," she said quietly to Callum and I. "But we should be swift and quiet, just in case."

"We should move," Callum said. He motioned for me to go in front of him, and I darted in front of him, following the rest of our group that was now moving much more quickly through the labyrinth of dragon eggs that lined either side of us.

Another rumble sounded underneath our feet.

We were running now.

Rachelle launched herself in the skies again, taking her hawk form as she circled above us.

The dragon's eggs seemed to tremble as the ground continued to shake. Was it an earthquake? Dirt continued to tremble under our feet as I sucked in air and tried to keep up with the rest of the group in front of me. We were halfway through the graveyard at this point, about to come up on the bone ribcage of the dead dragon. Then, we only had one last section of the dragon's egg field to go through until we reached the sand dunes that marked the start of The Eternal Sands.

I pumped my legs harder, praying that I would be able to keep up this pace even as my muscles began to burn. I wished for the strength that the others had, seeming not to tire as they ran ahead of us, the gap growing larger between me and the beginning of the group.

The rumbling intensified even more, the ground shaking with a horrible groaning noise. Above us, I could hear the screaming of a hawk—as if Rachelle was warning us about something.

Suddenly, the front of our group came to a halt, and I turned the corner of the last of the dragon's egg labyrinth on this side, coming to the clearing where the bone ribcage was.

I arrived just in time to see the dead dragon slowly peel itself out of the ground and begin flapping its bony wings. It yanked back its head, and let out a roar as fire emerged from its jaw.

46

The skeleton dragon unearthed its huge body with a roar. I could feel the heat of its fire as it flapped its horrible creaking bones, and I smelled the magic in the wind as it began to fly. Not by any laws of physics, but instead by some sort of dark power that allowed it to flap and hover above us, deciding who it would hunt down first.

"Run to the dunes!" Tristen shouted, and I saw him dragging his dark power out, shadows unspooling around him. His shadows tossed the dirt around us, creating a small dust storm to help obscure us from the dragon's view.

Priscilla, Issac, and Henry were already running, not wanting any part in this battle.

Rachelle flew circles around the dragon, who was blasting his fire at her. I froze, unable to tear my gaze away as she bobbed and weaved and dropped so quickly I thought she was falling out of the sky as she narrowly missed another spray of the dragon's fire.

"We have to go!" Callum yelled at me, grabbing my arm and pulling me after the others.

But Tristen held his ground, watching Rachelle and the dragon tangle in the sky.

"The others—" I started.

"Let them fight. We have to run!" Callum said, pulling me along until I finally started sprinting after him.

But as we dove through another maze of dragon's eggs, it was sparse enough on this side of the dragon graveyard that, when I looked over my shoulder, I could still see Rachelle struggle as she once again barely dodged the undead dragon's fire.

She was growing tired. I could tell by how she kept resorting to allowing her small hawk body to drop and nosedive to try and lessen the energy expenditure of her flapping wings as she tried to dodge the dragon and keep it distracted.

Tristen saw, too, and he shot out a wave of his shadowfire at the dragon, which caused it to turn its bony head and swivel its red beady eyes at Tristen.

They were going to die.

I stopped running after Callum and turned back.

"SAFFRON!" Callum shouted after me, but I couldn't leave them. I sprinted after them, my feet hitting the dusty ground below me as I made it to the clearing, steps away from Tristen and Rachelle.

The dragon dove at Tristen, but he shot out a massive wave of shadows and shadowfire that was a veritable wall of darkness. It was so powerful it shot the dragon backward, giving Rachelle enough time to land safely. She stumbled, and I realized she was about to pass out.

I ran behind Tristen and darted to her, catching her before she fell.

"It's okay, Rachelle, I got you," I said, holding her body to mine as her eyes dipped close.

Rachelle opened her mouth and only bird sounds came out, as if she hadn't fully realized she was human once more. I felt her body go limp against me as I struggled to hold her.

The dragon was diving again, and I saw Tristen rally his shadows and flames, charging up and then raising his hands at that dragon. Once more, a huge beam of magic flared from him, the dragon screaming as Tristen pushed it back.

Callum made it to my side.

"Take her," I told Callum.

"I can walk," Rachelle murmured, and held herself up—barely.

Callum was about to say something to me, but I pointed toward The Eternal Sands. "Go, Callum! Get her out of here!"

He put an arm around Rachelle, and started to help her out of the clearing. When she wasn't moving fast enough, he cradled her in his arms and took off running.

As they disappeared around one of the eggs, I turned to Tristen.

He was looking at me, his eyes wild. "You have to go if you want to live, Saffron," he said, and that's when I realized the edges of his body were being wrapped by his shadows. His power was starting to turn on him, feed on him. I remembered how that had felt when I had taken his power.

"Your magic..." I realized.

Tristen grimaced, and then threw his head back and laughed. It was a rough, low laugh that morphed into something more... dangerous. More unhinged. "Dead bones, dead bones. The dead bones are talking to me! They want our bones to join them and it will be so lovely," he called, his laughter growing more wild. "Saffron, won't you lie your bones with mine?"

His magic was starting to unravel his mind. As the dragon screeched and dove back toward Tristen and he raised his hands once more to the sky, I realized that the mad god's magic wouldn't let him walk away from this battle unscathed. Tristen was about to lose all of himself.

"NO!" I screamed, but Tristen was still laughing as his magic flooded out of him, blasting into the dragon as his shadows and flames exploded from him. But his shadows were wrapping around more and more of his body, his laughter more unhinged.

I was losing him.

"SAFFRON, *RUN*! It's him or you!" Callum yelled from across the clearing where he had climbed a hill on his way to The Eternal Sands, Rachelle still slumped in his arms. "YOU HAVE TO RUN!"

Callum shouted as Tristen pushed back the dragon, but this time it was a lot less far as Tristen's powers waned.

The dragon was preparing to circle back and dive once more toward us, its fire starting to recharge and glow in its bony maw.

"He's fighting for all of us! The least we can do is fight for him!" I yelled back. And it was true. I was paces away from Tristen, and I knew he would die the moment his magic faltered against this dragon. He couldn't kill it—if it even could be killed. *Where the fuck was the Bluesteel Blade when I really needed it?* Not to mention that I was powerless—

Wait. *Powerless.* That was it—I needed the only power that could rival the dragon's own strength.

I turned to the closest dragon's egg and placed both of my hands on the smooth, dusty surface.

I didn't know if this would work, but I needed to try. I pushed my palms against the dragon's egg.

Nothing.

"Please!" I begged, hearing the bony flapping of the dragon as it made its approach.

Then, under my hands, I felt it. A small ghost of a current of power. I coaxed it out, pulling with my own power, hooking as many of those invisible loops as I could. I dug deeper, searching for more power. I needed enough to win, enough to defeat this thing.

More, my power commanded, tunneling deeper into this dragon egg. Whatever was inside conceded, and there were more glowing loops. More power to draw from. I was greedy. With one huge pull, I hooked my mental claws around all of the loops, and dragged the power from the sleeping egg, my scream being ripped from my body with the effort. It felt like I was dragging a boulder up a mountain, the exertion so heavy as I pulled at the power within me.

It sat ancient and buzzing underneath my skin, and I didn't waste a second.

I ripped my hands off the egg, turning just in time as Tristen looked nearly completely overtaken by the shadows, his eyes all black —the whites of his eyes completely gone as his power was prepared to completely consume him as his shadowfire grew even larger at his hands.

"Stand aside!" I shouted at him, and my voice boomed and echoed with something *old*. Something from a different era.

Tristen stepped back, and as he blinked, I saw a shine of recognition in his eyes. I stood in front of him as the bone dragon began to nosedive once more. I raised my own hands, and called for my power to do... *something*.

Suddenly, a popping sensation covered every inch of my skin. I let out a strangled cry of pain, looking down long enough to see that my entire body was being covered in *scales*. I blinked again and suddenly my vision was beady and blood-red. *I had dragon eyes.* I threw my head back and roared—

—and suddenly, a stream of dragon fire burst from my mouth. It was so hot it nearly consumed me, but I let it flow out of me, the blast so hot and so powerful the bone dragon retreated.

Retreated, but did not stand down.

Something inside me tugged, and I lowered onto one knee, placing one hand on the ground.

"*Leave us. Return to your sleep,*" I begged in my mind. And then my mouth was moving, speaking in a language I did not understand, telling this creature of the dead to do my bidding.

Then, something slimy and dark slithered in my mind, the voice booming in every crevice of my soul. "*Why should I do what you say?*"

I replied with the only thing I could think of. "*Because these are my friends. And I need them if I am going to fulfill my destiny. As the Siphon.*"

I felt a pause in my mind. In front of me, the dragon flapped its wings, all of us watching. Waiting. Seeing what it would do.

Then, I felt that booming voice rattle my mind once more. "*We've been waiting for you, daughter of the sun and the moon. May the little one light your way.*"

The flapping slowed, and I stayed kneeling as the dragon lowered to the ground with a great rumbling sound. Slowly, it lowered its bone wings to the ground, and then its head. The lights in its eyes blinked out, its head resting as I heard it speak once more in my mind.

"*You may pass, brave one,*" it said, and with a *whoosh* my power left me, and I fell to my hands and knees as the scales rippled off my body.

We had survived.

To my left, Tristen swayed, and I hauled myself on my feet, forcing my leaden limbs to go to him just as he fell.

I nearly caught him before he hit the ground, his huge, muscular body so heavy against mine as I struggled under his weight.

"There she is. My *Sael,*" Tristen murmured, one of his shadow-wrapped hands reaching up to touch my face.

"Tristen..." I started, but his head lolled in my arms as he passed out.

47

Rachelle had volunteered to shift into a horse to carry Tristen the rest of the distance, but she only had enough magic left to transform into a pony. Well—Callum had called her a pony, and Rachelle shot back that she was just a small horse and had no more power left to be a normal-sized horse, but she definitely *wasn't* a pony. I could tell Tristen was too heavy for her, but she was too proud to let us know, and trotted on beside us as we continued through the graveyard.

Callum stuck by my side, occasionally casting glances at Tristen's limp body.

I caught one of those glances and glared at Callum. "We are not leaving him behind," I said.

Callum held up his hands. "Your idea, not mine."

I rolled my eyes. "Please, Callum, just let up on him already. He was willing to fight and die for us to give us time to escape."

Callum glared. "I would have helped if you hadn't sent me away with Rachelle."

I sighed, every cell in my body feeling bone-tired and weary. "She needed you."

"*You* needed me."

"I held my own just fine," I said. I hadn't processed what had happened, not really. The sun had started to dip in the sky and I knew we needed to get to the edge of The Eternal Sands before night fell.

"I know," Callum said, defensive. "But you went and fought for him."

My eyes flickered back to him. "Why is that a big deal?"

Callum fought to hide the hurt in his expression. "Because he wants you dead, Saffron."

"Let me pick my own battles," I said.

Callum shook his head. "I can't let you choose him over you. You need to survive these trials. Do you think a rebel assassin deserves to come out alive from this?"

Yes, a voice inside me answered. It was a small one. I didn't quite know why I wanted to defend Tristen against Callum's accusations. Tristen had caused the greatest injury of them all—he had stolen my memories. And he had shown no remorse when I confronted him about it. Yet, for some reason, we kept trying to die for each other. We kept fighting so the other one would live. Why would a heartless assassin put himself in harm's way for me?

A part of me dared to hope that Tristen cared about me. But why? He had a *wife*. One who was willing to make a deal with the likes of Cassandra to try and get him out alive. Not to mention a kingdom— Tristen was happily keeping his secret that he was the King of Stormgard, not just an assassin. What would happen to his people and his cause if he died here in these trials?

Was Tristen just keeping me around so he would have an easy victory in the final trial?

"We'll camp up here for the night," Callum said, and I looked up as we passed the outskirts of the dragon eggs. In front of us spilled endless dunes of sand, as vast and infinite as the ocean.

Priscilla, Issac, and Henry had already stopped, surveying the small clearing that marked the divide from the desolate flatlands of Dragon's Tail and the beginning of the endless sand dunes that were

The Eternal Sands—which did, in fact, look like a very eternal amount of sand stretching into the horizon. There were six sad-looking palm trees bent with thirst that provided a bit of shelter for the night, and some underbrush and branches beside them would that provide some kindling for the fire.

We reached the others, and Callum and I hoisted Tristen off of Rachelle's pony form and laid him down underneath one of the palms.

Issac walked over to us. "I'll watch over him if the rest of you want to go look for a water source to fill our waterskins."

I appraised the boy, but I saw a flash of something I didn't like in his gaze as he eyed up Tristen's form. Tristen was powerless. Limp. Exposed. Issac had been impressed by Tristen earlier in the trials— but I knew a part of him wanted to prove his dominance, and maybe by seeing to Tristen's own end.

I sat down crosslegged next to Tristen on the sandy ground. "It's all good," I said with a smile, unhooking my waterskin from my belt with a flourish and tossing it at Issac, who caught it with a frown. "I'm beat from saving you *and* transforming into a dragon. I think I'll rest here while *you* go search for water."

Issac frowned at me, and I saw his intention clear as day as his right hand twitched near his holstered dagger. He wanted Tristen dead before he faced him in a death match. I didn't blame him, but I wouldn't let anyone near Tristen in such a helpless state. I owed that much to him when he had been willing to die for us moments ago.

Callum glimpsed what I did, and clapped a hand on Issac's arm. "Now's not the time. Let's go."

Rachelle shifted out of pony form and then into an armadillo. She rolled around a bit, and then flashed back into a human form.

I raised an eyebrow at her. "An armadillo? That's new."

"I thought I'd be less thirsty in that form. Turns out I'm equally thirsty in all forms right now," Rachelle grumbled.

Priscilla stopped at the edge of camp. "Rachelle, would you be able to help us scout a water source?"

Rachelle sighed. "Sure, I'll be the linchpin holding the group together again." She leapt into the sky—but she was now a tiny sparrow, and I saw the effort it took her to keep her wings flapping as she fought against the breeze pushing her back.

She soared above as Priscilla led the way on the quest for a water source, Callum casting me one last glance before following the rest of the group. Henry and Issac followed after them as well.

As the others left me alone with Tristen, I turned back to the sleeping man lying beside me in the sand. The hard lines of his handsome face had softened in sleep, and he looked younger. More vulnerable. It reminded me of the rare few times I'd seen his brooding demeanor slip and he laughed or smiled—*truly* smiled.

I reached out my hand, brushing dark strands of hair out of his face, which had been soaked with sweat and exhaustion. The cool breeze coming off the sand dunes had made the air considerably colder, and the chill only intensified with the darkening night. If I wanted to, I could get up and stretch and get some movement in my body. But something kept me tethered to Tristen's side, pulling me to him as I continued to brush his dark hair out of his face. I traced the edge of his sharp jaw, and found my fingertips brushing over his lips.

A memory of us tangled in his tent before the second trial flashed in my mind, and I froze, feeling my body react to the memory. Something fluttered low in my stomach, and I moved to take my hand away, but Tristen's hand reached out and grabbed my wrist.

"Don't stop," he mumbled, his eyes still closed.

"Okay," I said, and my fingertips resumed their thoughtful exploration of his face, his neck, and I brushed them over his collarbones, stopping at his chest where the top of his shirt was unbuttoned. "You never wear any armor to these trials."

He opened one eye and grinned at me. "Don't worry, I'm hard to kill."

I frowned. "Didn't seem that way when your shadows made to make you their dinner earlier."

"Is that worry I hear?"

My eyes flickered back to his. "Maybe," I admitted.

His answering smile seemed to light up every corner of this darkening wasteland. "Seems like I should fight undead dragons in front of you more often."

"Please don't," I said, yanking my hand away. "You almost lost control today."

"Yes."

"Have you ever lost control of your power before?"

"Once."

"What happened?"

"I don't talk about it," Tristen replied.

"Because you can't. Right."

"No. Because reliving it..." he shuddered. "Being asphyxiated by the darkness is worse than death. The fear is still there. The realization that you are being swallowed whole by something greater than yourself is there. But there is no peace, no calm that you would get in death."

"I get that," I whispered. "I feel this swirl of nothing in the place of where my memories used to be. Sometimes I wonder if it will swallow me whole one day."

Tristen grimaced. "I'm sorry."

"For what? Taking my memories?" I shot back.

With great effort, he pushed himself up to a sitting position, facing me. "Yes and no. I said I would do it again and I meant it. Maybe in the future you'll understand why. But that doesn't mean I wish you pain. I don't. I wouldn't wish the emptiness of the void onto anyone."

"Thanks. But your apology isn't accepted," I said, but my anger didn't rise in me like it usually did. Maybe it was because I had heard the sincerity in his tone.

He chuckled. "I don't expect you to."

"Good."

Tristen looked at me, thoughtful. "You absorbed powers from the dragon's egg. That shouldn't be possible and yet... I saw you."

"What did I look like?"

Tristen gazed at me with a kind of wonder in his eyes. "You were still you. Mighty. Fearsome. Fire-breathing. Oh, and you had some very pretty scales."

"I'm glad you think my dragon form was pretty," I joked.

He reached up and tugged the back of my braid playfully. "Pretty terrifying, that's for sure. You were also speaking in tongues, saying things to calm down the dragon. Do you remember that?"

"I think so. But how did you know what I was saying?"

"Because I'm incredibly smart," he said, grinning.

"Yeah, sure," I said as I rolled my eyes.

"I also hear them when I sleep," Tristen said, the admission coming out sincere.

I quirked my head at them. "You hear the voices of dragons in your sleep?"

"More than that. I hear the voices of the ancient ones. The gods, the dragons—it's not the best way to fall asleep, but I've picked up a few words here and there."

"Why do they speak to you?"

Tristen hesitated. He looked so tired, so *exhausted*. "The god who gave me my power has plans for me. And I've been trying to avoid those plans for a very long time."

I felt the burden he bore in that moment, and it ran heavy and deep. "Can't you tell him no?"

Tristen laughed. "Of course you would have the courage to say no to a god, Saffron. You're braver than I."

"I don't know if that's true."

"Aside from all of the dragon slaying you've been doing lately? You snuck into my tent to steal a married man's powers using your feminine wiles. That's pretty brave."

"I would do it again," I said, throwing his words back at him before my brain fully registered what I had just admitted. *Fuck—what did I just say?*

Tristen looked up at me with surprise that quickly melted into a knowing smirk. "Oh, so you did walk away with something other than my power that night, did you?"

"Maybe," I said, not meeting his gaze even as I felt warmth pool into my veins.

In a flash, Tristen's face was inches away from mine as his finger-tips caressed my shoulder, one of his legs bent casually as he leaned against it. "You still think about our kiss, don't you?"

"I didn't say that."

"How long?" he asked, the words heating like hot coals as his gaze raked over me.

My mouth went dry as I tried not to lose focus from the way his fingertips dipped to the back of my neck, drawing slow circles on my bare skin. "How long what?"

"How long do you want me to wait? Because I'd wait an eternity for you. I'd watch kingdoms rise and fall into ash. I'd watch the cosmos rearrange themselves anew if it meant I could be with you."

"Tristen," I breathed, suddenly too aware of how close my lips were to his.

His fingertips dipped down my spine, and his light touch made me shudder and move closer to him. "I'd wait for you even if you chose another. I'd wait for you to see that he was wrong for you, wait for you to see that *I* was the piece that fit perfectly for you. If it's waiting you want me to do, I'd wait until the realms collapsed into utter oblivion if that's what it would take for me to have you. But until you tell me that what you need is time, I will fight for you. I'll die by your side and fight for you to see me the way that I do you. Waiting is easy. It's the fight that I want you to see from me. To know that I am worthy of you."

Every piece of me trembled at his words. His confession rearranged my heart, my mind, my soul. It struck something deep within me that I knew in that moment I would never be the same.

"What about your wife?" I breathed, trying to make sense of the rightness of him, of us.

"Melisandre, she's not—" suddenly Tristen was coughing. He turned to his side, spitting out blood on the sand beside him. It was as if something was keeping him from speaking.

Suddenly, a scream of a hawk sounded above us.

I turned away from Tristen as Rachelle landed in front of us and shifted back into her human form, hunched with exhaustion.

She looked at Tristen. "Good, you're awake." Her gaze shifted to me. "There will be no sleeping tonight. We need to cross the dunes. *Now*."

48

"What's going on?" I asked Rachelle as I scrambled to my feet. The sleeves of my white tunic fluttered in the slight cool breeze coming off the sand dunes. Dark had just about settled, and Tristen raised a hand and lit his shadow-fire so we could see her better.

"The others went looking for water, and they awoke something else."

"What?" Tristen asked, his expression hard.

"Dune Stalkers," Rachelle whispered. "They're holding them off, but we need to go and help—"

"Lead us to them," Tristen said without missing a beat.

We were running southeast, Rachelle running alongside us in her human form. She looked bone tired having used up so much of her shifting power, and was likely still as dehydrated as I was. Tristen didn't show any signs of slowing down, but I knew he must be even more spent than I felt. Every muscle in my body cried out with exertion, and my legs felt leaden as we crested sand dune after sand dune, the grains shifting under our feet as we ran as fast as we could.

As we skidded down another sand dune, the others came into view.

Callum, Issac, Henry, and Priscilla stood back-to-back in the sand. Around them was... nothing.

Callum saw us, and gestured for us to be quiet.

We slowed our approach, and Tristen split his flame into five levitating torches that he spread out around us so we could see clearly as the sun fully slipped underneath the horizon and we were bathed in utter darkness save his shadowfire.

We got within a stone's throw of the group, and we all drew our weapons, waiting, listening to the silent dunes.

Silence, except for a rough voice.

"Would you like to see, chosen one? Would you like a little taste?"

I whipped my head around, but saw nothing. None of the others seemed like they heard anything, so the voice... it must be talking to me.

"What do you want?" I asked.

"Closer, I have something for you," the rough voice asked, sounding like shaken gravel as it reverberated in my mind.

That's when I saw it. A slab of stone half-buried in the sand a few paces to my left, across from Callum and the others. Beside the stone stood half-buried marble legs of a statue, cut off at the knee. It was as if there was a great monument that had once towered above this swirling desert, but it had been mowed down in the face of some great violent act. I was mesmerized, my eyes unable to leave the glistening stone that seemed to shine in the desert light.

"What will you give me?" I asked the voice.

"A memory," it said.

I was already moving when Callum screamed at me to stop. I sunk down and placed my hands on the cool stone, and then I

d

r

o

p

p

e

d

into the suffocating dark.

~

FIGHT.

The instinct rammed through my body like a lightning bolt. I was somewhere high, somewhere on fire, somewhere shrouded in darkness.

Dual blades arced through the night sky. *My* blades. My body moved with such practiced ease as I sliced through an opponent whose sword clashed with mine. He didn't have time to scream as I kicked him off the battlements. His body fell below—amongst an army.

An army wearing Luminaria's colors.

"FIRE!" a voice shouted, and suddenly the air was filled with gunpowder and a huge *boom!* that had me stumbling slightly as a cannon fired. I was wearing a hood and a black bandana that was obscuring the lower half of my face—clothes of an assassin, or a fighter trying to hide their identity.

Screams of death and destruction filled the air—but suddenly, the sound seemed to hush amongst the warriors standing atop the stone wall.

"He's here," whispers came from the archers on the battlements.

"Thank the gods, we're saved," a warrior at a cannon said.

I turned, and saw *him*.

He was wrapped in shadows that slithered around him like snakes. As those trying to scale the wall, armed with terrible weapons, he flicked out his shadowfire and their ropes went up in flames and they fell, screaming to their deaths.

As he approached me, I felt no fear. No terror. Just awe.

"Luminaria has razed all of the neutral border villages," the version of myself in my memory said to him, the truth sinking like a stone as I sheathed my blades. "There were no survivors."

"Then we will destroy them and their forces," he said, stepping into the light of a nearby torch. He was stunning in the flickering light. Absolutely lethal, but with a kind of grace that kept my heart fluttering. "We will keep our people safe."

"We will. Together," I said.

And then in one short stride he crossed the distance between us, yanked down the bandana that covered my face, and captured me in a kiss.

It was everything and nothing like the kiss we had shared in the tent. In this memory, he kissed me like I was his last breath. All need and desire, nothing held back.

When he pulled away from me, he looked like he was about to say something else, when—

—an explosion rattled the battlements, the blinding light flashing as the memory

d

i

s

s

o

l

v

e

d.

49

"NO!" I yelled, trying to claw my way back into the memory, my hands scratching the stone slab underneath me. Wind picked up in the dunes, sand grains flying into my face. I choked on the sand as my mind whirred a hundred miles per hour.

In the memory I had been fighting with the rebels. With Tristen. I wanted to go back, to get the answers I so desperately wanted.

Suddenly, there was an explosion of sand behind me—

"SAFFRON!" Callum yelled, and he threw his shield out to cover me just as a huge spindly creature came screaming out of the sand, lunging at me. It had a massive, shiny brown body the color of sand. It was a giant arachnid twice my size with razor sharp legs and a dozen bottomless black eyes, all trained on me.

I spun around, my hands and feet kicking sand as the creature bounced off the shield. Just a second later and its sharp legs would have skewered me. It let out a cry and suddenly eight other sand spiders—Dune Stalkers, Rachelle had called them—shrieked as they shot out from underneath the sand.

Callum had shielded me, but him and the group were now vulnerable.

I saw it as it happened in slow motion.

Callum released his shield and unsheathed his sword, slicing right into one of the Dune Stalkers that had lunged for him. He was fast—but there was one that emerged slowly, silently from the sand behind him.

"CALLUM!" I screamed, pointing.

He turned, yanking his sword out from the spider it was embedded in. He raised his sword, but the spider seemed to sense his movements as if being tuned in to the vibrations on the sand. It stepped in the other direction, and then with one precise movement, it raised one of its razor-sharp legs...

...and stuck it right through Priscilla's heart, Henry and Issac looking on in fear.

I screamed as all hell broke loose.

Tristen's shadows held one down as he doused it in shadowfire, and it fell to ashes on the sand.

Rachelle shifted into a panther, dodging and weaving the sharp arms of another.

Issac and Henry were fighting with their swords now, and I saw Henry place a hand on one of the Dune Stalkers. The moment his hand touched the creature, its movements slowed by half. That was enough time for Henry to get a slash in with his sword, cutting off the creature's legs before his power loosened its hold on the creature. It was dead before it had a chance to retaliate.

I started into the fray, but realized I had no power to fight with. I looked back at the slab of stone, wondering if it could give me some sort of power just like the dragon's egg had, but it now seemed to glow with a kind of heartbeat that made mine feel skittish.

"*Everything comes with a price,*" that rough-as-rocks voice whispered into my ears. The guilt sliced through me as I saw Tristen's shadows struggle to hold down another advancing Dune Stalker. I had run to where the voice had promised me a memory without a thought to what would happen to my friends. I had been selfish, I knew, and saw two more Dune Stalkers emerge from the sands and scuttle closer to the fighting.

And as I watched my friends tire, I realized I would be forced to watch them die. That would be the price of my memory.

"No," I said, my voice hoarse. "I won't let it!" I screamed at the heavens.

"*Oh?*" the voice asked. "*So what are you going to do about it?*"

I squeezed my eyes shut. I barreled deep within myself. There had to be something. Something I could—

There.

The magic I had taken from the dragon's egg. There was a... whisp of some sort. Something small. It was barely a thread to yank on. Barely anything at all.

I pulled with all my might.

"LET THEM LIVE!" I shouted into the barren night, tears of rage and anguish rolling down my face.

A terrible *crack* split the night, but my friends were too busy fighting to notice. One of the Dune Stalkers got in a slash at Rachelle, and she yowled, tumbling down the side of the sound dune. Tristen turned, shooting out a pale blast of shadowfire that managed to distract the Dune Stalker about to go after her, and lure it to him instead.

Two more advanced on Tristen, and he dodged and parried with his sword, his flames, and his shadow. His power—even drained— was still so immense, but I could already see his shadows starting to weave around his body, threatening to douse him in that void he spoke of with such terror.

Callum fought one off, but the Dune Stalker seemed to grow tired of trying to kill him as he stabbed and parried its sharp leg. In one sweep, it knocked Callum off the top of the dune. As it approached him, it sliced Issac in half—who let out a gurgled scream before he fell to the ground.

The Dune Stalker pushed Issac's body aside and scuttled over to Callum, and raised its leg, aiming to pierce his heart.

I felt the pain and the fear bubble up in me, but before I could voice my horror, fire doused *everything*.

Fire that came from above.

I staggered back under the intense heat, and through the wavy haze of the fire, all of my friends looked to the sky. A flash of shadows grabbed Henry—who was in the path of a blaze—and swept him back. The flames burned the Dune Stalkers one-by-one, and their piercing cries seemed to echo in the quiet night.

When the fire stopped, we all could see what was above us clearly.

Flying to me on unsteady wings was a baby dragon.

It landed on the sand, skidding to a halt in front of me. And looked up at me. As if waiting for instructions now that all of the Dune Stalkers had been reduced to ash.

The group walked to me, looking as haggard as ever—but all of their eyes widened as they took in the baby dragon in front of me. It was just a bit larger than a housecat, with iridescent scales that glittered green and blue and gold in the desert sun.

"That's... impossible," Callum said as he stepped toward me. "The dragons are all dead."

The baby dragon looked up at me with warm brown eyes, and then hopped and down and... *chirped*.

I leaned down, and it jumped in my arms.

"Careful," Callum warned.

"It's okay," I said, feeling a sense of comfort as I ran a hand down his scales that were surprisingly soft. "He's here for me."

"He must have just hatched," Tristen said, helping a limping Rachelle to her feet.

"Rachelle!" I said, my eyes widening as I saw a gash in her side.

"Gods, he's so cute it hurts!" she squealed, clapping her hands before buckling over in pain.

"Are you okay?" I asked her.

"I will be when you tell me how you got the cutest baby dragon in all of Septerra to come save us," she said.

I looked down at the dragon. "I... I think I called him. For help. Using the tether to him I created when I took his power earlier when he was in the egg. But... how is it possible? Weren't those eggs just fossils?"

Tristen shook his head. "They must have been frozen in their hatching process. Your power must have awoken this one somehow."

Callum took a few steps closer, looking at the thing warily. "Regardless, he came just in time."

"Yeah," I said. The baby dragon flapped its wings, and I released it. It landed by my legs, and nuzzled me like a cat. "I'm naming him Pepper," I said with a small smile.

"Well, *Pepper* and the rest of us should get going," Callum said. "Who knows what else is waiting for us."

I waded through sand and reached Rachelle and Tristen. She was clutching her side.

"Is it bad?" I asked.

She lifted her shirt, and the cut looked deep. I tried to hide my wince.

Tristen met my gaze. "We have to get to the end of this trial. I can help her walk, but we need to get going."

"I can help, too," Henry said, pulling himself up. He was battered and bloody, but not nearly as bad as Rachelle.

Tristen shook his head. "Maybe later. I've got her for now."

"Okay," I said. "Let's head out."

"This way," Callum said, and started leading the way through the dunes.

I followed him and Pepper kept to my side, skipping through the sand and chirping in surprise whenever we slid down a sand dune.

We trekked for hours through the night. Whenever we heard a scuttling among the sand, we all stopped and Callum threw his shield around us. As we got deeper and deeper into The Eternal Sands his shield flickered out faster and faster, unable to hold for as long whenever we paused at a strange sound.

Four or five hours into the trek, we paused for a break, drinking the last of our water.

"Here," Callum said, offering me his waterskin, but I shook my head.

"You need it for your shield," I said, trying to ignore the grainy feel of sand coating my mouth.

"We're almost there," Callum said.

"Yeah," I said, and I looked down to see Pepper leaning against my leg, as if dozing off. I picked up the small dragon and cradled it in my arms. It let out a satisfied chirp before nuzzling into my tunic.

I smiled, but it vanished as my thoughts returned to what we had lost already. Priscilla. Issac. Nearly everyone else. Without Pepper, we would all have been dead. If I hadn't followed that voice...

"It's not your fault," Callum said.

I met his gaze. He looked exhausted, going on two nights without sleep, but his expression was still warm.

"It was, though," I said. "I wanted... I saw a memory. *My* memory. Of fighting alongside the rebels. With Tristen."

Callum's expression hardened. "The stone you touched? That was the marking of where the dead god of The Eternal Sands slumbers, Saffron. They plant all sorts of false lies in your head."

"It felt real," I said.

"You're not a rebel," Callum said as he met Tristen's glare from across camp as he sat crouched next to Rachelle.

"I know what I saw," I said.

"Have something to say to me?" Tristen asked, standing and strolling over to us.

"Please," I said. "Let's not do this now."

Tristen's shadows swirled around him. "I know you've been trying to poison her against me, Callum."

"And so is the island, apparently. Maybe it's a sign?" Callum spat.

Tristen's eyes widened and he turned to me. "Did Nocterin speak to you? Did you hear him?"

"Nocterin?"

"The God of Shadows and Madness. He is buried here, somewhere in The Eternal Sands. I bet the stone you touched was his grave marker. What did he say?"

"He showed me one of my memories. Of me—of us—fighting against Luminaria—"

"He's the God of *Madness*, Saffron," Callum countered.

Tristen ignored Callum, stepping closer to me. "Those with gods' blood have the power to restore that which is forgotten. That's within their power. So what you saw was real."

Before I could react, Callum was lunging at him, but Tristen sent up his shadows, deflecting Callum's blade with ease.

Callum roared, the anger flashing across his face—

"STOP!" Rachelle screamed.

We all turned and saw Rachelle flat on the ground, Henry crouched over her with a dagger.

"Get off her!" I screamed, and Pepper screeched and took flight with a flap of his wings.

I made a move to run to them, but Tristen was already there, yanking the dagger from Henry's hand.

Henry froze, rising to his feet. His head turned to Tristen—and then kept turning in a horrific *360-degree motion*. He opened his mouth, his teeth covered in blood as he gnashed them, his eyes wide and bloodshot.

"How nice it is to see you, *Tristen*," a voice that was both Henry's and not Henry's boomed with something ancient and terrible. "Come to slay me at last?"

Tristen didn't hesitate, blasting Henry with shadowfire—enough that he should have been reduced to ash. But instead, Henry's body went flying.

"Stay away from him!" Tristen shouted at all of us. "Nocterin has his body."

Henry's body stiffly rose and walked back up the dune toward us. His gait was awkward, his bones broken from the blast. He was like a puppet being moved forward by cosmic strings. "She got a taste, but she didn't pay the price. She must pay the price." He raised a broken arm, leveling a pointed finger at me. "She must pay the price."

"She's paid enough," Tristen said, shadowfire at his hands—more faint than it had been all day.

"Put up your shield around all of us, Callum," I said, turning to him.

Callum shook his head. "Let Tristen fight it."

"No," I seethed through gritted teeth. "Put up your shield."

"Let him make his own decisions," Callum said, his glare leveled on Tristen.

"Like you do mine?" I said, and before I could stop myself, I had placed my hands on Callum's bare arms.

Callum looked down at me in surprise, but I didn't stop. I pulled with all my might, yanking his power away from him and into me.

I had never taken power so quickly before, and I gasped as I stumbled back, but I threw up the shield all around us, blasting it up and over us, over Tristen, Rachelle, Callum, Pepper, and I. It glittered above us as Henry's re-animated body stopped at the edge of it.

Henry's eyes—now black and depthless—locked onto mine as I stood panting, my body and my power feeling run ragged.

"You have a role to play. And you will play it," said that gravely voice that sounded older than the sand beneath us.

One moment Henry was standing there. The next, he exploded into hundreds of beetles, and slipped below the sand. Pepper keened, crying in fear and nudging my leg.

A moment of silence. Two. Then I let the shield drop, and fell to my knees, my stomach heaving as I vomited all over the sand.

Callum fell to my side. "Saffron—"

"We have to move," Tristen said. "I can carry Rachelle. Can you carry Saffron? We have to get to the threadwell. *Now*."

Callum didn't look up, just brushed my hair back as I sat back on my feet and wiped my mouth on my tunic sleeve.

"I got her," Callum said.

Tristen went to Rachelle, slipping his arms around her legs and back and holding her to him.

"Can I pick you up?" Callum asked me.

I only had enough strength to nod, managing to sweep a trembling Pepper up in my arms just as Callum cradled me in his.

Callum and Tristen crossed the dunes, climbing through the darkest part of the night. Slowly, as we continued through the dunes, I saw it.

The first precious rays of morning light were rising. Not only that, they were shining on a glittering body of water.

"The threadwell pool," Callum breathed. "We made it."

50

Tristen had already set down Rachelle by the threadwell when Callum and I arrived. Callum set me down by the edge of the glimmering water that was being dusted by the early rays of morning light. Around us were marble pillars that were broken at odd angles, as if they had been cut down halfway. A relic of a temple or small ruin that once covered the pool.

"We have to pass one at a time into the threadwell for it to work," Tristen said. "Rachelle first."

Rachelle's face looked ghost white from blood loss. "If you insist," she said. "What do I do?"

"Just jump in," Tristen said. "Keep your arms close to your chest, hold your breath, and don't let the current scare you—it will drag you through the island's underwater tunnels and spit you out in the attached threadwell pool by the Stone Coliseum."

Tristen helped her to the edge of the glowing waters that seemed to ripple with a humming energy. Rachelle turned to Callum and I, and stumbled a dramatic bow. "Illumia be with you, my companions."

Then, she crossed her arms across her chest and fell backward into the pool. I stepped closer, watching as the ripples smoothed on the water's surface, and Rachelle was just... gone.

"Did she make it?"

"She did," Tristen said. "You next, Saffron."

"No," I said, turning to Callum. "You go, Callum. I don't trust leaving you two alone."

"I don't trust leaving you with *him*," Callum said.

I glared at Callum. "I have Pepper. It will be okay."

Callum's gaze softened when he looked at me. "I'm sorry. I just... I've come so close to losing you too many times to count today."

I felt a tug in my heart at that. "I know. Please go. I'll be right behind you."

Callum nodded, but he stepped closer, tilting my chin up to him. He bent down, brushing a kiss to my lips. Then, he leveled a glare at Tristen, who was standing stone still a few paces away. "If I don't see her come through in sixty seconds, I'm coming back for her."

Tristen's gaze was murderous. "The woman has a godsdamn dragon, Callum. She can handle herself."

Callum looked back at me, then turned to the water and dove in. Once more, the water's ripples smoothed, and he was gone.

I looked up at Tristen, whose body was still tight with tension.

"What I saw," I said, taking a step toward him. "It's true? We fought together?"

Tristen opened his mouth—as if he was trying to form words that wouldn't come. "We—" suddenly, he cut off, coughing. He wiped at his mouth, blood on his hands. "I keep not learning my lesson trying to share these things with you."

"What... what is that?" I asked. "What's hurting you?"

He brushed the blood off on his sand-dusted leather pants. "Don't worry about me." He paused, as if thinking through something. "Even gods of madness can't promise something they can't give. If they promised you a memory, they gave you a memory."

"So that's a yes?" I asked softly. "I saw you. In my memory. You kissed me."

A war raged behind Tristen's gaze. In that moment I wished nothing more than to be in his mind, to know what he was thinking.

Tristen took my hands in his. "Do you love him?"

The question took me off guard. "What?"

"Do you love him? Callum?"

"I..." I trailed off. "I think so."

Tristen's hands tightened around mine. "Don't think. *Know*. Love isn't something that sneaks up on you. It's a truth that you feel in your bones. Not with your head."

I nodded, feeling warmth spread under my skin. Being so close to Tristen—it was like a drug. His presence was intoxicating. It was more than just his finely cut features, his dark beauty. There was something about him that struck deep. He felt like destiny in a way that I couldn't explain. Couldn't process.

"You're next," Tristen said, nodding at the pool. "And you probably should keep Pepper away from the palace for now."

I looked at the baby dragon, who seemed to understand. It let out a sad cry, and landed on my shoulder. Why did it feel like I was saying a string of goodbyes?

My words were hard to say, but I forced them out anyways. "You have to go, Pepper. I'll come for you again when this is all over."

Pepper gave another sad yowl, then jumped into the skies, flapping away.

I couldn't stop a tear from rolling down my cheek, feeling weirdly attached to the small creature that had saved our lives.

But as I turned back to Tristen, I had more to say. "Tristen—"

"Go!" Tristen shouted, and suddenly I saw a group of shadows emerging from the dunes. Not just shadows—but the silhouettes of nearly a dozen people, about to converge upon Tristen.

"Wait!" I said, but it was too late.

Tristen had pushed me into the threadwell pool, and I was yanked underneath the surface by the current as he was left alone to fend for himself as the shadows surrounded him.

PART IV

THE SACRIFICE

51

G oing through the threadwell was like being catapulted through a riptide. Water tore at me as it thrust me through a dark tunnel, and I tumbled through its grip. Finally, the twisting underwater tunnel seemed to start to shoot upward, and a glow could be seen from above. I was shoved above the surface where I gasped for air, emerging into chaos.

It was dawn in front of the Stone Coliseum, and I was dragged out of the threadwell pool by guards. All around me, confetti and streamers floated in the early rays of the morning light. Courtiers from Luminaria and from kingdoms far and wide surrounded the threadwell pool, the Stone Coliseum stretching up behind us.

As I got to dry land, the courtiers grew quiet as King West stepped forward. He grabbed my wet hand and yanked it into the sky with his. "My favored lives to see the final trial!"

Cheers erupted all around us, and I caught sight of a dripping wet Callum and a pale-faced Rachelle standing beside the other guards. It looked like we were the only ones to survive the fifth trial.

I looked back at the pool. Tristen—

"Now, we celebrate!" King West said, and suddenly I was pushed and prodded into a loud parade, two guards by my side. No iron bands were placed on my hands as I was forced forward.

"Tristen, he—" I said to one of the guards.

"Get moving, missy," one of the guards said to me. "We have to get you washed up before the celebrations tonight. The King has quite a night planned for all of you. Be on your best behavior now that you're freed from your iron bands—one wrong move and you're done for." The other guard snickered.

I swiveled my head, looking behind me, past the priestesses and courtiers following us in the procession.

The threadwell pool remained placid and calm. Tristen did not emerge from it.

~

THE GUARDS RETURNED me to the same chambers in the Saltspire Palace that I had resided in previously. Leah was tending to the roaring hearth when I closed the door behind me.

She turned. "You're back. Is Rachelle—"

"She's safe."

Leah's stoic demeanor crumbled, and she rushed to me, throwing her arms around me in a rare display of affection. "Thank you."

"It's the least I could do—thank you for everything you did to help us."

A knock at the door had me pulling away from Leah, and I went to answer it. As I opened the door, Zara slipped inside—as soft and quiet as the whispering fabric of her skirts. She closed the door behind her, her white scribe's robes flowing around her.

She fixed those odd gray eyes of hers on me. "I need to speak with you. Alone."

I shook my head. "I trust Leah. You can say what you need to in front of her."

Zara took a look at Leah as if assessing her, and then turned to me and nodded. "As you may have guessed, I am no scribe. I am a spy in service of an ally of yours."

"An ally of mine? Who?"

"I cannot say," Zara said. "But I'm here to get you out. Tonight."

"How?"

Zarah raised her hand, holding it in front of her...

...and then her arm up to her elbow disappeared, going invisible.

"My power is useful for stealth, and I can shield two people at one time. Pick who you would like to come with you and I can be sure they are safe and out of reach of the island and the forces who control it by this evening."

Two people. I turned to Leah, whose eyes had gone wide. "Take my sister. *Please.*"

The choice was obvious, and I didn't have to think about my answer as I faced Zara once more. "Don't take me. Take Rachelle and Leah," I said, gesturing to Rachelle's sister. "Callum and I will find our own way out."

Leah's hands flew to her mouth to cover a gasp.

Zara quirked her head. "You would give up your freedom? For two strangers whom you've met in these trials?"

"They aren't strangers. They're my friends. And they've given up more for me than I could put into words."

A smile slipped across Zara's lips. "You truly are everything they say you are."

"What do you mean?"

But Zara was already in motion, heading to the door as she glanced at Leah. "I'll meet you back here at midnight, Leah. Pack light and don't be late."

Zara had disappeared from the room just as Leah burst into tears. I went to her, pulling her into another hug.

"Why?" Leah asked me as her sobs subsided, finally pulling away.

"Because my greatest fear—and my greatest weakness—is losing those I care about," I admitted. "If you and Rachelle are safe, that means Callum and I can focus on escaping the final trial alive. Plus, I don't want the King to retaliate against anyone else if I'm found missing tomorrow morning."

Leah nodded, wiping at her tear-stained face. "Speaking of the

King, I need to get you ready for tonight. Here, let me start on your hair."

∼

LEAH PUT me in a gold and ivory dress with a tight square bodice and a voluminous gown that trailed on the floor. My hair was swept up in a delicate updo, just a few curls spiraling down to frame the angles of my face.

I was whisked away to the ballroom, where the most raucous party I had seen yet was underway. King West was roaring drunk, parading me around to the other kingdoms like I was a prized mare. Rachelle, who had been seen by the healers, sat beside Callum at the far end of the table as endless wine and food were served. I kept my distance from Rachelle as to not arise suspicion—and I could barely escape the King and his court despite my disdain for them.

My gaze kept sliding to the doors of the throne room.

Doors that Tristen did not enter.

The night continued in a blur as the festivities reached a fever pitch.

I couldn't take it anymore, and as soon as King West was distracted, I slipped from the ballroom.

∼

SILENCE AWAITED me in my chambers. My guards were missing—likely drunk with the rest of them in the main ballroom, the revelry overflowing like the cups of everyone in the palace.

I stepped inside on wobbly legs.

Tristen had been alone and drained of his power when those shadows had emerged before he had pushed me through the thread-well. He hadn't come back through the pool. He must be... he couldn't be...

I felt tears burning behind my eyes, and I sunk down on the lush carpet of my room, feeling the weight of the trials bearing down on me.

Everything was too much. How was I supposed to show up to the sixth trial and kill Callum? How was I supposed to come to terms with the fact that Tristen had likely died, alone in the dark dunes of The Eternal Sands? There had been so many dark figures that had emerged from the shadows—surely too many for him to fight off himself.

Tears flowed faster now, and I felt a sob make its way up my throat.

"I can't," I whispered to myself in my cavernous room. "I can't accept this."

Behind me, I heard the door of my room open and close.

My heart fluttered, hope coming alive as I turned—

—but as Callum entered, I swallowed my disappointment.

"Callum," I said, and he helped me to my feet.

"Figured that I'd check on you and let you know that they just announced the last trial is tomorrow."

"Tomorrow," I said, still feeling in a state of shock as his hands took mine. "That's so soon."

"I know," Callum said, squeezing my hands. "I got away as soon as I could. Everyone's distracted. I wanted to... see if you wanted to spend the night together. In case it's our last."

My heart was squeezing, threatening to explode. "It can't be our last," I said, my voice sounding so small. Unbidden, the memory of everyone I cared for being murdered in the underwater palace came back to me, and fresh tears rolled down my face. "I can't have this. I can't keep saying goodbye to the only people I know in the entire world. I can't keep wondering what small joy in my life will be extinguished next. I can't... I can't win these trials and keep my soul, too."

I looked up at him, and he reached up and brushed away my tears. "Don't think about all that. Just be here. With me."

He leaned down and kissed me then, but for some reason his touch felt wrong.

Callum felt wrong.

Something under my skin tugged. As Callum's mouth moved with mine, I felt the pull again.

Let me free, it seemed to say.

So I did.

And Tristen's stolen power fizzled through me, opening Callum's mind to me with a

f

l

a

s

h.

52

Riverleaf had fallen.

In his memory, I saw through Callum's eyes as he surveyed the burning homes of our little village. He went into charred homes, rooting through the rubble only to find charred corpses of families who had been trapped inside. I felt his anger boiling until he broke into a run, sprinting toward the edge of town as wails of the survivors filled the air.

Callum stopped in front of the bakery—*my* bakery—where the door had been melted open and the inside burned to a cinder. He stepped inside, as if worried he would find me amongst the remains.

"Saffron? Are you here? Anyone?" he called out, but there was no reply. Then, something caught his eye and he lowered to one knee, reaching down to the soot-stained rubble to pull out the blue ribbon —*my* blue ribbon, and the one he had kept at his bedside. I felt his emotion swell as he pocketed it.

"Missing something?"

Cassandra stood in the doorway with three of her priestesses, flanked by six Luminaria guards wearing white and gold. The darkening sky cast an eerie light across her face, and she smiled at Callum.

He didn't hesitate and blasted them back with his shield, sending them flying, out of the bakery and back onto the dirt road. But Cassandra seemed to float on some sort of wayward wind, and Callum unsheathed his sword, leaving the burned down bakery and advancing toward her.

"Leave our village."

Cassandra raised her arms, turning to the other Luminaria soldiers beside her. "He speaks!"

"Back off!" Callum yelled, and I heard the fear in his voice.

Cassandra stepped closer. She tilted her head. "Oh, I'm sorry. You aren't even just a soldier. You're..." her eyes dipped a symbol in his armor of a six-pointed star. "...a *captain*. Oooh, how special. You must be privy to your little militia's plans, aren't you?"

Callum roared, and his steel rose to slash at her. She merely reached up and *gripped his blade*, blood sliding down her palm from where her skin met the hilt.

His eyes went wide. "You're a witch."

Cassandra smiled as she melted his blade in her fist, and silver droplets landed on the soil beneath her. "High Priestess, actually."

She raised another hand, and power blast out of her at him, but he fell to the ground, calling out his shield to protect him just in time. I felt his fear run through his veins as he realized he was outmatched.

Cassandra blasted waves of power at the shield again and again, but it did not waver. "You're a strong one, aren't you? Your power could be... useful to us, you know."

Callum didn't answer, grunting under the strain of keeping his shield up. But Cassandra threw more power at the shield, and he cried out in pain as it started flickering. *He was losing.*

He knew it, too.

That's when his hand dipped underneath his chest, reaching for a hidden dagger there.

A hidden dagger to pierce his own heart crystal and blow everything to hell.

Even as just an observer in Callum's memory, I saw the moment his resolve clicked into place as he prepared to sacrifice his own life to end Cassandra's.

Cassandra saw it, too, and suddenly, she shot out a fresh beam of power—a force streaked with a rainbow of color from all of the stolen heart crystals she had absorbed. It overwhelmed his shield in an instant, snapping it with a cry as Callum's dagger dropped to the ground.

Callum dove for his dagger, but Cassandra was on him instantly, and with a horrible crunch she broke his leg.

He screamed, but Cassandra was on top of him. She held his dagger at his throat.

"Now now, don't make such a fuss," she chided. "I saw you were going to introduce us all to the gods a moment ago, but that would be a waste of your heart crystal and the power stored there."

"*Fuck. You,*" Callum spat at her, but pain wracked his face. She pressed on his broken leg and he let out another horrible scream.

"Be still, soldier. I heard that you lost someone today, didn't you?" Callum froze.

Cassandra smiled, and through his eyes I could see how wicked that smile was. "I know the Shadowfire Assassin left this village with something that didn't belong to him. A *girl*. If my sources are true... *your* girl. What if I told you that I could bring her back?"

Callum swallowed. "What do you mean?"

"It's simple, *captain*. You fight for Luminaria for one year and help us put a stop to these silly neutral villages that are aiding the Stormgard rebels, and in return I will see to it that you will be reunited with your dearest Saffron."

Even as I witnessed Callum's memory, a part of me began raging at him. To stop. To not consider this.

"I'll find her myself."

Cassandra looked down at him, pointedly. "You think I'd let you live? That's cute," Cassandra crooned. "And even if I did, do you think the bloody remains of your militia will brave another fight after what has happened here? Here, I'll even offer you a *blood oath* that I will bring her back to you if you work for us willingly."

"If she was taken by the Shadowfire Assassin, how can I be sure that he has not warped her mind? That he has not taken her for his own?" Callum asked, his voice cold.

"You're right. Then here are my terms: you will share with me all of the militia plans for all of the villages on the border and serve in Luminaria's forces for just one *tiny little year* as we see fit to quell this rebellion. In exchange, I will spare the rest of the surviving civilians here in Riverleaf and return Saffron to you. And I will ensure she will be... *unencumbered* from any man who thinks to lay claim to her. Deal? Or would you prefer death?"

Callum hesitated, and I felt the warring emotions in his mind even as the terror started to give way to finality.

His decision was made.

"Deal," Callum said as I watched the memory unfold with growing panic. "We seal it in blood?"

"Why of course," Cassandra grinned, and rose to her feet. Callum stood as Cassandra took her dagger and in a smooth motion, she split her hand open, handing the dagger to Callum, who did the same.

They clasped hands, their blood mixing with a spark of power, and I *screamed and screamed and screamed* as the memory

d

i

s

s

o

l

v

e

d

around me.

~

I STUMBLED back from Callum in my chambers, gasping for breath, for truth.

"You..." I whispered, shaking my head.

Callum was gripping the chair behind him, his face ashen. "You looked into my mind. You... *stole Tristen's powers to look into my mind.*"

I didn't let myself think of how it had been possible for me to unintentionally take Tristen's powers—and how if I *had* taken them, he had been truly defenseless against those shapes that had emerged from the dunes. I had sealed his death with my unknowing touch, but I shoved away that rising guilt and let it boil over into raw fury.

"You made a deal with her," I said, my eyes wide. "With Luminaria! When you watched them torch our village and *burn everyone in it!*"

Callum held up a hand. "The destruction was done. Tristen had stolen you from me. Everyone we loved... they were all dead. I made a deal to salvage what was left. Us. I made that deal for *us.*"

Tears, hot and angry, flowed down my face. "You gave them information to help them take down the other neutral villages, didn't you, Callum? The ones at the border that were aiding the Stormgard rebels? Those *innocent* people?"

Callum shook his head. "I did what I had to do to bring you back to me, Saffron. I told you before, my wish was to see you again."

Truth flashed through me. "You... you're the reason I'm *here*. In these godsforsaken trials. Cassandra said she'd bring me to you—and this is where she brought me!"

Hurt and anger flashed through Callum's eyes. "I should have clarified my blood oath with her. I messed up, Saffron. I never thought... never thought she'd bring you here. Like this. I just... I just wanted you to survive. Everything I have done is for you. Please... believe me..."

He took a step forward, but I took two steps back. "*No.* You've betrayed *everyone* for me. What about my memory? Are you somehow responsible for that, too?"

"No," Callum said. "The sphinx told you that Tristen had done that. Probably so that you couldn't see all of the horrible things he must have done to you behind enemy lines."

"Behind *enemy* lines?" I said, and wild laughter slipped from my lips. "I *am* behind enemy lines. And all I see is my *true* enemy."

Callum took another step toward me, but I couldn't bear it. I couldn't bear to look at the man who I had wished with all of my heart could have been the missing piece to a forgotten love story— but in truth was the reason my life had turned into a living nightmare.

I flung myself out of the door of my room and down hallways, down stairs, past drunk courtiers and guards and priestesses.

Out. Out. Out. I have to get out.

My feet obeyed, and I made it to the gardens before I realized I was out of breath from running. I stopped at the foot of the sweeping gardens, the ocean glittering beyond in the dying light.

My hands were shaking as I took unsteady steps down the small staircase and onto the wet grass. Behind me, I could still hear the revelry of the party happening above. In *my* honor—the honor of the King's favored who would win The Ash Trials and help the King of Luminaria in his quest to destroy the Stormgard rebels—and any innocent civilians that stood in his way.

"A beautiful night, is it not?"

I whirled to see Cassandra strolling toward me out from behind a fog-lined hedge.

"*You*," I said, my anger rising as I took sight of her. "You are the reason I'm here."

Cassandra smiled, the image of piety and sweetness. A candy apple rotten to her core. "You should be *thanking* me. I brought you back to the man who loved you. It's not my fault he just happened to be here of all places."

"He chose me over innocent people. He let Luminaria destroy those neutral villages."

"In the name of love, was it not? A lot of people do silly things for the name of love. Just like your husband-to-be. Don't think I believe for one second that Tristen just *happened* to be caught after you showed up here."

Husband.

Suddenly, I was brought back to the first memory I had in this version of myself. Lying on the cell of Ashguard, looking down to see I was dressed in a torn wedding dress.

It wasn't Callum who I had chosen to be wed to.

It was Tristen.

53

Cassandra took a few more steps toward me, her catlike smile growing wider. "I see you're putting the pieces together, aren't you?"

I felt my heart shatter into a million pieces. There was so much I hadn't said to Tristen, so much time we had lost...

...and I hadn't seen him since he pushed me into the threadwell pool.

There was a good chance I had just lost my greatest love once more. The revelation started to undo me, piece by piece.

My eyes flashed with fury as I looked up to Cassandra. "You knew."

"Of course I did. Who do you think whisked you away from the altar? But it doesn't matter now. You will do your *duty* to the King just like I had to do. Like *all of us* had to do. You don't get to run away with the rebels and think you can remake your kingdom somewhere far away from this. Wartime means sacrifice. And it is time for you to sacrifice, Saffron."

A roaring filled my ears. "I have sacrificed enough."

I pulled the dagger I had stored in my bodice and lunged at her.

She laughed and disappeared. I stumbled into the empty space where she once stood, a hedge cushioning my momentum.

"I am the High Sorceress. You don't have enough power to defeat me, *girl*," Cassandra crooned, and I spun to where she had appeared behind me.

I raised my dagger again, but this time she moved lightning-quick, catching my arm mid-swing. "Enough of this." She whipped her head around. "Take her!"

Guards streamed out of the palace, heading to me. Cassandra let me go and I took a step back. I was surrounded.

"You may be the King's favored, but I will still enjoy watching you break as you murder your way to the finish line tomorrow," Cassandra said. Her priestesses emerged from behind the fog-filled garden before her, their blue hoods drawn as she waved at the guards. "Take her away."

"You'll pay," I spat at her. "I swear it."

"I've paid enough," she said, mocking me. "But keep that energy. It'll serve you tomorrow."

She swished away with her blue dress and robes, her priestesses falling in step behind her as she returned to the palace.

Two of the palace guards stepped out and wrestled my wrists into iron bands. I felt the first drops of rain fall from the sky as I was dragged to the cells below the Saltspire Palace to await the final trial.

54

I awoke to a shudder of thunder jolting me awake on the cell floor. I blinked, pushing myself up, my body aching and my thin gown barely keeping my body warm in the cold. There were no windows in the cell, but time had passed. It must be nearly morning.

A few vines had crept into this old cell beneath the palace. On one of the vines bloomed a moonflower. I crawled closer to it, the white petals blooming from a starfish-like shape at the center. The moonflower was so rare, and it only bloomed in the darkest hours of the night.

I reached out my hand and brushed the pure white flower. It had fought so hard to unfurl its soft petals in this dingy cell.

Far away, I heard the clanking of keys and the unlocking of a door. I watched as polished boots made their way down the steps. *Too* polished. These were boots that never saw mud or true terrain. Only fine rugs and smooth palace floors.

I made my way to my feet, keeping my head high as King West strode in front of my cell, his nose wrinkling as he took in my dirty dress and unkempt hair. "Pity. I gave you every opportunity to arrive at your final trial in glory. And instead you try and attack my High

Sorceress? You deserve for all of the allied courts to see you as the filth you truly are."

I leveled a glare at him, no longer trying to hide my hatred. "At least I'm not the filth that pretends to care about his people and then turns around to murder innocent villagers."

He quirked his head. "Innocent? They chose to fight with the rebels and sealed their fate. Those villages were far from neutral and had to be put down." He took a step closer to the bars. "I will destroy every last one of the rebel forces after this is over. And you'll help me."

"I will not—"

King West reached out and grabbed me, yanking me to the bars. I felt something pierce my arm, and I looked down to see one of his extravagant rings was twisted open to reveal a hidden sharp blade just the length of a thumbnail, but wicked sharp. Blood slid down my arm where he had used it to slice my skin. "You will do what I say." Suddenly, my blood was levitating as he raised his free hand.

King West was a blood magic wielder.

I tried to hold back a whimper as that horrific sensation crept through my veins, the blood starting to march at his command.

"Never," I whispered, pushing down my panic as I held his piercing stare.

He grinned. "You're a feisty one. You'll need that. I'm already planning all of the ways in which I'll force your body under my command. I will learn how to best... *provoke* your siphon powers. I've already promised you to my best warriors who will use you as they see fit on the front lines."

I felt a chill sweep through my body as I realized the full truth of what lay ahead of me after this sixth and final trial.

A fate truly worse than death.

"I'll never help you," I said, but my voice wavered.

"You have no choice," he said, tightening his grip on my blood and I felt my heart skip a beat as he paused the blood in my veins, keeping it from flowing.

I opened and closed my mouth, no oxygen coming in or out. Stars started to cloud my vision, and I felt myself teeter on the brink of passing out.

Then, my blood rushed back into my heart, and I slumped against the bars, the King pulling away with a low chuckle.

"You will always submit to me, Saffron. Oh, and I did you a favor."

It took too much effort for me to lift my head to face him, my breath coming in gasps.

King West took out a small gold handkerchief, cleaning the blood off his ring as he hid the dagger within it, sliding the crest of Luminaria back into place. "You'll only have one opponent in the final trial."

"What?" I asked, fear slicing through me.

"I sent one of my men to take care of the shifter for you. Just to make sure there was no way you'd lose. And just for good measure, we closed up the threadwell pool by the coliseum with a grate of metal stakes. Just to ensure that any... *unexpected guests* would get an equally unexpected surprise."

My mouth went dry. *Rachelle. Tristen.* No. Surely Zara would have reached Rachelle in time and the King was lying. And Tristen... gods, I hoped he was still alive.

"You fucking bastard—" I threw myself at the cell, wishing I had the strength to break it down and strangle him.

But King West had already turned on his heel, heading to the guards stationed at the stairs. "Put on a good show today, Saffron. How you'll be treated after you win will depend on it."

I screamed, shaking the bars. But the sounds were swallowed up by the cell. I slid to the floor, my body shaking with rage.

I was all alone, withering on the damp stone floor as the night-blooming flower slowly closed its petals as dawn made its death march.

55

I didn't speak as the guards tossed a pair of fighting leathers into the cell, not turning to give me privacy as I changed out of the dress and into them instead.

I didn't speak as three of them dragged me out of the palace gates, ornate ships of all of Luminaria's allied courts floating beyond the cliffs in the sea below.

I didn't speak as I was escorted down the dirt path that led to the Stone Coliseum, the crowd loud and restless from where they waited inside.

I didn't speak as I was led through one of the tunnels, and found myself standing in front of a gate that led into that dusty pit at the base of the coliseum. The stands were once again full with courtiers and nobles, the chosen few who were allowed to watch the final trial.

The trial that determined whether Callum or I emerged alive.

I could see as the guards brought him to his own stone grate, across the coliseum from mine.

At the center of the coliseum sat a pile of weapons.

Weapons we would have to kill each other with.

He was too far away for me to make out his expression, but I saw he stood resolute. Stone still like a true commander about to face down his death.

I kept a firm grip on my heart as the door behind me closed, and my iron bands fell to the floor.

The King rose and made a speech, but I didn't hear it. His words were no longer of concern to me. Then, trumpets from the side of the arena started to play a war march. The final music one of us would hear before crossing over into the next realm.

Slowly, the gates began to rise. The crowd's roar grew louder, and I stepped out onto the dusty floor of the coliseum, the blood from the first trial long replaced with fresh sand.

Callum and I walked slowly to the center of the coliseum. Neither of us made a move to the new pile of weapons. There was a stone atop the pile, but the Bluesteel Blade was notably absent.

Callum stopped a few paces from me. I could see his expression now. It was one of torment, of anguish. Of a man who was thoroughly broken.

I opened my mouth to speak, but he shook his head.

And dropped to his knees in front of me.

"Do it, Saffron," he gritted out, not meeting my gaze. "Kill me and *live.*"

The coliseum roared, the audience wanting blood. I looked up at them. Saw what they wanted. I turned to the pile of weapons. The screaming grew more shrill as I withdrew a crooked dagger from the pile. I stepped back in front of Callum, his eyes shining as he raised his head to me.

"I love you. I always have," he said.

I shook my head, slowly. "I didn't," I said, the words slicing him like no dagger ever could. "And you took me from the one who had truly earned my heart."

Callum's eyes flashed. "He manipulated you, Saffron. This whole time—"

I shook my head. "No. That was you, Callum."

"Saffron—"

I raised my dagger, and he squeezed his eyes shut. Waiting for his death. For his punishment. For a fate he sealed when his jealousy had caused him to lash out at Tristen and choose to enter the trials.

With my raised hand, I tossed the dagger in the sand beside him.

Callum's eyes snapped open. "No."

"There are fates worse than death," I spat out. "And I intend to make my last stand. Right here, right now. Are you with me?" I held out a hand. I could see him searching my eyes for an answer, and he took it. I pulled him to his feet.

The cheering and screaming of the coliseum turned to jeers and boos. Callum and I dove for the pile of weapons, grabbing blades. We stood back-to-back with swords aloft. We would fight, and we would die. But I was no longer afraid.

I was no longer that fearful girl cowering in an Ashguard cell.

I was a warrior. And I would die for my right to freedom, on *my* terms.

We faced the crowd, waiting for the guards to stream in and fight us.

But then there was a rumbling. On the far end of the coliseum, the last gate began to open.

Gasps and cries of surprise echoed in the arena.

He strode in, strolling into this final trial as if he was death's messenger. His shadows trailed him with a crackling energy, spinning and undulating like chaos given form.

His clothes were torn, muddy, and covered in blood. But he was alive, and walking straight toward us.

Tristen, the Shadowfire Assassin—the man I was to marry—was alive.

56

Tristen stopped a few paces in front of us, the arena holding its breath as Tristen appraised us.

I lowered my sword, taking a step toward him.

"I know everything," I said, and I couldn't chase the quiver of my voice. "I—"

"Not here," Tristen said, his stony expression unreadable. His eyes flickered to Callum. "We need to fight our way out."

Callum stepped in front of me, pointing his blade at Tristen. "She's not going with you."

Tristen turned to me. "Will you?"

I stepped out from behind Callum, pushing his sword away from me. "I am."

Callum watched me, his eyes helpless. I felt a twinge of guilt—but it disappeared as he refocused on Tristen. "Then you will die, Assassin."

Callum lunged at Tristen, and I screamed.

But Tristen had regenerated his magic, and his shadows lashed out, batting away Callum's sword as the two men circled. The arena was swelling with noise once more, the spectators finally getting the fight they had been promised.

"This is your problem, Callum. You're fighting a losing battle. There is no prize for you at the end of this," Tristen said.

Callum spun, landing a hard blow on one of Tristen's shadows, another one spearing out to parry his next slice as he went to cut Tristen down again and again with a flash of steel. "She is not *your* prize."

"You're right. She is no prize. She is the tempest at the eye of the most vicious storm. She is the precious last breath a soldier takes before he dies. She is the giver and taker of life. And she is *mine*."

His words struck something deep and primal within me. My body reverberated as if his words had pulled the cord of a forgotten bell that was finally rung.

Tristen sent a wall of shadows at Callum, throwing him back. Callum tumbled, throwing his shield up.

The King was yelling something, and then I saw the guards flooding the arena.

Tristen turned to see them, and locked eyes with me.

"You need to call your dragon. And I'm not talking about Pepper."

"I can't."

Tristen stalked to me, taking my face in his hands. "You can, and you will."

He crouched down, placing my hands on the dusty ground of the coliseum. "Don't let your fear distract you."

Callum was barreling toward Tristen again, and Tristen rose to his feet, his shadows lashing out and shadowfire growing at his hands as Callum assaulted him with impressive blows—blows he still fought back with ease.

But the guards had hit the floor of the coliseum now, running toward us. No doubt here to kill Callum and Tristen so I could be declared the winner and fulfill the duty that the King and Cassandra had set out for me.

I reached into the ground, picturing the sleeping creature in that graveyard at Dragon's Tail. I called for it, begging the island to be my conduit. Begging that the slivers of supernatural energy that slumbered at our feet would hear my call. I pulled any drop of magic I could from the soil below me, calling out for that thing I knew could give us our shot. Could allow us to walk away from all of this.

A rumbling answered my call, and the earth began to shake beneath my hands, the ground underneath our feet cracking and splintering.

"*Come to me!*" I cried out.

The rumbling froze. Nothing happened. I looked up, seeing Callum and Tristen still fighting. The guards were running now, so close as they unsheathed their swords, ready for slaughter.

I had failed. My heart pounded in my chest, and I tried to hide my disappointment. If I couldn't use my power, I would use a blade to cut down those who would see us dead.

I got to my feet, picking up the sword as I did, ready to fight to the death for them.

For Tristen.

For *us*.

The soldiers had reached us when I heard it.

That scraping sound of bone wings flapping in the air. And the humbling roar of a dragon's cry.

I felt the heat and smelled the stink of singed flesh as the dragon fire dipped down low enough to light up some of the guards behind us.

Every head in the coliseum swiveled up as the bone dragon arrived, answering my call. I laughed, relief washing over me as the dragon opened its bony maw, fire blazing in the sky as the screams began.

Callum realized what was happening, and he swiveled to fight off some of the distracted guards, culling their ranks—and giving Tristen and I a chance to escape.

"Now," Tristen said, grabbing my arm, and we ran. Chaos emerged as we sprinted to the gate I had entered on the southern-most end of the coliseum.

"Faster!" Tristen called, and I sprinted to keep up with him as we reached the gate. Tristen didn't hesitate, sending a massive blast of shadows and shadowfire from his hands. It ripped through the stone, leaving a gaping hole where the gates had stood. On the other side, guards were fleeing into the woods.

Tristen grabbed my hand and we ran through the hole in the coliseum's walls, and sprinted across the dirt road that encircled the building. Behind us, I saw Callum fighting off guards as he followed. He was overwhelmed, blasting his shield again and again to keep the massive number of guards at bay.

"They're going to kill him—" I started.

"Don't worry, Callum's strong enough to hold them back and make it out," Tristen said, and as if on cue, Callum let out an even more massive blast of his shield that tossed the guards around him away like they were toy soldiers.

He turned, starting to run to us, and we continued to make our escape once more. As we put more distance between us and the Stone Coliseum, I tossed another glance back, and saw as another line of guards stopped Callum, and he began fighting them off just as Tristen and I disappeared into the heart of the forest.

The screams continued to echo behind us as we slid through paths in the forest, dodging trees as we ran. I felt my lungs burning with the exertion, but I forced myself on, trailing just slightly behind Tristen.

We finally broke through the treeline, stumbling on a beach just south of the Saltspire Palace.

Several men were readying two small rowboats as we arrived.

One of them with a mop of ivory hair and a big grin who I recognized as Aldric turned to us. "Heard the screaming. Thought it was time go."

"Good timing," Tristen muttered.

I stumbled on the beach beside Tristen, and Aldric grinned. "Glad you made it out alive, Your Highness."

I looked behind me—had Melisandre somehow showed up?—but there was no one there. I turned back to Aldric, and he tracked my confusion. He cast a sideways glance at Tristen, an eyebrow raised. "She doesn't know...?"

"You know I still can't say anything about fuck all," Tristen growled, stalking to the rowboat and turning to me after taking a few steps into the surf. "Get in, we have to go before the island starts to ignore the fact that I stole this from Callum." Tristen held out the Illumia Crystal that Callum had used to help us break free of the island's clutches before.

"You have a way out of here?" I asked.

"Yes, we have a ship glamored off the coast, ready to take us back to Stormgard," Tristen said, motioning again for me to get into the rowboat that Aldric had just jumped into, bobbing on the current.

"Okay," I said, shelving my questions for later as I started wading into the ocean.

"Going on a little trip?" The female voice had us all frozen and turning to where Cassandra and her hooded priestesses approached from the treeline.

Tristen took a few steps toward me. The men from the second rowboat disembarked immediately, one of them charging at her with a gleaming sword.

He swung for her, and she stepped out of his way. She placed a hand on his bare arm where his armor didn't cover him. From where she touched, his skin began aging rapidly. He let out a pained cry, crumpling to the ground as her power took hold of him, spreading quickly to the rest of his body, undulating as her magic aged him so fast he was crumbling to dust before her in a blink.

She dusted her hands off on her skirts, turning to the rest of Tristen's men. "Would you like to be next?"

They shrank away, but Tristen stepped forward. "Leave us, Cassandra."

She clucked her tongue, swaying her hips as she approached him. "You stupid, stupid boy. You could have had your rebellion *and* your kingdom. Yet you risked it all just because you couldn't let your princess go."

Tristen stared her down. "She's not my princess. She's to be my *Queen*." Tristen began to cough, and spat out blood on the sand next to him.

Cassandra watched him wipe the blood from his mouth, and

flickered to my expression. "I see my silencing spell is breaking down. Tell me, Saffron, do you remember what you traded for his life?"

I looked at Tristen, and he glanced at me, his gaze heavy.

"Show me," I begged, needing to know what she was talking about.

"Go ahead," Cassandra motioned. "I'll even lift the spell so he can show you the truth. All of it." She unclipped a small dagger and made a small cut on her wrist, murmuring a language I didn't understand as her blood hit the sand before us. A small blast of power hit Tristen, something invisible, but I could still taste the metallic aftertaste of magic as he rocked back slightly on his heels.

Tristen kept his eyes on Cassandra until the last moment, flickering them to me. He slipped his hand in mine. "My memory. Of the last time I saw you."

My hand grew warm, and suddenly I was

g

o

n

e.

57

I n Tristen's memory, he was standing in a field of softly swaying grass. As a small band began to play, he swept his gaze across the small audience of gathered people wearing the red and black of Stormgard, who rose to their feet and turned.

There, from underneath dripping willow trees, I emerged. Walking down an aisle, escorted by an older woman—

—a woman, I realized, with shock, was my mother. *Aurora*. That was her name—*Aurora Vale*. My mother, resplendent in a simple gold dress that shone like the sun in the soft light of sunset. Her ice blue eyes and long blonde hair matched mine. The realization would have overwhelmed me had I not been hit by the force of Tristen's emotions as his eyes absorbed every detail of me. My eyes, the way the setting sun hit my skin, and my wedding dress. The same dress that would later be torn to shreds on my body as I awoke on a prison cell floor in Ashguard.

But here? As I walked down the aisle to him, rose petals leading the way, I saw myself from his perspective. Felt the adoration and love as he drank me in. My dress was white with a flowing train, and had an off-the-shoulder style with long lace sleeves and a lace cape draped behind me. My hair was braided and curled with flowers. Not any flower—the night-blooming roses that had been magically spelled to stay open as they dripped from my hair.

We stopped in front of the altar, Aurora throwing her arms around me as she whispered in my ear. "Go have your happy ending, Saffron. Cherish every moment."

When she pulled away, tears were in her eyes, but she looked so vibrant and youthful, even with the soft wrinkles lining her face.

Then, I stepped up to the altar, across from Tristen as Aldric stood between us with some official-looking leather bound book. On the front of the book was the crest of Stormgard, I realized—a fist holding a lightning bolt. The same emblem that had embossed the handkerchief that I had found beside my ruined dress when I had awoken in Ashguard.

There were words being spoken by Aldric, a ceremony happening that he was officiating, but in Tristen's mind—all of that was background noise.

He was focused on nothing but me as I stepped up on the altar beside him, my ice blue eyes shining as Aldric made some joke and the audience softly laughed with warm humor. My eyes never left Tristen's, not even as crowns were opened from velvet boxes. Even as a crown was placed on my head—a beautiful thing made of delicate golden spirals twisting into leaves and inlaid with diamonds and pearls—I couldn't tear my gaze from Tristen's. The electricity between us was humming. It had always been there, I realized in that memory, but it was something I had ignored, brushed off as just my attraction to his beauty.

But now, as I felt that moment through his memory, I knew our feelings for each other ran much, much deeper than anything I could have ever imagined.

"My parents would have loved to be here," Tristen whispered to me as Aldric made more jokes to the audience, going off-script. "I'm glad Aurora could make it."

"Me too," I whispered.

"These two can never really stop breaking the rules, can they?" Aldric said to the audience of our closest friends and family members, a few guards posted around the ceremony. "If you don't care about my speeches, let's skip to the good part, shall we?"

A ripple of laughter went through the crowd.

"By the light of a thousand stars and the blessing of every realm, do you declare your undying devotion to take Saffron Vale as your beloved Queen, now until the end?"

"I do," Tristen said, his words uttered like a prayer. Aldric was nudging me, and I smiled at Tristen as I slipped a wedding band on his finger.

The same wedding band I had seen him wear during all of the trials.

Aldric turned to me. "As two paths become one road eternal, do you, Saffron Vale, declare your undying devotion to take Tristen Grewyood as your beloved King, now until the end?"

Tristen's answering smile was sunlight, moonlight, and all of the light in-between. He withdrew a ring from his pocket, and my breath caught as I saw it in the light. A diamond was placed between two twin sapphires the color of my eyes, and the gold of the band was etched with lightning bolts.

He held out the ring, about to slide it on my finger. "I—"

"Oh, how sweet," a female voice rang out. It slithered underneath my skin, and I felt the flash of fear as Tristen pulled me behind him.

We all turned as Cassandra walked down the aisle. Tristen's shadows were already out, unfurling as she approached.

"Get out, Cassandra," he said, low and deadly.

"I can't do that, *Prince*. Or is it Shadowfire Assassin? It's so hard to keep track of all of your identities these days."

Tristen snarled, and his shadows speared for her, but she blocked them with a wave of her own magic. Screams rang out as royal guards in Stormgard red and black helped the guests from the pews, evacuating them. One of them grabbed my mother, who fought against them. *She was trying to get to us.*

"Now, is that how you treat your guests?" Cassandra mocked.

"Aldric," I whispered, and he looked at Tristen, who nodded. Aldric slipped away, going to get Aurora out of the outdoor wedding space—and out of harm's way.

"What do you want, Cassandra?" I asked as our guests cleared out, our guards and trusted soldiers creeping closer to where we stood facing Cassandra on the altar.

Cassandra looked me up and down. "A secret wedding. Why, I wonder? Are you afraid Luminaria will realize that the long-empty thrones of Stormgard are about to get filled, and you might just find yourselves with some unaccounted for wedding guests?"

"Speak or die," Tristen warned, angling his body in front of mine.

"I'm here to fulfill a blood oath," Cassandra said, her hips swaying as she approached. "I made a certain promise to a man that he would have her—and I'm glad I caught you before you tied the knot. It would be so sad to lose a bride after she's truly yours, would it not be?"

"We're not losing anything," I asserted.

Cassandra sniffed at me. "You smell powerless." Her eyes lifted to Tristen. "You really think taking a *hollow* as a wife will help you stave off Luminaria's eventual reign of your lands?"

The shadows grew longer at Tristen's feet. "So you do admit they're our lands?"

"Semantics." Cassandra tilted her head back to us. "Your wards are down. I had a little help with that part."

From the treeline behind us, a row of her hooded priestesses appeared, their hands glowing with power.

Far away, a screeching sound echoed through the darkening forest. Not of an animal, but of a monster.

"Soon, you'll have other concerns, but I'll get what I came for. Blood oaths demand either fulfillment or life itself—and I never break my word."

Cassandra rammed a blast of colorful power at Tristen, and he flew backward, his shadows stretched thin as he kept them in front of me and the fleeing guests. He hit a tree with a terrible crack, blood running from his head as he struggled to his feet.

Cassandra charged up another blast of power at her hands.

"STOP!" I screamed, stepping in between Cassandra and Tristen. "You will not touch him."

"That's the problem, Saffron. I promised that you would be delivered without any troublesome romantic entanglements."

"Delivered to whom?" I asked, my voice cold.

"That's not my information to share," Cassandra said with a smirk. "But it was made clear that you are not to be with another when I am to take you. And it looks like you and the prince are *quite* intertwined."

"Then let me make a deal with you," I said.

Cassandra's power flickered out at her hands. "Oh?"

"I'll have him erase my memories. He'll be as good as dead to me, which will fulfill your blood bargain. But you must promise that he lives."

"No," Tristen said, pulling himself up and stalking toward us. But his shadows were starting to double back upon him, and I knew he was pulling more from his power than he should as he protected all of those we loved who were fleeing.

Another roar sounded in the distance, the monsters starting to encroach upon our lands.

"I must," I said, turning to him. "The wards are down. Everyone will die if you don't go and stop what's coming in. If you sacrifice yourself for me, our kingdom won't survive it. The rebellion won't survive it. Luminaria will win, and I'll be as good as dead if that's the price we have to pay."

"I'll pay any price," he said, and in his memory I felt the anger rippling through him, raw and painful.

I reached for a dagger, slicing my hand. I flipped the dagger so its hilt faced Cassandra. "We have a deal, then? You let Tristen live and in exchange he'll wipe my memories so you can fulfill your blood oath to whoever sent you."

"Saffron, no—" Tristen said, grabbing my arm, but I didn't look at him.

Cassandra studied us. "What do I get out of this?"

My eyes flared. "If you decline my offer, we will both die tearing you limb from limb."

Cassandra considered, weighing her options. Then, she smiled.

"One one condition: after he erases your memory—and I do mean *every* memory—I get to place a spell on him where he cannot remind you of your past memories... should those pesky things return if he does come across you once more. Just a simple silencing spell."

"Deal," I said, shifting a pleading gaze to Tristen. "It's the only way."

"It's not—"

"It is," I said, and he paused at the pain he saw there, his own emotions rippling with a heavy intensity.

Cassandra studied me. "Fine. Let's end this the civilized way, shall we?"

Tristen tried to yank me away but it was too late—Cassandra sliced her hand with my outstretched dagger, and we shook. Magic sparked from our blood oath, and when our hands dropped, a feline grin stretched across her face. "Make it quick. I have places to be."

I shot a glare at Cassandra, and she sighed, walking a few paces away to give Tristen and I privacy for our goodbyes.

"You shouldn't have done that," he said, his voice coiled with pain and absolute devastation.

I fought back tears that fell anyways. "Stormgard need you. Right *now*. If I'm being taken behind enemy lines into Luminaria—they can't know what I know about the rebellion. Erasing my memories will protect everything that we have built from Luminaria. No mindweavyr will be able to look into my mind if it is blank."

"I won't stand for this—" Tristen said, and I could feel his fear cresting as he took me in, memorizing every detail of my face.

"You *have* to. You have to get the wards back up, secure the borders, watch after the people we love, go marry godsdamn Melisandre if you have to so you can claim the crown and rule before everything falls to pieces—"

"Saffron—"

"You have to give us a fighting chance against Luminaria. You have to keep fighting. For me. *Promise me.*"

Tristen's voice was raw as he responded, his hands going to cradle my head. "I promise that I will find you. That I will fight to bring you home. Even if you don't remember me, remember us—" he sucked in a breath, and I felt his heart breaking in his chest, "—I will fight for you. You will be my Queen, and we will win this war. I swear it."

"Tristen," I breathed, and his lips were on mine. Loving, wanting, desperate. Even as everything was slipping from our fingers, even as our home was in danger, we crashed together with an intensity that left me breathless when he pulled away. "I love you," I said, but he was shaking his head.

"This is not goodbye, Saffron. So don't be telling me goodbye."

"I love you," I echoed again.

"Gods*dammit*," Tristen seethed, clutching me to him. "I love you, too. But this is not goodbye. Swear it."

"I swear," I said, tilting my head up to him.

"Now or never," Cassandra called, looking back at us.

Tristen placed his hands on either side of my head. "I love you, Saffron. I will find you again. Now, breathe for me, darling—I'm so sorry, but this will hurt." His voice shattered like all of the pieces of my heart, and as his magic lifted to his fingertips, I began to scream as every precious memory of mine was ripped away from me.

58

"No," I said, the word tumbling from my lips as I stumbled away from Tristen on the beach, my hand clutching my heart as it raced. I turned my gaze to Cassandra, who was smiling. "You—"

She shrugged. "Me? Oh please, I was just fulfilling a blood oath, nothing personal. But since I so generously let you have that memory, Tristen is fair game. But I'll give you one last gift—you can watch him grow old by your side before I reduce him to ash and we return to the King."

Cassandra was advancing toward Tristen, and I screamed, wanting to call for someone—*anyone*—to help as Tristen shot out his magic toward her, his shadows wrapping around is own body so quickly after so much use today—threatening to overtake him once more. Cassandra was powerful—maybe not as powerful as Tristen, but close. But he was at a disadvantage.

"Go!" he yelled at me, but I couldn't run. My sword and dagger had been abandoned at the coliseum, lost in the rush to get to the beach. I was defenseless, and as Cassandra's magic started to overpower Tristen, I felt the lump in my throat grow.

I was losing him.

Cassandra pulled back her magic, and then with a blast, sent a ray out toward me. Tristen panicked, stretching out his shadows to intercept it—

—giving her just enough room to blast him backward into the sand.

"Please! Stop!" I begged, but Cassandra was advancing on Tristen. He was still on his back, his magic writhing like a living thing as he struggled to his feet. She raised a hand—not to send more of her raw magic at him, I realized, but to drain him of his youth. Of his life. Of our future together.

Horror hit me as she was just two paces away, and I felt everything move in slow motion.

One moment, she was standing over Tristen, leaning forward to take everything from him. Then, her fingertips went to touch his skin.

She frowned, looking at Tristen in a twisted kind of awe. "Oh. So you're not normal, are you? Does she know?"

The next moment, a glittering blue dome shot over him, tossing her away like a piece of trash on a strong wind.

I knew who that shield belonged to.

"Callum!" I yelled as he emerged from the forest line, his sword on the ground as his arms were crossed overhead, kneeling as he channeled all of his strength around the shield that covered Tristen, stretching it to cover me and the two rowboats.

"You need to leave, now!" he yelled.

I nodded, and ran to Tristen, helping him up. Cassandra was on her feet, stalking to Callum. He shifted his shield so it covered him as well, forcing the glittering dome to expand as I slung one of Tristen's arms over my shoulder and dragged him through the water to the boat. Aldric helped us into the rowboat just as Cassandra launched an attack at Callum, his shield holding strong—but just barely.

We started to row, and I turned back to shore. "Callum, come with us! We need to leave!"

Callum looked back at me, sweat beading on his face as he struggled to hold his shield against Cassandra's onslaught, keeping it glimmering over us, too. "Paddle hard. I'll see you soon, Saffron."

And the realization swept over me as Cassandra emptied her horribly colorful magic into his shield.

Callum would die here, so that I could live.

"Callum—" I shouted.

"I'm sorry, Saffron," he called back, and I could see the tears streaking his face. "I'll love you now until my dying breath."

"Thank you," I choked out, my voice breaking as the waves carried us out of earshot. But Callum's shield held, and I heard him give a battle roar that would move mountains.

As we rowed, our little boats got caught by the current that helped to sweep us out to a ship that had just sailed out from behind a rock formation right off shore.

It flew red flags for Stormgard. The rebel forces. *Our* people.

Callum's shield continued to stretch over us as we reached the ship, growing weaker and weaker with every second. My tears fell hot down my face as I abandoned the oars and clutched the edge of the rowboat, watching him hold the shield against Cassandra's relentless press of magic until I was torn away from the rowboat, dragged onto the larger ship that awaited us out at sea.

As we were hauled aboard the ship and the shore was no longer visible, I heard it before I saw it.

A great explosion, originating from a power supposed to be rationed over a lifetime that was instead let loose in a second. It sent a shockwave of his glittering shield so large, it could almost hold all of the sky within its safe confines as we made our way safely on the ship.

There was a great puff of smoke and flash from the shore as Callum's shield blinked out.

59

I t was a warrior's sacrifice. A choice of death to give others life. A choice that had me falling to my knees on the ship's deck.

Tristen kneeled beside me.

"I know," Tristen said softly. "I know."

I threw my arms around Tristen, sobbing. Callum had taken so much from us, but he had done what he had thought was right. And he had chosen death to give me a future. A future with Tristen.

As the crew gathered on the deck, Tristen turned to them. "A moment of silence for the sacrifice given to us by Commander Callum Wells, please," he said, and silently, the crew began to kneel all around us.

I kneeled beside Tristen, beside Aldric, beside all of the others. The silence was carried on the breeze, honoring what he had given us even as I felt my heart constrict. In that moment, the wind carried my braided hair away from my body, and I noticed the blue ribbon I still had tied there.

The ribbon of mine Callum had kept, as a reminder of me. The same ribbon that would now be *my* reminder—of him and what he had chosen to give up when he had chosen to detonate his heart crystal to give us a chance to escape.

I rose to my feet, even as sobs tore from me as the truth sank in—Callum was dead. Even though Callum had doomed me—and Tristen—with his choices, he had atoned for them.

Tristen held me to him. "I know."

My tears subsided, and I looked up at him. "It's not fair."

"I know," Tristen said again. "Luminaria will pay for what's happened here."

I nodded, wiping at my face. We could honor Callum's sacrifice by fixing what was broken—and repairing what Luminaria had taken from us.

"Saffron!" I turned, and a woman with fiery red hair bounded out from the people on a crowded deck. She hugged me. "You're alive!"

Behind Rachelle, Leah stood nearby—and I saw Zara with her ephemeral scribe's robes appearing like a specter on the ship as she followed behind.

"You're all here!" I said, my heart warming as I realized I wouldn't have to bear any more casualties.

Then, screams started up on deck as people started pointing to the sky, readying crossbows.

An annoyed squawk had me shouting, "Hold your fire!"

I ran to the edge of the boat to see a very tired—and very annoyed—baby dragon flapping its way to our boat.

It landed with a tumble on the deck, letting out an indignant screech.

"Pepper!" I cried, sweeping up the creature in my arms.

Rachelle clapped her hands, jumping up and down. "He made it!"

Pepper nuzzled his scaly head in my arms, and I swore he let out some sort of sigh. "I think he's annoyed we almost left him behind."

Tristen sighed. "To be fair, I *did* look for Pepper before getting here. He flew away when my men and I were battling the Thousand-Fanged Scorpion King after you left. Turns out Pepper is a lot *less* inclined to help when you're not around," Tristen grumbled.

I frowned, turning to Tristen. "A Scorpion King with *how many* fangs?"

Tristen shrugged. "Doesn't matter. We're here now."

"How did you escape The Eternal Sands? Those men who came out of the shadows to kill you—"

Tristen shook his head. "They were fellow rebels, not enemies. They arrived right on time to help me set up the escape plan. It was all very well-orchestrated, but I won't bore you with all the details. All I'll say is that Zara had swiped Callum's Illumia Crystal from his old quarters in Ashguard before getting Rachelle and Leah out last night. We tried to spring you and Callum last night as well, but you both were too heavily guarded. So we opted for Plan B. And now we're going home."

"To Stormgard," Aldric said, stepping up beside us on deck.

"To Stormgard," echoed the voices of those on board. Slowly, those gathered on deck crossed their right hands over their chests, their fists at their heart. I watched as they all watched me with a fierceness that belied hardship and a loyalty that ran deep.

"What's going on?" I asked Tristen. Rachelle and Leah looked confused, but Zara just placed her fist over her heart like the others— the ultimate chameleon, able to blend in with any group.

"They're honoring their future King and Queen," Tristen said, watching my expression. "If you'll still have me."

"You've always had me," I said.

Tristen's obsidian eyes lit up like stars shining through the night sky. In one fluid movement, he crossed the distance between us and captured my lips in a kiss. Cheers shot up around the deck, and I pulled away, my cheeks reddening from all of the attention.

"Finally," Aldric grumbled. "You have no idea how insufferable this one was when we were scouring the world looking for you."

"Shut up, Aldric," Tristen said, and wound an arm around my waist. "Set sail for Stormgard. Let's go home."

"You heard him! Let's put as much space as we can between us and this godsforsaken island," Aldric said, turning and shouting instructions to the crew.

Rachelle grinned at me as Tristen was pulled away by some of the warriors and sailors on the ship.

"I heard. Everything. You're to be a *Queen*, Saffron!" she squealed as the sails caught wind and we started flying over the water. "Do you remember it? Everything that's happened? With you and—him?"

Tristen caught my gaze across the ship, a small smile creeping across his face as he took me in before turning back to the conversation he was engrossed in.

"Only what I've been shown," I said. "I'm hoping it will come back over time. But if not? It'll be a good excuse to make new memories."

Pepper chirped in my arms, and Rachelle reached out a questioning hand. "Can I?"

"Here, you can hold him," I said, and I put Pepper in her arms.

Pepper let out a content squeak as Rachelle held him close.

Zara stepped up, her eyes flickering a bit warily to Pepper. Seeing her trepidation, I walked to the edge of the ship as Rachelle and Leah cooed over Pepper, scratching his neck the way he liked.

"Thank you. For getting them out," I said to Zara.

Zara smiled. "A promise is a promise."

"So you're not a scribe?"

"Oh, I am. A scribe's training pairs best with a spy's ear." She lowered her voice. "Which is why you should be careful when you return to Stormgard."

"You're not coming with."

"Not now," Zara said. "I will part ways once we reach land. But you should know that the people of Stormgard have been without true leaders since Tristen's parents were slaughtered by Luminaria. Ever since, the kingdom has awaited its sole heir to marry, and when Tristen chose you over Melisandre—*especially* after you were taken by Cassandra and he refused to chose her or another—there have been some who have grown distrustful of his future reign."

"What are you saying?" I asked, careful.

Zara just gave me a small smile. "Enjoy your new future. Just know that underneath every seat of power lives a den of vipers. Stormgard is no different."

I nodded. "I understand."

"And I'm sorry for your loss today," Zara said.

"Thank you. Luminaria will pay for everything they've done." I looked out at the island, growing smaller as we made our escape.

"Revenge may be necessary to balance the scales, but don't forget to cherish the gifts of those you've lost left behind," Zara said.

"I know," I breathed, "He would want me to be happy."

"He would," Zara said, and her eyes dipped to someone approaching behind me.

Footsteps sounded on the deck, and I turned to see Tristen standing a few paces away from us. "Can I borrow her?" he asked Zara.

Zara smiled, stepping away like a cloud drifting on a soft breeze. "Borrow away."

I ducked my head, trying to hide my blush as Tristen's hand went to my lower back, leading me to his quarters.

~

TRISTEN'S QUARTERS were at the front of the ship, windows sprayed with the salty sea as the prow carved through the deep blue water. A four-poster bed was hidden away in the corner, with a lounge area surrounding tables covered in maps at the center. A small metal bar cart with a decanter filled with liquid of an amber hue sat by one of the tables.

Tristen had led me to a small bathing room where I washed off, stripping off my wet and bloody clothes and stepping into a warm bath. I didn't linger, my skin already feeling hot. I pulled on a simple white gown with capped sleeves and criss-crossed laces across the front of the bodice that I left loosely tied, the dress dipping open across my breasts as I ran my fingers through my wet hair that was starting to dry in curls thanks to the salty sea spray.

Then, I wandered out into the spacious bedchambers to see Tristen dressed in a fresh tunic and pants—both in black, his favorite color, it seemed—his dark hair still damp.

"You bathed," I said.

He smiled. "I used Aldric's chambers to give you some space. May I?" Tristen asked, going to pour me a drink.

"Sure," I said, suddenly feeling a sense of eager anticipation in his presence as the tension between us continued to crackle like invisible electric sparks.

Tristen motioned to one of the couches. "Sit," he said.

I did, and he poured two drinks into crystal glasses, walking over to sit beside me. He propped an arm on the top of the sofa, the other one tracing the rim of his glass.

I took a sip of the liquid and started coughing. "What the fuck is this?" I ground out in-between coughs.

A small smirk quirked his lips. "Oakspirit. It's a favorite that's imported from the Kingdom of Verdanroth."

I set down the glass on the low table by my feet. "Well it's definitely not *my* favorite." My eyes flickered up to him. "Or is it?"

He shook his head. "You're still the same person you were before. What you like is what you like." Warmth danced in his eyes. "You were impartial to Grimwine before. I just don't have any on our ship."

"*Our* ship," I echoed.

Tristen downed the rest of his drink, setting the glass on the low table with a slow, careful movement. "Everything you see is yours, too. If you want it."

The undercurrent of his words was clear. He still wanted to know if I wanted *him*.

I bit my lip, and his eyes tracked the movement. "So Melisandre... she wasn't... you never..."

"*Never*," Tristen growled. "Clearly, she was trying to position herself in a place of power at Stormgard. To claim she was my wife was a dirty lie, even for her, but our people..." his eyes shifted back to mine, and I saw the pain there, "they're desperate for a path forward. I've hurt them by being away for so long, but I couldn't bear returning without you."

"And if I hadn't wanted to return?"

Pain flashed through Tristen's eyes, and he lifted his gaze to me like it took effort. "I knew from the moment that I entered Ashguard and joined the trials that there was a chance you wouldn't fall for me again. There was a chance that our love... that it made sense for your last life, but maybe not in this one. When I arrived and I saw you protecting Callum, I faced that fear head-on. But I couldn't let you go. Even as I tried to convince myself that you would be safer with him, that if you had picked him it was for a reason—even then I couldn't fathom not having you by my side once more. And when I smelled him on you, saw how he looked at you..." Tristen closed his eyes, shaking his head. He blew out a breath, and locked eyes with me once more. I saw they were rimmed with tears. "I knew it would destroy me if I failed at winning you over, so that couldn't be my mission. So, I made it my mission to make sure you survived—at all costs. Even if you didn't choose me."

I inhaled sharply, feeling the full weight of his sacrifices. "You've done so much for me. Why?"

Tristen's hand slid into mine, and his obsidian eyes warmed like a spring night. "I don't know if I've made it clear to you in this version of your life, but I want you to know that it's an honor and a privilege to remind you each day of why I fell for you. You may not remember it yet, but when your village was crumbling, you chose to stay and help the other villagers evacuate. And when you saw me fighting the Luminaria forces? You picked up one of their blades and, even though you didn't have a lick of training, you wanted their blood. You were a baker's daughter with a warrior's heart, and you saw as I did that Luminaria had no more care for human life. So you joined us. Trained with us. Fought beside us. You were considered hollow without a drop of power, but you made your determination your power."

"I wasn't the Siphon before?" I asked in disbelief.

Tristen shook his head. "No. Which is why your bravery was even more stunning. You fought with your whole heart against Luminaria troops and their magic. You found your own ways to be clever and cunning as we rebuilt the border and helped villagers escape into our territory, and you even fought your way into my heart." His lips quirked up into a smile that set my heart on fire.

"As did you," I said, and as the words left my lips, they felt more true than anything I'd ever said before. "Because I choose you, Tristen."

"And I choose you," he said, his voice soft and his eyes wide as if he couldn't believe his luck. "I will *always* choose you."

I bridged the gap between us, my lips meeting his. He tasted of the salt of the sea, his scent of pine and spice overwhelming me. I felt his fingertips brush my neck and then wind into my hair, pulling me into him and angling my lips toward his. His kiss was warm and fervent and it promised a kind of sinful escape that made me lose himself in him.

I pulled away, his forehead meeting mine as the current between us grew stronger.

"How do you know I'm not just here to steal your powers?" I teased.

"I'd like to see you try," he said as his eyes darkened.

He pulled me onto his lap, and I arched into his touch as his fingertips traced up my thighs, lifting the hem of my dress. His touch was like a wildfire, and I wanted to be devoured by it. His lips moved, tracing my jaw and reaching the shell of my ear.

"You have no idea how hard it was to keep my distance," he murmured in my ear, "when every day, all I wanted to do was strip you bare and claim you as *mine*."

The small gasp that escaped my lips was swallowed up as his mouth crashed against mine. Heat pooled at the apex of my thighs, and as his right hand slid up my dress, I moved against him and felt his hardness through the fabric of his pants. My hand fisted in his shirt as I chased the friction of our bodies sliding against each other, Tristen's left hand pulling me against him.

My fingers went to the buttons of his shirt as I pulled away from his kiss. "Off," I commanded, a little breathless.

Tristen's answering smirk was hidden as he stripped off his shirt, tossing it aside in a flash—he was just as impatient as I was. In the blink of an eye, he picked me up, his lips hungrily finding mine once more as he strode to the four-poster bed.

He broke from our kiss and then tossed me onto the bed before climbing over me.

"Off," he growled as he caged me in with his body. He nipped at my neck as he tugged at my dress.

I pressed a hand on his bare chest, heady with lust as I pushed him off me. I guided him to the bed as he let me straddle him. I undid the laces at the front of my dress, and the straps of my dress slid down my shoulders as the material spilled at my waist, baring my breasts to him.

"Saffron," Tristen breathed, sitting up to brush kisses at my collarbone... lower... "You're beautiful."

He flipped us once more, undoing the rest of my dress and pulling it off me. I hadn't bothered wearing anything underneath, and Tristen's gaze turned absolutely lethal as he took me in, flickering back up to me as I lay sprawled before him.

"I knew what I wanted," I said with a half-smile.

"You're what *I* want," Tristen growled, a feral grin stretching across his face as he moved off me, standing at the edge of the bed. He took my legs and yanked me to the edge of the mattress and I let out a yelp of surprise.

He sank down to his knees before me, his strong hands going to cradle my leg. "There were so many times I was jealous," he murmured, kissing my ankle, my shin. "But you know when I was most jealous?"

"Mmmm?" I said, my skin burning with each kiss as he worshipped my body.

"I was the most jealous of that fucking ice cube."

My mind shot back to the Temple of Orsi, the aphrodisiac we had all been drugged with—and how Tristen had cooled down the most sensitive parts of my body with the ice cubes. I sucked in a breath as he kissed my knee, my inner thigh, climbing higher.

"I promised myself if I found myself between your thighs again I wouldn't let it go to waste," Tristen said, finally reaching the sensitive area between my legs. Before I could breathe, he licked the seam of me, his tongue hitting my clit as I arched my back with a cry.

Lightning rocketed through my body as he worked, eliciting breathless moans from my lungs as my core dripped with desire.

"Gods—you're so wet," Tristen said against me. The hum of his voice made me shudder with pleasure, but he didn't give me a second to recover. He added one of those strong, talented fingers of his, moving inside of me as he sucked on that sensitive bud.

Every cell of my being teetered on the precipice of oblivion as Tristen worshipped my body, energy buzzing underneath my skin and sensations crested like waves, growing stronger.

"*Tristen,*" I gasped, his name coming out like a prayer from my lips.

"Come for me, Saffron," he commanded, slipping in another finger into my dripping core.

His demand sent me over the edge, and I unraveled. My pleasure shot through me like lightning—he was a force of nature in his hold on me.

He withdrew, my body trembling in the aftershocks of how he had consumed me. Each moment had felt like the colliding of stars, but I wanted *more*.

As Tristen rose to his feet, I saw the impressive length pressing against the seams of his pants. Gods, he was huge—I would be lying if I said he didn't intimidate me.

Then, his shadows swept out with a soft touch—surrounding me as I was brought up to a sitting position at the edge of the bed in front of him. I laughed in surprise at the feel of them.

"Happy?" he asked with a mischievous grin.

"I want you," I said, but it came out like a breathless plea as I reached for him over his pants. His blazing eyes locked with mine, and through the haze of lust I saw an unbridled joy in his gaze.

"You do?" he asked, as if he hadn't dared himself to hope that I would choose him. Choose *us*. And that it was still a surprise to hear it from me.

"I want you. Forever. But especially right *now*," I said, unable to keep the neediness out of my voice as I tugged at the waistband of his pants.

"You have me," Tristen said, shedding his pants and tossing me back onto the bed.

I laughed, but in a flash, he was upon me, a hungry kiss devouring my laugh as he rested in the cradle of my spread legs. I could feel his massive velvety length pressing against me, and I felt my hips buck against his—desperate for the friction, for the fullness I craved.

"Please," I begged as Tristen teased his cock at my entrance. "I need you inside of me, Tristen."

"So impatient," he whispered in my ear, and then sheathed all of himself inside of me.

I sucked in a gasp as he slid inside, pleasure echoing deep into my bones as my back arched once more and I clamped down around the delicious fullness of him.

His gaze met mine, his body stilling as I adjusted to him.

He reached down, brushing a piece of hair from my face, his gaze tracing my skin like an artist preparing to paint a portrait of his beloved. The gesture was so loving, so filled with care that I nearly burst, so many sensations rushing through me at once as I felt my hips move against him on their own accord, wanting him deeper.

Tristen groaned, his forehead falling against mine as he started to move, withdrawing and then thrusting deeper inside of me. "Fuck, you feel perfect, Saffron."

I let out an answering moan as his lips went to the sensitive juncture where my neck met my shoulder.

He started moving faster, and I felt my core coil tighter like a spring building to release as we moved together, my moans breathy and urgent. I felt the whispering feel of his shadows ghosting over my body like a lover's caress or a light breeze, and then a stream of them slipped underneath my low back, propping me up to allow Tristen to thrust even deeper inside me.

His hand dipped between us, and as he found my clit and toppled me over the edge of my desire once more. He thrusted into me at a punishing pace that hit every nerve ending deep within me.

Waves of release shuddered through me as I cried out, and I clung to Tristen as he followed, filling me with his seed.

I went boneless in his arms as he held me, my head on his chest. We lay together as our breathing slowed, still joined. Then, he reached down, brushing my hair out of my face once more as I looked up at him.

"I love you, Saffron," he said, the words resonating through me like a perfectly struck chord. "I loved you as you were before, and I love you as you are now."

"You're a hard person to hate," I said, and he laughed.

"I'll take it," he said, leaning down to kiss me. Every unspoken feeling he had held back in the trials tumbled into that kiss.

When he pulled back, I reached up and brushed a stray piece of his dark hair from his obsidian eyes. "I love you, Tristen. What memories I have of you so far don't do you justice."

He grinned. "The real thing is much better, isn't it?" Then, he pulled away and disappeared into the bathing room. I heard running water, and then he returned a moment later with a damp washcloth.

"May I?" he asked, and I nodded as he went to gently clean me with the warm towel, his movements reverent, kind, gentle.

He stood once more, placing the towel in a clothing basket by the side table before returning to bed with me, scooping me back into him as he held me, our bodies fitting perfectly together.

"You feel right," I murmured.

"Do I now?" Tristen asked, and I pulled myself closer to his warm body, marveling at the feared Shadowfire Assassin—the sole heir to Stormgard—who had kneeled before no one, except me. Who had loved no one, but me.

Who had knowingly entered The Ash Trials, knowing he might have been going to his death—all to save me.

I tipped my head back up to look at him, to admire the one I had chosen to share a bed with—only to see him already watching me with a smile so bright it chased away every corner of the dark that followed him.

60

We didn't leave Tristen's quarters the rest of the day—or night. At one point that evening, food was brought to us, one of the ship's crew knocking on the door. Tristen pulled on a pair of low slung grey lounge pants that looked downright indecent on him, the bulge of him causing my body to heat with desire as he went to the door and I pulled the bedsheets higher to cover my chest.

Trays of hot food were brought in, but Tristen just placed them on the table in the center of his large quarters. When we were alone once more, he devoured me instead as the food went cold.

The moon glinted off the sea out the windows as I traced circles on his bare chest hours later, my head resting on his chest as his heartbeat and the sway of the ship threatened to lull me back into sleep. Stars glittered like diamonds out the panoramic windows of his cabin.

"Were we always this..." I paused.

"Insatiable?" Tristen asked, and I could hear his smirk in his voice. "You have no idea."

"You'll have to *remind me*, then," I murmured as I moved my head, kissing his chest. "I don't want to leave this bed."

"You don't have to, *Sael*," he said.

I raised my head. "You've called me that a few times before. What does it mean?"

His expression shifted. A look of admiration filled his features. "I couldn't tell you... before. Because of the silencing spell Cassandra had me under."

"Tell me what?" I breathed.

"*Sael* is a word from the ancient language. It's a sacred term for the one who is meant for us in this life and every one after that. Our Soul Bonded."

I stilled. "I'm your..."

"Soul Bonded. Yes, you are. You always have been," he said. "Those who are Soul Bonded always find each other in every life, every world. You can reject the bond, but it doesn't weaken it. If you accept it, through ceremony and the exchanging of blood similar to a blood oath, your heart crystal hums at the vibration of your partner's, and the bond grows stronger. Sometimes granting those who are Soul Bonded additional powers. But at its core, those who are Soul Bonded can feel each others' presence, like an invisible tether. Can even sometimes sense emotions. It grows more complex the longer the bond is in place."

I froze as Tristen's eyes flickered over my face.

"I don't want to overwhelm you—" he started.

"I knew it," I whispered, my heart racing. "Why I always felt pulled to you. Why I couldn't stay away. Maybe a part of me remembered you, but it was more than that. *Is* more than that."

Tristen rose from the bed, going to a golden chest by the window.

"What are you doing?" I asked.

Tristen removed a small box. I sat up, stepping out of bed to join him as the moonlight bathed us in its pure white glow.

"I'm doing what I'd do in every lifetime," he responded, dropping down to one knee as he opened the box, revealing the diamond ring I'd seen from his memory, inlaid with the twin sapphires. "Will you do the honor of becoming my wife, Saffron *Greywood*?"

The words ricocheted through me, and I felt my heart hum. I said the only word that felt right, the only word that could begin to express the depths of what I felt for him. "Yes."

With that, he slipped the ring on my finger, and pulled me into yet another devastatingly perfect kiss.

61

The morning light started to drip into Tristen's cabin, and I felt Tristen's body curled around mine, his arm pulling me to him. I nestled into his embrace, not wanting the dawn to disrupt our slice of paradise as my ring glinted in the morning rays, tossing glints of blue light from the sapphires that shone from where they were inlaid in the gold of the ring around the diamond. We would be arriving in a day or so, he had said—

—but the ship was still.

My body tensed, and I felt Tristen jerk awake behind me.

"What's wrong?" he asked, his voice rough with sleep.

But I didn't speak, just threw back the covers and stumbled to the windows.

Instead of the endless sea, the front of the ship faced land.

Not any land.

We were back at the Isle of Embermere.

I turned to Tristen, but he was already pulling on his clothes.

"We're still here," I said, my voice strained.

His expression was grim as he went to his weapons. "Everything will be okay."

I knew it was a lie.

~

I PULLED on armored fighting leathers, strapping daggers onto my body as I hurried out of Tristen's quarters and joined him and the others as they gathered at the deck overlooking the front of the ship —and the Isle of Embermere, our prison and worst nightmare.

"How are we back?" I breathed.

Tristen turned to Aldric. "Did we lay anchor?"

Aldric shook his head, pointing to something in the water. "Look."

Tristen and I leaned over the railing of the ship to see writhing, serpentine bodies boxing the ship into its current position.

"Sea serpents," Tristen said, and he pulled out a spyglass. He extended it, pointing it at the island, closing one eye as he brought the other to the spyglass. A moment passed, all of us looking at him, and then he lowered it. "We have to go ashore."

"I'll ready the boats—" Aldric started.

"No," Tristen said, grabbing his arm. "Not boats. Just one. Only Saffron and I can go."

I looked at him, confused. "Why?"

Rachelle stepped up, joining us. "I should at least come with."

Tristen shook his head. "No. You're staying. Saffron and I have to go and make a deal."

"Make a deal with who?"

Tristen turned to me, his jaw tight. "The gods of the island."

"Here, let me look—" Rachelle snatched the spyglass, angling at land.

Her eyes were already looking through it as Tristen pulled it away. "No—it only takes one look from the gods to be able to use their compulsion on you. If you lock eyes with them, they can slip into your body. Remember what happened to Henry?"

Rachelle shivered. "Yes. That was horrible. But why are you able to look?"

"I'm different."

"What do you mean?" I asked Tristen.

Tristen took in a shuddering breath. "The gods are already in my head."

~

You won't be able to leave this island with what you want most until you win the final trial. Otto's words rang in my head as the small rowboat was lowered to the water. Had the seer been talking about this? I wasn't sure what Otto had seen in his vision, but it probably wasn't good. Tristen and I were both armed to the teeth, but I didn't know how much steel could do against a god.

When Tristen took me by the waist and placed me on one of the seats of the rowboat, I went to go for the oars—but they were nowhere to be found.

"The oars—"

"We don't need them," Tristen said.

He was right. As soon as we were both sitting in the rowboat, a smaller sea serpent broke off from the group that was caging in the ship and started nudging our boat to shore, circling it to create a kind of current and pressing us forward.

"What are we walking into?" I asked Tristen, who was gripping the side of the boat so hard that I thought it might splinter under his hands.

"I'm not sure. Don't speak to them, don't take any bargains, and let me handle it."

"What aren't you telling me?" I said, and he looked at me.

With true *fear* in his eyes.

But then he blinked and it was gone, replaced by the mask of catlike arrogance and smooth confidence. "These cranky bastards are just salty they didn't get their annual entertainment. It'll be fine."

It didn't feel fine.

~

THE ROWBOAT NAVIGATED past the rocky outcropping of Siren's Rest, where I swore I could see the glittering tails of mermen glittering underneath the surf. To my right was Dragon's Tail, and straight ahead was where the dunes of The Eternal Sands met the sea, the powdery white sand slipping straight into the crystal blue of the Cimmerian Sea.

"We're going back to The Eternal Sands," I said, not a question.

"We are," Tristen said, and his whole body was tense.

Finally, the boat reached the shore, and we stepped out into the surf, climbing up the steep incline to get to the top of the sand dune.

Instead of the endless sand dunes, we arrived at an open air temple amidst a sea of sand. It had four columns of marble holding up a roof, and a smooth floor.

As we stepped onto the shiny marble floor, Tristen pulled me behind him. I was about to protest, but then I felt *it*. A vibration below our feet warned of a huge presence. A crackling of power that rivaled Tristen's own. From the dunes across from the temple, he emerged.

The god was massive, a foot taller than Tristen and much wider. He was bare-chested and surrounded by fast-moving shadows that swam around him and sparked as they clashed, like an eternal storm. His eyes were not just black, they were the absence of light, color, sound. Swirling black holes that seemed to suck up everything around it. But when he saw us, he smiled. It was a grin so full of destruction that I felt my body beg me to let it drop to its knees. It took every ounce of my strength to stay standing.

The god stepped forward until he was in front of Tristen, looking down at him. "I thought you knew better than to cheat us of our hero, *boy*."

Tristen shrugged. "And here I was thinking that you must have something better to do than watch some stupid fighting ring."

The god shifted its gaze to me, and Tristen moved to block his eyesight, but the god simply shot him a look, and Tristen took a small step to the side, allowing the god to see me but not get too close.

"So this is her," the god said, those bottomless eyes boring into me.

"You brought us back here," Tristen said, trying to pull the god's attention back to him. "What do you want, Nocterin?"

The god of madness and endings. The god who controlled Tristen's powers. I held my breath, trying to keep my terror tamped down.

Nocterin tore his gaze back to Tristen. "What, I need an excuse to see my son?"

Son. I stared at Tristen in shock. "You're a god," I whispered.

Tristen clenched his fists at his side. "No. A Brightborne," he said, his eyes still locked on his father. "A human granted a drop of a god's power."

"Oh, so you didn't tell her?" Nocterin said. "Maybe you should stop wearing that useless fucking glamour so she can see you clearly."

Nocterin waved his hand at Tristen, and suddenly a wave of suffocating power hit Tristen as he stumbled back.

Before me, I saw Tristen change. His transformation claimed him like an inheritance finally come due, power erupting through his form not to devour, but to crown. His jet-black hair unfurled into living shadow, cascading down his back in waves that would make midnight itself burn with envy. His olive skin pulsed with veins of silver-black radiance as though the darkest realm itself ran through his blood, marking him as its chosen prince. But his eyes—gods, his eyes—were where dominion truly burned through, deepening from their usual darkness into something that made me understand why empires fell for a single glance. His twin eyes of black obsidian were rimmed with chaos-fire, the kind of gaze that could break kingdoms and make you thank him for the privilege. He towered even taller, an apex predator, fully formed.

He stood in front me, Tristen, *my* Tristen, but *more*. Power rolled off him in waves thick enough to drown in, his presence a gravity well of beautiful destruction that turned heads and stopped hearts. He was still himself, still the man whom I promised forever to—but now his familiar, devastating beauty was wrapped in shadows that whispered to me everything that was concealed. He was now the kind of being armies would kneel for, that queens would start wars over, the kind who made me finally understand why they say only the chaos of darkness could make the stars so beautiful.

Tristen's eyes blinked—those familiar yet wholly new godlike eyes—and his gaze landed on me, and concern was written in his expression. Concern as if—

"She *should* be afraid of you. Afraid of what you are," Nocterin sneered. "You should have never involved yourself with a mortal girl, Son."

Tristen had been breathtaking before, but I didn't let the astonishing power rippling off him scare me. I twined my hand in his. Reassuring him even as I felt my heart skip a beat as I took in the glowing man in front of me.

"I'm not afraid," I said, and forced myself to meet Nocterin's gaze.

"Good," Nocterin said with a curl of a smile. "Because I should take him from you for what you've done."

Ice skittered down the back of my neck. "No."

"No?" Nocterin roared. "You dare tell a god *no*?"

Lightning-quick, Tristen pushed me behind him. A blast of Nocterin's shadows shot to where I had been standing just a second earlier.

Tristen's shadows rallied in response, but did not strike. "Stay away from her."

Nocterin's eyes blazed, swirling and tumbling over themselves. "The island demands sacrifice. And she is still marked, despite how you may feel about her."

I looked at my left hand where the blazing fire of The Ash Trials still inked my skin. "What sacrifice will the island accept?" I asked.

"None from you," Tristen said, backing us up a few steps, still angling his body in front of me. "Let us go, Father."

"Not until the final trial is complete."

Fear cut through me like a knife. "I cannot and *will not* kill Tristen," I said to Nocterin. "There must be another way."

"There is," Nocterin said. "But first my son must leave you and return to the ship."

"*No*," Tristen snarled.

"Tell me," I asked, fighting to keep my voice steady.

Nocterin's eyebrow lifted. "A brave mortal. Or a stupid one. I suppose it remains to be seen."

"I'm not leaving her behind," Tristen said, his shadowfire growing at his hands.

"Then you must decide which of you will die."

"I accept your sixth trial," I said in a rush, and before Tristen could do anything, a pulse of magic rippled through the island.

"NO!" Tristen yelled, but a swirling mist encased his left hand and the flame that signified his participation in The Ash Trials disintegrated.

Setting him free.

There was a rumbling underneath us, and out of the sand behind the open air temple, two figures made wholly of shadows appeared out of nowhere—Nocterin's guards. They disappeared and then reappeared at Tristen's side, holding him back.

"Please," Tristen said to his father as he fought against the shadow beings that restrained him. "Let me take her place. I'll do *anything*."

Nocterin laughed, the sound fraying in my ears as if the laugh held within it a kernel that could break minds. "You can do nothing against such ancient magic. Take him back to the beach."

The shadows yanked him back, but he thrashed against them. "Saffron," he said, his gaze fierce. "Show them what you're made of. And then come back to me."

"I will," I said, and Tristen struggled against the hold of the shadows as they dragged him down the dunes, back to the sea.

I turned back to Nocterin, alone with the god. "What would you have me do?" I asked, fighting the fear his power elicited within me as it continued to shed from his form in waves.

"Simple," Nocterin said, "kill the one who would see you leashed."

Then, Nocterin turned his head to where a man had just crested a sand dune beside us.

Not just any man. King West, wearing other people's blood on him and murder in his eyes.

62

Nocterin disappeared, and in his place, a blade clattered to the stone floor of the open air temple.

I recognized it as the Bluesteel Blade—back once more.

"Thanks for coming this time," I muttered to the blade. It glowed in acknowledgement—no longer deigning to speak to me like the first time it had called to me.

I rushed to pick it up, falling into a fighting stance as King West slowly descended from the dune, every step promising death as he approached the open air temple.

"*You*," King West said. "You have ruined *everything*."

"Why? Because I didn't allow you to use me for your slaughter?" I spat at him as he reached the marble floor. A wind whipped errant sand particles through the temple, but King West continued his slow approach.

"You were mine to use," he said, withdrawing his sword from his scabbard, and I held my ground in the center of the open air temple.

"Spoken like true spoiled royalty," I said, and then in several swift steps, our blades were clashing.

The Bluesteel Blade was heavy, but I hefted it against every strike of his sword, my footwork fast and agile against his punishing power. I stayed focused on preserving my energy, the adrenaline coursing through my veins as we circled each other. He was strong, but he was just a pampered royal. I was a *warrior*.

I always had been.

He pulled back, watching me as we circled each other. "You think you're special? You're not. You're just a baker's daughter who stumbled into being the object of a godsdamned prophecy. Even fate wants you to do its bidding. Why do you think that sword keeps showing up when you need it the most?"

With that, he sliced out at me, and my blade arced up to meet his, our swords crossing. I fought against his strength as he bore down on me.

"I don't care as long as I can use it to kill you," I ground out, and took a sidestep, releasing my blade and stepping aside just as he rushed at me.

He stumbled slightly, but then we resumed circling each other. A slow smile spread across his lips. "You're not even curious what the goddess Orsi wants from you? After all, you've been given every advantage you've needed to win these trials. Allies, weapons, a new power..."

I had, hadn't I? How much had my fate been written in stone, and how much had I done myself? The thought clanged through my mind with so much force that I was caught off-guard by King West's next advance, and I ducked—narrowly missing his blade as he slashed out at me with surprising agility.

I took a few steps back, resuming my fighting stance. *Get it together, Saffron.*

"I will win these trials fair and square," I said, and I meant it. I wasn't going to be able to get close enough to him to use my Siphon powers on him even if I wanted to.

"You sound just like me when I entered my first Ash Trial," he said, and my mouth went dry.

"You... you were a contestant in one of the Ash Trials?"

King West grinned. "Oh, dear Saffron. I wasn't just a contestant—I was a winner. See? We're not so different, you and I. Despite being of noble blood, I wanted to prove to the gods that I would be a worthy warden for this island, and so I entered the trials when I came of age to do just that. I beat murderers and shifters and monsters of all different kinds. I killed them all to prove my allegiance to these sleeping gods. That's why they let me preside over the games each year. And that's why they'll let me kill *you*."

Then, King West lunged at me, and we were a clash of steel and force once more. But this time, his prim manner devolved. He became a swift, agile fighter.

He had been holding back on me.

The Bluesteel Blade began to grow heavy in my arms as I fought off his onslaught. Maybe he was right—maybe the gods had only let me get this far because I was some agent of fate. Maybe I had never been worthy of the blade or the title of winner.

No.

You do not *choose death for yourself.*

Tristen's words ignited a fury within me. Even if I had gotten help from my allies, from the gods, from a mysterious power, I was still *me*. I may not win this fight with pure strength or agility, but I could try and outwit the King. He had been locked away in his gilded palace for so long, allowing his men to fight his battles for him. The ingenuity demanded of a battlefield was something he was no longer intimate with.

But I was.

I took a jab forward, allowing my left side to be exposed—hoping he would take the bait. When he saw it, he lunged for me. But I spun out of the way, slashing my sword against his side.

His blood spilled immediately, and as I stepped backward to get out of his path, I saw that I had landed not a killing blow, but one close enough where my next strikes could be fatal if he slowed down.

I grinned, realizing that I was about to win this.

But then King West straightened as well, a mirror of a grin on his face.

I frowned as a drop of blood hit the sand-dusted marble below me. The crimson droplet marred the marble floor, and as I looked down, I saw that he had cut me on my arm. Not deep, but enough for me to bleed.

And that would be enough for him to destroy me.

I clamped my arm against my chest, trying to keep the blood from him, but he just reached inside his jacket pocket, unscrewing a vial of something.

"It's a shame, really. We could have accomplished so much together," he said, and then raised his other hand.

I screamed as my blood shot for him, my vein emptying as his blood magic pulled it to him. But as it reached him, he simply overturned the vial, a liquid intermingling with my levitating blood droplets. Then, with a flick of his wrist, he sent my blood back to my body.

I stumbled back, trying to shield my wound from it, but his power was too precise. As my blood squeezed back into my veins, I knew something was wrong as my body reacted.

I stumbled back, suddenly feeling hot and heavy.

Poison.

"Not... fair..." I ground out, staggering a few steps backward to the edge of the temple where the sand dunes lay behind me.

"You think I would fight fair?" he asked, and threw his head back, laughing. "This is why you will die, Saffron Vale. Your morality is your greatest weakness. You don't have the stomach for true victory."

It was the lapse in attention I needed.

I turned, sprinting to where the marble dropped off into sand behind me, grasping for a handful of sand. As I hurtled back to him, he lowered his gaze to me, and I threw the sand in his eyes—a move that I had seen Callum use. *Still helping me, even now.*

He screamed and dropped his blade. At his heart, he was still a member of royalty who couldn't stomach a moment of discomfort even in amidst a fight to the death.

As he clutched at his eyes, I grabbed his fallen sword. It was heavy, and the edges of my vision were beginning to darken, my tongue growing fat in my cotton-dry mouth as the poison burned through my veins like wildfire.

Then, I stood to my full height, wielding both his blade and mine.

Just like my memory of when I fought with the rebels and by Tristen's side.

King West raised his head, and in that moment he saw his death.

"May Illumia be with you," I said. In one smooth movement, I sliced both swords through his neck, severing it.

His head rolled to my feet.

I had won the sixth trial.

My swords clattered to the ground, the King's blood staining the floor of the temple.

I fell to my knees, the world swaying as the poison took hold, blurring my vision.

"Saffron!" I heard Tristen's voice, felt him as he caught me before I hit the floor.

I reached up to touch him as he held my head in his lap, my vision doubling. "You came back."

"I got back as soon as I could. You're hurt—"

"Poison," I mumbled, the words falling heavy from my mouth.

"No," he said, gripping me to him. "It can't be."

"I love you," I said, fighting back the pain as every piece of me felt as if it had been set on fire. "I wish we had more time. That's all I want."

Tristen's eyes were full of anguish. "You can't leave me, Saffron. You *can't*. I just found you again."

My heart started beating faster, the poison creeping deeper into my fragile human organs, starting to turn them off one-by-one as my skin grew hot and then cold. "I fought, like you told me to."

"You did. I'm so proud of you, but you need to *keep fighting*," he said, his voice full of panic. "NOCTERIN!" he screamed.

My vision grew hazy. I thought I saw another swirl of shadows, but as the world slanted and slipped around me, I couldn't be sure.

"It will cost you," that voice rumbled.

"I will pay any price," Tristen said. "*Please*. Save her."

The last thing I saw before I passed out was a lightning bolt that shot from the sky, and I felt Tristen buckle in pain, crying out, gripping me harder against him as he screamed again.

63

I fell, thrashing through water, and it filled my lungs and shot through me, shoving out the fire that was searing my veins.

I was dying.

I was being dragged down to dark depths, and I couldn't open my eyes. I couldn't scream, couldn't hear, couldn't breathe.

You need to keep fighting.

Tristen's words rushed through me. How? How could I keep going after all that I had endured? The sixth trial had ripped me apart. I had given everything, and I had nothing left. All of those who had told me I wouldn't be able to survive them had been right.

At the end of it all, I had tried to be brave, tried to be strong, but the current was dark and I was growing cold.

The current slowed, and ahead I could see a bright light, winding with warmth and a promise of the end of pain. But as the current released me from its grip, I did not swim to it even as my breaking body begged me to.

Memories started flashing through my mind, the precious few I had. Not memories of the death and pain of the trials, but memories of him. Of Tristen. Our wedding day, even as it was cut short, and the way he gazed at me like I was his salvation. His *Sael.*

"Why do you pause?"

I opened my eyes. The dark water was still crushing down on me, the pressure crunching my bones and tearing my organs. Before me floated a goddess, her hair the color of the rainbow as it fanned from her glowing skin in the current. I remembered her statue at the Temple of Orsi.

"I want to go back to him," I choked out, my voice weak.

She quirked her head. "Peace awaits you, my child. Why would you turn away from it now?"

I shook my head, the effort extraordinary so far underwater. "I do not want peace. I love him."

"Love is a terrible thing," she said. "Love always precedes loss. You will always be in pain as long as you love."

"I will take any pain," I said, and I meant it. "I want to return to him."

"Have you learned nothing?"

I remembered my offering at her temple. "Haven't I killed enough for you? It was you who gifted me the Bluesteel Blade, wasn't it?"

She sighed. "It was. Your bloodline has much left to do with it, still."

"Then let me continue to fight."

The Goddess Orsi examined me with her otherworldly eyes. "He has fought for you, too. He's still fighting for you to return. And... I will allow it, even though what lies ahead of you is great pain. Yours will not be an easy love."

I almost laughed. "I do not choose easy. I choose *him*. I choose life."

She took one hard look at me, and then nodded. "Very well. The waters of Aetherna have parted for you, and for his sacrifice and your role to play in all this, I will give you what you're owed."

The current encircled me and broke every bone in my body. I screamed, but it was wordless as the water crushed my lungs.

The goddess leaned forward, punching her hand through my chest, and in a pain more blinding than anything I'd known, she squeezed my heart until it burst.

In that moment, I became the darkness.

～

IT WAS DARK, but this time I was floating about the still water.

I opened my eyes to the night sky. It was so sharp, so clear. Had the stars always shone this brightly?

Suddenly, I heard a splashing noise.

"Saffron!"

My head was heavy, and I couldn't turn it. Couldn't even tilt it to see who was calling my name. But their voice was deep and rough with emotion. I heard their emotions like music notes. Did voices always sound like that?

"Saffron," the voice said, so urgent. Finally, the owner of the voice came into view, leaning over me.

He was the future King of Stormgard, the Brightborne of Madness and Endings, and the owner of my heart.

"Tristen," I said, wanting to reach for him, but my hand wouldn't move.

His eyes widened as he took me in. "You're... she really did it."

"Did what?"

"We need to get you out," he said, already slipping his hands underneath my legs and cradling my neck.

"Where am I?" I asked, my body limp in his arms as he waded to shore.

"Lake Aetherna," he said, barely able to take his eyes off of me as he carried me to shore. "The waters of the Temple of Orsi flow down here, and it's a place of healing and rebirth. You..."

"I died. The goddess Orsi killed me," I said. "This must be heaven if you're here."

Tristen reached the shore, and gently set me down on the grassy bank. The night sky glinted on the lake behind him.

I tried to move my limbs, but they felt weird and wobbly as if blood was flowing to them for the first time.

Tristen cradled my head. "Don't panic, Saffron."

I frowned up at him. "Why would I panic?"

"You're no longer human," he breathed.

Even though he told me not to panic, I found the strength in my arms to finally push me upright. I rose on unsteady feet, Tristen by my side. I approached the shore, and in the placid waters of the lake, I saw myself.

My long blonde hair seemed to float off my body, which was coated in a warm glow. My blue eyes seemed to sparkle and swirl like mist atop an endless ocean, and my facial features were the same, yet different. There was a subtle harmony to the proportions of my face and my body that did not look ordinary. My slight frame had elongated into a willowy hourglass shape, and my jawline was sharper, my lips more plush and my skin more youthful. I held out my left hand, where the mark of the Ash Trials had disappeared. Looking back at the reflection in the water, I put together all of the pieces.

"I'm a Brightborne," I whispered in awe, turning to Tristen. He was still in his true form, and he had a slight glow to him. "Like you. How?"

"The Goddess Orsi decided to grant you a favor. I'm so glad she brought you back to me," Tristen said. He looked relieved, but there was still a strange tension to his features.

"I remember... you made a deal. What did you do?" I asked, knowing there was more to this.

"I just asked my father for a favor."

Nocterin. "What did it cost?"

"Nothing. He did it for me. For us. Now we have to go," Tristen urged me. "The other gods won't like what you've become."

Tristen started to lead me back to a moonlit path, but a strange noise made me pause. It was a whispering on the wind, a chorus of many ancient voices.

I was now hearing the conversations of the gods as they grew in strength.

64

y gown was wine red with sheer sleeves and gold detailing. As I stood in the hallway of this palace—my new home—I could hear the roaring beyond the curtains. We had traveled by ship for a few days before we reached the sea port of the capital of Stormgard, and we had made it to the sprawling palace just in time to address the people. *Our* people.

"Ready?" Tristen said, entering the hallway and closing a door behind him.

"Yes," I said, my heart doing tiny flips as he entered, dressed in a black brocade jacket and finery with gold trim that matched the gold I wore. He was truly embodying the King of Stormgard.

Tristen took my hand in his, giving it a comforting squeeze. Then, we pushed past the curtains, stepping into the afternoon sun.

We let our glamours drop completely as we stepped onto the balcony, and the crowds gathered before us cheered in adoration. They waved crimson banners in the same shade of my dress, the official seal of Stormgard inked on them in gold—a hand gripping a lightning bolt.

"Today is one of celebration," Aldric said to all of the spectators, who hushed just long enough to hear his magically amplified voice.

"For today, our one true Queen returns, and we gather here today to see her crowned and joined together in a Soul Bond with King Tristen Greywood, heir to the throne."

More cheers, and Aldric takes a box from a pedestal, opening it and presenting it to Tristen. In it lies a gold crown of fire, a tiny phoenix at the center of the crest.

"Long live Queen Saffron Greywood," Aldric said, and the crowd shouted in glee as Tristen reached for the crown and placed it on my head. Aldric closed the box with a flourish, and then returned with a second one, opening this one to me.

"Long live King Tristen Greywood," he said, and I took the crown and placed it on Tristen's head. The smile that lit up his face was like the glow of a hundred sunrises and sunsets. Eternal, hopeful, and the most stunning sight on all of the horizon.

"Bow to your rulers, who will once and for all lead Stormgard into our future as a free kingdom," Aldric called, and Tristen pulled me into a kiss as the crowd shouted our praises from below.

Tristen pulled away and then took my hand, leading us to the end of the balcony, where we stopped to look out at the crowd below.

A hush settled, and Aldric took a step back as Tristen addressed our subjects below.

"When I left, I promised that I would return with our Queen, and I did." Cheers threatened to overwhelm the crowd, but he held up a hand. "Not only that, but she has returned blessed by the goddess Orsi as a Brightborne. I look forward to proving myself worthy of her —and of you. I know we're all fighting a war against the Kingdom of Luminaria. But rest assured, we have returned to lead you—all of you —to victory. And my Queen will fight by my side to ensure your safety."

Shouts and applause peppered the crowd below as Tristen turned to me.

I took a deep breath, smoothing my skirts as I addressed my new subjects. "A lot has transpired since I have seen you last, but one thing remains the same. Stormgard will remain free. We will not bow to Luminaria's reign of terror, and I will be on the frontlines beside your King to ensure it. Thank you."

I took a step back. Tristen nodded at the crowd, and we turned back to the doors, disappearing into our palace.

Our home.

~

TRISTEN and I walked back inside, his hand squeezing mine.

"Not too shabby after being at sea for the last day," he said.

"I'm just glad that the floor stopped moving," I said, smiling at him, taking in his features. Not only had we survived The Ash Trials, but we had made it back. Made it *home*.

Tristen suddenly pulled us down a small hallway, and before I could say anything, he pushed me up against the stone wall of a small alcove, his lips and body pressed to mine. His kiss was insistent, hungry—his need for me never ebbing since we first came together.

"Tristen," I said, a small noise escaping the back of my throat as he kissed my neck, his hands pulling me against him.

"You're mine," he growled against my skin. "No one will take you from me ever again," he promised, his lips ghosting against my jaw as his promise made my heart flutter.

I was about to reply when a scream split the air.

Tristen broke away from me in a heartbeat. With my new Bright-borne hearing, I heard the rush of footsteps down many halls as Tristen and I started running toward the origin of the sound.

We sprinted until we reached the main hall of the palace. As we burst into the cavernous rooms, a woman with bright red hair stood in the center.

I knew as I ran toward her who she was, even as she slowly raised her face to me.

"Rachelle!" I called, but she didn't look like herself. Her blue eyes were instead replaced by dark voids, and she was dripping in blood. Behind her lay the bodies of several guards.

Her mouth stretched back into a grin, and when she spoke, I

heard not just her voice, but the voice of a god who was channeling through her.

"You think you escaped us, Saffron?" she said, her voice echoed by that awful, ancient one that felt like it scraped down the innermost recesses of my mind. "Until you return, you will be hunted. Those you love will be killed, one-by-one. And do you know who will be waiting for you when you are forced to finally face us? The one you left behind."

Rachelle threw back her head, emitting a high-pitched cackle.

"Let go of her!" I yelled to the god who had a grip on her body, and Tristen prowled closer to her, his shadows snaking out.

Then, there was a flash of steel as Rachelle's arm shot up, a dagger in her hand.

Not a dagger aimed at us, but a dagger aimed at her own heart.

"NO!" The words ripped from my lips as I lunged for my friend, but Tristen's shadows reached her first. They wound around her wrist to keep her from plunging it into her heart, but she was unnaturally strong. I got to her and gripped her hand as well, also trying to keep her from puncturing her own heart as she struggled against us. A line of blood formed on her chest where the dagger was starting to embed itself within her.

"Please! Let go of her!" I begged the forces who had possessed Rachelle.

"Stand back," Tristen said, and I saw him charging up his shadowfire in his hands.

"You can't kill her—"

"I won't—"

"If I let go she's done for!" I screamed.

"We'll do it fast. On three..."

I struggled with the blade, fighting against Rachelle as the spirit possessing her tried to drive it deeper within herself.

"Two..." Tristen said.

Rachelle's eyes shifted back to her familiar pale blue color. "Saffron—help me!" she said, and I saw the agony in her eyes.

"You have to fight, Rachelle!" I pleaded, and I saw a flash of resolve as her arms fought against the spirit possessing her, withdrawing the blade just slightly from her bloody skin.

"NOW!" I screamed as I let go of the blade, just as the black pits of nothingness eclipsed her eyes.

I jumped back and Tristen's shadowfire shot out, blasting the blade with precision. The spirit that possessed Rachelle screamed, trying to crush the blade into her heart, but it had been frozen by Tristen's power and it merely shattered into a thousand frozen pieces at her feet.

Rachelle's eyes flashed blue once more and she turned to me, forcing her words out as if each one cost her all of her energy. "They won't let you live, Saffron," Rachelle said to me as she fought the thing inside of her. Then, her eyes rolled back into her head, and she fell to the ground.

I ran to her as Tristen turned to the guards spilling into the space.

"Get a healer!" he called.

I ran my fingers through her curly red hair, my breathing unsteady as Tristen crouched beside us, checking Rachelle's pulse.

She was still alive—barely.

~

RACHELLE HAD BEEN DRAGGED into a sleep so deep she barely breathed, kept in a state that the healers could only describe to me as a form of stasis. I stayed at her bedside that night, unable to sleep while Tristen paced the hall outside, having long discussions with his advisors and generals.

We had only just returned, only just claimed our rightful place at the throne—only to be haunted by everything we had faced on the Isle of Embermere. We had escaped, but clearly we were not free of the gods that seemed to be growing more restless there.

One part of what Rachelle had said—what the spirit or god inside her had said—kept repeating itself within my head, over and over again.

And do you know who will be waiting for you when you are forced to finally face us? The one you left behind.

There was only one meaning to those words.

Callum was still alive.

～

I HAD FALLEN asleep in a chair in Rachelle's bedchamber, morning rays of light waking me. As I sat up, I saw Tristen sitting alert in a chair across from me, keeping watch over both Rachelle and I, his dark hair messy and his eyes rung by dark circles.

"We have to go back," I said without greeting or niceties.

Tristen's gaze hardened. He knew exactly what I meant. "I know," he said.

It was time to send a message to the gods.

AUTHOR'S NOTE

I f you enjoyed The Ash Trials, I have a secret cheat code for how to get me to write the next book faster. Just leave a review on Amazon and Goodreads and tell your friends about the book, and my typing speed will magically increase!

All jokes aside, I do read every review and I really appreciate you helping other readers find this book. You can leave a review on Amazon and Goodreads by scanning either of the QR codes below:

Review on Amazon:

Review on Goodreads:

Want to stay in touch? Join my newsletter at FromtheDeskofAmy Suto.Substack.com or join with the QR code below:

ACKNOWLEDGMENTS

The Ash Trials would not be here without the support of Kyle Cords— my editor, partner, and a literal creative genius. Thank you for your endless support and incredible pitches. I'm reminded on a daily basis why I'm the luckiest girl in the world, and I'm grateful to be able to do life with you.

Thank you to Ashley Munson, who designed such a gorgeous cover—per usual! It's such a treat working with you again on this book. Your artwork really brought the story to life, and seeing the illustrations come together even as the draft was (very much) in-progress was such a cool feeling.

Thank you to Melissa Nash for your stunning map design for the book. Your cartography skills added a layer of reality to the Isle of Embermere that helped me visualize the story as I was writing it.

Thank you to my proofreader, Sierra Campbell. You really helped the manuscript shine, and I can't wait to work with you on the next one!

Thank you to my beta readers, Anna and Presley, for reading my working draft on such a short notice and giving great feedback. It's always a bit scary to get feedback when the draft is just barely completed, and I appreciate how thoughtful you were in your notes.

Thank you to my family for always encouraging my love of reading and writing. I wouldn't be living my dream without your support.

Lastly, I'm sending so much gratitude to you, my readers. This book marks my first foray into the romantasy genre, and I look forward to writing more books for you very soon.

ABOUT THE AUTHOR

Amy Suto began her career as a Hollywood TV writer before hitting the road and becoming a digital nomad and freelance writer, which was the subject of her nonfiction book *Six-Figure Freelance Writer: A Holistic Guide on Finding Freedom in Freelancing*. Suto has published two works of fiction: her debut romantasy book *The Ash Trials* (which you're reading now!) and her mystery short story collection *The Nomad Detective: Volume I* inspired by her travels as a digital nomad. Suto runs a Substack newsletter called *From the Desk of Amy Suto* teaching others how to make writing their job. When she's not writing, Amy travels the world and works remotely from cafes in Cusco, Peru—or is learning the ways of the samurai at a dojo in Kyoto, Japan. You can learn more about Amy at: AmySuto.com.

ALSO BY AMY SUTO

Six-Figure Freelance Writer: A Holistic Guide on Finding Freedom in Freelancing

The Nomad Detective: Volume I

Made in United States
North Haven, CT
02 March 2025